W/O

HAND IN GLOVE
The death of a young English poet in the Spanish Civil
War casts a shadow forward over half a century.

'Cliff-hanging entertainment'
GUARDIAN

CLOSED CIRCLE
1931, and two English fraudsters on a transatlantic liner stumble
into deep trouble when they target a young heiress.

*'Full of thuggery and skulduggery, cross and
doublecross, plot and counter-plot'*
INDEPENDENT

BORROWED TIME
A brief encounter with a stranger who is murdered soon afterwards draws
Robin Timariot into the complex relationships and motives of the dead
woman's family and friends.

*'An atmosphere of taut menace...heightened
by shadows of betrayal and revenge'*
DAILY TELEGRAPH

OUT OF THE SUN
Harry Barnett becomes entangled in a sinister conspiracy
when he learns that the son he never knew he had is languishing
in hospital in a coma.

'Brilliantly plotted, full of good, traditional storytelling values'
MAIL ON SUNDAY

BEYOND RECALL
The scion of a wealthy Cornish dynasty reinvestigates a 1947 murder
and begins to doubt the official version of events.

'Satisfyingly complex...finishes in a rollercoaster of twists'
DAILY TELEGRAPH

CAUGHT IN THE LIGHT

A photographer's obsession with a femme fatale
leads him into a web of double jeopardy.

'A spellbinding foray into the real-life game
of truth and consequences'
THE TIMES

SET IN STONE

A strange house links past and present, a murder,
a political scandal and an unexplained tragedy.

'A heady blend of mystery and adventure'
OXFORD TIMES

SEA CHANGE

A spell-binding mystery involving a mysterious package, murder and
financial scandal, set in 18th-century London, Amsterdam and Rome.

'Engrossing, storytelling of a very high order'
OBSERVER

DYING TO TELL

A missing document, a forty-year-old murder and the Great Train
Robbery all seem to have connections with a modern-day disappearance.

'Gripping...woven together with more
twists than a country lane'
DAILY MAIL

DAYS WITHOUT NUMBER

Once Nick Paleologus has excavated a terrible secret from his
archaeologist father's career, nothing will ever be the same again.

'Fuses history with crime, guilty consciences and human fallibility...
an intelligent escapist delight'
THE TIMES

PLAY TO THE END

Actor Toby Flood finds himself a player in a much bigger game when he investigates a man who appears to be a stalker.

'An absorbing display of craftsmanship'
SUNDAY TIMES

SIGHT UNSEEN

An innocent bystander is pulled into a mystery which takes over twenty years to unravel when he witnesses the abduction of a child.

'A typically taut tale of wrecked lives, family tragedy, historical quirks and moral consequences'
THE TIMES

NEVER GO BACK

The convivial atmosphere of a reunion weekend is shattered by an apparent suicide.

'Meticulous planning, well-drawn characters and an immaculate sense of place... A satisfying number of twists and shocks'
THE TIMES

NAME TO A FACE

A centuries old mystery is about to unravel...

'Mysterious, dramatic, intricate, fascinating and unputdownable'
DAILY MIRROR

FOUND WANTING

Catapulted into a breathless race again time, Richard's life will be changed for ever in ways he could never have imagined...

'The master of the clever twist'
SUNDAY TELEGRAPH

LONG TIME COMING

For thirty-six years they thought he was dead...
They were wrong...

'When it comes to duplicity and intrigue,
Goddard is second to none'

BLOOD COUNT

There's no such thing as easy money.
As surgeon Edward Hammond is about to find out.

'Mysterious, dramatic, intricate,
fascinating and unputdownable...
The crime writers' crime writer'

BEYOND RECALL

ROBERT GODDARD

CORGI BOOKS

TRANSWORLD PUBLISHERS
61-63 Uxbridge Road, London W5 5SA
A Random House Group Company
www.rbooks.co.uk

BEYOND RECALL
A CORGI BOOK: 9780552164184

First published in Great Britain
in 1997 by Bantam Press
an imprint of Transworld Publishers
Corgi edition published 1997
Corgi edition reissued 2011

A CIP catalogue record for this book
is available from the British Library.

Addresses for Random House Group Ltd companies outside the UK
can be found at: www.randomhouse.co.uk
The Random House Group Ltd Reg. No. 954009

The Random House Group Limited supports The Forest Stewardship
Council (FSC), the leading international forest certification organisation. All
our titles that are printed on Greenpeace approved FSC certified paper carry
the FSC logo. Our paper procurement policy can be found at
www.rbooks.co.uk/environment

Typeset in 11/13 Giovanni Book by
Phoenix Typesetting, Auldgirth, Dumfriesshire
Printed in the UK by CPI Cox & Wyman, Reading, RG1 8EX.

1 3 5 7 9 10 8 6 4 2

In fond memory of Terry Green, friend, colleague and boon companion, on whom time was called far too early.

ACKNOWLEDGEMENTS

I am indebted to the following for help and advice gener-
ously given to me during the planning and writing of this
novel: Christopher Street, who supplied background
information on the classic car restoration business;
Charles and Thelma North, whose recollections of
grocery and credit drapery before, during and after the
Second World War proved invaluable; and in particular
Malcolm McCarraher, who tirelessly vetted the legal
ramifications of the plot and was considerate enough to
provide ingenious solutions to any problems he
identified.

TODAY

The air is different here, purer somehow. The light is clearer, the edges of the leaves and the lines of the buildings as sharp as the memories. Recollection invades my senses through the unchanged brightness of this place called home. I raise the window on the evening, cool and sweetly washed by late afternoon rain. I touch the wood and test the paintwork with my thumb. I watch a rabbit, disturbed but not startled by the squeak of the sash, hop away into the trees. The direction of his leisurely retreat draws my eyes towards St Clement's Hill, where I can make out the roofs of Truro School, and just to the north, the white dots that could be sheep in a field but for the regularity of their spacing, sheep safely grazing rather than the headstones of the dead resting for ever on a familiar hillside.

I didn't ask for an east-facing room. I didn't let slip my connection with Tredower House when I booked in. I didn't even disguise my name. The receptionist was too young to remember anyway, probably too young even to care. Pure chance, then, puts me here, in this particular room, where my great-uncle kept his vast old

15

daybed and his jumble of assaying equipment and his battered leather trunks and cases, laid out as if in readiness for a journey. Maybe he rested here, listening to the cooing of the doves and sniffing the summer air, before setting out that last time, nearly fifty years ago. Just up there, half a mile away at most, his bones are dust beneath a slab of Cornish granite. I stood beside it a few hours ago, waiting to be met; waiting, but also willing to be forced to remember. I read the inscription, cursory and reticent, declaring just as little as propriety demanded, and thought of how carefully my grandmother would have chosen the wording. 'Brevity and seemliness,' I imagined her saying to the monumental mason. 'His name.' *Joshua George Carnoweth*. 'His dates.' *1873–1947*. 'The customary initials.' *RIP*. 'That, I rather think, will suffice.'

And you must have thought it would, mustn't you, Gran? You must have been so confident, even when your own life ebbed away twenty-five years later. No cold grave on a windy hilltop for you, of course, but neat hygienic cremation. Well, some things can't be burned, or even buried. You must have thought they could be. But you were wrong. Only you're not here to face that fact, are you? I am.

I was early for my appointment at the cemetery. Not by much, but early enough to recover my breath after the climb and draw some calmness from the scene. The wind was up, heralding the rain that hadn't yet arrived. The speeding clouds shifted the sunlight around the city below me, lighting first the single copper spire of the cathedral, then its taller central tower, then the long pale line of the viaduct and the deep green fields beyond; and finally, closer to, a flight of birds above the cemetery chapel, tossed up in the breeze like a handful of shingle

16

on a gale-ripped beach, lit and seen and swiftly lost.

The houses have crept up the slopes around the cemetery since Uncle Joshua was buried, crept up unsuspected, like some besieging enemy by night, unnoticed until suddenly perceived. The thought struck me just as I saw her approaching up the path, walking fast and straight, anonymously dressed, thinner and gaunter and older than when we'd last met.

She stopped a few feet away and stared at me, breathing steadily. Hostility, if it was there, was expertly masked. But what else would I have expected? She'd always worn a mask. I just hadn't always known it.

'You've aged well,' she said neutrally. 'Still off the drink?'

'As a matter of fact, yes.'

'That must be it, then. Unless it's the effect of marriage and fatherhood.'

'How did you find out?'

'I made it my business to. Where are they – your wife and son?'

'Switzerland.'

'Handy for the banks, I imagine.'

'Is that what this is about – money?'

'What else? I'm short.'

'Didn't they pay you enough for those imaginative memoirs of yours?'

'Not enough to keep me indefinitely in the manner I'm accustomed to.'

'You mean you've run through it all.'

'Something like that.'

'Well, bad luck. You'll get nothing from me.'

'I'll get as much as I need from somebody. You – or the highest bidder. And I think the bidding will go pretty high for the story I have to tell. Don't you?'

'Maybe.'

'If the truth gets out, a lot of people are going to look very stupid.'

'Worse than stupid, in your case.'

'That's why I'm willing to keep my mouth shut. At a price.'

'What price?'

'Half of what I stood to net last time. You can afford it. Just half. Isn't that fair?'

'No, not in the least.'

'I'll give you twenty-four hours to think it over. Meet me here this time tomorrow with your answer.'

'Why here?'

'Because this is one grave I know the exact location of.' She almost smiled then. It would have been an admission that something beyond greed and envy were at work, but the admission never quite came.

'I don't believe you have the courage to drag it all into the open now.'

'I don't need courage, just a lack of alternatives. I've had to scrape by on a budget lately, leading the kind of dull deadening life I swore I never would. Well, I've had enough of that, and this is the only way to escape it.'

'Isn't it better than prison?'

'Oh, I've no intention of going back there. With what the papers will pay me for the truth, I can leave the country and become a different person. You know how good I am at that.'

'Yes, I do.'

'But that's not an option for you, is it? Now you're a committed family man. Think about it. We made a deal before. We can make another. It's simple enough.'

'If you really believe—'

'I believe anything you say now you might look back on as rather foolish when you've had a chance to weigh up the options. Take my word for it. I've been weighing them for a long time.'

'And I get twenty-four hours to do the same?'

'Exactly. Generous in the circumstances.' She held my gaze for a moment. Whether she felt the same strange complicity with me as I felt with her I had no way of telling, and I'd never have dared to ask, for fear of the answer. We'd set ourselves up for this years ago, by agreeing – however reluctantly – to share and conceal the truth. What is a secret without trust but a bargain waiting to be broken? 'Until tomorrow?' she added.

I nodded. 'Until tomorrow.'

So there it is. The threat I've lived with since we first struck our deal. The dilemma I've liked to pretend I didn't anticipate. Well, if it had to happen, let it happen. Here and now. There's no more fitting place or time. And I have until tomorrow to reach a decision. Who needs more than that?

I look from the window down at the sloping flank of the lawns and listen to the roar of the traffic accelerating up the hill. I remember a time when there was so little of it you could hear a single car cross Boscawen Bridge and labour up the road towards the Isolation Hospital. Just as I remember a time when I knew nothing of the truth about Uncle Joshua's death except the little that the average newspaper reader on the Clapham omnibus knew. For more than thirty years, as child and man, I inhabited that happy state. Then, early one Sunday morning in September 1981, on the path near the rhododendrons down there, where my gaze lingers, I caught my first sight, partially blocked by undergrowth, of what brought that phase of my life to an abrupt and horrifying end. And set the next in motion. Moving towards this day. And tomorrow.

I lower the window and shut out the noise. But not the memories. They rush in and surround me as I slowly cross the room and lie down on the bed and close my eyes, the better to confront them. I'm not going anywhere. I'm not running away. I have until tomorrow to relive them all. As it seems I must. Before I decide.

YESTERDAY

CHAPTER ONE

By September 1981, the murder of my great-uncle, Joshua Carnoweth, had ceased to be a shocking and lamented blow to Truro's peaceful image of itself. Thirty-four years had transmuted it into a quaint footnote of civic history. Most of the many things said about it at the time had been forgotten, and all of the passions stirred had been dissipated. It wasn't that nobody remembered, it was just that nobody cared enough to call the events to mind. Three decades of the affluent society had cast the rationed pleasures and abundant pains of 1947 into relative antiquity, and with them the memories of those who'd failed to outlive the year.

Even within the family, of which old Joshua had been a semi-detached member, his name was seldom mentioned. Some of us lived in his house. All of us – to varying degrees – prospered thanks to the fortune my grandmother had inherited from him. But most of us had trained ourselves to pretend he'd played no real part in transforming the Napiers from humble shopkeepers into company directors and absentee hoteliers. He hadn't intended to, after all. He hadn't wanted to shower his wealth on us. He'd probably have been outraged that his murder should have such a consequence. To that extent, perhaps our neglect of his memory was justified. Perhaps anything beyond collective indifference would have been like dancing on his grave. That's how I'd have defended it if I'd had to. But then I was among the least witting of his beneficiaries. I thought I knew the whole story, but I didn't know the half of it. I thought I remembered it exactly as it had been, but what I remembered was a cunningly wrought fiction that had worn dangerously thin without anyone noticing. And by September 1981, it had reached breaking point.

Saturday the fifth of September was the day my niece, Tabitha Rutherford, was to marry Dominic Beale, a good-looking and highly eligible young merchant banker. It was also, by happy contrivance, my parents' golden wedding anniversary. A full-scale family celebration was therefore arranged. The wedding was to be at St Mary Clement Methodist Church in the centre of Truro, followed by a reception at Tredower House.

Since my grandmother's death, the family home had been converted into Cornwall's premier hotel and con-ference centre (according to the brochure), managed by my brother-in-law, Trevor Rutherford. This had been my father's solution to the problem of what to do with Trevor when he sold off the chain of six Napier's Depart-ment Stores which Gran's inheritance from Uncle Joshua had helped him establish in the Fifties. He'd done that almost as soon as death had neutralized her veto on such a conservative move, and retired with my mother to Jersey. A few years later, realizing Cornwall really did have a claim on their souls, they'd moved back to what must still be the most desirable residence on the Helford estuary. Tredower House Hotel had meanwhile begun to live up to its reputation, thanks more to my sister Pam's organizational abilities than any managerial excellence on Trevor's part.

The hotel was closed for the weekend, so that the vast gathering of friends, relations and business associates could revel in our hospitality. And on Saturday morning, reluctantly obedient to Pam's summons, I drove down from Pangbourne to join in the merrymaking. I'd given the Stag a tune-up for the journey and made it in four hours dead, little short of a record in those days. Pam had wanted me to go down on Friday, but I'd claimed an open-top drive against the clock was just what I needed to blow away some end-of-week cobwebs.

That was an excuse, of course, as I'm sure she realized. I couldn't boycott an event of this magnitude, but I could minimize my exposure to it. A last-minute arrival and a prompt departure the following afternoon: I had it all planned. I'd be there, but with any luck I'd feel as if I hadn't been.

There'd been a pretty classic falling out between me and Dad. It went back twenty years, to when I'd walked out on a managerial traineeship at the Plymouth store and the generous allowance with which he rewarded filial obedience. I was making a living now, and not a bad one, but there had been times, too many for comfort, when I hadn't. I'd not asked to be helped out of any of them, and Dad hadn't offered. Pride got in the way on both sides. He wanted me to admit my mistakes without acknowledging any of his own, and he probably thought I wanted the same of him. So an armed truce was what we got. It left me with a unique status in recent generations of my family: that of a more or less self-made man. Self-remade was actually nearer the mark, in view of a sustained attempt at drinking myself to death in the late Sixties. But the upshot was the same. I wasn't in and I wasn't out. I was one of them, but it didn't feel much like it – to them or to me.

Something of the same ambivalence characterized my relationship with the city of my birth. Truro's both what you expect and what you don't of a cathedral city at the damp and distant tip of the south-west peninsula. A place of long, steep, curving hills, of bright light falling on rain-washed stone, of Georgian elegance cheek by jowl with malty warehouses and muddy wharves, of poverty and deprivation crammed in with the tourism and the Celtic romance and the strange, stubborn sense of meaning. None of the features of it I can most readily picture – the huge out-of-scale cathedral, the viaduct soaring above Victoria Park, my old school high on its hill to the south, the house in Crescent Road where I was born, Tredower House itself – none of them were much more than a hundred years old then. Yet what I carry about with me of Truro, and can neither discard nor visualize, seems both older and stronger. We Napiers are partly incomers. One of Grandfather Napier's principal attractions as far as my grandmother was concerned was that he *wasn't* a Cornishman. But the Carnoweths are as Cornish as saffron cake. Their Truronian roots lie deep, and some stem reaches me, however far or long I stray.

All this rendered any visit of mine to Tredower House a venture into well-charted waters that were nonetheless turbulent. It stood, bowered in trees, near the top of the hill on the St Austell road, a Gothic mansion that must have looked stark and ugly when built for Sir Reginald Pencavel, the china clay magnate, back in the 1870s. But the maturing of the grounds and the weathering of the sandstone had given it a sort of acquired avuncularity, like an old acquaintance you suddenly realize has become a friend.

The last of the Pencavels was killed on the Somme.

When his widow remarried in 1920, she put the house up for sale. Its buyer was a prodigal son of the city, my great-uncle Joshua Carnoweth, who'd just returned from a long and self-imposed exile in the gold fields of North America with a greater fortune than anyone had thought him capable of amassing. The purchase of Tredower House was both a rebuke to his doubting contemporaries and a declaration that his wandering days were over. He was forty-seven; too young, I'd have said, for subsiding into Cornish squiredom. But he had reasons enough, and no way of knowing that those reasons would one day conspire to destroy him.

I was glad, in a way, that the house had become a busier, brasher place since it had ceased to be my home. A modern conference suite to the rear, a car park in what had been the orchard and a scatter of signposts and security lights proclaimed its commercial identity in a way that subdued more personal memories without ever quite erasing them. Even weddings had become a regular branch of the business, though none of the receptions laid on for clients could ever have required a larger pinker-draped golden-ribboned marquee than the one I glimpsed through the trees as I sped past in the Stag that morning, *en route* to the church.

The ceremony went off flawlessly, without so much as a fluffed line, and was followed by a mass transit to Tredower House. With so many people eager to congratulate the bride and her grandparents, Pam distracted by her responsibilities as hostess and Trevor having for once a good excuse to ignore me, I drifted with little resistance to the margins of the event. An hour at least of champagne and canapés loomed ahead. For a reformed alcoholic on edgy terms with his relatives, this promised to be a torturous interlude. So I took myself off, as discreetly as possible, to a shady corner of the lawn, propped myself against the croquet bench that had been moved out of harm's way beneath the beech tree, and gazed back at the party. Laughter mixed ripely with the jazz band's lazy melodies in the still summer air. Colourful outfits swirled like a slowly wound kaleidoscope in the hazy sunshine. Light sparkled on champagne flutes. Joy, pleasure and satisfaction mingled. And trying desperately not to feel dog-in-the-mangerish, I toasted them all with orange juice.

My parents, along with the bride and groom, were out of sight within the marquee. They'd still be busy greeting the guests, and I knew they'd be doing it with tireless aplomb. Gran had trained my father well in the social obligations that went with the status she'd carved out for him. She'd taught him to project a bluff glad-handed image of himself that had smoothed his path in the world of big business and local politics. It was an image old age seemed only to have strengthened. You needed to have been close to him to see and know a different kind of man.

But my mother had been closer than anyone for the past fifty years and I knew her devotion to him was no act, so I reckoned there must always have been more that was genuine in him than I'd been prepared to admit. I suspected Gran had manoeuvred them into marriage in the first place. The provision of a wife for her son and a mother for her grandchildren wasn't something she'd have left to chance, that's for certain. But, if so, her manoeuvring had paid off, as usual. I'd never had cause to doubt that my parents loved each other. The only question in my mind was whether they truly loved me.

Pam would have dismissed such an idea as nonsense, and with good reason. Her upbringing had turned her into a practical and affectionate woman, with a daughter who was a credit to her. Tabitha had her mother's shrewdness and clarity of vision, as well as her fine-boned looks and graceful bearing.

I caught sight of the father of the bride then, moving artfully through the crowd. Middle age had improved Trevor, smoothing out the gaucheness and insecurity I remembered from when Pam had first introduced me to him. The public relations side of hotel management was something he excelled in. It clearly agreed with him. He drank heavily, without showing any ill effects, which naturally I hugely resented, while secretly regarding him as a fool, which was, in turn, what he probably thought me. And both of us could have called on some substantial evidence to support our claim.

I don't think I heard anything to make me look round at that moment. Maybe I sensed that I wasn't the only one observing the scene, that a change had occurred, a thread been pulled from the fabric of the day. I'm not sure. It doesn't matter, anyway. The fact is I did look round, and saw a man standing beneath the stretching branches of the old horse chestnut that dominated the north-east corner of the garden. He was about my height, but thinner, with matted greying hair and beard. His clothes were ragged and dusty, threadbare jeans and an open-necked check shirt worn beneath an old mackintosh. The mac was what made me think he must be a tramp. Who else would wear one on such a sunny day? He was trembling too, which couldn't be from the cold. His face was in shadow, but I had the impression he was looking at me rather than the wedding party spilling across the lawn.

I stood upright and rounded the bench. As I did so, he took a step towards me, a step that carried him into a pool of sunlight. I saw his face clearly for the first time. If he was a tramp, he'd not been on the road long. His eyes weren't dull enough, his skin wasn't rough enough. I felt instinctively that I knew him, but I didn't trust the instinct. His mouth twitched. A smile or a grimace, it was hard to tell which. He mumbled something. Even without the noise of the reception, it would have been difficult to catch. But catch it I did. 'Chris.' My name. Spoken by somebody I could no longer take for a stranger.

'Do I know you?' I said, frowning.

Then he did smile, lopsidedly and familiarly. He glanced up at the thick bough of the horse chestnut above his head, raised his arms slowly towards it and moved them back and forth, miming the action of someone propelling himself on a swing suspended from the branch. I felt my mouth drop open, remembering how I'd swung from that very branch as a child, how my boyhood friend Nicky Lanyon and I had—

'Nicky?' I should have known at once. Between the ages of seven and eleven, I suppose we'd spent more time with each other than with any other single person. We'd been the most inseparable of pals for those four years straddling the end of the war. Chris and Nicky; Nicky and Chris. But all that had ended in the summer of 1947. All that and much more. 'Is it you?'

I hadn't seen him for thirty-four years. I'd done my very best to forget him. But forgetfulness, I realized as I looked at him, was only a pretence. I remembered him as if shabby middle age were merely a disguise he'd cast off at any moment, as if the eleven-year-old boy he'd once been could step suddenly into view, hair shorn, eyes sparkling, face tanned by a Cornish summer, shirt hatched from some woodland scramble, trousers grass-stained, knees muddied, socks rumpled, shoes scuffed; as if every fragment of a lost friendship could be miraculously gathered and reassembled. There was a moment – a fleeting instant – when I was happy, so very happy, to see him. Then guilt and caution and something like contempt rushed to defend my part in his ostracism. I felt myself stiffen and draw back. Then saw him flinch, as if he too had watched the portcullis slam down between us.

'What are you doing here?' My tone had altered without my meaning it to. It must have sounded cold and stiff and forbidding.

'Came to see . . .' He spoke slowly, slurring the words. His gaze lingered on me with a strange mild curiosity. 'Came to see . . . you.'

'Me?'

'Read . . . about this.' He tugged what looked like a scrap of newspaper from the pocket of his mac and held it up. I took it for a cutting from the local paper, and guessed Trevor might have inserted some notice about the wedding. But what was Nicky's interest in it? He didn't even live in the area. Did he? 'Knew . . . you'd be here.'

'You've been . . . waiting for me?'

'Mum's dead.'

'Your mother? I'm sorry. I . . .'

'My sister too.'

Nicky's younger sister, Freda, had died of whooping cough during the war. Mentioning her death, of which he must have known I was aware, seemed pointless, if not perverse, but I assumed it had some significance only he could understand. 'What do you want, Nicky?'

'Mum and Dad . . . together.'

'Perhaps they are now.'

'Not with me.'

'When did your mother die?'

'Six months . . . ago.' He stuffed the scrap of paper back into his pocket. 'Cancer.'

'I'm sorry to hear that.'

His gaze hardened. 'Why should you be?'

'Because I liked her.'

'Liar.'

31

'It's true.'

'Liar!' He shouted the word this time, his face flushing with a rush of anger. '*Liar!*'

'Calm down, for God's sake.'

'Why . . . should I?'

'This is my niece's wedding day. We don't want any . . . unpleasantness.' I regretted the words as soon as I'd used them. His own life had contained more than enough unpleasantness, and it was certain he'd wanted none of that either. 'What are you . . . doing these days?'

'Looking.'

'For what?'

'The answer.'

'To what?'

'You know.'

'No. I don't.'

'But do you . . . know the answer? Do you, Chris?'

'The answer to what?'

'Who killed my father?' The question was so bizarre, yet so evidently sincere, that I simply stared at him in response, trying to read in his despairing gaze the harshness of the road he'd trodden since the summer of 1947. 'Who did it?'

'What the hell's going on?' Trevor's voice, raised and peremptory, cut through the seclusion of our exchanges. I turned round and saw him striding towards us, drink and disapproval darkening his expression. 'What's the shouting about?'

'Nothing. It's all right. There's no need—'

'Who's he?' Trevor glared past me at Nicky. 'Looks like some bloody dosser.'

'Nothing of the kind. I can—'

'This is a private party,' said Trevor, cutting across me. 'Get the hell out of here.'

'Hold on, Trevor. You don't understand.'

But lack of understanding had never restrained my brother-in-law. He marched towards Nicky, one arm gesturing in the direction of the road. Nicky stumbled back, raising his hands and lowering his head submissively. Sorrow – and guilt – lanced into me at this show of weakness. I called his name, but it was too late. He turned and began to run, stooping beneath the branches, heading for the part of the wall we'd often scaled together as boys, with Trevor in token pursuit. It was no contest. Nicky ran like a fox before the hounds, vanishing into the deeper shade of the trees. In my mind's eye, I saw him climb by the remembered footholds up on to the wall, drop down the other side, descend the bank to the pavement below, then jog away along the road.

'The bastard's gone,' panted Trevor as he rejoined me by the bench. 'Legged it.'

'So I see.'

'You should have sent him packing yourself. Drunks and derelicts. You can't afford to give them any encouragement.'

'He was as sober as I am, and no derelict.'

'You talk as if he was a friend of yours from Alcoholics Anonymous.'

'A friend? Yes. Well, as a matter of fact he is.' I sighed. 'Or was.'

'A friend of yours? Should I know him, then?'

'In a sense, you do.'

'Really? What's his name?'

'Nicky Lanyon.'

'*Lanyon?*'

'Yes. Son of Michael Lanyon.'

'What? The man who . . .'

'That's right. The man they hanged for Uncle Joshua's murder.'

*　　*　　*

33

'*The man they hanged for Uncle Joshua's murder.*' The phrase lodged in my mind, with dormant recollections clinging to it like cobwebs on a musty old signpost. Trevor hadn't known us in 1947, hadn't even lived in Cornwall. To him the Lanyons were just an irrelevant piece of second-hand history. Even so, he didn't want their name mentioned on a day set aside to celebrate our family. He was aware that the Lanyons represented nothing so substantial as a threat, but something unsatisfactory, unresolved and faintly disturbing. Nicky's presence in Truro didn't worry him, but he'd have preferred him to be somewhere else. Anywhere else, in fact.

'Let's keep this to ourselves, shall we, Chris?' he said as we walked back across the lawn. 'It's the last thing Melvyn and Una need to hear about on their anniversary.' The reference to my parents was a direct appeal to my sense of family responsibility. But I suspected that Mum and Dad weren't the people he was really worried about, as he tacitly went on to admit. 'And I don't want anything to spoil the day for Tabs.'

'Would she even recognize the name?'

'Probably not. But I'd like to keep it that way.'

'What about Dominic? Does he know how we inherited this place?'

Trevor pulled up sharply. I stopped as well and turned to look at him. His expression suggested that he was trying hard not to be riled. 'In a couple of hours, my daughter and son-in-law will be on their way to Mauritius for their honeymoon. Is it asking too much for you to do your best to make sure they get a happy send-off?'

'No. It's not.' I gave him a man-to-man smile. 'Let's forget about Nicky. I reckon we've seen the last of him.'

I did rather well, if I say so myself. I discovered the secret of how to amuse Dominic's mother, nearly sold his father the Bentley Continental then taking pride of place in my showroom back in Pangbourne, made an impromptu speech wittily blending the role of grateful son and gratified uncle, and generally threw myself enthusiastically into the proceedings. I saw Mum and Dad share at least one glance of pleasurable surprise at my contribution and was happy they shouldn't have the faintest idea what lay behind it. I was trying my damnedest to shake off the guilt and shame that Nicky's sudden appearance had left me with. I was trying to shake them off before I had too long to wonder why I should be prey to them in the first place.

By late evening, I'd more or less succeeded. Tabitha and Dominic had departed for Mauritius, and the disco laid on for their friends had begun to wind down. My mother had started to tire, but my father still seemed to be enjoying himself, so I suggested a frame of snooker before they went home, knowing how much he relished beating a younger opponent. He rose to the challenge and we took ourselves off to the billiards room, mercifully distant from the beat of the band.

The room was kept up for the use of guests, but was pretty much as it had always been, with a full-size table, original leather seating and faded hunting prints around the walls. The setting made me think of Uncle Joshua, despite his disdain for all things sporting. Even so, it was the nostalgic bent of my father's conversation, as he plodded round the table building a break, that undermined my resistance to memories of Nicky Lanyon – and *his* father.

'It's been a great day. Really has. Your mother's had a wonderful time. So have I. Far cry from *our* wedding day, I can tell you. Oh yes. *Very* different.'

'In what way?'

'Well, it was the middle of the Depression then, wasn't

35

it? We were living in Carclew Street. Didn't move to Crescent Road until after Pam was born. And the shop was really only ticking by. There wasn't money to throw around taking honeymoons on the other side of the world. Your mother and I had three days in Penzance. *Three days.* Can you believe it?'

I chuckled. 'I think so.'

'As for the reception, that was in a function room at the Royal. No marquee on the lawn up here for us.'

'But Uncle Joshua was at the wedding. I've seen him in the photographs.'

'Oh, he was there all right, looking down his nose at me and your mother.'

'He was never the type to—'

'What would you know?' Dad straightened up from squinting along his cue to look at me. 'You never saw the hard side of his nature. He could have done something more for us than just turn up to the wedding, couldn't he? He had money to spare and a big house here to rattle around in. But did he ever offer to help us out? Did he hell.'

'He helped us in the end, though, didn't he? Inadvertently, I mean. He got himself murdered by the man who stood to inherit everything. The money *and* the house.'

'Yes.' A faraway look came into my father's eyes. 'So he did.'

'Michael Lanyon.'

'I know his name, boy. I know it well.'

'Funny, isn't it?' Why hadn't it occurred to me sooner? That's what Nicky must have been thinking, as he watched the grand and wealthy people admiring each other on the lawn. That they could have been *his* friends, attending a party at *his* house, eating *his* food, drinking *his* champagne. But for his father's conviction for the murder of Joshua Carnoweth. Because the law doesn't allow a murderer to profit from his crime by inheriting his victim's estate. Though it does allow his son to be ordered off what would otherwise be his property – without compunction.

'What's funny?'

'How things turn out.'

Dad's potting went off the boil after that, but mine did too, so he still won comfortably. We went back to the lounge, where Mum had fallen asleep, and Trevor was swiftly volunteered to drive them home. After they'd gone, I planned to stage a speedy retreat to bed. But Pam insisted I have some coffee with her, and somehow I felt sure it wasn't for the pleasure of comparing notes on Tabitha's going-away outfit.

'Trevor told me about Nicky.'

'Ah. Did he?'

'What's he doing in Truro?'

'I've no idea.'

'He was your friend.'

'You make that sound like an accusation.'

'I'm sorry. I don't mean to. I'm tired and . . . I wouldn't want anything to mar the day.'

'Nothing has marred it.'

'No, but . . . Was it a coincidence, do you think? Him showing up here this afternoon.'

'Not sure. He said he'd read about the event.'

She frowned. 'That must be the piece in last week's *West Briton*. Mum and Dad's golden wedding tied to some free publicity about our reception facilities. Trevor thought it was a good idea.'

'But you didn't?'

'Well, they hadn't actually got to the day then, had they? And Tabs and Dominic . . . I just thought it could have been better left till afterwards.' She sighed. 'I don't believe in tempting providence.'

'Don't worry. It looks like providence has resisted temptation.'

'Let's hope so.' She gazed at me with sisterly concern. 'Was it a shock, seeing him after all these years?'

'Naturally.'

'How did he look?'

'Rough.'

'How did he *seem*?'

'Confused. Fuddled. Distressed.'

'Not all there, Trevor reckoned.'

'Maybe not.'

'Where's he living now?'

'He didn't say.'

'Nor why he's come back?'

'No,' I lied solemnly. 'Not a hint.'

I didn't dream about Nicky that night, which was a victory in itself. I slept soundly in the room I'd occupied when we moved into Tredower House early in 1948. It was a sentimental gesture on Pam's part to allocate it to me. She wasn't to know I'd have preferred a room with fewer footholds in the past.

When I woke, early, to birdsong and the trafficless hush of Sunday morning, I found myself recalling the day of the move from Crescent Road. Gran had planned it like a military campaign and must have been pleased by how smoothly it went. She'd had long enough to refine her plans, of course. She'd known we'd end up there since Uncle Joshua's death the previous August. Assuming the man he'd willed the house to was convicted of his murder, as in due course he was.

It was then already nearly six months since I'd last seen Nicky. Six months that were to stretch to thirty-four years, thin and hard, across our adolescence and adulthood. Even then, he was lost to me. And I was glad. It meant I could do what everybody wanted me to do: forget him.

Looking back, I could forgive my behaviour. The enormity of murder – the black stain of my friend's vicarious part in it – would have suborned most eleven-year-olds. Especially when my family and half of Truro seemed so happy to fasten guilt by association on *all* the Lanyons, whatever their age. But that wouldn't do any more. I was no longer a child. I'd had all my adult life to track down Nicky and learn if I could help him cope with having a murderer for a father. But I hadn't. Instead, I'd let *him* track *me* down.

I took a shower, put some clothes on and walked out into the grounds, confident that nobody else would be up and about so early. The marquee was still in place. The lawn was littered with paper serviettes, discarded cocktail sticks, cigarette butts, champagne corks and miniature drifts of confetti blown across from the drive in the course of the night. The caterers would be back later to clear up, but for the moment everything was still and desolate, yet strangely peaceful.

I found myself wishing that Nicky would arrive *now*, when I was prepared for him and free to speak as I wanted to, when there was nobody to object or interfere. I followed the path the long way round the lawn towards the spot where I'd seen him the previous afternoon, hoping somehow that he'd come back and was waiting to give me a second chance. It wasn't much of a hope, more a fantasy really. Life doles out second chances with a sparing hand. I knew that. It's why I started in surprise when I first made out the figure beneath the horse chestnut tree.

I raised my hand and quickened my pace, smiling uncertainly. But there was no response, and as I neared the top of the rise between us, I saw why. More clearly with every hurrying step. There was somebody there, dressed like Nicky. He wasn't standing, and he wasn't swinging either. He was hanging by a single length of rope from the bough I'd seen Nicky stretch his hands towards. Hanging with arms limp, head bowed and feet dangling.

CHAPTER TWO

I could see the crown of the horse chestnut tree, green and sleepy in the thickening sunlight, from my chair near the tall windows of the lounge. Not the branch scored by the rope, nor the bosky patch below, where they'd zipped Nicky into his plastic shroud. Just the dense green cumulus of the big old tree we'd climbed in and knocked conkers from and swung beneath in heedless childhood days. My gaze rested on it with my memory, while in the present metal chinked on metal as the pink and gold marquee slowly came down and Detective Sergeant Collins laboriously checked the facts one more time.

'We're sure it *is* Nicholas Lanyon, are we?' Our certainty on the point, given that we admitted he'd been beyond our ken for more than thirty years, clearly puzzled him. 'Mrs Rutherford?'

'Yes,' said Pam. 'I mean, that is, I haven't actually—'

'The dead man is Nicky Lanyon,' I put in. 'You can take my word for it.'

'For the moment, we have to, sir. He didn't seem to be carrying any identification. In fact, he didn't seem to be carrying anything at all.'

'No money?'

'Less than two pounds in loose change.'

'What did I say?' remarked Trevor gloomily. 'Down and out. There's your motive, I suppose.'

'But why come here, sir? That's what I don't understand. You said his family left Truro years ago.'

'Thirty-four years ago,' I softly specified. 'If he was planning to kill himself, coming back here to do it makes perfect sense.'

'Chris,' pleaded Pam, 'do we really need to bother the sergeant with all that?'

'I should think he'd want to be forewarned of the interest the press will take in this.'

'Minimal, I'd guess, sir. Suicide's not—'

'Murder, Sergeant. That's why they'll be interested. Nicky Lanyon's father and another man murdered the owner of this house in 1947.'

Collins frowned. 'In that case, you're probably right. Hanged, were they?'

'Nicky's father was. Enough to start the crime correspondents rooting through the archives, do you think?'

'More than likely, sir. Any idea at all about next of kin?'

'Nicky said his mother was dead.'

'Any brothers or sisters?'

'None living.'

'*Anybody* in Truro who might still have been in touch with him?'

'Not that I can think of.'

'Hold on,' said Pam. 'Wasn't there an aunt?'

'Yes,' I responded, amazed for a moment at how easily and completely I'd forgotten. 'Nicky's mother had a sister who married into a farming family down on the Roseland – the Jagos. He used to spend a week with them every summer. I . . . went with him one year.'

'Then you'll know where we can find them.'

'Yes.' My eyes focused on the horse chestnut tree again. 'I know.'

Detective Sergeant Collins looked as if he hadn't even been born in 1947. No wonder the name Lanyon meant nothing to him. It was so long ago. But not as long ago as the start of it all. You had to go back much further for that. To the turn of the century and beyond. To a time when Truro Cathedral was only half built, a scaffolded giant slowly taking shape in the heart of the city it would eventually tower over, an Anglican cuckoo swelling and soaring in a nest of Methodism.

There was a framed photograph of the west front of the cathedral *circa* 1900 hanging in the hotel bar. It showed the western half of the building as no more than a shell, with the stonemasons and surveyors pausing in their toil to gaze down from their lofty platforms at the camera. My great-grandfather, Amos Carnoweth, wasn't one of them. I knew that for a fact, despite stonemasonry having been his craft and the cathedral his last place of work. I knew because he'd died in a fall from scaffolding at the other end of the cathedral back in the spring of 1887. His son Joshua was fourteen years old then; his daughter Adelaide, my grandmother, was eight. She told me once that *her* grandmother claimed the tragedy was God's judgement on a Methodist daring to turn his hand to Anglican granite. Those were the good old days.

Great-Grandfather's death meant a move from the family home in Old Bridge Street. Gran and Uncle Joshua had grown up there, next to the stables of the Red Lion Hotel, a mere drove's throw from the cathedral, in air tinged with dung, harness oil and granite dust. They found cheaper lodgings in Tabernacle Street, just off Lemon Quay, where mud and fish and sailcloth were the prevailing scents.

The past is always closer than you think. The Red Lion was finished off by a runaway lorry in the late Sixties, and the river flowing past Lemon Quay was covered over in the Twenties. I only ever remember the triangular space between Lemon and Back Quays as a car park, with the cathedral looming to the north as a complete and permanent edifice. But somehow I also seem to remember what my grandmother remembered: a different, darker, sweeter Truro, six hours from London by the fastest train, but in many ways as remote as Constantinople.

Uncle Joshua became the family breadwinner after his father's death, labouring in a tin mine out at Baldhu twelve hours a day. Gran used to take a freshly cooked pasty out to him for his lunch, wrapped in a cloth to keep it warm. Three miles there and three miles back. There must have been loyalty between them then, a trusting tenderness, and no reason in this world to think it wouldn't last their lifetimes. Their mother's health, mental as well as physical, declined, but they held their life as a family together.

Gran left school at fourteen, despite her academic promise, as she often later lamented. Maybe, if her father had still been alive, it might have been different, but with her mother no longer even up to taking in washing, there was a living to be earned. She took a job as a seamstress-cum-sales-assistant at Webb's drapery store in Boscawen Street. Another assistant of her own age, Cordelia Angwin, struck up a friendship with her and became a regular visitor to the house in Tabernacle Street. Cordelia was an energetic and vivacious girl rapidly blossoming into a beauty. At first Uncle Joshua paid her little heed, but then, as time passed, and she grew older and more composed and more and more beautiful . . .

Uncle Joshua never told me any of this and Gran was

never an entirely reliable chronicler of events involving herself, so a lot had to be guesswork. Deduction, I prefer to call it. Joshua Carnoweth when I knew him was a taciturn and watchful man, seemingly incapable of grand romantic gestures. But things were different then, and so was he. He fell hopelessly in love with Cordelia Angwin and pleaded with her to marry him. But she wanted to wait and preferably find a husband capable of elevating her in society, which no mere tinner was likely to be able to do. The rift between Gran and Uncle Joshua dates from this period. Reading her character as well as I can, I should think she was at first embarrassed by his pursuit of her friend, then angry at both of them when she realized just how deeply he adored her. Neither was behaving as she wished – something she never could abide.

Matters came to a head in the summer of 1897. Cordelia was eighteen and had made it clear to Uncle Joshua that she wouldn't even consider marrying him until she was twenty-one. The implication, I suppose, was that she thought a better choice of husband might cross her path by then. Uncle Joshua must have reckoned that gave him three years to transform himself into an irresistible catch. News had just seeped out of a big gold strike in the Canadian Yukon the previous year. The word reaching the tin-mining community via the dockside taverns of Falmouth was that there were fortunes to be made by those with the right skills. Uncle Joshua was offered a cheap passage on a cargo vessel bound for Nova Scotia. He took it, reckoning he could work his way across to the west coast and reach the Yukon by spring. He extracted some sort of parting promise from Cordelia to wait for him, promising in return that he'd be back before the three years were up, pockets bulging with gold dust.

Gran regarded this as an unforgivable betrayal, since it

left her to support their ailing mother alone. She thought that if there were rich pickings to be had in the Yukon, there'd be none left by the time her brother got there. It was a realistic assessment. But young love and realism are mutually exclusive. Uncle Joshua went off to chase his dream.

A few letters reached Gran and Cordelia in the course of the winter and spring, reporting his progress across Canada. Then – nothing. No news; no word; no contact of any kind. Joshua Carnoweth vanished from sight and, eventually, as the years passed, from mind. Dead, or too ashamed to come home and admit his failure – nobody knew which. But, either way, he didn't return. In three years, or six, or twelve, or twenty.

Back in Truro, Gran started going out with a young man named Cyril Napier. No hopeless love match for her. My grandfather was chosen as just the sort of level-headed but ambitious young man she needed as a companion in life. His parents were originally from Worcestershire. They'd moved to Cornwall some years before and opened a grocery shop in River Street. His father was in poor health and had hoped the milder Cornish air would agree with him. It may have done so, but only up to a point. He died shortly after Gran and Grandad got engaged. They brought forward the wedding, so as to be able to take over the running of the shop as a married couple, and moved into the Napier home in Carclew Street with both mothers to save money. Grandad's mother helped in the shop, of course, which meant they didn't have to employ anyone. It was hard work, trading from seven in the morning till eight at night, six days a week, but it was their own business, and Carclew Street was a little higher up the hill, both topographically and socially. My father's birth in 1905 meant they were working to improve the lot of the next generation as well. Gran was setting out her stall for the future.

So, in a sense, was Cordelia Angwin. She left Webb's and went into service at a big house on the Falmouth road. She waited for Uncle Joshua – or a better proposition, depending how cynical you want to be – until she was twenty-one, and well beyond. She and Gran lost touch, although they must have bumped into one another from time to time; Truro's too small a city for them not to have. What they said or thought on such occasions I don't know.

About ten years after Uncle Joshua's departure for the Canadian unknown, Cordelia married. Her husband worked as a junior clerk for the city council. His name was Archie Lanyon. They moved into a small house in St Austell Street, where their first and only child was born in 1910. They christened him Michael.

The cathedral was finished that same year, and the stonemasons had to look elsewhere for work.

Detective Sergeant Collins was long gone and most of the caterers' clearing-up crew likewise. I stood on the lawn, watching the men from the marquee hire company stowing the last of their gear on to a lorry parked halfway down the drive. The afternoon was still and sultry, the sunlight warm on my face. Some small creature was rooting through the leaf litter beneath the trees beyond the flower border. With very little effort of the imagination, the discovery I'd made that morning could have been consigned to the realm of delusion. But its consequences couldn't be ignored. They were still queuing up to remind me of the reality of Nicky's crooked lolling head, his chin crusty with dried spittle, his tongue swollen and protruding, his eyes dead and staring – straight at me.

'Chris!' I heard Pam call to me from the house and

47

turned to see her walking down to join me, jangling a set of keys in her hand. 'Are you all right?'

'Yes. I think so.'

'I'm going to drive down and let Mum and Dad know what's happened. Better than a phone call, I thought.'

'Good idea.'

'Do you want to come?'

'No thanks. I . . . um . . .'

'Have somewhere else to go?'

I smiled uneasily. 'Yes. I probably will . . . take a drive while you're gone.'

'To see the Jagos?'

'It seems you've read my mind.'

'I reckoned it was either that or you'd head straight back to Pangbourne.'

'No. I . . . think I'll probably stay for a few days. If that's all right.'

'No problem.'

'Of course, if you need the room . . .'

'I said there was no problem.'

'Yes. So you did. Thanks. I . . .'

'Chris, there's something you should know. About the Jagos. They had a son, didn't they?'

'Yes. Tommy. A few years younger than Nicky and me.'

'He died. A while back. I read about it in the paper. A farming accident. A tractor rolled over on him, I think. Something like that.'

I glanced away. 'Oh, great. That's just great.'

'I was going to mention it to you, but by the time we next heard from you . . . I must have forgotten.'

'Never mind.' I put my arm round her in a fleeting gesture of brotherly affection. 'Tell Mum and Dad I'm really sorry if this has spoilt their anniversary.'

'It's not your fault.' She sighed. 'At least it didn't happen the night before.'

'It couldn't have.'

She frowned at me. 'Why not?'

'Because I wasn't here then. That's why it *is* partly my fault. He was waiting for me. He wanted me to be here when he did it, and to see what he looked like afterwards.'

'You can't know that.'

'I think I can.'

'But why? What would be the point?'

'I'm not sure. But I'm going to try and find out.'

'And you think the Jagos can help you?'

'Maybe. I have to start somewhere.'

'You don't *have* to start. It's not compulsory.'

'No? Well, I'll tell you this, Pam. It certainly feels as if it is.'

Uncle Joshua never spoke openly of his years in North America. The most detailed information I ever had out of him was when he found me looking at a map of Alaska and the Yukon territory of Canada one day. It was in a big old atlas in the library at Tredower House. He'd bought most of the books in the room from Lady Pencavel as a job lot, as a way of filling the shelves, I assumed, since you'd never have called him a literary man. But maps he seemed to like. Maybe they reminded him of the wandering life. It must have answered some need in his soul, otherwise he wouldn't have followed it for so long. And, not surprisingly, the atlas always seemed to fall open at that particular page.

Juneau, Sitka, Skagway; Whitehorse and Dawson City; Valdez, Fairbanks, Nome. He knew them all. That was obvious from the way he spoke about them. He had his memories: of the tented city on the beach at Nome, where gold sparkled in the black sand of the Bering Sea; of the mud-steeped streets and smoke-filled saloons of Dawson; of the smokestacks and aerial tramways of the

Treadwell gold mine stretching along the shore of Douglas Island across the channel from Juneau – so big it was a town unto itself; of the long sunless winters, when the snow drifted higher than the houses and the temperature dropped to 50 below; and of the short nightless summers, when the flies and mosquitoes could literally drive a man mad. He spoke of such things that afternoon more freely and fully than at any other time. I don't know why. Maybe my curiosity and his nostalgia for the land that had been his second home peaked simultaneously by pure chance. It was a day in the early spring of 1947, cold enough to remind him of Alaska; a day in the last spring he ever saw.

Fairbanks, deep in the Alaskan interior, was the place he said most about. He'd spent more time there than anywhere else. Years, it seemed. He talked of when it was just a scatter of tents and log cabins, but also of when it was a large and bustling town, laid waste by fire one year but rebuilt by the next. He described the annual sweepstake on the date the ice would melt in the Chena river. He recounted the celebrations that greeted the news of Congress granting Alaska the right to self-government. And he mentioned an organization I knew nothing about: the Northern Commercial Company. I absorbed these names and events with the wonder – and lack of understanding – of the child I was.

After his death, when the true scale of his wealth became apparent, I borrowed every book about Canadian and Alaskan history that Truro Public Library held. There weren't many, but from them I gleaned enough to put some flesh on the skeleton of his past, to trace the outline of the life he led during his twenty-three-year exile from Cornwall. Mum and Dad disapproved of my interest in the subject. They said it was disrespectful of the dead. Even then, I knew that was eyewash. With secretive zeal, I went on, while other boys were collecting stamps and birds' eggs and cigarette cards. More than once, I wished I had Nicky to impress with my discoveries. But that wish had to be protected with even greater secrecy than my historical researches.

Joshua Carnoweth left Cornwall in the autumn of 1897, bound, like thousands of other optimistic fortune-seekers around the world, for the Klondike goldfield. That's a fact. The rest is my reconstruction of what he must have done – but it's as close to the truth as we're ever likely to get.

Anybody who came as late as Uncle Joshua to the Klondike was bound to be disappointed. Gran was right on that score. The goldfield was compact and accessible – if you were lucky enough to be there at the start. But that was in 1896/97. If, like Joshua Carnoweth and countless others, you were still working your way up the coast of British Columbia in the spring of 1898, you were chasing a wild goose, not a golden one. And the chase was hard and long. You reached Skagway, a ramshackle crime-ridden port just over the Alaskan border. If you weren't robbed and/or murdered there on a mud-smeared plank-walk, you headed north across the mountains via the notoriously heartbreaking Chilkoot Pass to the Canadian border. You repeated the journey as many times as it took to stockpile the year's supply of food which the Mounties insisted you have before entering Canada. Then you trudged on to Lake Bennett and scrambled for a berth on a riverboat up to Dawson. And when you got there, you rapidly realized that there wasn't even a living, never mind a fortune, waiting for you. In the summer of 1898, 20,000 people, Joshua Carnoweth among them, confronted each other and their collective folly on the muddy streets of Dawson City. The Mounties ensured they were at least safer than they'd been in Skagway, but rich they weren't – nor ever likely to be. The gold was all gone or spoken for, and glitter was in short supply. Uncle Joshua must have despaired, realizing he'd come halfway round the world to gain nothing but an insight into his own stupidity. What was he to do?

The question answered itself that winter when word reached Dawson of a bigger better gold strike at Nome, on the far western coast of Alaska. The stampeders were off again, in mad pursuit, sledging or walking down 2,000 miles of frozen river. Uncle Joshua went too. On foot, I reckon. If he did have money, it wouldn't have been enough to buy a sledge *or* dogs to pull it. Maybe he knew by then that it was hopeless, that as soon as you heard of a strike it was already too late to profit from it. But there was no alternative; he had to follow the course he'd set.

Nome was in fact kinder than most goldfields to the small-timer. The metal was right there for the panning, laced through the sand along the beach. There was no premium on expensive machinery, but, as elsewhere, priority counted for everything. The best claims were taken by the spring of 1899. For the rest, there was gold to be had, but not enough – and certainly not quick enough – to yield a fortune. Uncle Joshua must have crossed from alternating hope and despair into a hard new realism on the tented foreshore at Nome that last summer of the century. You could sift a living of sorts from the sand, but if you reckoned up the profit and loss, you came out scarcely better than even. Two of the three years Cordelia had granted him were up, and it was obvious the last of them wasn't going to be any better. It was over, finished, done with. The gamble was lost.

What did he do? Here the evidence becomes sketchier. I think he realized his only chance of making good was to learn the craft of gold prospecting and to apply the knowledge in areas where none had so far been found, but where there was some reason – however slender – to believe it might be. If so, he must also have realized that the effort could take years and still go unrewarded, but I think he preferred that to creeping home, destitute and defeated. How he set about it I don't know. His familiarity with Juneau and the Treadwell mines suggests he may have worked in them to raise funds for his grand effort. As an experienced miner, it would have been a logical recourse when he left Nome even poorer than he'd left Dawson. He may have laboured there, salting away his wages, for a year or more. Then . . .

Fairbanks. The strike there broke the gold rush trend, because most of the gold lay inaccessibly deep. It took time and heavy machinery to exploit its potential, so the town of Fairbanks grew as a stable forward-looking community, spared the worst excesses of boom and bust. Uncle Joshua made it his home for the rest of his time in Alaska, and that decision made his fortune.

I think he was in from the start: July 1902, when an Italian prospector named Felix Pedro struck gold near a trading post, that was all Fairbanks was then, on the Chena river. I think he may even have been in partnership with Pedro. I remember Gran speaking scornfully once in Uncle Joshua's hearing of the Italian prisoners of war the Jagos had been lent to help with the harvest. The old man had flown to their defence, describing the Italians as 'good and honourable people'. I didn't know then that it might have been Felix Pedro he was really thinking of.

Uncle Joshua remembered Fairbanks when its permanent structures could be counted on the fingers of one hand. Which means he must have been there that first summer. He remembered the town's great fire, which swept through the business district in May 1906. And he remembered news reaching the town of President Taft signing the Alaskan home rule bill in August 1912. I think it's safe to assume he was there continuously from 1902 until the outbreak of the First World War, slowly accumulating a fortune from what must have been highly lucrative mining interests. The Fairbanks region produced 63,000,000 dollars' worth of gold between 1902 and 1914, a statistic that's stuck in my mind ever since I first came across it. Uncle Joshua presumably formed a company to administer production at his mines. Maybe he also had a stake in the Northern Commercial Company, the outfit he mentioned to me. The NCC established a virtual monopoly on road and river transport to the coast and supplied the town with water, electricity and steam heating. Maybe he invested in some of Fairbanks' other industries as well, like brewing and logging, and made generous donations to the schools and hospitals. Maybe he became a pillar of the community and decided to settle there permanently, helping civic values to establish themselves in the Alaskan heartland. For what it's worth, I believe he'd have ended his days in Fairbanks, nourishing his memories of Cordelia, yet reconciled to never seeing her again – but for the war.

That was a phase of his life he never once discussed: the four years he spent in the Canadian army, fighting on the Western Front. Some patriotic instinct must have prompted him to leave Fairbanks and volunteer his services to the military authorities in Canada. He had plenty of good reasons to stay put in Alaska. He was over forty and documents that came to light after his death showed he'd already been an American citizen for more than ten years. But still he went. Gran found some campaign medals and frayed epaulettes in an old tobacco

54

tin when she was clearing out his effects. It's only because of them that I know he was a major in the Royal Canadian Engineers. His mining experience probably meant he was a valuable recruit. Maybe he oversaw trench construction and tunnelling operations. We'll never know, because he never said – so much as a word. The only certainty is that he emerged from the conflict with mind and body intact. Unlike Cordelia's husband, Archie Lanyon, who ended *his* war with a German bullet lodged in his brain, an injury that was to prove all the crueller for not being fatal.

Uncle Joshua knew nothing of that when he was de-mobilized. Even so, something had changed in him. He wanted to go home, and home, it seems, meant Cornwall. The death and destruction he'd seen in France must have made him yearn for the land where his life had begun. I suppose he went back to Fairbanks to sell off his business interests and settle his affairs. That would explain why he didn't reach England until the spring of 1920 and had only liquid assets with him when he did, assets on a scale that must have shocked the manager of Martins' Bank in Truro when he made it clear just how much he meant to deposit with him. The fact was that Joshua Carnoweth had returned to the city of his birth a millionaire – several times over.

I felt a haunting affinity with Uncle Joshua in the distant hour of his homecoming as I drove out of Truro late that afternoon. There's a point at which absence becomes its own sustenance. Beyond that point, any return to the place and people you've abandoned becomes im-possible. Not in the physical sense, of course. You *can* go back, but only to discover that what you remember is no longer there.

I was heading for the Jagos' farm down on the Roseland peninsula, following the same route as in August 1946, when my father had driven Nicky and me down to Trelissick in the grocery van and seen us on to the King Harry Ferry, satisfied that Dennis Jago, Nicky's uncle, was waiting for us with the dog cart on the other side of the river. Petrol was rationed then, holidaymakers in cars hadn't been seen since 1939 – which meant never in my recollection – and horse-drawn traffic was commonplace. The ferry was an ageing steam-powered craft that looked as if it had been in operation since before the internal combustion engine was invented. Travelling on it without adult supervision – even if we were under observation from both banks – was a great adventure. As the ferry limped across, I stared over the rail at the tree-lined windings of the river, imagining a galleon in full sail gliding up from Falmouth in times gone by, or smugglers stealing out by night on secret errands.

Something of that childish wonder was still with me as I approached the ferry that afternoon. It was a sunny Sunday afternoon and I wasn't surprised to find a queue winding back up the hill at Trelissick. I had to sit out one crossing before getting aboard. It might well have been quicker to drive the long way round through Tregony. But I didn't care. The thickly wooded banks of the Fal, as it stretches languidly towards Carrick Roads, hold more associations for me than I could tire of in a whole day of waiting.

When I reached the other side, I took the St Mawes road, letting my memories soak in with the heat of the sun and the familiar green folds of the fields and hedges. No vehicle followed me when I turned off down the deep fern-shuttered lane. It had been less overgrown in 1946, on account of wartime traffic to and from a nearby anti-aircraft battery. But the sign at the end of the track leading to Nanceworthal was exactly as I remembered it, sagging on its post at what seemed the very same angle.

I passed a half-built brick structure, visible through a gap in the hedge. The grass was nearly as high as its walls, suggesting its construction had been abandoned a long time ago. That was the only change I noticed as I approached the house, tucked beneath the brow of the hill just where the land began to descend towards the cliff top. The fences looked in good order, the cattle in the fields healthy and numerous. When I pulled into the yard, though, I noticed a Dutch barn that hadn't been there in the Forties and a bigger more modern milking parlour. Nanceworthal had moved on, if not exactly with the times.

There was a dog already snapping around the car when I climbed out. I heard Ethel call it to heel before I saw her, watching me from the door of the cob and slate farmhouse. She was about sixty-five, but looked older in a frayed brown dress and green cardigan, her hair lank and grey as a winter's dusk, her eyes dimmed by a surfeit of misfortune. I was suddenly lost for words, capable of nothing beyond a smile and a vague gesture of the hand, offering sympathy without consolation.

'Hello, Ethel,' I said, sensing the incongruity of the greeting; I'd never addressed her by her first name before.

'Hello, young Christian.' Her Cornish accent surprised me. I'd forgotten how strong it was. 'Reckoned as how it was you.'

'Have you heard . . . from the police?'

'We been told 'bout Nicky, if that's what you mean.'

'I'm sorry. I wanted to . . . Can I come in?'

'Come in and welcome. There's tea in the pot.'

I followed her down the passage and into the kitchen. It would have been cleaner and better aired in former times. The grimy range and unwashed dishes stacked in the sink implied it wasn't just her own appearance she'd ceased to care about. She'd been a

57

bright-eyed thirty-year-old back in 1946, with glossy brown hair and a bubbly laugh. But she'd had a son and a sister and a nephew then. And her brother-in-law hadn't been hanged for murder. Ceasing to care was probably about the only way she could have survived.

She poured me some tea and we sat down at the table. I drank in silence for a moment, aware of her studying me. Then she said, 'I got no saffron buns for 'ee.' I nearly choked, remembering how freshly baked saffron buns had been waiting for us in that room every afternoon when Nicky and I returned from some scramble round the field-end, swinging little Tommy between us. How I'd looked forward then to our promised week at Nanceworthal the following summer. But it hadn't happened. This was my next visit – more than thirty years late.

'I was really sorry to hear about Tommy.'

'You saw his bungalow down the lane?'

'What – half-built?'

'That's it. No sense finishing it, was there? 'Twas meant for him. Planning to get married, see. Nice party she was, too.'

'How long ago . . . was this?'

'Seven year.'

I sighed. 'How's Dennis?'

'He's out in the fields. Don't trust himself to do much but work these days. When they told us about Nicky . . . he just nodded and went back out. 'Tis either like that or he gets so angry with me . . .' She shook her head. 'What's a body to do? You don't expect it, do 'ee? Not to lose so many so young.'

'Nicky said . . . his mother had died recently.'

'March it was when Rose went. A mercy, really. She was that ill.'

'Where was she living?'

58

'Essex. They didn't stop when they left here till they got to the east coast and could run no further.' She caught my eye. 'They all felt hounded. Then and later.'

'What did they do? I mean—'

'Rose married again. Feller called Considine. Some sort of 'lectrician.'

'And . . . old Mrs Lanyon?'

'Cordelia died within a twelvemonth of leaving Truro. Cancer, like Rose. Or heartbreak. Take it as you please.'

'Was Nicky living with his mother when she died?'

'*She* was living with *him*. Little flat in Clacton. Left her husband last year. Wanted to die with one as loved her proper, I dare say. That Considine never was a bit of good to her. Always one to rattle the bucket and run.'

'So Nicky was left on his own after Rose died?'

'That he was.'

'No family of his own?'

'Never married, if that's what you mean. Never settled to nothing, did Nicky.' She gazed dolefully into her tea. 'What happened to his father . . . He couldn't get the other side of that. 'Twas always in his mind.'

'Did you see a lot of him?'

'Less and less as he grew older. Rose'd tell me what he was about in her letters, o' course. But that weren't much, seemingly. Had a job in the public library in Clacton for a long time. Gave it up so as he could nurse his mother. Since she died . . . Well, when I went up for the funeral, I saw the change in him. Turned in on himself. Living more and more in the past. And this family's past is no fit place to dwell, is 'un?'

'Was that the last time you saw him?'

'No. He came here last week, see. And how he was . . . made me fear the worst. When we heard . . . I weren't so very surprised. You could tell he weren't right. Sat where you're sat now, he was. He'd been on the road a while, I

59

reckon. Clothes all lampered. And he looked so tired. I asked him to stay with us, but he wouldn't hear of it. Said as he had somewhere else to go. And I reckon he did, but you'll not find it on any map.' She turned away and dabbed at her eyes with a handkerchief she'd plucked from the sleeve of her cardigan. There was a thickness in her voice when she added, 'Let's hope he's happier there.'

'I spoke to him yesterday afternoon,' I said, unsure how much of our conversation it was wise to reveal. 'He seemed preoccupied with . . . his father's death.'

'Like I told you. He never could let go of that.'

'He asked me who killed him.'

She gave me a long thoughtful look. 'What did you tell him?'

'What *could* I tell him?'

She pushed out her lower lip and shook her head in answer, then gathered herself in her chair and glanced up at the clock. 'Dennis'll be bringing them in directly for milking. Best move your car, I'm thinking.' I sensed she wanted to find a reason to be rid of me, though whether she was worried about letting her tongue run away with her or by how Dennis might react to my presence I couldn't tell.

'I must be going anyway,' I said, finishing my tea at a gulp as I stood up. 'I only came . . . well . . . you know.'

She looked up at me. 'Yes. Reckon as I do.'

'Can you let me know when the funeral's to be? I'd like to attend, if I may.'

'I'll do that for you, Christian.'

'You can contact me at Tredower House. Or they'll pass a message.'

'Your sister's made a handsome job of running that place.'

'Yes. I think she has.' The remark drew my thoughts back to Nicky and the past he'd dwelled in overlong.

'Perhaps if Nicky's sister had lived, there might have been somebody to . . . well, I don't know . . . give him some support when he needed it. He mentioned her yesterday, strangely enough. So long ago and—'

'He mentioned his sister?' Ethel frowned at me.

'Yes. He did. I thought it odd at the time. After all, she's been dead for years.'

'Who's to say she's dead?' Ethel's frown was turning hostile, affronted somehow.

'Sorry?'

'Rose talked herself into believing she was dead, and I suppose Nicky went along with her until he believed it too. But nobody can be sure.'

I stared at her in amazement. 'I don't understand. Freda died of whooping cough, didn't she?'

'Oh, Freda did, yes.' She coloured. 'I see what you mean.' Hurriedly, she stood up and moved towards the door. 'I'd best see you out before they cows dabber up your car.'

'Hold on. A second ago, you said nobody could be sure. What did you mean?'

'Nothing. It's just . . .' She looked at me, pleading, it seemed, not to be pressed. 'I didn't rightly understand.'

'What didn't you understand?'

'Which . . .' She looked away. 'Which sister you meant.'

'But there was only one. Wasn't there?'

'No. Rose had another daughter, see. After they moved to Essex.'

'What happened to her?'

'Disappeared one day on her way home from school about fifteen year ago. Vanished without a trace. Rose convinced herself she was dead, but no body was ever found. She could be alive to this day.'

'And she'd be Nicky's half-sister?'

'No. They were brother and sister, fair and square.'

'I still don't understand. Surely, if Rose had a daughter by this man Considine—'

"Tweren't by Considine. Michaela was born before Rose even met that whitneck.'

'*Michaela*?' Before Ethel could respond, I guessed what the name must signify. 'You mean . . . she was Michael Lanyon's child – born posthumously?'

Ethel hesitated for a moment, then nodded in solemn confirmation.

'Good God.'

'Yes.' Her eyes held mine. 'But sometimes I wonder if he is so very good. When I look at what he allows.'

CHAPTER THREE

Pam was waiting for me when I got back to Tredower House. I felt so taken aback by what Ethel Jago had told me that I found it difficult to remember where she'd been and why. Another more distant memory plucked at my thoughts and whispered inside my head: Nicky as he'd been that long-ago summer when we'd had the run of Nanceworthal and the run of the world to look forward to; Nicky as he'd been before fate chose him as its perpetual victim. My own misfortunes were so much more trivial than the tragedies he'd tried and failed to endure. A father hanged for murder; a mother dying for want of love; a sister missing for year upon vanished year. How was he supposed to win against such odds – without a friend to turn to?

'How were the Jagos?' Pam asked.

'Bowed down. Beaten by life, more or less.'

'As bad as that?'

'I'd say so, yes.'

'Perhaps you shouldn't have gone.'

'Perhaps I shouldn't have stayed away so long.'

'But you hardly know them.'

'True. But I do know them slightly. Why is that, Pam?'

'Because you spent a week with them when you were ten.' She frowned. 'What do you mean?'

'Never mind.' I tried to shrug off the niggling doubt my visit to Nanceworthal had left me with. Now I'd been lured into thinking about it, setting up a farm holiday with Nicky for me seemed a strange way for my parents and grandparents to demonstrate the disapproval they'd expressed of the Lanyons. 'How are Mum and Dad?'

'Fine. Rather shocked, of course, but . . . they want to talk to you about what happened.'

'Do they?'

'Yes. I told them you were staying on for a few days. They suggested you go down there for lunch tomorrow.'

'Right.'

'Shall I phone them and say you'll be there?'

'Why not? It'll give me a chance to ask them.'

'Ask them what?'

'The question you didn't understand.'

Pam's frown deepened. 'I don't know what you're talking about.'

'No, but they will.'

The ability of my family to edit its own past has always been marked. The origin of my friendship with Nicky Lanyon was one example. My grandfather's exemption from military service during the First World War was another. The ill health that dogged him during those years had seemingly relented by the time I knew him and it certainly didn't prevent him living to a hale and hearty old age. Could it be that my grandmother, though the most strident of patriots, took a poor view of his chances of survival and decided she couldn't spare him? If so, I doubt it would have been beyond her to manipulate the medical facts to that end. Which might explain, among other minor mysteries, why Dr Truscott went on receiving a lavish complimentary hamper from us every Christmas long after he'd retired from general practice.

Archie Lanyon didn't have the benefit of Gran's far-sightedness. He went off to war in good health and excellent heart, returning well before the Armistice with the brain of a child and the body of an invalid. He didn't die for many years, but his life was over. Cordelia must have been as close to destitution as despair. She had a young son to rear as well as a helpless husband to care for. And the steadily more prosperous premises of Napier's Grocery in River Street to pass whenever she needed reminding how much kinder life could have been to her if it had seen fit. I don't know how she coped from day to day, nor whether she ever asked Gran for a favour or a loan or a helping hand. Maybe she was too proud to. Or maybe she knew what answer she'd get. Gran owed her nothing, and Gran made a point of paying only what she owed. Either way, Cordelia must occasionally have thought of Joshua Carnoweth. But never, I imagine, as her potential saviour. Never, I strongly suspect, as a wanderer who was about to return.

But, in the spring of 1920, he did precisely that. To a city scarcely altered from the one he'd left twenty-three years before. The cathedral was complete, of course, and there were a few private cars and motorized taxis to be seen, but otherwise all was much as it had ever been, with most road transport horse-drawn, the River Kenwyn not yet covered and the streets still lit by gas. The war had brought significant economic changes, though. The cost of living had soared, which was good news for my grand-parents, who could build a little extra profit into rising food prices, and a matter of no consequence whatever to a man of such practically limitless means as my great-uncle. But for somebody in Cordelia's precarious circumstances, it posed a real threat. The rent of her home had doubled since before the war, but her ability to pay had plummeted.

Uncle Joshua's reunion with his family seems to have been a cool one. Gran always said he took a dislike to Grandad and let them know he thought mere shop-keepers beneath him now he'd acquired wealth and status. It's a version of events my father always went along with, but, frankly, it's never stood up to examination. The Joshua Carnoweth I knew could be prickly enough, it's true, but he was no snob. The extent of his wealth was all the more surprising for its lack of effect on him. He owned a big house, but he lived simply and dressed plainly. He was the least ostentatious of men. I don't doubt there was a rift between brother and sister, but it had nothing to do with Uncle Joshua's opinion of my grandfather, poor though it undoubtedly was. It had to do almost entirely with his employment of a house-keeper. Because the housekeeper he employed was Cordelia Lanyon.

What was *their* reunion like? How did Cordelia greet the man who'd come back to find, as he must have expected, that she hadn't waited for him? How did Uncle Joshua explain himself – his tardiness, his transformed circumstances, his distance from the lovesick tinner he'd once been? I imagine them, standing awkwardly in the tiny front parlour at the house in St Austell Street, looking at each other, fumbling for the words to encompass the experiences their diverging lives had comprised, while Archie lolled in a chair in the corner, dribbling and mewling, and young Michael gaped at them from the doorway. Cordelia was still beautiful. Even in old age, as I remember her, her looks were pale and gentle, imprinted with the beauty that had been. Uncle Joshua was strong, handsome and well-dressed. They looked at each other and saw what might have been. If he'd come back sooner; if she'd followed him; if Archie had died, instantly and mercifully . . . But she loved her husband. She didn't wish him dead. And Uncle Joshua admired her for that. Nothing would have been said outright, nothing declared, but they came to an understanding.

The Lanyons moved into Tredower House within the month. Cordelia took charge of the domestic staff. Uncle Joshua engaged a nurse to care for Archie and a tutor to bring out the cleverness he detected in Michael. To those who knew nothing of their past association, it must have seemed unremarkable enough, though singularly generous on Joshua Carnoweth's part. Cordelia's duties as housekeeper were genuine and demanding, even if her rewards were lavish by the standards of the day. But some took a less charitable view. They suspected and whispered and implied . . . that Joshua Carnoweth's relationship with his housekeeper was not that of an employer with his employee. They were right in one sense. And in the other sense . . . I don't know, but I don't think so. Not while Archie Lanyon lived, at any rate, and he lived a long time.

Michael Lanyon turned out to be a bright boy. At twelve, he won a scholarship to Truro School. Uncle Joshua would presumably have paid his fees if he'd had to. He certainly supported him financially when he went up to Oxford in 1928, and during a post-Oxford year spent broadening his horizons on the continent. I assume he also eased his subsequent passage into a junior partnership at Colquite & Dew, the long-established Truro estate agent and auctioneer. There's really no room for doubt that Uncle Joshua did everything he could to help and encourage Michael. He came to look on him, I suppose, as the closest to a son he was ever likely to get. Which only gave the rumour-mongers more to chew on, and my grandparents more to resent. The grocery business was doing better and better, but it didn't run to an expensive private education for my father. His university was the shop in River Street, his destined profession not auctioneering but the world of bacon, bread and flour; of matches, mustard and soap; of thirteen trading hours per day, six days per week. It must have galled him – as it galled Gran – to see Michael Lanyon swanking past in his office suit. My father had married my mother by then. Pam had been born. The enlarged family had moved to the house in Crescent Road where I was to arrive on the scene. They weren't doing badly. In fact, they'd have thought they were doing as well as anyone – but for the unavoidable comparison with the occupants of Tredower House.

In April 1935, Michael Lanyon married Rose Pawley, the elder daughter of Truro's stationmaster. My parents and grandparents were invited to the wedding. It was a gesture of reconciliation they weren't inclined to reject, however many resentments they were obliged to stifle. The future had to be considered. As Uncle Joshua grew older, their doubts about who he meant to bequeath his wealth to assumed disturbing proportions. Gran knew when to put pragmatism before principle, and this was such a time. So they went, and wished the happy couple well.

The newly-weds had no need to seek a home of their own. Tredower House was large enough to accommodate as many children as they might be blessed with. It had become, in many ways, the Lanyons' home, even though Cordelia remained technically a mere live-in house-keeper. Gran can have liked none of this, but she didn't deem it politic to say so. Instead, she did her best to ensure her brother didn't forget how much thicker blood was than water. For his part, Uncle Joshua remained warily amiable. The proportions of his wealth – and how he intended to dispose of it – remained a matter between him, his conscience and Mr Cloke, his solicitor, in whose office safe in Lemon Street his will had long lain.

Rose Lanyon's first pregnancy happened to coincide with my mother's second. In March 1936, either side of Hitler's reoccupation of the Rhineland, Nicky Lanyon and I entered this life – and with it this story.

Monday morning brought the press to Tredower House. It was scarcely a zoom-lensed siege, just one or two of Fleet Street's second-division snoopers, hoping to nose out the background to what was so far just a page-five suicide with strings. Too idle to read their own papers' thirty-four-year-old cuttings, they were unaware of all the reverberations of the event and, naturally, we left them that way. Trevor claimed a guest had found the body, which was almost true, but he didn't mention that the guest was his brother-in-law and that he was still on the premises.

I left early for lunch with my parents and followed a rambling route down to the Helford estuary through the sun-warmed countryside. Lanmartha was a low-pitched, mellow-stoned house on the heights above Helford Passage, with a glorious sub-tropical garden descending in leisurely terraces towards the river. Here my mother pursued her passion for camellias, hydrangeas and Mediterranean exotics, while, at the golf course that backed on to the property, my father pursued his passion for hitting a pimply white ball into a hole. Such occupations seemed superfluous to me, when you needed only to glance out of the window to see the greenest of head-lands and the bluest of skies mirrored in sparkling water. But I lived in landlocked Berkshire and knew the rarity of such scenes. To my parents, who seldom left Cornwall, it was simply what you looked at while eating your breakfast.

They greeted me sympathetically, as if expecting me still to be distressed by my experience. I was, but not in the way they'd expected. The physical shock had been supplanted by a creeping unease, which no amount of sympathy was going to dispel. We sat out on the terrace above the top lawn with our aperitifs – pink gin for Dad, sherry for Mum and home-made lemonade for me – while Mrs Hannaford, the housekeeper, prepared lunch. The setting made the sombreness of our discussion seem all the stranger. We should have been sharing our pleasure at how well the wedding had gone. But Tabitha and Dominic were for the moment forgotten. They, after all, had the good fortune to be on the other side of the world.

'I'm sorry for anyone who's desperate enough to take their own life,' said Mum. 'But what I don't understand is . . . coming all this way to do it.'

'One shouldn't speak ill of the dead,' Dad chimed in, 'but, damn it all, it seems almost spiteful.'

'In what way?' I enquired as I sipped my lemonade.

'Well, doing it at Tredower House guarantees embarrassment for us, doesn't it? It means the press will remind everyone of the murder.'

'Why should that embarrass us?'

'It's something we could certainly do without,' said Mum. 'Saturday was so . . . altogether lovely. Then . . . this.'

'Gather from Pam he spoke to you that afternoon,' said Dad.

'Yes, he did.'

'Make any sense?'

'Not much.' I paused. 'He asked me who killed his father.'

They both frowned at me in puzzlement for a moment. Then Dad said, 'Mad, you think?'

'Confused, certainly. But I suppose you'd have to be to do such a thing. You know the tree he used – the horse chestnut? It's the one we used to swing from.'

'I don't remember a swing,' said Mum. 'But we visited Tredower House so seldom in those days.'

'I virtually lived there in the summers.'

'Did you?'

'You know I did.'

'I know you and . . . Nicky . . . were quite friendly.'

'*Quite friendly*? We were best pals.'

'An exaggeration, surely, dear.'

'No, not at all. If we hadn't been, why would I have spent a week with him at Nanceworthal the summer before?'

'Was it as long as that?'

'We were due to go again that summer too.'

'Really? I can't recall.'

'You encouraged the friendship.'

Dad snorted. 'Why should we have done that?'

'To keep in with Uncle Joshua, I suppose.'

A small but stubborn silence fell between us. Dad cleared his throat and swallowed some gin. Mum flicked a wasp away from the lemonade jug and rose hurriedly from her chair. 'I'd better see how Mrs Hannaford's getting on. Excuse me.'

As soon as she was out of sight, Dad looked across at me and said, 'You were brooding on all this before he killed himself, weren't you? I remember you were in an odd mood during our game of snooker. You should have told me what it was all about then.'

'I didn't want to spoil your anniversary. Besides, if meeting him had been the end of it, I'd probably have been able to put it out of my mind.'

'You should try to do just that now. There's no point agonizing over whether we thought it might be . . . beneficial . . . for you and him to get acquainted when you were both children. We're talking about forty odd years ago, for God's sake.'

'But did you . . . think it might be beneficial?'

He pursed his lips. 'In a sense. Your grandmother was worried Uncle Joshua would forget about his family in favour of the Lanyons. And with good reason, as it turns out. But remember: it was your future – yours and Pam's – we were trying to safeguard. I don't see that as something we need to apologize for.' He threw me a challenging glare.

'Neither do I. It's just that I can't help feeling responsible in some way for Nicky ending up as he did.'

'That's ridiculous.'

'Is it? He was my friend, however long ago.'

'And his father murdered your great-uncle, however long ago. Have you forgotten that?'

'No. But it's more complicated than you think. I went to see Ethel Jago. According to her, when Rose Lanyon left Truro, she was—'

'*Chris!*' It was my mother, calling to me from the French windows that led into the drawing-room. 'Phone call for you.'

'Who is it?'

'Says he's an old friend, though I've never heard of him. Don Prideaux.'

'Your mother's memory's not what it was,' Dad said softly. 'You were at school with a boy called Prideaux, weren't you?'

'Yes. Afterwards, he became a—'

'Journalist with the *Western Morning News*.' Dad nodded. 'He still writes for them.' Then he treated me to a mirthless smile. 'That's friendship for you.'

I let the remark go, rose and hurried into the drawing-room. My mother had vanished, but she'd left the telephone on the sideboard off the hook. I picked it up and said warily, 'Hello?'

'Chris, you old bugger. It's Don Prideaux.' His voice was lower and huskier than I recalled, but unmistakably his. 'Any chance of a few words about poor old Nicky Lanyon?'

'What do you want to know, Don?'

'Could we meet for a chat?'

'I'm not sure. I—'

'I'm in Truro. How about the City Inn at opening time this evening? The drinks are on me.'

'Don, I'm really not sure I can make it. It's . . . difficult.'

'I have to do this piece, Chris.' His tone altered, some of the mateyness draining away. 'You wouldn't want me to get anything wrong, would you?'

'No. But—'

'So I'll see you there?'

I sighed. 'All right.'

'Great.' He chuckled throatily. 'Knew I could count on you.'

Strictly speaking, I'd known Don Prideaux longer than I had Nicky Lanyon. We met in the first year of Daniell Road School in the autumn of 1941, thrown together across the narrow aisle between our desks by alphabetical chance. He was large for his age, mischievously pugnacious and irrepressibly curious. The Second World War had been going on for two years by then, but since we were too young to remember much about life in peacetime, it had effectively been going on for ever.

I have no memory of the outbreak of hostilities in September 1939, although the scene at Crescent Road is so enshrined in family tradition that I feel as if I do. We'd

73

been to Perranporth for the day, in the splendid old dove-grey Talbot that was destined to spend the next six years laid up in the garage in sulky grandeur. We'd picnicked among the dunes and paddled on the beach. We'd passed a normal seaside Sunday. Then we'd driven back to Truro in time for the six o'clock news on the wireless and heard the dread announcement in perfectly modulated BBC English, which had so transfixed Gran that she hadn't noticed half my egg soldier drop into her tea and had gone on drinking it without complaint.

Many of the features of life I became aware of as a child were actually wartime exigencies I mistook for permanent states of affairs. Rationing meant Napier's Grocery became less a private business than a branch office of the Ministry of Food, with registered customers, fixed prices and a perpetual discussion of points, coupons and legendary pre-war delights like pineapples and bananas which I had difficulty even envisaging. Call-up meant half the adult males in the neighbourhood vanished to distant parts, occasionally reappearing on forty-eight-hour leave with bulging kitbags and severe haircuts. My father was one of them, departing in the spring of 1940 for a war spent administering army food supplies from behind a desk somewhere in Yorkshire. The blackout and restrictions on travel didn't mean much to me, although Pam frequently complained that we never went to Perranporth any more. Whether she'd have wanted to scramble over barbed-wire defences to reach the sea, supposing we'd had enough petrol to drive there in the first place, is another matter, of course.

Cornwall was spared the worst of the Blitz, so nights huddled in an air-raid shelter didn't figure in my child-hood. Gran pointed out a glow on the eastern horizon to me one evening and told me it was Plymouth burning, but I had no conception of what that really meant. On spring and summer nights, I heard the dull and random thumps of bombing raids on Falmouth Docks, but nobody seemed to think they were likely to come any closer. They thought again in August 1942, when a bomb hit the Royal Cornwall Infirmary, just the other side of Chapel Hill from us. Don Prideaux, whose family lived in Redannick Lane, that bit closer to the hospital, reckoned the blast had vibrated him out of his bed, but even then he had a proto-journalistic gift for exaggeration. We walked down to look at the damage together next morning and thought it all great fun, unaware as we were that real people had been crushed to death beneath the rubble.

The Lanyons were shadowy figures to me at this time. In my mind, they were relatives of some kind, cousins perhaps, but there always seemed to be an ambiguity about our connection with them. Gran took Pam and me to Tredower House for tea with Uncle Joshua on several occasions and the atmosphere was never one of a brother and sister at ease with each other. Uncle Joshua had taken in a Belgian family who'd fled the German invasion in 1940 and ended up on a cargo boat in Falmouth Harbour. Gran seemed to disapprove of them somehow, possibly because Uncle Joshua gave them such a free run of the place and didn't appear to distinguish between their children and the Lanyons' – Nicky and little Freda. Michael Lanyon was in the RAF. The prominent place in the drawing-room Uncle Joshua had accorded to a photograph of him in pilot officer's uniform was another irritant to Gran, as I could tell by her surreptitious glares at it. But she kept up a stubbornly amicable front, the greatness of my unwitting expectations ever fixed in her mind. And at the end of my second year at Daniell Road, she played a trump card she'd been fondling for a long time.

Pam was about to start at the County Grammar School. No money had been spent on her education and it had never been implied that any would be spent on mine. But Gran had been putting funds aside for some time, apparently. She wanted to enrol me at Truro School. The reasoning behind this was obscure to me. I had no wish to leave Daniell Road and the circle of friends I'd acquired there, Don Prideaux among them. But my wishes were hardly relevant. 'It'll be the making of him,' Gran averred. 'And what's good enough for Cordelia Lanyon's grandson' – here we came nearer the mark – 'is good enough for mine.'

There was no doubt in my mind that Gran resented, even disliked, Cordelia Lanyon. I couldn't understand why, given the old lady's gentle manner and quiet, white-haired beauty. She wore mostly black at this time, in Victorian-style mourning for her recently deceased husband, and was all dimple-cheeked kindness to me when we met. Gran described her as Uncle Joshua's housekeeper, but her daughter-in-law Rose, a chubbier less elegant woman, though just as kindly, was the one who served tea whenever we visited Tredower House; Cordelia seemed to occupy a more exalted position. Pam referred darkly to family secrets I was too young to be entrusted with, probably because she hadn't been entrusted with them either. But I was the one whose schooling was being disrupted on account of them, which made me all the more determined to find out what they were.

In September 1943, I was packed off in my stiff new blue and grey serge uniform to Truro School's prep department at Treliske, a converted manor house a mile out of the city along the Redruth road. That mile seemed more like a hundred, so remote did my friends at Daniell Road suddenly become. As it turned out, I was to be reunited with Don Prideaux five years later, when he won a scholarship to the senior school and caught up with me there. By then, the war would be over. So would the friendship I was about to form with Nicky Lanyon. And so would the lives of Joshua Carnoweth and Michael Lanyon. It's just as well we can't foresee the future, otherwise the past wouldn't be such a carefree place.

I hadn't seen Don in twenty years. We'd revived our schoolboy friendship when work took both of us to Plymouth in the late Fifties. He was chafing at the tedium and triviality of provincial journalism then, just as I was chafing at the tedium and triviality of department-store management. We'd become drinking companions, swapping dreams of our glamorous cosmopolitan futures; his in Fleet Street, mine in the music business. However you looked at it, life hadn't played along. The Don I found propping up the bar of the City Inn that evening had lost a lot of hair and gained a lot of weight. But he was still a long way from Fleet Street. And when he heard what I wanted to drink his horrified grimace suggested he didn't think I'd handled the intervening years with much more success than he had.

'Perrier water?' he spluttered. 'You must be joking.'

'I'm afraid not. I've been teetotal for more than ten years now.'

'In God's name, why? With all your money, you could be rinsing your teeth in vintage champagne.'

I sat on the bar stool next to his and smiled ruefully. 'Doctor's orders.'

'That bad?'

'The big city didn't turn out to be very good for me. Think yourself lucky you never made it to Fleet Street. They might have weaned you on to something harder on the system than beer.'

'I'd have been willing to take the chance.'

'Why didn't you?'

'It never came. I got bored before I got famous. And now . . . it's too late.'

'Surely it's never too late.'

'Easy for you to say that, sitting pretty on the Carnoweth millions.'

'You know as well as I do, Don, that I've had to stand on my own two feet since leaving Plymouth. Not a penny of those millions has come my way.'

'But you've got them to look forward to, haven't you?'

'I'm not sure. Except that the contents of my father's will are definitely none of your business.'

Don raised his hands in a gesture of pacification, smoke curling up from the cigarette gripped between his two most nicotine-stained fingers. 'OK, OK. I'm sorry. It's just that from where I'm standing you haven't had things so bad. That singer you married – what was her name?'

'Melody Farren.'

'Divorced yet?'

'Since you ask, yes. A long time ago.'

'How did I guess? You must have done well out of that. Still get a cut of her royalties?'

'There aren't any royalties to speak of. And, even if there were, I wouldn't be entitled to a share.'

'What does she do now?'

'Keeps goats. On a smallholding in North Wales.'

'What a waste. She had a good voice, and an even better body, as I recall. But then you'd know all about that, wouldn't you?'

'Yes, Don. *I* would. But *you're* not going to.' I certainly ought to have known, but my marriage to Melody Farren – real name Myfanwy Probin – had been so blurred by my alcoholism that I'd have been hard put to dredge up many of the details, even supposing I'd wanted to. After what I'd put her through, she was probably wise to plump for celibate goat-keeping in Snowdonia.

'Which year did she come third in the Eurovision Song Contest?' Don asked musingly. 'Must have been when miniskirts were at their shortest, because the one I saw her wearing on the telly for that fandango . . .' He gave up as my expression hardened. 'Well, all water under the bridge, eh? You're in the classic car game now, is that right?'

'Who told you?'

'Nobody. Saw one of your ads in a magazine. Napier Classic Convertibles of Pangbourne.'

'That's me.'

'You might be interested in my Morris Minor. Bags of character, but not much performance. Bit like its owner.'

'Why don't we come to the point?'

'All right. Nicky Lanyon. He turned up at Tredower House on Saturday and spoke to you. Hanged himself that night. You found him the following morning. Correct?'

'So far.'

'His mother died recently. No other close family. So Nicky gets depressed and decides to end it all. But he comes all the way here to do it. That shows a nice sense of, what, irony? Hanged, like his father, on property you could say his father was hanged *for*. No wonder the brat pack's down from London. It's a gift, isn't it? Or it would be, if they could be bothered to check out all the angles.'

'Which is where you come in?'

'Exactly. You and Nicky were buddies, Chris. Seen him at all since forty-seven, have you? Before Saturday, I mean.'

'No.'

'You'd forgotten all about him, I expect. But he hadn't forgotten about you.'

79

'Apparently not.'

'What did he say to you on Saturday?'

'Nothing coherent.'

'Oh, come on.'

'It's true.'

'Something about his father, wasn't it?' Don's eyes engaged mine. 'I spoke to Ethel Jago this afternoon. I wrote a piece about her son's death a few years ago and she mentioned her connection with the Lanyons then. She also happened to think my article was a restrained and tasteful piece of journalism. So, she was more communicative with me than she might have been if some leather-jacketed oik talking in a cod cockney accent had turned up. I'm several steps ahead of them. I know about you and Nicky, which they don't seem to. And I know he's been protesting his father's innocence for the past thirty-four years. Which is what I suspect he was doing when you met him. Correct again?'

'No.'

'Then I must be losing my sense of smell. Which I'm not.'

'He couldn't accept his father was a murderer. That's not the same as believing he was innocent.'

'I can pile on the pathos for this piece if I have to, Chris. I can portray Nicky as a sad and lonely victim of life, deserted by his best and oldest friend.'

'What's stopping you?'

'The possibility that there's a bigger story behind it all. Ethel told me about Michaela as well.' He smiled faintly at my flinch of surprise. 'Michael Lanyon's posthumous child. Now, that could be a real scoop.'

'Looks like it's yours for the writing.'

'Not quite. I need more information. And as far as I can see, the only likely source is Nicky's stepfather, Neville Considine.'

'Why are you wasting your time with me, then?'

'Because Considine lives in Clacton, and my editor isn't going to pay me to travel to the Essex coast to follow up a Cornish story. But he'll be down for the funeral, won't he? Bound to be. It's this Friday.'

'You know more than I do, it seems.'

'The point is, Chris, I need somebody to steer Considine into my waiting arms. Somebody to recommend me as the boy scout of my profession. There might be a few rivals sniffing around by then. I need somebody to push me to the head of the queue.'

'You mean me?'

'You're bound to meet him at the funeral. He must know you and Nicky were friends, so he won't quibble if you introduce me as another of his—'

'You'll be there?'

Don shrugged. 'Ethel didn't seem to mind.'

'Then why not get her to introduce you?'

'Because you'll do it better. I told her the three of us were at school together. Only you know that's technically not true.'

'And that the nearest you came to being a friend of Nicky's was shouting insults at him and me when we walked down Chapel Hill in prep school uniform.'

Don gave another shrug, accompanied this time by a grin. 'It's a small enough distortion. It'll justify my presence at the funeral and help me win Considine's confidence. Not much to ask in return for keeping your name out of the story.'

'So that's it, is it? Blackmail.'

'Look at it this way. The publicity might throw up a clue to Michaela's whereabouts. There's no reason to assume she's dead, is there? It would give some sort of purpose to Nicky's death if his sister could be reunited with what's left of her family.'

'Why do I have the impression that isn't your primary concern?'

'Because you're a mean-minded cynic who thinks all I'm after is a cracker of a story that I might be able to sell on to one of the nationals.'

'Your big break.'

'You were the one who said it was never too late.'

'So I did.'

'You'll play along, then?'

'All right. On the strict understanding that I won't read about myself in your paper.'

'Great.' Don finished his beer and signalled to the barmaid for a refill. 'Another Perrier, Chris? Or are you driving?'

CHAPTER FOUR

Don Prideaux kept his side of the bargain. His *Western Morning News* piece about Nicky's suicide mentioned neither me nor Michaela Lanyon. He was biding his time where she was concerned, awaiting the chance I was going to gift-wrap for him to draw all the strings of the tragedy together. Since the nationals had apparently lost interest in the case by the middle of the week, his strategy was a clever one. When he broke the story, his rivals would all be a long way away.

So, come to that, would I. The ease with which Don had been able to pressurize me had shocked me out of my sentimental reverie. Nicky was dead and the time to help him was past. I'd go to his funeral because I wanted to pay our friendship an overdue homage, but that would be the end of it.

I drove back to Pangbourne on Tuesday morning, intent on putting in a therapeutic couple of days at the workshop before returning to Truro for the funeral. Napier Classic Convertibles' public face was a quarter-share in the forecourt and showroom of Grayson Motors, Station Road, Pangbourne. I tried to spend as little time as possible sitting behind a potted palm there, waiting for customers, preferring to devote my efforts to the messy but satisfying task of hands-on restoration at the two Nissen huts, disused barn and adjoining yard I rented from a nearby farmer. Mark Foster, my only full-time employee, had Wednesday off. That was fine by me; a solitary day of purposeful tinkering with the Austin-Healey I was putting back together for one of my prompter payers was just what the doctor had ordered.

The morning went well and I was beginning to think about taking a break for lunch when a noise that sounded like a biplane landing alerted me to the arrival of a car in the yard. It was an abominably kept Fiat 500, with more rust than paintwork and an exhaust system that made me think a sudden fog had descended.

The owner, a tall, thin old man wearing a cheap blue-black suit and grubby shoes with cracked uppers, unwound himself from the driving seat and hesitantly walked towards me. He had thick greasy hair and eyes as bright as a magpie's, but I'd have put him at seventy even so. He breathed shallowly and trembled faintly. The smell of something unsavoury clung to him like a tawdry memory, and when he smiled, the expression was nervous yet somehow predatory at the same time. 'I'm looking for Mr Napier,' he said cautiously.

'You've found him.'

'My name's Neville Considine.' He held out a hand and I was strangely relieved to be able to display my oil-blackened palms as an excuse not to shake it. 'They told me at the garage in Pangbourne that I'd find you here.'

'You'd better come in.'

He followed me past the stripped-down Austin-Healey to the tiny office at the back of the workshop. I offered him a seat and a cup of coffee, hoping he might decline at least the latter. But he didn't.

'Are you on your way to Truro, Mr Considine?'

'Yes. For Nicholas's funeral. I gather from Mrs Jago that you'll be attending.'

'I will, yes.'

'The police told me you were the one who found him.'

'Yes. It's an awful business. You have my—'

'That's all right, Mr Napier. I'm the one who should offer sympathy. Coming across him like that must have been a dreadful shock.'

'Well, it was, of course, but—'

'You must understand I've seen very little of Nicholas in recent years.' His voice was low but grating. 'And it's not as if he was a blood relative.'

'No. Well, I'm sorry anyway. And about your wife, of course.'

'Thank you.' He made his thanks sound like an indecent proposal. I was glad the kettle boiled at that moment. As I made the coffee, he added, 'Nicholas often spoke of you, Mr Napier.'

'Really?' I handed him his mug and sat down with mine.

'Rather more often than he spoke of anyone else he'd known in Truro. And that was seldom.'

'What did he say about me?'

'That you were his best friend, of course. That's why I'm here.'

'Well, if there's anything I can do . . .'

'They were an ill-fated family, you know. When I married Nicholas's mother, I thought their bad luck was at an end. But I'm afraid it wasn't. First Michaela. Then Rose. Now poor Nicholas. All dead, and only me left.'

'Ethel told me about Michaela. Isn't it rather defeatist to assume she's dead?'

'Realistic, I should have said. They got a man for a string of teenage sex killings in the Colchester area around the time she disappeared. The police seemed certain she was one of his victims. He never admitted it, but there didn't seem much room for doubt.'

'I didn't know that.'

'It's a long time ago. You learn to live with it.'

'I suppose you must.'

'You learn to live with most things, don't you? You have to, if you're to survive. Nicholas never was a survivor.'

'No?'

'I always thought he might have inherited some character flaw from his father.'

'But you never knew his father, did you?'

'No.' His tone didn't alter. I had the impression it never did. But he started blinking rapidly, as if afraid he'd offended me. 'That's true, of course. And, at all events, Nicholas is out of his misery now.'

'Is that what his life was – a misery?'

'Much of the time, I fear so.'

'Who's to blame for that?'

He frowned at me, sipped his coffee and frowned at me again. 'Suicide always leaves the living feeling guilty, I suppose.' It was a good answer, a better one than I'd have thought him capable of. 'We must do our best for him now he's gone, mustn't we?'

'Yes. We must.'

'I've assured Mrs Jago I'll meet the cost of the funeral.'

'That's good of you.' He was right about guilt. It stabbed at me in that moment. I should have thought of the undertaker's bill myself.

'The fact is, however, that such an unexpected outlay will place a considerable strain on—'

'Let me take care of it.'

'Oh, I couldn't possibly—'

'Really.'

'Well, if you . . .'

'I insist.'

'More than generous of you, Mr Napier. Thank you.' He smiled at me over the rim of his mug. I felt certain then that he'd come to Pangbourne to touch me for money – quite possibly *before* making any kind of offer to Ethel Jago – and for no other reason. I should have been eager to discuss Nicky's life with him, but all I really wanted was to be rid of him. The only blessing of his visit was that it cleared my conscience where setting him up for Don was concerned. Neville Considine was a man who positively invited deceit. What kind of a substitute father he'd been to Nicky – if any kind at all – I preferred not to imagine.

'It's not, alas, the only expense I may be put to as a result of Nicholas's untimely demise, but—'

'What else?'

He cleared his throat, without noticeable effect on his voice. 'Nicholas left one or two debts behind him in Clacton, I'm afraid. He'd had no work for more than a year, but was too proud to claim unemployment benefit. There are some arrears of rent on his flat and a loan from a finance company overdue for repayment. No doubt his death writes off such debts in law, but I feel obliged to make some effort—'

'How much?'

'It could amount to several thousand pounds.'

I looked at him, letting him read the scepticism in my face. He probably thought, like Don, that I was rolling in money, willing and able to write him out a fat cheque there and then. It was all depressingly predictable. 'Tell you what, Mr Considine. You get these . . . creditors . . . to submit detailed accounts of what Nicky owed them, and I'll see if I can help out.'

He swallowed his disappointment with the last of his coffee. 'Too kind, Mr Napier. Really too kind.'

'Least I can do.'

'I'd best be off. Long journey ahead of me, you know.'

'Quite.'

He stood up. As I did the same, he said, 'There's no need to see me out.' But there was. With a man like him, an assurance that he'd definitely left was well-nigh essential. I followed him out of the office and back to the yard, watching him eye the Austin-Healey as he went. 'Nice car,' he remarked. 'It must be pleasant to be able to indulge a hobby for this kind of thing.'

'It's not a hobby. It's my living.'

He made no response, content, it seemed, to have registered his point. We reached his Fiat and I waited while he clambered in, then, when he wound down the window to say goodbye, I decided to risk a single question about his relationship with Nicky.

'Tell me, did Nicky ever talk much about his father?'

'Not to me. But, then, I didn't encourage it.'

'Why not?'

'Because I wanted him to stop living in the past.'

'And did he?'

He frowned thoughtfully whilst coaxing the Fiat's engine into noxiously spluttering life, then, just as he started to move off, gave me his parting reply. 'It doesn't look like it, does it?'

Living in the past. It's always said pejoratively, as if the past is necessarily inferior to the future, or at any rate less important; nobody's ever condemned for looking forward, only back. But the truth is that we *do* live in the past, whether we like it or not. That's where our life takes shape. Somewhere ahead, however near or far, is the end. But behind, shrouded in clouds of forgetting, lies the beginning.

For Nicky and me, the real beginning was the autumn

of 1943. Truro School's prep department was a much smaller and more secluded institution then than it is today, so I was bound to become better acquainted with Nicky than occasional teatime encounters at Tredower House had made possible. But friendship requires something more than proximity. Nicky and I shared a dreamily inquisitive nature that would probably have drawn us together even if our families had been totally unconnected.

A routine established itself whereby Nicky called for me on his way up Chapel Hill in the mornings. Pam would walk with us as far as the County Grammar School, then we'd go on together to Treliske. Going back in the afternoon, we'd wait for Pam to come out of school, then walk with her down Chapel Hill into Truro to call at the shop. Grandad would set off in the van on his delivery round while Pam helped Gran behind the counter. Nicky and I went with him, Nicky dropping off at Tredower House *en route*. On Saturdays, I'd go up there to see him and we'd play tennis with the Belgian children, or restage Montgomery's North Africa campaign on his bedroom floor with toy soldiers and matchboxes for tanks, or climb the horse chestnut tree to watch out for imaginary German soldiers marching in from St Austell, or take turns on the swing Uncle Joshua had rigged up for us on a stout lower branch.

So it was that we became, with the easy imperceptibility of childhood, each other's best friend. During school holidays, we'd mount all-day expeditions to Idless or Malpas or out along Penweathers Lane towards the open moorland, unwittingly retracing the route Gran must have walked fifty years before with Uncle Joshua's lunch. But we knew more about the Norman Conquest than we did about our families' recent past. That was one book we weren't encouraged to open. When we saw

Nicky's grandmother and my great-uncle strolling across the lawn at Tredower House together, we didn't have a clue what they might be talking about. There were greater and more immediate concerns in our lives, like whether we could cadge any chewing gum from the GIs coming and going at the American army camp in Tresawls Road, or name-spot a new jeep hurtling along the lanes. To us, the war was the best game ever invented.

The reality of its dangers only became apparent to me in the aftermath of Freda Lanyon's death from whooping cough early in 1944. Nicky stayed with us at Crescent Road for a week to minimize the risk of infection. We both thought this a great lark, until shocked into an early awareness of mortality by his sister's sombre fate. Michael Lanyon came home to comfort Rose and his heavy limp proved that the crash landing on a Kentish airfield Nicky had told me about wasn't just a thrilling 'prang'. People really could be hurt. Events, it seemed, had consequences.

And the war, it also transpired, would eventually run its course. Most of the American troops vanished across the Channel after D-Day in June 1944 and a more humdrum pattern of life established itself in Truro. Michael Lanyon was transferred to a radar base down on the Lizard. This meant he spent most weekends at Tredower House. According to Nicky, he wasn't as much fun as he'd once been. No doubt the stresses of active service, not to mention physical injury and the loss of his daughter, accounted for that. The limp, and presumably the memories, didn't go away. But I always found him kindly, almost gentle, in his manner. His slick-haired good looks, his smart flight lieutenant's uniform and the oddly graceful way he carried his stiff leg became an ideal of manliness in my mind. My own father, whose captain's uniform never seemed to fit quite as well and whose vital contribution to the war effort had never involved the slightest personal danger, was a disappointment to me when measured against the same standard. I never said so, of course, but I envied Nicky such a glamorous parent. Everything Michael Lanyon did, whether it was smoking a Player's Airman cigarette or challenging us at French cricket, whether cutting back the rhododendrons or simply staring into space with that quizzical lopsided smile Nicky had inherited from him, he did with elegant panache.

School life proceeded in comforting isolation. Nicky and I lost our Cornish accents and acquired some polished ways to set us apart from the likes of Don Prideaux. But the differences didn't go very deep. We all followed the celebratory Floral Dance from the football ground down to the cathedral on VE Day in May 1945. And did the same three months later for VJ Day.

The war was over. Michael Lanyon went back to Colquite & Dew and my father returned to the shop, allowing my grandfather to ease his way into retirement. Gran remained actively involved, though, and not just in the grocery business. As I grew older and my understanding of the subtleties of tea-table conversation at Crescent Road deepened, I began to see for myself that she had as many fears as hopes riding on her brother's generosity. 'I'm doing my best to ensure Joshua makes proper provision for his family,' she announced more than once in the style of a sermon. 'I expect you all to do the same.' And by *his* family she meant us, of course, not the offspring of Cordelia Angwin. Uncle Joshua was seventy-two that last summer of the war. Time was running short. And not just for him.

The sun shone for Nicky's funeral as it had for my last meeting with him. There was no preliminary church service. The mourners, all five of us, proceeded straight to Penmount Crematorium and met in one of the two chapels there. Another much better attended funeral was going on in the other chapel, which gave a hole-in-the-corner feeling to our sparse gathering. It was made all the worse by the tangibility of Ethel Jago's dislike for Neville Considine and my own suspicion that it was obvious Don Prideaux and I were in cahoots. Dennis Jago probably came out of it best, by remaining wordless throughout, other than to utter the appropriate prayers more distinctly than anyone.

The clergyman Ethel had recruited made a hasty departure after his perfunctory conduct of the service. There were no wreaths to inspect, none of us having apparently thought it fitting to send one. All that remained was to thank the undertaker and assemble awkwardly in the car park, aware that at any moment we'd be overrun by the other party, while above us smoke drifted in seemly shreds from the furnace chimney.

'Didn't realize you were at school with Nicky till you told me so, Mr Prideaux,' Ethel said to Don, dabbing away the last of her tears.

'Oh yes,' Don replied. 'I was never as close a friend as Chris, of course, but . . .'

'I'm glad you came,' put in Considine. 'Nicholas's mother would have appreciated the gesture, I know.'

'God rest her soul,' murmured Ethel.

'We were thinking . . .' Don began awkwardly. 'What I mean is, would you all like to join Chris and me for lunch? We thought we'd go to the Heron at Malpas.'

'That would be most agreeable,' said Considine, in a tone that somehow implied we'd already offered to stand him the meal.

Ethel glanced at Dennis before responding. How he conveyed his wishes was unclear, but by a meek little nod she seemed to acknowledge them. 'We'd best be getting back, Mr Prideaux. We can't leave the farm for long, see.'

'No. I suppose not.'

'Goodbye then, Ethel,' I said, stepping forward to kiss her.

'Goodbye, Christian.'

'Dennis.' He shook my hand firmly, his face stiff and expressionless. Then they both headed off towards the mud-streaked Land Rover that cast their immaculate funeral clothes in such odd relief. I sensed this was a final goodbye to both of them and that it warranted more words, a greater show of feeling. But who would that have been kind to? 'I can hardly suffer to think of it all,' Ethel had said earlier. So why force her to? I let them go with no more than a farewell wave.

Considine had travelled to Penmount in the undertaker's limousine, so he rode with Don when we left and I followed. We drove back into Truro past Tredower House, with the roofs of Truro School showing above the trees to our left, then took the Malpas road down past Boscawen Park. I was alone, but at every twist of the lane could remember Nicky's company on fishing expeditions and aimless rambles long ago. We'd often enough walked the way I was now driving, down to Malpas, the village clinging to the headland at the junction of the Truro and Tresillian rivers. Sometimes we'd taken the ferry across to Tregothnan and staged daring forays on to Lord Falmouth's estate. And sometimes we'd just ambled up the track towards Tresillian, watching the sailboats coming and going across the silver-grey water. All those unremarkable days had conspired in my memory to become a Shangri-La to which I could never retrace the route. The past is a room you only realize you've left when you hear the door close behind you.

Don hadn't wasted his journey from Penmount on

yearning reminiscence. That was obvious when I caught up with him and Considine at the Heron Inn. It seemed as if they'd already struck some kind of deal. Don had stationed a running tape recorder on the table by Considine's elbow and it was apparent he'd shown his journalistic colours. I was there as a guarantor of his good faith, required to do little but watch and listen.

'How did you meet the Lanyons, Mr Considine?' Don was venturing when I joined them.

'Electrician's my trade.' Considine paused to sup his brown ale, then went on. 'I'm Clacton born and bred. I used to do a good deal of work at Butlin's holiday camp – all the lighting and so forth. It was a really smart place back then – big name performers and every chalet taken in the season. Rose worked in the kitchens. I knew her to pass the time of day with, nothing more. I never heard a whisper about her late husband and what he'd done. She'd come to Clacton to put all that behind her, of course. Early Fifties this would be. Her mother-in-law was dead by then. Rose and the children – Nicholas and little Michaela – lived out at Jaywick, a holiday town just west of Clacton. Wooden bungalows mostly, intended for summer use only, chucked up in the Thirties. But it was the cheapest accommodation going and a lot of hard-pressed families settled there permanently, the Lanyons among them.

'Jaywick was always prone to flooding. That's why the council had tried to stop it being developed in the first place. Well, a lot of it was swept away in the floods of fifty-three. The sea just washed over it. Dozens of people were drowned and hundreds made homeless. Rose and the kids got out with their lives and nothing else. When I heard what had happened, I offered to take them in. Mother and me had plenty of room at our house. It would have seemed a crime not to do what we could for them.

'That's how we got started. Rose was a fine woman: a good mother and a hard worker. Before it came time for them to leave, I let her know how I felt about her and we decided to get married. She told me about the murder then. She didn't want me to find out later and feel let down. But it didn't make any difference to me. None of it was her fault, was it? Or the children's. We married that summer.'

'And remained so until her death?' asked Don. 'Ethel seemed to imply . . .'

'There was a separation before the end,' said Considine levelly. 'But no divorce. I reckon the illness affected her mind. She'd have come back to me, I'm sure, if she'd lived.'

'No doubt,' said Don with a reassuring smile. 'How did you get on with Nicky? He'd have been, what, seventeen when you married his mother.'

'Well enough. An adolescent and his stepfather . . .' Considine sighed. 'It's never easy, I dare say. Nicholas wasn't troublesome, I'm not saying that. But he was guarded, yes, very guarded. Introverted, the trick cyclist would have said, I expect, if we could have afforded to send him to one.'

'Did he have any kind of employment?'

'He worked at a laundry out on the St Osyth road. My, the fleas he used to bring home from that place. But it was honest work, and he was taking evening classes to better himself. Nicholas tried hard to make a go of life, no question about it. He passed some exams and got a respectable job at the public library. Rose was really pleased about that. Career; wife; children: she had it all mapped out for him in her mind.'

'What went wrong?'

'Oh, several things. He got mixed up with those anti-nuclear campaigners. You know – CND. All on account of some girl, actually. She was no good for him. And being seen waving a banner in Trafalgar Square wasn't any good for his career in the library service either. I tried to set him straight, but he wouldn't listen. Then the girl chucked him and . . . things went from bad to worse. It wasn't all his own fault, mind. When Michaela disappeared, well, it really shook him. It shook his mother too, of course. And me. I loved the girl like she was my own. But Nicky . . . just couldn't come to terms with it.'

'What exactly happened?'

'She was in the sixth form at the County High School, doing really well. She was a bright girl, just turned seventeen. April of sixty-five, it was. Her first week back at school after the Easter holiday. Well, one afternoon, a Thursday, she just didn't come home for tea. Some friends had seen her leaving by her normal route, across the recreation ground behind the school. Then – nothing. There wasn't a sign of her. No sightings, no clues – nothing. She'd vanished. The police thought at first she might have run away. But she had hardly any money and no change of clothes. Her school uniform would have made her conspicuous. And she hadn't said anything – even to schoolfriends – to suggest she was thinking of such a thing. Besides, Rose and I were sure she *wasn't* thinking of it. She was happy. A real homebird, you know? Not one to wander.

'The police changed their tune later. Several young girls had been murdered in the Colchester area over the previous couple of years. They arrested the culprit about six months after Michaela went missing. He was the worst kind of sex maniac. A real animal. Rape, mutilation and God knows what. He ended up in Broadmoor. Perhaps you remember the case. Brian Jakes, his name was.'

'Can't say I do,' said Don, glancing at me.

I shook my head. 'Nor me.'

'I'm not that surprised,' said Considine. 'The Moors Murderers were grabbing all the headlines then. Their trial and Jakes' coincided. Anyway, the police reckoned – and so did we – that Michaela was one of his victims. There were several missing girls he wouldn't say he'd murdered, but wouldn't say he hadn't either. He lived on his own in a caravan on a site just outside Colchester. He was a rat-catcher by trade, travelling from job to job in his van. And on the day Michaela disappeared he'd done some work for a farmer up near Thorpe-le-Soken, just a few miles from Clacton. He must have dropped down to Clacton afterwards, waylaid Michaela at the rec, over-powered her, bundled her into his van, driven away and . . . Well, perhaps it's best we never found out exactly what he did to her, if the mess he left some of the others in is anything to go by.'

'And you said Nicky took it pretty badly?'

'Yes. He was very protective towards his sister. He seemed to think he should have prevented it happening. There was no way to reason with him. It wasn't a *reasonable* view. But he held to it, firm and solid. He was to blame. Rose reckoned he'd always thought he should have saved his father as well. He had this way of loading the responsibility for misfortune on his own shoulders. It didn't make a scrap of sense – except to him. I tried to help him, of course, but I suppose getting Rose over the worst of her grief took up most of my attention. My mother died in the middle of it all, too. It was a grim time, I don't mind admitting. And we were only just beginning to come out of it when Nicholas came by some infor-mation that set him so far back he never really caught up with himself again.'

'What information?'

'I don't know how he found out, but he did. A few years after Michaela's disappearance – sixty-eight or sixty-nine,

I'm not sure which – they let Edmund Tully out of prison.'

Edmund Tully. Michael Lanyon's accomplice in the murder of Joshua Carnoweth. The lucky recipient of a commuted sentence of life imprisonment. Across the years, I felt the fading aftershock of what the news must have meant to Nicky. His father had hanged, but Edmund Tully, the man who'd struck the fatal blow, had served scarcely more than twenty years in prison – and then he'd walked free. He was out there somewhere, breathing the clean fresh air, while Nicky's father rotted in a prison grave and his sister . . .

'That seemed to make everything worse for him. He started to go downhill around then. His appearance deteriorated. He lost a lot of . . . self-respect. He used the library to get hold of all the press cuttings about his father's trial and went through them over and over again. I don't know what he was looking for. I'm not sure he knew himself. He moved out into a flat of his own. It wasn't much of a place, but he was adamant he wanted to be on his own. He seemed to spend more and more of his time that way. I suppose he turned into a bit of a recluse. It can't have been any good for him. He lost his job at the library in the end – or gave it up, I'm not sure which. Either way, he was in a downward spiral even before his mother died. I've seen nothing of him since then, but from what I've heard . . . he was heading for what happened last weekend for a long time.'

'You don't think there's any chance Michaela might still be alive, do you?' asked Don.

'Jakes murdered her. I reckon that's plain enough.'

'But he's never admitted it?'

'Not as such, no. As far as I know.'

'Did Nicky believe she was dead?'

'Oh yes,' I said in an undertone. 'He told me so himself.' Looking up, I found the other two staring at me, disconcerted by my intervention. 'Well,' I added defensively, 'so he did.'

'There you are then.' Considine eyed me. 'Nicholas had no doubts, it seems.'

'But there's no proof,' persisted Don. 'Whereas there *was* proof his father murdered Joshua Carnoweth. And it seems he *did* doubt that.'

'True,' agreed Considine.

'Why?'

'I don't know. Loyalty to his father's memory, we must suppose.'

'No other reason?'

'What other reason could there be?'

'Maybe he turned up something trawling through those cuttings you mentioned. An inconsistency in the evidence. An element of doubt.'

'I don't think so.'

'Why not?'

'Because, if he had, he wouldn't have killed himself. The possibility of clearing his father's name would have given him a reason to live. Don't you agree, Mr Napier?'

'Sorry?' My mind had wandered to my encounter with Nicky at Tredower House. He'd told me then what he was looking for. But what he was looking for couldn't be found. Maybe he'd finally realized that. 'He . . . that is . . .'

'Never mind,' cut in Don. 'I think I've got enough.'

'I'm afraid it's all a great tragedy,' said Considine, the faintest hint of self-satisfaction souring the mournfulness of his words. 'Poor Nicholas never really stood a chance.'

There was a time when Nicky *had* stood a chance. I remembered it well. Back in the summer of 1946, when we'd had our carefree week together at Nanceworthal, his prospects had been as bright as mine, his future every bit as cloudless. He had Tredower House for a home; a mother and father who loved him as much as they did each other; and my great-uncle to confer on him just as many advantages as he might need. As a start in life, I'd have had to say it surpassed my own. But I was too young to dally with such thoughts, and consequently free of the resentment that simmered away inside my parents and grandparents – all the more perniciously because it could never be expressed.

I've often wondered if they'd have been able to hold their tongues had they realized just how much there was for them to resent. They knew – everyone knew – that Joshua Carnoweth had come back from his travels many years ago a wealthy man, but what that actually meant in pounds, shillings and pence was never even guessed at. But then wealth didn't entitle you to an increased butter ration, and most of the luxuries you might have dreamed of spending it on simply weren't available. In post-war England, wealth was largely theoretical. The Talbot came out of the garage, but petrol rationing meant it couldn't be taken to Perranporth very often, let alone further afield. Customers queued back out into the street at the shop, but goods were few and prices were fixed; the business couldn't expand as Dad had hoped it would when he came home from the war. The fruits of victory in the Napier household amounted to an occasional and much celebrated banana.

Gran, however, was never one to be daunted by adversity, let alone austerity. In the autumn of 1946, she started a credit drapery business in the room over the shop, having bought the stock of a certain deceased Miss Odgers for £100. According to her, credit drapery was cleaner, easier and potentially more profitable than grocery. She proceeded to win a name for herself the following spring as the only outlet in Truro for New Look fashions. I've often wondered what would have happened to her sideline in the long run, whether eventually it would have eclipsed the grocery business altogether. We'll never know, of course, because their relative economic merits were about to be swept into irrelevance by a far greater upheaval in our lives.

None of us had any inkling of that during the long cold winter of 1946/7. The nation was in crisis. I knew that because of my father's frequent tirades against the Labour government, whom he held responsible for every difficulty. Turning out Mr Churchill was where the country had gone wrong, according to him. To Nicky and me, it seemed that an endless supply of snow to play with and thickly frozen ponds to skate on constituted a pretty whizz-bang state of affairs. We had a lot of time for the snowman we made on the lawn at Tredower House and christened Mr Dalton in honour of the then Chancellor of the Exchequer, principal target of my father's wrath. Our Mr Dalton didn't melt till March and we were sorry to see him go.

Strangely enough, the privations of that winter drew my family closer to Uncle Joshua than ever before. The pipes froze solid at Crescent Road, but hot water was still to be had at Tredower House, where a vast store of logs meant there was a fire to sit by as well, coal shortage or no coal shortage. For a good couple of months we took baths and meals there, and many of the unspoken differences between the two households thawed long before the weather did. It was during this period that Uncle Joshua volunteered some of his gold-hunting experiences to me. He and Gran spoke more readily and freely to each other than I could ever recall. Even she and Cordelia discovered some common ground to tread. It was a perversely happy time, symbolized in my memory by a party on the Sunday between Nicky's eleventh birthday and mine. There weren't any candles on our cake – they were as scarce as knobs of coal – and it wasn't exactly a big cake either, but it was a wonderful party, even for the adults. Gran and Uncle Joshua danced together and my father and Nicky's chatted like old friends. The spring of 1947 arrived early for the Napiers and the Lanyons.

There was plenty to look forward to as well. The summer for a start, when Nicky and I were hoping to spend another week – maybe longer – at Nanceworthal. Then the autumn, when we'd penetrate the glamorous mysteries of the senior school.

We left the prep department for the last time one hot afternoon in July after a classroom tea party and a hopeful hymn. We took a long rambling route home up Treliske Lane as far as the ford, then along the path beside the River Kenwyn into Truro. This brought us into the city along St George's Road, under the viaduct and into Victoria Gardens, where we sat on a bench near the bandstand to compare our latest cigarette card acquisitions and dispute whose batting average in the house cricket team had been the higher. It was mine, though not by much. Nicky vowed to reverse that the following season. We bet his Douglas Bader to my Denis Compton on the result. I doubt we'd have remembered the bet a year on, but I remember it now, as clear as the air that afternoon in Truro. Because that was our last schoolday together. There would never be another.

Don Prideaux and I stood between his car and the railings above the beach, on the other side of the road from the Heron. Considine was still inside, relieving himself after four brown ales and a three-course lunch. The ferry was chugging back to the Tregothnan shore with a party of walkers on board, while the afternoon sun turned the scene into a picture-postcard vista of waterside ease. Only in my mind were storm clouds racing across the sky.

'Is he worth what you're paying him, Don?'

'I'm not paying him anything.'

'Come off it. He wouldn't have been that forthcoming just for a pub lunch.'

'He's on a promise, if you must know. It depends on whether I can sell the story on. My editor wouldn't put money up front if you offered him Lord Lucan's address and telephone number.'

'And can you sell it on?'

'I shan't know till I try. I'll have to check up on Jakes first. If they've let the bastard out, which I wouldn't put past them, I could play up the "free to kill again" angle. But if he's still inside – and especially if he's confessed to killing Michaela Lanyon – then it's just ancient history.'

'Not as ancient as my great-uncle's murder.'

'You're thinking of Tully? It was to be expected he'd be out by now. Life seldom means life.'

'But it makes hanging Michael Lanyon seem so . . . pointless.'

'You surely didn't think they'd locked up Tully and thrown away the key?'

I looked out across the river. The ferry had reached the other side. Its passengers were stepping ashore. 'I'm afraid the problem is, Don, I didn't think at all.'

CHAPTER FIVE

A fortnight passed. Nicky didn't fade from my memory, but he did from my thoughts, as they found more everyday concerns to dwell on. His suicide had certainly aroused public interest in a thirty-four-year-old murder, but the effect didn't last. Don Prideaux sent me a copy of his *Western Morning News* article about the tragedy of the Lanyon family, but in an attached note admitted he'd been unable to find a market for it elsewhere. No pay-off for Neville Considine, then, who nevertheless didn't seem in much of a hurry to supply me with the details of Nicky's creditors. I had the feeling – not an unpleasant one – that I wasn't going to hear from him again.

The only new information I gained from Don's article was bleakly inconclusive. Brian Jakes had been murdered by a fellow inmate at Broadmoor in 1974. If he *had* killed Michaela Lanyon, he'd taken the knowledge to his grave. As for Edmund Tully, the Home Office confirmed his release on licence back in 1969. But that was as much as they were prepared to reveal. Don speculated that he had a new name and identity by now. The man who'd done more than anyone to lay waste to Nicky's past had apparently been granted official protection from his own.

My family reflected the general tendency to brush off the Lanyons' misfortunes as a bundle of life's vagaries. A week after their return from honeymoon, Tabitha and Dominic invited me to dinner at their smart home in Chelsea. Dominic's best man and his girlfriend were there, as was Trevor, who'd left Pam in Truro while he spent the weekend cultivating contacts at an international hotel catering fair being staged at Olympia. I was asked to describe my discovery of a hanged man at Tredower House as if the passage of three weeks had turned Nicky's death into nothing more than a cheaply thrilling anecdote. Why did I play along? Because I was too ashamed of my neglect of him to admit what his death really meant to me. None of the people I was eating and drinking with had been in Truro in 1947. None but Trevor had even been born. They didn't know. They couldn't imagine. And I didn't want them to.

'Do you remember much about the murder, Chris?' Dominic asked me at some point.

'Not really,' I unhesitatingly replied. 'It all went on at several removes from me. The trial was up in Bodmin, and I was too young to read the newspaper reports. We didn't even have a television then.'

'The other murderer – this man Tully. Was he local?'

'No.' I smiled. 'Sorry to disappoint you, but I never so much as set eyes on him.'

I noticed Trevor studying me as I spoke. I wondered if he was in any position to know I was lying. Something in his expression suggested he was. But, if so, he wasn't about to draw it to the others' attention.

My attention, however, was a different matter. As became apparent when I gave him a lift back to his hotel at the end of the evening.

'I'm surprised you're not staying with Tabs and Dominic,' I remarked casually.

He grinned. 'I didn't want to cramp their style. Besides, they've their own lives to lead now. I don't mean to get in the way. I'm only glad they don't seem unduly bothered by the Lanyon ghastliness. But like you said—' He turned in his seat to look at me. 'It never had anything to do with you and Pam, did it? Or Melvyn and Una.' He paused before quoting my words back at me. 'It all went on at several removes from the lot of you. Just as well, really. I mean, if any of you *had* seen something significant, you might have had to testify at the trial.' There was another pause. Then he added, as if unable to resist making the question explicit, 'Mightn't you?'

But I never had seen anything significant. Not for certain, anyway. If only I had. I was an eleven-year-old boy. To me, certainty meant tea on the table when I got home; the Cornish Riviera Express pulling into Truro station at a quarter to five in the afternoon; the cathedral bells ringing for evensong; the coming up of the sun and its going down; the fret and play of an average childhood. None of that measured up to what began for me and Nicky and his father one afternoon in late July, 1947. None of that helped any of us.

On account of his duties as Colquite & Dew's roving valuer of art and antiques, Michael Lanyon enjoyed a comparatively generous commercial petrol ration for his car – a handsome 1937 Alvis Silver Crest. He had an appointment in Helston that afternoon and, finding Nicky and me kicking our heels in the garden when he returned to Tredower House for a snatched lunch, bundled us into the car and took us along. It was a rare and exciting treat and we made the most of it, persuading him to take us down to Porthleven after his business was concluded to buy us an ice-cream each. We sat by the harbour eating them, while he smoked a cigarette and gazed out to sea and the gulls wheeled overhead and the fishing boats creaked at their moorings and the sun sparkled on the wavetops. I don't know whether he felt happy, but he certainly seemed contented, taking his ease there in the sunshine, with his son beside him and his wife waiting for him at home. He was thirty-seven years old to my father's forty-two, but he looked a lot more than five years younger, with his unlined face and his clear-eyed gaze. He looked, to tell the truth, like a man with nothing to worry about.

It was gone six o'clock when we got back to Truro. Michael said he'd only have to pop into the office for a few moments, then he'd take me home. The office was above Colquite & Dew's showrooms off Lemon Quay. When we pulled into the yard, it looked deserted, with the premises closed for the night. At Porthleven there'd been a refreshing breeze, but here in Truro the evening was close and airless. The inside of the car smelled of hot leather and Airman cigarettes. The sky was a bruised blue-grey. A hooter was blowing in the gas works behind us. Hazy sunlight was washing across the western towers of the cathedral. A cat was stalking something near the wall at the back of the yard. Nicky was winding the string of his catapult round and round his fingers. All these things I remember. All these details. But nothing significant.

As the car coasted to a halt, a figure detached itself from the deep shadows beneath the overhang of the warehouse roof. It was a man, dressed in a baggy double-breasted suit and battered fedora. He was smoking a cigarette. A tightly folded newspaper was wedged into his jacket pocket. He took a few steps into the sunlight, stopped and looked towards us, expectant and unhurried. Michael turned off the car engine. The hooter sounded louder, but so did the motionlessness of the scene. So did everything. I heard Michael catch his breath. Nicky let the catapult string fall slack. The man moved closer, stopped again and cocked his head. We could see his face now – pale and narrow, with the smudge of a clipped moustache beneath a flattened nose. Michael ground out his cigarette in the dashboard ashtray and grasped the door handle.

'You boys wait here,' he said with quiet emphasis. 'Don't leave the car.'

He climbed out, slammed the door behind him and walked slowly across the yard to where the other man was standing. They didn't shake hands. They didn't even nod in greeting. But they weren't strangers. You could tell that by their stance, by the way they looked at each other. I heard them speak, but they were too far away to catch more than an odd phrase. 'Long time . . .' 'Never thought . . .' Their tone was even yet uneasy, neither hostile nor affectionate. The man in the fedora sniggered. He drew on his cigarette before flicking what was left of it away. Michael glanced round at us, then laid his hand on the other's shoulder, stepping towards the showroom entrance as he did so, urging him, it seemed, to move back to where he'd been waiting. Slowly, they went, then stopped, completely out of earshot now.

They spoke for maybe three minutes. Nicky and I watched them in silence. Something was wrong. Something wasn't normal. I saw Michael reach inside his jacket, take something out and hand it to the man. The hooter died. The man looked down at what he'd been given, then slid it into his pocket and smiled broadly. With that he turned and walked away, casting a single glance across at us as he moved towards the gateway on to Lemon Quay. He caught my eye for a second and I wished he hadn't. Still he was smiling.

'Who is he?' whispered Nicky.

'I don't know,' I replied. 'But I don't like the look of him.'

'Neither do I.'

The man vanished from sight but Michael stayed where he was for another minute or so, staring after him. Then he turned on his heel and strode back to the car, speed exaggerating his limp, the soles of his shoes sounding like gunshots on the cobbles of the yard. He climbed straight in and started the engine.

'Aren't you going into the office, Daddy?'

'No, son. I'm not.'

'Who was that man?'

'Nobody. Don't worry. You won't see him again.'

He was right there; we didn't. Not even when we drove out of the yard and turned along Green Street towards Boscawen Bridge. He was nowhere to be seen. But we recognized his photograph in the newspapers a few weeks later. There wasn't a shadow of a doubt in our minds. He was Edmund Tully.

I was in the habit of putting in a few hours at the showroom on Saturday afternoons. If there was such a thing as a passing trade in classic convertibles, that was the time for it. You wouldn't have known it that Saturday, though. A week had passed since Tabitha's and Dominic's dinner party, a full month since their wedding. Autumn had announced itself in a succession of wet and windy days, which can't have made anyone eager for open-top motoring. The leaves were yellowing on the trees across the road and there was a chill edge to the breeze. It hardly promised to be a classic afternoon for business.

And so it proved. Depressingly so. Until a smart red MGB GT pulled into the forecourt. Sports cars driven by attractive young women are an ad man's ideal of glamour, of course, but this particular example didn't quite conform to type. The woman who got out was certainly young – thirtyish, I reckoned – and strikingly attractive, with short dark hair that only seemed to magnify her large sparkling eyes, but she was dressed in a strangely formal black suit and white blouse, as if for the office. Though not the outer office, if the cut of the suit and the flashing gold of pendant and brooch were anything to go by. She didn't look like anyone's assistant but her own. The self-assured expression on her face suggested she knew the impact she made.

She paused by my lovingly restored Bentley Continental – which Dominic's father claimed he was still seriously considering – and ran an approving glance over it. I rose from my chair and went out to meet her. Somehow, I already knew we weren't going to be discussing cars.

'Thinking of trading up?' I ventured.

'Hardly.' She peeled off one of her pale kid gloves and the thought flashed through my mind: how many women of her age still wore gloves to drive in? Approximately none. But then she wasn't in the least like anyone else. She seemed both older and younger than I'd have said she was, and she had a smile that was effortlessly superior and winsomely appealing all at the same time. 'You're the proprietor?'

'Of Napier Classic Convertibles, yes. Chris Napier.'

'Pleased to meet you, Mr Napier.' We shook hands. 'Pauline Lucas.'

'Of course, if it's new you're interested in, Miss Lucas—'

'No, no. Actually, it's you I'm interested in, Mr Napier.'

'Me?'

'Yes. You've been running Napier Classic Convertibles for some time, haven't you?'

'Eight years. But I don't—'

'It looks as if you're doing well. The showroom. This beauty. And the other ones tucked away up at Bowershaw Farm.'

'You've been to the workshop?'

'Yes. Mark didn't seem to mind showing me around.'

I'll bet he didn't, I thought. But what I said was: 'Are you a buyer, Miss Lucas?'

'No.'

'Then what?'

'A solicitor. Acting on behalf of your ex-wife.'

'Miv? What the hell does she want with a solicitor?'

'Why don't we sit down? Then I can explain.' She smiled sweetly, as if I were being obtuse. I was certainly grateful that there were no customers about and that Les, the Grayson's salesman, was busy on the telephone. I hadn't heard from Miv – token Christmas cards apart – in years, and I hadn't expected to. Certainly not through a legal intermediary.

We sat down and she handed me a business card. *Pauline A. Lucas, LLB (Hons)*, with an address in Llandudno. The solicitor who'd handled the divorce for Miv was based in London, so I suppose I shouldn't have been surprised that she'd found a new one in North Wales. But as for setting her on me, that did surprise me.

'Mark said you live and breathe classic cars.'

'Did he?'

'He also said business was booming.'

'He doesn't see the books.'

'No. But then neither does your ex-wife.'

'Why should she? It's *my* business, not hers.'

'That's not entirely clear, Mr Napier, is it?'

'What do you mean?'

'Well, didn't she put up some of the capital?'

'What if she did? It was a gift. A parting gesture of goodwill.' Miv had always been generous – as well as forgiving. She'd been awash with royalties from 'Lover Come Back' at the time I'd set up Napier Classic Convertibles. She'd known I couldn't turn to my family for help, so, she'd stepped in. And I'd been grateful. She'd made it clear, after all, that it *was* a gift. Not a loan – of any kind. But she hadn't had a legal adviser like Pauline Lucas then. 'You're not going to tell me she wants the money back?'

'No. I'm not.'

'What does she want, then?'

'The point is that her gift, loan, call it what you will, constitutes a share in the business – a stake in the profits.'

I gaped at her. 'You're not serious.'

'Completely. Of course, she doesn't want to play an active role, but as, in effect, your sleeping partner, she's certainly entitled—'

'*She's not entitled to a thing!*' I instantly wished I hadn't shouted. Les was staring at me across the wide expanse of the showroom, telephone mercifully still clamped to his ear. 'This is absolutely ridiculous.'

Pauline Lucas cocked an insouciant eyebrow. 'Do I take it you deny she's entitled to a share of the business proportional to her original contribution?'

'Yes. Please do take that.' I leaned across the desk for emphasis. 'As my last word on the matter.'

'I fear it's unlikely to be that.'

'It was an outright gift. With no strings attached.'

'Not according to my client.'

'Fallen on hard times, has she?'

'I can't discuss her financial affairs with you, Mr Napier. But certainly your own prospects are considerably rosier than hers.'

'What the hell do you mean by that?'

She lowered her voice. 'I'm referring to the Carnoweth inheritance.'

I suddenly felt sorry for Miv. That she should have been reduced to carping about what might or mightn't come my way when my parents died, given the contempt she'd always expressed for the moneyed classes in general and my relatives in particular, was little short of pathetic. But pathos clearly wasn't going to cut any ice with Pauline Lucas. She was there to see what she could get for her client, and I honestly didn't know which to offer her: a pay-off, or the bluntest of rejections. I ended up somewhere in the middle.

'When Miv and I got divorced, Miss Lucas—'

'I wasn't acting for her then.'

'Perhaps that's just as well.'

'Perhaps it is – for you.'

'Tell her if there's something she wants to talk to me about, then that's what she should do – *talk to me*.'

'That's all you have to say?'

'Yes.'

She smiled. 'Well, this visit was really only intended to clarify the situation in my mind. It's certainly achieved that.'

'Oh, good.'

'I'll pass on your comments. And then . . .'

'Yes?'

'I'll be in touch.' She rose effortlessly from her chair and smiled again. 'Goodbye for now, Mr Napier. And thank you for seeing me.'

I watched her walk back out to the MG, slip elegantly into the driving seat and start away. As the car flashed out of sight beneath the railway bridge, Les ostentatiously cleared his throat. He was no longer on the telephone.

'Wife trouble, Chris?' he asked with a sympathetic grin.

'*Ex*-wife trouble, if you must know.'

'Ah. The worst kind. At times like this, you must regret giving up the booze.'

'Very funny.' But it wasn't, of course. Not at all. It was actually far truer than it was funny. By a long way.

In a sense, I've lived my whole life in the shadow of the Carnoweth inheritance. There was a time when I knew nothing about it, and another longer time when I didn't care about it, but it was always there. I was always involved in it, wittingly or not, willingly or not. I remember telling Miv once how grateful she should be that there was no money in her family. She'd thought I was satirizing her politics, but not so.

It wasn't Uncle Joshua's fault. He was simply trying to share his good fortune with those dearest to him. It's hardly an unworthy motive. Why shouldn't he put the Lanyons before his own family if he wanted to? Gran would have said blood ties were indissoluble, but if her brother had returned penniless from Alaska and looked to her for charity, she might have changed her tune.

Ironically, it's possible Uncle Joshua *did* decide to feather-bed our futures as well as the Lanyons' – just before the end. Maybe he'd been mulling it over for years. Maybe, as the two families grew closer together and old age softened his differences with Gran, he came round to thinking of all of us as his beneficiaries. If so, it would explain what he'd meant the last time I ever spoke to him. Which was also the last time any of us spoke to him.

It was the afternoon of Thursday 7 August 1947, steamily hot and languidly still. The cathedral shimmered in the haze. Doves cooed in the trees around the lawn at Tredower House. Life itself seemed stunned into slow motion. Nicky and I were playing tennis at walking pace, too drowsy even to dispute points, when Uncle Joshua ambled down from the house and waved to us. He was wearing a three-piece linen suit, an open-necked shirt, a straw hat with the brim turned down and the stout boots he favoured in all weathers. He looked if anything older than he was, on account of his snowy white beard and aldermanly paunch. But his walk was that of a much younger man – firm and jaunty, with his shoulders pushed back. He never carried a stick and I'd never had to slow down to let him catch up. That measured stride of his had a momentum of its own. It bore the strength of his past.

'Your mother wants you, Nicky,' he called.

'What for, Uncle Josh?'

'For a good reason,' he said gruffly. Then he grinned. 'It could be to ask what you'll be wanting to take to Nanceworthal next week. Why don't you go and find out?'

'Righto, Uncle.' As Nicky scampered off, I shouted after him that I'd probably set off home for tea before he came back. He waved an acknowledgement and went on.

'I'll walk with you into town if you like, Christian,' said Uncle Joshua. 'I'm going that way.'

So it was agreed and we set off down the drive. I asked what he was going into town for and he tapped his nose, grunted and eventually delivered a one-word answer.

'Business.'

'Dad says it's too hot for business.'

'He's right. But this has waited long enough. I'll not postpone it just because the mercury's rising.'

'I hope the fine weather lasts all summer.'

'It probably will. Looking forward to starting up there next month?' He nodded towards the outline of Truro School on the south-eastern horizon.

'I think so.'

'Hah! You've got it about right there, young 'un. The future's a two-edged sword.' He sighed. 'But you can't always be leaving it in the scabbard, can you?'

'I don't know, Uncle.'

'No. And why should you, eh? Don't listen to me. I'm just an old man rambling on.'

No more was said until we'd descended the hill into Truro and started along St Austell Street. The silence was by no means uncomfortable. It was congenial and utterly normal. Despite what he'd said, Uncle Joshua was never one to ramble – on foot or in speech. He always had a direction in mind. But he didn't always reveal what it was. When we stopped outside one house in a drab terrace and he gazed fixedly at the front door, I realized it must be the house where the Lanyons had once lived. But why he'd stopped there – and what he was thinking – I couldn't guess. He scratched his beard and tilted his hat back and gave a soulful sigh. And then we went on, round by Old Bridge Street into Cathedral Close, where we paused again in the welcome shade. There he lit a cigar and puffed it approvingly into life. He was the only man I knew who smoked such a thing. Woodbines and foul-smelling briars were the norm among the post-war manhood of Truro. Uncle Joshua's cigars were just one more proof that twenty-three years away from Cornwall had left their mark.

'I need some advice, Christian,' he said at length. 'Reckon you could give me some?'

'Me, Uncle?'

'Why not? You're young enough to be impartial.'

'Nobody's ever asked me for advice before.'

'Then it's time somebody did.'

'What's it about?'

'It's about the difference between family and friends. Who do you put first?'

'I'm not sure what you mean.'

'Well, imagine your sister Pam was in some kind of trouble. What would you do?'

'Help her out of it.'

'And if your friend Nicky was in trouble?'

'Help *him* out of it.'

'But if they were in trouble at the same time, who would you help first?'

'Well, I . . . I mean . . .'

'Tricky, ain't it?'

'I know.' I grinned triumphantly. 'I'd find a way to help both of them . . . simultaneously.' And my grin broadened with pride at being able to slip in such an exotic adverb.

Uncle Joshua laughed and patted me on the shoulder. 'That's a good answer. Mind you remember it. I will.'

'Is it valuable advice, Uncle?'

'Yes, young 'un. I reckon it is.' He wedged his cigar between his teeth and we wandered round into High Cross. 'Are you going home – or to the shop?'

'Shop.'

'Then we part here. I'm for Lemon Street. Give my best regards to your parents. And to Lady Fan Todd, of course.' He'd started applying this humorously disrespectful dialect nickname to Gran since her move into credit drapery. 'Tell her . . .' But he seemed to think better of asking me to pass on a message. He smiled. 'It can keep. Off you go.'

'Bye, Uncle.'

'Bye, Christian.'

I'd covered no more than a few yards when he called to me. 'What is it, Uncle?'

'Nicky said you and he wanted to see the Wyatt Earp film they're showing at the Plaza.'

'*My Darling Clementine*? Gosh, yes, we do.'

He grinned and tossed me a coin from his waistcoat pocket. It flashed silver in the sunlight. As I caught it, I saw that it was a half crown.

'Mind you get the best seats, then. No sense skimping.'

'Crikey! Thanks, Uncle.'

'Now be off with you.' He gestured with his cigar in affectionate dismissal, then turned and strode away along Cathedral Lane, while I made off towards River Street.

I never did get to see *My Darling Clementine*. Somehow, I hadn't the heart to spend Uncle Joshua's half crown so frivolously. Not when I knew I'd never see him again. The police traced his movements later and established that he'd called at his solicitor's office in Lemon Street just after five o'clock, only to find that Mr Cloke had gone to visit a client at Chacewater and wouldn't be back that day. He'd made an appointment to see Cloke at eleven o'clock the following morning. He hadn't said what he wanted to discuss, so nobody can ever know whether it concerned the terms of his will, because the appointment wasn't kept. Joshua Carnoweth was murdered that night.

Moving to Pangbourne in 1970 had turned out to be one of my better decisions. Miv and I had just split up and I'd realized that if giving up alcohol was to be anything more than a vainglorious boast, I'd have to get out of London. Drink had already cost me my driving licence, so it was by train that I'd begun exploring the Thames Valley for a cheap but comfortable hideaway. The one I'd found and still lived in eleven years later was number four, Harrowcroft, an end-of-terrace cottage in The Moors, a potholed lane off the High Street, with a lean-to garage for the Triumph Stag I'd promised myself at the end of my suspension and a small garden running down to the banks of the Pang.

It was no more than a five-minute walk from Grayson Motors and I should think I made it in about three that afternoon. Les's presence had prevented me telephoning Miv straight after Pauline Lucas's departure, but I didn't propose to wait long before demanding an explanation from her. Fortunately for my blood pressure, she answered the first time I rang.

'Hi there.' The Americanism chimed oddly with the Welsh accent that seemed to have reasserted itself since her retreat to Snowdonia.

'It's me. Chris.'

'Chris? This is a surprise, I must say.'

'It shouldn't be. I've just been speaking to Pauline Lucas. Or rather *she's* just been speaking to *me*.'

'Oh yes. Who's she?'

'Stop playing games, Miv. Pauline Lucas. Your solicitor.'

'I've never heard of her. I suppose old Warboys is still my solicitor if anyone is. Is she his assistant?'

'No, of course not. You know damn well who she is.'

'I don't. Honestly, Chris. You're not making any sense.'

'She came here today and told me about your so-called claim to a share in my business.'

'But I don't have a claim to a share in it. Come to that, I don't want a share in it. Who'd you say this woman was?'

'Pauline Lucas. A solicitor from Llandudno. Hold on.' I plucked the card she'd given me from my pocket. 'Pauline A. Lucas, 32A High Street, Llandudno.'

'The name means nothing to me. Besides, Llandudno hasn't got a high street. As for getting involved in your jalopy racket, forget it. It's the last thing I need.'

'I'm not asking you to—'

'Are you sober, Chris?'

'Yes, of course I'm bloody well sober.'

'You don't sound it.'

'Neither would you if—' The doorbell jangled through the confusion of my thoughts. I saw a shape moving beyond the frosted-glass crescent window set in the door. 'Are you saying that you haven't asked Pauline Lucas – or

119

anyone – to chase me up over the money you gave me towards starting the business?'

'That money was a gift. I don't go back on gifts.'

'*Is that what you're saying?*'

'Yes.'

The doorbell rang again. The caller could probably see me standing in the hall, but I decided to ignore them anyway. 'Then how did she know about it?'

'Haven't a clue.'

'You must have told her.'

'But I've never met her. Not that I know of, anyway. What's she like?'

The doorbell interrupted my stumbling efforts to describe Pauline Lucas, the caller giving the bell three imperious stabs. It seemed they weren't going to give up, though clearly one of us was going to have to. I took a deep breath. 'Listen, Miv, can I call you back?'

'If you feel you must, sweetie. Or I could give you the number of a good psychiatrist.'

'Thanks a lot. Bye.'

I slammed the telephone down, marched to the door and flung it open. A woman was standing on the mat, hand raised to give the bell another jab. She was slim, almost petite, curly dark-brown hair framing a pale, soft-featured face. She was wearing blue jeans and a red polo-necked sweater beneath a fleece-lined flying jacket. The jeans were flared, several years behind the fashion, frayed and faded enough to be genuinely old. My first impression was that she was some kind of student, but it was obvious she had to be the mature kind. I'd have put her age at thirty-odd. Strangely, however, there was nothing in the least mature about the skittering look of panic that flashed into her eyes at the sight of me. She bit her lower lip and withdrew her mittened hand from the bell.

'Yes?'

'Er . . . Chris Napier?'

'That's me.'

'Oh . . . right.'

'What do you want?'

'Well, it's a bit . . .'

'I'm in a hurry, so I'd be grateful if—'

'Michaela Lanyon.'

'What?' I genuinely thought I must have misheard.

'I'm Nicky's sister.' She looked at me for a second or two in silence, then swallowed hard and repeated her name, as if sharing my disbelief. 'Michaela Lanyon.'

CHAPTER SIX

'I suppose it must be . . . a shock. I mean, if you thought, like the guy who wrote about me in the paper . . . that I'm . . . that I was . . .'

'Dead?'

'Yeh.' She looked at me across the sitting-room, into which I'd distractedly shown her. We were standing either side of the window, each confronting a familiar shadow cast by a total stranger. 'God, I wasn't sure whether to . . . I mean . . .'

'You're Michaela Lanyon?'

'Yeh. Well, I call myself Emma Moresco, actually. Have done for years. Ever since I . . . ran away.'

'You weren't murdered.'

'No.'

'You just . . . vanished of your own accord.'

'I had to.'

'Leaving your family to think you were dead.'

'There was nothing I could do about that. Not without—' She turned aside and bowed her head. 'I didn't like it, you know. I didn't enjoy it. But I had to get away from there. From the life I was leading.'

'Why?'

'That doesn't matter. It's not why I came. I came because of Nicky.'

'Too late. He died, believing you'd been murdered by Brian Jakes.'

She sighed and ran a hand over her face. 'This isn't easy. Christ, I don't even . . .' A shudder ran through her. 'Could I sit down?'

'Yes, of course. I'm sorry.' I ushered her into an armchair, her vulnerability undermining my anger. 'Look, do you want some tea?'

'You haven't got anything stronger, have you?'

"Fraid not.'

'Tea, then. Yeh. Fine.'

I walked into the kitchen and put the kettle on. As I measured some tea into the pot and arranged cups and saucers on a tray, I reeled mentally before the mundane reality of Michaela Lanyon's return from the dead. For a second, I almost believed she wouldn't be there when I went back into the sitting-room. But she was, hunched forward in the armchair, just as I'd left her. She looked up as I entered and smiled weakly.

'Sorry about this. Honest.'

'You don't have to apologize to me.'

'No. But I reckon I have to explain.'

'Teenagers run away from home every week. And a good few never come back. What's there to explain?' My tone sounded harsh, even to me. 'Sorry.' I grinned ruefully. 'Now we're both apologizing.'

'Perhaps we both need to. In our different ways, we each ran out on Nicky, didn't we?'

'Yes. I suppose we did.'

'If I'd known he was likely to commit suicide, I'd have . . .' She shrugged. 'Done something.'

'Me too.'

'I had no idea Mum was dead or that Nicky was so . . . desperate. Truly.'

'I believe you.'

'He used to talk about you so much. His good friend Chris Napier. He would never have a word said against you, would never admit . . .' She shook her head, sparing me, it seemed, the words of condemnation I could as easily have uttered myself. Then the kettle came to the boil.

I filled the pot, put it on the table and stood beside it, waiting for the tea to mash. 'How did you find me?' I asked, as much to fill the silence as to satisfy my curiosity.

'I phoned Tredower House. The receptionist gave me Grayson's number. That's how I knew where you were. I followed you from there. Even when you got here, though . . . I hesitated.'

'Why?'

'Sixteen years is a long time to be thought dead. You get used to it. It becomes a habit. And habits aren't easy to break.'

'So why did you break it?'

'Because Nicky's death ties you and me. We can't walk away from him now. He's forced us to listen, hasn't he? He's forced us to take notice.'

'Notice of what?'

'His belief. His certainty.' She watched me as I poured the tea, nodding yes to milk and sugar. I carried our cups across and sat down in the armchair opposite her. 'I'm taking a bet he spoke to you before he hanged himself. That's why he went to Truro. To see you, in the place where you'd been friends. Am I right?'

'Yes. You are.'

'Then I'll take another bet. But this is a safer one, because it's only what he was forever saying to me when

I was a little girl. He thought our father was innocent – a wronged man. He told you that, didn't he?'

'In his own way, I suppose he did.'

'But you didn't believe him. No more than I did, when I was old enough to grasp what had happened. Nobody ever believed Nicky.'

'Not even your mother?'

'She wanted to. But she didn't have the strength of mind to withstand Considine's drip-drip-drip campaign to portray himself as the noble saviour of a murderer's widow.'

'It doesn't sound as if there was much love lost between you and your stepfather.'

'*Love*?' There was real passion in her voice now. 'I hated that man. I still do. He made my life hell.'

'How?'

'How do you think?' Her stare challenged me to draw the obvious conclusion. 'It was him I was running from. I preferred to let my mother and brother believe I was dead rather than let Considine think there was even a possibility I might still be alive somewhere. Because he'd have come looking, for certain. Searching and prying and probing and—' She broke off. 'I'm sorry. You don't want to hear this.'

'Michaela—'

'Call me Emma. Please. That's who I've been for sixteen years.'

'All right. Emma. Where have you been for those sixteen years?'

'London. Isn't that where all the runaways go? It wasn't so bad. There was this guy I met in Clacton that last Easter. He was on holiday there. Well, we sort of hit it off and . . . he offered to put me up if I needed a place to stay in the big city. Nice bloke. Gay, actually. Maybe that's why he was so nice. Anyway, he gave me a start. Since then, it's just been . . . an ordinary life. I work shifts on a super-market check-out. Home's a high-rise flat. Not much, is it? No husband, no children and a dead-end job. But it's what you have to expect if you do a runner from your own identity. And I've never regretted it. Never once. It's been worth it to be out of Considine's reach.'

'Aren't you taking quite a risk by coming forward now?'

'I'm not coming forward.' She set down her cup and stared at me intently. 'Nicky told me I could trust you, Chris. And that's exactly what I'm doing. Nobody must know I'm alive. If Considine ever found out . . .'

'It can't be that bad.'

'I couldn't sleep at night if I thought he knew.' She folded her arms defensively around herself. 'There's nothing he's not capable of.'

I held up my hand reassuringly. 'All right. OK. Don't worry. I won't tell anyone. Especially not Considine. You can trust me. For Nicky's sake, if you like. You're right. I let him down. But tell me this, Emma. What can I do, now he's dead, to make up for that?'

'You can prove him right,' she replied without even a momentary hesitation. 'You can prove our father didn't murder your uncle.'

I thought I was dreaming at first. And so I was, in a way. The ringing doorbell became a bumble-bee buzzing in my ear, ever louder and more threateningly, as I traversed some soon to be forgotten landscape of my sleeping mind. Then I woke and realized it was the real solid brass doorbell of our home in Crescent Road that was ringing. It was pitch-dark in my bedroom, but there was a light visible round the door and a sound of movement along the landing. I rolled over and peered at the luminous dial of my alarm clock. It was a quarter to three, the very middle of the night. Yet there was somebody at the door.

126

Whoever they were, whatever they wanted, I knew the time meant something very serious had happened.

There were footsteps on the stairs now and a strengthening of the light as another switch was thrown. Then a creaking of the floorboards in Gran and Grandad's room. I clambered out of bed, walked to the door and edged it open, letting my eyes adjust gradually to the brightness. Mum was standing by the banisters in dressing-gown and slippers, looking down into the hall. I assumed Dad had gone down and that it was him I could hear fiddling with the bolts. The letter box rattled as he pulled the front door open and a gruff but subdued male voice said, 'Mr Napier?'

'Yes,' Dad replied. 'What can I do for you, Constable?'

'Sorry for disturbing you at this hour, sir. I have some bad news. Could I step inside?' The door closed behind him and his voice sounded louder in the confines of the hall. 'It concerns your uncle, Mr Joshua Carnoweth.'

'Is he ill?'

'I'm afraid he's dead, sir.'

Gran and Grandad emerged from their room just as the words were spoken. I couldn't see them, but I could see Mum glance round at them. 'Did you hear that?' she murmured.

'I heard it,' said Gran, 'but I can't quite believe it.' She started down the stairs, with Mum and Grandad in pursuit. 'What's happened?' she demanded as she reached the hall. 'Did you say my brother Joshua's dead?'

'I'm very sorry to say that he is, madam.'

'But he was in perfect health when I last saw him, only a couple of days ago.'

I stepped out on to the landing and tiptoed to the banisters for a view. Then I saw Pam standing at the top of the stairs. She frowned at me and pressed a finger to her lips.

'When did this happen, Constable?'

'He was found . . . just a couple of hours ago, madam.'

'He died in his sleep?'

'Not exactly. When I say found—'

'What *do* you mean? Out with it.'

The constable sighed. 'I mean, madam, that Mr Carnoweth was found dead in Barrack Lane just after midnight tonight.'

'Dead – in the street?'

'He'd been stabbed several times.'

'Good God almighty,' mumbled Grandad.

'Murdered?' said Mum disbelievingly.

'It seems so, madam.'

'Who did it?' demanded Gran.

'We don't know yet, madam. But we have a good description of a man seen running from the scene of the crime and you can be assured no effort will be spared—'

'Murdered?' put in Dad. 'Here in Truro?'

'Yes, sir.'

'But why?'

'It's too early to—'

'Money,' announced Gran, as if there could be no room for doubt, as if she'd always feared such a fate might overtake him. 'It'll have been for his money.'

'Nanceworthal, summer of forty-six,' I said as I handed the photograph I'd taken of my ten-year-old friend to his sister all of her lifetime and more later. Nicky was grinning down at me from his perch halfway up an uneven haystack on the Jagos' farm in a snapshot of his childhood and mine. 'We never went back,' I added as she scanned the faded print.

'You never can,' she murmured. 'Still, when you see something like this, you feel as if it might almost be possible, don't you? As if you could step into the black

128

and white past and lead Nicky out of it. But you can't. He's still there. But he'll never be here again.'

'Doing what you did – running away – must have meant turning your back on every kind of keepsake.'

She shook her head. 'Not really. I didn't have any. I'm not sure how much Mum kept when she left Cornwall, but whatever there was she lost in the flood.'

'You mean the flood at Jaywick in fifty-three? Considine told me about it.'

'Yeh? Well, he wasn't there, was he? But you're right. Jaywick, January fifty-three. It's just about my earliest memory – Nicky waking me in the middle of the night with water lapping around my bed. It was so cold. Like ice. And the bungalow was moving. It seemed like the end of the world. Nicky got Mum and me on to a mattress and we floated up with the floodwater. He stayed calm while Mum just wept and I was too frightened to do anything. I remember watching him swim to the front door and pull it open, letting in a rush of water. Then he swam to the back of the bungalow and broke through the wall with a saucepan. It was only a plank wall, of course, but it took some doing. I thought he'd gone mad, that he was trying to drown us, but he'd realized you had to let the water find its own level or the whole bungalow could turn turtle. Then he got us up into the roof space, where he said we'd be safe. We sat up there all night on the rafters in the freezing cold and pitch-dark. Nicky smashed a hole in the roof and shouted for help, but there was no answer. We found out later our nearest neighbours had all drowned. When it got light, we looked out and all you could see was grey swirling water on every side. There were bungalows actually floating by us. And dustbins and cars and God knows what. Our bungalow was wedged against a brick shed by the current. I suppose that's what saved us. But, actually, without Nicky, Mum and I would have drowned for certain. He saved our lives. That's literally all we got out with when the rescue boat came for us: our lives. Everything else – clothes, furniture, the lot, down to the smallest possession – ended up in the North Sea. But thanks to Nicky we were still alive. I suppose that's why I can't accept that he died in vain.'

'You may have to,' I said gently. 'I wouldn't know how to start trying to prove your father innocent – even supposing I thought he was.'

'Can't you give him the benefit of the doubt for Nicky's sake?'

'I can. But where does that get us?'

'I've been thinking, you see.' Her eyes sparkled with sudden enthusiasm. 'That journalist—'

'Don Prideaux.'

'Yeh. He said Edmund Tully was released from prison twelve years ago. Well, he's the one man who knows the truth, isn't he? The absolute truth.'

'If he lied at the trial, he'll lie now. Besides, we have no way of contacting him. He could be anywhere. He could be dead, for God's sake. If he was the same age as your father, that would make him seventy now.'

'Wouldn't the Home Office have told Prideaux if he was dead?'

'Maybe.'

'So it's odds on he's still alive.'

'Even so—'

'And Nicky became more and more obsessed with the case after I left. That's what Considine said, wasn't it? Collecting press cuttings about the trial. Going through the evidence, over and over again, searching for the answer. Don't you see? He's bound to have gone looking for Tully.'

'So?'

'He kept everything. He always did. If Nicky found

Tully, there'll be a record of his whereabouts – at the very least a clue to them – amongst his possessions. And where are those possessions now?'

'With Considine, presumably.'

'Exactly.' She fixed me with her appealing gaze. 'That's why I can't do this and you have to. For Nicky *and* me. It has to be you. There's no-one else.'

I might have found it more difficult to absorb the shock of Uncle Joshua's death if Gran and my parents had been open with me about the details. As it was, their determination to keep me in the dark – or shield me from the gruesome facts, as they no doubt saw it – provided me with a mystery to puzzle over. This gave me more than enough with which to occupy my thoughts as early morning blended into a long day of dislocation and uncertainty. Dad and Gran departed straight after breakfast for Tredower House, leaving Mum to open up the shop, assisted by Pam. Grandad stayed at home with me. He was to remain there in case of messages and I was to remain with him on the grounds that I'd be a nuisance anywhere else.

What I wanted to do above all was to see Nicky, knowing that I could rely on him for a full account of the facts. I reckoned he was bound to know more than me, since he actually lived at Tredower House, which I imagined to be the nerve centre of police investigations. I assumed that was why Dad and Gran had gone there; that and the wish to share their grief with the Lanyons. But when I suggested as much to Grandad, he indignantly rejected the idea and unintentionally revealed what may have been their true motive.

'He was your gran's brother. He was no relative of the Lanyons. It's not for them to take charge of his affairs – much as they might like to.'

So, amidst the dismay of bereavement, the lineaments of a power struggle were beginning to appear. The spring truce was over, broken by Uncle Joshua's death. Gran had gone to Tredower House to stake out her territory. But was it her territory – or Cordelia Lanyon's? It had taken only a few hours for bereavement to turn to rivalry.

And what of Uncle Joshua? How could he be dead, when I'd seen him, stout and proud and striding, the previous afternoon? Banished to the back garden, I played tennis against the garage wall as the day dragged on, my thoughts coming back to him all the time. He'd seemed so permanent, so indestructible – like some outcrop of granite up on the moors. You couldn't break granite with a knife. Something more than a thin steel blade would have been needed to topple Uncle Joshua, something more profound and elemental. A blood feud perhaps, like in several of the Sherlock Holmes stories I'd read. Maybe some secret society had reached out its vengeful arm from Alaska to strike him down. I was already convinced, despite Grandad's scepticism, that Uncle Joshua had gone to Barrack Lane to meet somebody by appointment. It was the other side of the city from Tredower House, after all. Why else would he have been there at midnight? He'd been heading in that direction when I last saw him. On urgent business, by his own admission. Had he returned to Tredower House in the interim? If not, where had he been? And why?

But answering my questions was top of nobody's agenda. Enlightenment of a meagre kind came only when Dad and Gran returned with Mum and Pam at six o'clock. A family conference of sorts was staged around the tea table, with everybody too taken up with events to bother keeping any of them from me. The murderer had apparently been apprehended. A clerk at the railway station had recognized his description as matching that of a passenger he'd sold a ticket to for the first train to London that morning. The man had been taken off the train at Plymouth and was presumably back in Truro by now, being interrogated by the police. His name and motive had not been disclosed – supposing them to be known at all. Only the nature of his crime was clear: murder. None of us expressed any doubt of his guilt.

Gran had been to see Uncle Joshua's body. That much I gleaned from her description of him as looking 'uncommonly peaceful'. I wanted to ask *where* she'd seen him, but couldn't summon the nerve. Perhaps that was just as well, in view of the temper she flew into when Pam asked about the Lanyons.

'Anyone would think he was Cordelia's brother, not mine, from the way they're carrying on. What were they ever to him except . . . hired help? They're sitting there in Joshua's house like it was their own, with never so much as a by your leave. Disrespectful, I call it.'

'There'll be time enough to sort out such matters later, Ma,' said Dad.

'Time enough? That's what Mr Cloke had the nerve to tell me. "All in due course, Mrs Napier." But whose course? That's what I'd like to know. We've the right to be told now.'

'Uncle Joshua went to see Mr Cloke yesterday,' I remarked, eager to involve myself in the discussion.

Suddenly, silence consumed the room. All eyes were turned on me. The significance of my words was slowly absorbed. Then Gran said, 'What do you mean, Christian?' She stared at me, her brow furrowing, as I stumbled through an account of my walk with Uncle Joshua twenty-four hours before. She seemed to find it hard to believe he'd sought my advice about anything, but *'business in Lemon Street'* meant his solicitor. About that she was certain. And from that certainty it was a short jump to a disturbing conclusion. 'I told you, Melvyn,' she said, turning to Dad. 'This is about money. Solicitors and murderers have that much in common. Money's at the root of it, and Joshua had more than was good for him.'

'But the real question is who's he—' Dad broke off, regretting, I think, the hint of greed in his voice. Uncle Joshua was only eighteen hours dead and a long way from being buried. It was too soon, too offensively premature, to be pondering who'd profit by his death. But it was in his mind, as it was in Gran's, and it couldn't be dislodged.

'I mean to find out sooner than Mr Cloke might care for,' said Gran, slowly and deliberately, as if Dad had finished the question. Then she added, without any apparent awareness of irony, 'I owe it to Joshua.'

'No-one's interested, are they?' mused Michaela Lanyon, alias Emma Moresco, as she read the note Don Prideaux had sent me with the copy of his newspaper article. 'That's why he couldn't sell the story on. Because nobody really cares.'

'I do.' I intended the remark to be consolatory, but she gave no sign she'd so much as heard it.

'Do you know what the weirdest thing is? Until I saw his photograph in the paper – some old police mugshot – I didn't even know what my father looked like.'

'Did he know about you – before he died?'

She glanced up at me. 'No. Mum was only three and a half months pregnant when he was hanged, and I was a small baby, so she was hardly showing. She told me she'd thought it kinder not to tell him, but I'm not sure she didn't regret that later. I've often wished she *had* told him. It would mean there was something between us, something real, not just . . . a biological fact. As it was, I felt one worse than an orphan. I was always afraid people would find out – neighbours, schoolfriends – and label me the murderer's daughter. Considine threatened me with just that several times when I wouldn't . . .' Her expression faltered. She rose and moved away across the room, resuming with her gaze trained on the world beyond the window. 'I suppose I was running away from Michael Lanyon as well as Neville Considine when I left Clacton that day.'

'Had you been planning it for a long time?'

'Thinking, yes – a long time. But actually planning? No more than a couple of weeks. Since meeting Norman in a coffee bar over Easter. Without his offer of accommodation, I wouldn't have had the nerve. I bought some second-hand clothes and hid them in my locker at school. I took them with me in my bag when I left school that afternoon, changed into them in the loos on the recreation ground, then hung round for an hour before catching the five o'clock train to London. Norman knew who I was, of course, but nobody else. Then or since. I haven't trusted a soul with the truth in all those years.'

'Apart from me.'

'Yeh. Apart from you.' She looked back at me. 'So, it's pretty important you don't let me down.'

'I can't guarantee to prove your father innocent, you know. I can't promise the impossible.'

'I'm only asking you to try. Not much, is it?'

'Not *too* much, certainly.'

'Does that mean you'll give it a go?'

'Yes.' A smile suddenly flashed across her face. 'I suppose it does.'

A police spokesman confirmed last night that the man arrested earlier in the day after being removed from a London-bound train at Plymouth North Road station, Edmund Tully, has been formally charged with the murder in Truro on Thursday night of Joshua Carnoweth, a wealthy and highly respected resident of the city. The spokesman said that Tully would appear before Truro magistrates on Monday, and added that a further arrest in connection with the case could not be ruled out.

So ran the front-page article in the *Western Morning News* of Saturday 9 August 1947. I first read it craning over Pam's shoulder in the kitchen at Crescent Road while we were supposed to be washing up after breakfast. It told me two things that I found tantalizing as well as baffling. Firstly, the murderer was somebody I'd never heard of, presumably a stranger who'd come to Truro for the specific purpose of doing Uncle Joshua harm; my theory about an Alaskan equivalent of the Ku Klux Klan was thus partly vindicated, at least in my own mind. Secondly, there might be a second murderer, an accomplice or accessory of some kind; the police spokesman could only have declined to rule out a further arrest because he was actually expecting one.

I decided there and then to go and see Nicky. It was only what I'd normally have done on a Saturday morning anyway and Gran and my parents had evidently been too preoccupied to think of prohibiting it, so my excuses were ready-made. Nicky might know more than I did. Above all, he might be able to help me start believing in the reality of Uncle Joshua's death. The event still seemed like a cross between a bad dream and a James Cagney gangster movie. It was going on out there somewhere, but my brain refused to register it as a fact. Uncle Joshua was dead – but not to me.

So, as soon as the washing-up was done, I told Pam I

was going down to the railway station to do some train-spotting, instead of which I made for Tredower House. I planned to take a circuitous route via Daniell Road, Strangways Terrace and Gas Hill in order to avoid passing either the shop, where Mum might waylay me, or Mr Cloke's offices at the bottom of Lemon Street, where Gran and/or Dad might be intending to put in an appearance. This route had the additional advantage of crossing Lemon Street at its other end, close to its junction with Barrack Lane. If there was anything to be seen there, I meant to see it.

And there *was* something to see, something that achieved what the protracted agonizing of my parents and grandparents had failed to. At the top of Lemon Street, dead opposite me as I emerged from Daniell Road, stood the Lander Monument, a tall granite column supporting a statue of Richard Lander, the famous Truronian explorer of darkest Africa. At its foot, a man in overalls was working with a broom and bucket, scrubbing at the paving stones. An acrid smell of cleaning fluid drifted across to greet me and I stopped, puzzled by the intensity of his efforts. A dark and patchy stain straggled round from the monument towards Barrack Lane, but at first I couldn't think what it might be, nor why its removal should be so important.

Then, as I stared across the road, it came to me. Uncle Joshua's blood, spattered along a length of Truro pavement. It *was* real. In my mind's eye, I could see the moonlit struggle at the foot of the monument, the flash of the blade, the fatal lunges. I could see Tully turning to flee while Uncle Joshua reeled and stumbled towards the corner of Barrack Lane, blood gouting from his wounds. I could see and believe it all.

Suddenly I was running down Lemon Street, the slope speeding me on. The diversion was forgotten now. I just wanted to be as far as possible from the bloodstained pavement. Uncle Joshua had roller skated down this very hill as a youth; Gran had told me so. I thought of him, young and lean and eagle-eyed, outpacing me as I ran. I must have passed Mr Cloke's offices at the bottom, but I didn't notice. I dodged through the bustling shoppers in Boscawen Street and darted along Cathedral Lane to the spot where I'd last seen Uncle Joshua. There I stopped. But there he wasn't. I could summon the scent of his cigar from my memory, the curve of his grin as he tossed me the coin. But already the lustre of immediacy was gone. He was fading, like a photograph exposed too soon. He was slipping away, and I could see it happening.

I began following the route we'd taken from Tredower House on Thursday in reverse, past the Lanyons' old home in St Austell Street, across Boscawen Bridge and up Tregolls Road. My pace slowed as I neared my destination. For some reason, I was beginning to dread arriving there, whereas earlier I could hardly wait to. Curiosity had turned to foreboding.

When I reached the entrance to the drive, I stopped and crouched down to tighten my shoelaces. They weren't loose, but I was now seriously worried about the wisdom of visiting the Lanyons. I wanted to see Nicky, but I didn't want to learn what that dark suspicion forming at the back of my mind really was. I couldn't stop thinking about the man who'd met Michael at Colquite & Dew's yard; about their anxious secretive talk. I couldn't stop being afraid of something I couldn't have named.

As I stood up, I heard a car labouring down the drive in low gear. It emerged slowly into view round the bank of the raised lawn and I blinked at the sight of the bell on its bumper and the police sign across its radiator. It drew to a halt gently beside me and the driver started checking for traffic, glancing to right and left. As he did so, I looked into the rear seat and saw, wedged between two burly constables, Michael Lanyon. Our eyes met and he smiled faintly, as if to assure me there was nothing to worry about, as if the whole thing was just an amusing embarrassment. Then the car pulled out into the road.

At the same moment I heard rapid footfalls behind me, approaching down the drive. As I turned, they stopped. And there was Nicky, panting and tearful, staring at me from ten yards away.

'What's happened?' I called to him.

'They've arrested him,' said Nicky. 'They've arrested Daddy.'

'You do realize, don't you,' I said as we entered the outskirts of Reading, 'how compelling the evidence against your father was?' I'd volunteered to drive Emma into Reading when she left, late-night trains from Pangbourne being few and far between.

'Oh yeh,' she murmured. 'I realize.'

'He was seen handing an envelope to Tully in a pub a couple of nights before the murder. That envelope, with his fingerprints on it, was later found in Tully's possession, stuffed with five hundred pounds' worth of fivers. A witness overheard him telling Tully to do what he was being paid to do soon, otherwise it would be too late. And Tully said that was to kill old Joshua before he could change his will, under which your father was the sole beneficiary. Now, how could Nicky ever have hoped to overturn all that?'

'I don't know. And I'll never know – unless we find out what progress he made over the years.'

'If any.'

'Yeh. It could be none at all. I understand that. In a way, I'd almost prefer that.'

'Why?'

'Because then running out on my family wouldn't seem so bad, would it?'

'It sounds as if you had a good reason.'

'Maybe my father had a good reason too. For doing the things that incriminated him.'

'If so, Emma, I honestly don't think Nicky found out what it was.'

'But can you be sure?'

'No, I can't. That's why I'm going to Clacton tomorrow.'

'I'm grateful, Chris. Really.'

'There's no need.'

'And I'm sorry, too. That I can't trust you with more than my telephone number. I suppose I'm out of practice at relying on other people.'

'That's understandable. So would I be in your position. But relying on people isn't always a bad thing, believe me.'

'No.' I saw her uncertain smile reflected in the neon-lit windscreen. 'I'm sure it isn't.'

CHAPTER SEVEN

It rained all the way from Pangbourne to Clacton, intensifying as I neared the coast. Water hurled itself at the car, as if the sea were rushing up across the flat grey Essex countryside to meet me, rushing as it had that winter's night when all the Lanyons' yesterdays were washed away but still not cleansed.

The front at Clacton looked as dismal as only a seaside resort on a wet Sunday can. The pier was empty, the amusement arcades closed, the season over. Emma had given me Considine's address, but instead of going straight there I headed west past a rainswept golf course to Jaywick, where the sea wall rose higher than the roofs of the ramshackle chalets and the clouds crouched low over the dank refuge the Lanyons had run to thirty-four years before. As far as could be imagined from the cliffs of Cornwall and the comforts of Tredower House, they'd hidden from scandal and rejection. And all they'd found had been flood and despair – and Neville Considine.

Wharfedale Road was a long straight street of terraced houses in the Victorian heart of residential Clacton. I sat outside number seventeen for several minutes, finalizing my explanation for this unexpected visit. I hadn't phoned ahead, but I was confident I'd find him in. The pubs weren't yet open and I didn't have him down as a church-goer. No, I reckoned I knew exactly where Neville Considine was.

And I was right, though the time he took to answer the door, while I sheltered from the rain in the shallow porch and examined the peeling paintwork, sufficed to stretch my nerves.

A sour mix of stale cooking and damp plasterwork wafted out to meet me as he opened the door. He stepped back in momentary surprise, then gave me his thin-lipped smile. At once, I thought of Emma and why she'd have gone to any lengths to escape this man. 'Mr Napier. What an unexpected pleasure.' He was wearing a baggy dandruff-flecked cardigan over a shirt so old and worn that the collar looked as if it might soon detach itself completely. His trousers were threadbare and mottled with stains, crumpled at the ankles over bizarrely brand new Rupert Bear slippers.

'There's something you might be able to help me with, Mr Considine. Mind if I step in?'

'Not at all. But you must take me as you find me, natur-ally.' He led the way down a dingy passage, rain-marbled light falling sparsely from a landing window down the narrow stairwell. 'I don't get many visitors, you under-stand.' We passed two closed doors to our right and arrived in the kitchen, where Considine's breakfast still seemed to be in progress, to judge by the scatter of tea leaves, breadcrumbs, jam-crusted knives and egg-smeared plates on the table. The sink was piled high with dirty pots and pans; water was dripping from the tap on to the blackened base of one. The stove was spattered with scabs of old fat and the filthy lino sucked at my feet. Grimy tea-towelled likenesses of the Prince and Princess of Wales stared at me from a rail above the grill, while a guinea pig, or some such rodent, scurried about amidst a litter of wood shavings and shredded newspaper in a cage on top of the ominously buzzing fridge.

'Can I offer you some tea, Mr Napier? Or a sherry, perhaps.'

'Nothing, thanks.'

'Well, what can I do for you?'

'It's . . . about Nicky.'

'I supposed it must be.'

'You never did let me know about his creditors.'

'I decided to deal with them myself. After your generosity regarding the funeral expenses . . . But *what* about Nicholas? Has there been some . . . new development?'

'No.' Over-anxious to cover Emma's tracks, I added, 'Nothing of the kind.'

'Then I don't quite understand.'

'It's about his . . . possessions.'

Considine frowned. 'Oh, yes?'

'I just wondered . . . You may think it's silly, but I was rather hoping to have something to remind me of him. A memento, if you like.'

'I see your conscience *has* been stirred.' He sniggered disconcertingly.

'I assume you have them.'

'It depends what you mean. Nicholas lived in a small furnished flat. The landlord asked me to remove his possessions, such as they were, shortly after his death, which I did. I donated the clothes to a charity shop, though they were hardly in a usable condition. The rest was . . . well, rubbish for the most part. I threw it away.'

'You kept *nothing*?'

'There was nothing to keep. Of Nicholas's, anyway. Apart from his scrapbook, that is. I believe I told you how

Nicholas started collecting press reports of his father's trial after we lost Michaela. He kept them in a large scrapbook which I came across when I cleared out the flat. Well, I hadn't the heart to throw it away. Not after all the time and effort Nicholas must have devoted to it.'

'Could I see it?'

'By all means. Of course, it contains nothing to remind you of Nicholas as such. The cuttings aren't *about* him.'

'Even so.'

He gave me a strange little half smile. 'Come into the parlour, Mr Napier. You'll be more comfortable there.'

We went back down the hall and he opened the farther door, revealing a surprisingly neat little sitting-room, furnished with a three-piece suite and some glass-fronted cabinets in which an excess of Victorian knick-knackery called up the spirit of his dead and probably domineering mother. The fireplace had been panelled in and a two-bar electric heater installed on the hearth. Considine bent over it and activated one bar, which began to glow weakly. He waved me to an armchair, then dragged a tea chest out from a recess between the chimney breast and a cabinet.

'This contains some things of Rose's I removed from the flat. I've been meaning to sort it out, but . . .' He toyed with a bead necklace, then dropped it back into the box. 'Here's the scrapbook.' It was a large spiral-bound board-covered volume. Considine pulled it out and handed it over to me. 'Take a look.' As I opened it, I heard him sigh and was aware of him lowering himself to his knees by the tea chest and delving further into it. I was also aware of the rain drumming at the windows and the metalwork of the electric fire creaking and clicking as it heated up. There was a smell of singeing dust in the air, a consciousness of old ground being trodden after long desertion.

The cuttings were photocopies drawn from the microfilmed archives whence Nicky had pursued his father's ghost, but scissored and pasted as if assembled at the time of the events they described, beginning with a report of Uncle Joshua's murder and Edmund Tully's arrest. This was followed by a fulsome obituary notice in the *West Briton* and then . . . Even as I turned the scrapbook page and saw the headline, I remembered first reading it on an August morning in Truro thirty-four years before. *Truro auctioneer charged with patron's murder.* It was the moment when Michael Lanyon's complicity in the murder of Joshua Carnoweth had ceased to be a whispered horror and become a legal reality. It was the moment when I realized that nothing could be the same as before.

'This is a terrible business,' declared my father, slapping the newspaper down on the bureau and commencing a prowling patrol of the space between it and the window. 'A damned awful business.' He was grappling with the pipe in his waistcoat pocket as if it were a creature he was determined to subdue. 'And it isn't going to get any better.' He swung round to face Pam and me. 'You two are going to have to display a great deal of fortitude in the months ahead. Which is why it's important—' He broke off and glanced across at Gran, as if in search of confirmation that what he was about to say really needed saying. She gave him a spine-stiffening glare and he cleared his throat. 'Which is why it's important that you understand what's happened.'

'What *has* happened, Dad?' I asked ingenuously. 'How can anyone think Mr Lanyon murdered Uncle Joshua? Surely that other man—'

'Tully was put up to it by Michael Lanyon, Christian. That's what it amounts to. Paid, I assume, to kill Uncle Joshua. And that makes both men guilty of murder.'

'It is true, then?' put in Pam. 'About Mr Lanyon?'

'I'm assured the police have clinching evidence. We must work on the assumption that it *is* true.'

'Aren't people supposed to be innocent until they're proved guilty?' I had the immediate impression that this wasn't what I was supposed to say. 'I mean . . . aren't they?'

Dad narrowed his gaze. 'Of course they are. Michael Lanyon will get a fair trial. This isn't about that.'

'What is it about, then?'

'It's about how we deal with the Lanyons between now and the trial,' snapped Gran, her impatience seemingly directed equally at Dad and me. 'As far as I'm concerned, they all have my brother's blood on their hands.'

'Gosh,' I mumbled, subdued by the recollection of the bloodstains at the foot of the Lander Monument.

'It seems best to your grandmother and me,' said Dad, with a hint of emollience in his tone, 'that we have nothing to do with them, *at all*, until . . . this is settled.'

'But . . .' I hesitantly began, thinking of Nicky, whom I'd last seen, tearful and confused on the lawn at Tredower House, as the police drove his father away.

'That includes Nicky. I'm sorry, Christian, but I must forbid you to see or speak to the boy. People might misconstrue your friendship.'

'But we *are* friends.' Denial of this seemed to hover around me in the silence that followed. 'I understand why our holiday at Nanceworthal had to be cancelled,' I stumbled on protestingly, 'but surely that doesn't mean—'

'His father had a hand in your uncle's murder,' Gran declared angrily. 'To my mind, you shouldn't *want* to see him, let alone still be complaining about a cancelled holiday.'

'I'm not complaining.'

'It sounded to me as if you were. Your uncle's funeral

is on Friday. That's more important than how you occupy your spare time, my lad.'

The injustice as well as the irrelevance of this last jab left me dumbstruck. As if to defuse the tension, Pam said calmly, 'Why is Mr Lanyon thought to have done this dreadful thing?'

'It appears he's the sole beneficiary under Uncle Joshua's will,' Dad replied. 'We can only suppose—'

'Not a penny for his own flesh and blood,' said Gran to no-one in particular. 'That's a crime in its own right. But it's bred a worse one.'

'We can only suppose,' Dad plugged on, 'that he wanted to forestall the possibility of Uncle Joshua changing his will.'

'More than a possibility,' said Gran. 'It's why he wanted to see Cloke last Thursday.'

'Which brings us to your walk down with him from Tredower House, Christian,' said Dad. 'Didn't he more or less tell you that's what he was planning?'

I puzzled over the question for a moment, unable to believe Dad had so grossly misunderstood my account of our conversation. Eventually, since an answer of some kind seemed essential, I said, 'Not really.'

'Mmm.' Dad frowned at me. 'Well, you can only describe things as you remember them, I suppose. As you'll have to this afternoon.'

'Why? What's happening this afternoon?'

'A policeman's coming to see you. Inspector Treffry. He wants to ask you some questions.'

'What about?'

'Just tell him as much as you can, Christian. That's all you need to do. There's nothing to worry about.' He stepped over and gave me an encouraging pat on the shoulder. 'Easier than an end-of-term exam.'

'Can I ask something else, Dad?' Pam said hesitantly.

'What is it?'

'About Uncle Joshua's will. You said Mr Lanyon's the sole beneficiary. Does that make him wealthy now?'

'No. It doesn't.'

'Why not?'

'The murder changes everything. He can't inherit if he's convicted.'

'Then who will?'

Dad grimaced and looked away. The question seemed to discompose him. But not Gran. 'I will,' she declared with quiet firmness. 'As I always should have done.'

I flicked on through the scrapbook pages. Michael Lanyon's committal and trial with Edmund Tully for the murder of Joshua Carnoweth was faithfully chronicled in photocopied newspaper reports spanning the late summer and long autumn of 1947. The Nicky who'd worked away his twenties and thirties as a librarian had compiled this, calmly and methodically, in secret tribute to the wronged man he believed his father to have been. There were no scrawled protests in the margins to speak of what he felt. I had to imagine that as I scanned the successive headlines. LANYON AND TULLY SENT FOR TRIAL. PROSECUTION OPENS CASE AGAINST LANYON AND TULLY. EDMUND TULLY CHANGES PLEA AND DESCRIBES MURDEROUS CONSPIRACY WITH MICHAEL LANYON. JURY FINDS MICHAEL LANYON GUILTY OF MURDER – HE AND EDMUND TULLY SENTENCED TO DEATH. EDMUND TULLY REPRIEVED – SENTENCE COMMUTED TO LIFE IMPRISONMENT. MICHAEL LANYON TO HANG TODAY – NO REPRIEVE EXPECTED. Nor was there any. I knew that, just as Nicky had known. Maybe it explained why he'd refrained from including a report of the hanging itself. There was no more to be said – or read – after the morning of the execution. Only blank pages and a blank life running to its end.

But that wasn't quite true. As I closed the book, a loose edge of paper slid out from the back. Reopening it at the last page, I saw a cutting had been slipped inside the rear cover, as if Nicky had planned to trim and paste it in but had forgotten to do so. It was a genuine cutting, as distinct from a photocopy, and more recent than the others. The *West Briton* for 25 May 1967 was a journal he shouldn't logically have had access to, given how far Clacton was from Truro. But there it nevertheless was. And the article he'd cut out of it was nothing less than a retirement tribute to Detective Superintendent George Treffry of the Cornwall Constabulary, the man who twenty years before, as a mere inspector, had found himself tackling the most sensational case of his entire career, in the course of which he'd called at the Napier house in Crescent Road, Truro, to interview its youngest occupant.

He was a big man, taller and squarer than my father, but about the same age, with a bristling moustache and spiky hair. He wore a faded brown mustard-striped suit that made him look like a figure in a sepia photograph and seemed even more uncomfortable than I felt, twitching at his shirt collar and dabbing at his sweat-sheened forehead with a red handkerchief large enough to make a pirate's hat. It was certainly hot, stiflingly so where Mum had installed us in the sitting-room, with the sunlight streaming in through the conservatory. But I had the impression there was more to Inspector Treffry's discomfort than that. Perhaps he wasn't at his ease with children. Perhaps he wasn't at his ease with the Lanyon case at all.

'Your parents tell me you're at Truro School, Christian,' he remarked with what was supposed to be a reassuring smile.

'I start next month, sir.'

'Excited about it?'

'Well, I haven't thought about it much really. Not with
. . . everything that's happened.'

'No, of course not.' He gulped down some of his tea.
'It's on account of what's happened that I asked your parents if I could speak to you. You don't mind, do you?'

'No, sir.'

'I gather from them that you saw your uncle just a few
hours before . . .' He left the sentence hanging and waved
his hand by way of conclusion.

'Yes, sir. We walked down from Tredower House to the
cathedral together.'

'Did he say where he was going on to?'

'Lemon Street.'

'To see his solicitor.' Treffry nodded. 'Did he say why?'

'Not exactly, sir.'

'What did he say – *exactly*?'

I recounted our conversation as accurately as I could,
even mentioning Uncle Joshua's parting gift of half a
crown.

'There's a coincidence,' said Treffry. 'I wanted to see *My
Darling Clementine* myself, but something cropped up.'
He sighed. 'Did your uncle seem . . . angry about
anything, Christian?'

'No, sir. He was . . . fairly jolly, actually.'

'And Michael Lanyon. Last time you saw him. Was he
. . . fairly jolly?'

'Yes, sir.'

'Ever see him with this man?' He handed me a photograph. I recognized the subject at once, and nodded in
reply. 'Where?'

'Colquite and Dew's yard, sir.'

'When would that have been?'

'Towards the end of last month.'

'Friendly, were they? To each other, I mean.'

'Not really friendly, no. More . . .' He cocked an

150

eyebrow at me, waiting patiently for me to continue. 'More like they knew each other, but not as friends.'

'Did Mr Lanyon give him anything – that you saw?'

'Something. But I don't know what it was.'

'Money?'

'It could have been.'

'You're an observant boy, aren't you, Christian?'

'I don't know, sir.'

He stretched out his hand and retrieved the photograph. 'Know who this man is, do you?'

'No, sir. But I'm wondering . . . if he might be . . . Edmund Tully.'

'Ever see him on any other occasion?'

'No, sir. Definitely not.'

'Well, I think that's all I need to know.' He finished his tea, stood up and glanced out into the garden. 'Looks like it'll stay fine for the Test Match. Think Compton will score another century?'

I knew he was patronizing me. I was used to adults doing that and usually played along. But the sense that I was being excluded from events had grown during our interview. I had to tell people everything I knew, but it never seemed to work the other way around. It wasn't fair and it wasn't right. What I said next was as much a protest against that as a plea for information. 'Did Mr Lanyon really hire Tully to kill my uncle, Inspector?'

Treffry gave me a kindly frown and I realized the conventions of our relationship weren't to be so easily overborne. 'That's not for me to say, Christian. That'll be for the jury to decide.'

'He *is* going to be tried, then?'

'Oh yes. He'll be tried all right.' He smiled, hoping, I think, to console me, but utterly failing to. 'And then we'll know.'

*   *   *

151

And now we did know. The law's answer, anyway.

Michael Lanyon was found guilty yesterday at the conclusion of his trial at Bodmin Assizes for the murder of Joshua Carnoweth, his wealthy patron, in Truro last August. The jury returned its verdict after a six-hour retirement. Lanyon and fellow defendant Edmund Tully, who changed his plea to guilty three days ago, were sentenced to death, although the judge, Mr Justice Goldfinch, said that he would be recommending the Home Secretary to exercise clemency in the case of Tully on account of his altered plea, his evident remorse and his outstanding war record. But for Tully's experiences as a prisoner of the Japanese, he would probably have had the moral strength to reject Lanyon's vile proposal of murder at the outset. As for Lanyon, the judge said that although he had not personally struck the fatal blow, his guilt was the greater, rooted as it was in a ruthless avarice. No words could properly express the repugnance every decent man and woman would feel at his total lack of—

I slammed the scrapbook shut and looked up at Considine, who was perched on the edge of the sofa, staring soulfully at a framed picture. 'Finished?' he murmured, glancing across at me.

'I think so, yes.'

'Not pleasant reading, I fear.'

'No. Not pleasant at all.'

'Everything else that I kept belonged to Rose. She had this by her bedside when she died.'

He held the picture out for me to see and I took it from

him for a closer look. It was a set of three photographs, displayed in oval compartments in the mounting. The central photograph was of Nicky as I'd never seen him, in his late twenties probably, leaning against the front door of the house in a checked shirt, his hair Brylcreemed, his face smiling. The left-hand photograph was of a baby girl sitting up on a studio cushion fondling a ball: Freda, I assumed. The right-hand photograph was of Michaela as a teenager, posing on the beach in a coyly skirted swim-suit. She wasn't smiling and I recognized the wary look in her eyes at once. It had been there even then.

'All dead now,' mumbled Considine. He caught my eye. 'Sad, isn't it? So much vitality, so much promise, snuffed out.'

'Yes,' I replied, choosing my words carefully. 'Very.'

'I think of Michaela a lot, you know. What sort of a woman she'd have become. You can't help yourself, you really can't.'

I looked at the swimsuited girl in the photograph and the moist-lipped hint of remembered lust in Considine's face. I knew what sort of a woman she'd become, of course. I knew what I mustn't allow Considine to discover – at any price.

'Aren't you going to rebuke me for assuming Michaela's dead, Mr Napier?'

'Why should I?'

'You did last time.'

'Whistling in the wind, I suppose. Nothing more. It's probably best to be realistic.'

'I do so agree. I was fond of her, of course.' He paused as if for effect. 'Extremely fond of her.' Then he smiled. 'But still one has to face facts.'

'Quite.'

'Do you want to take the photograph?'

'I'm sorry?'

153

'The snap of Nicholas. You said you wanted a memento of him.'

'Oh, I see what you mean.' I handed the picture back to him. 'Actually, no. Thanks, but I . . . wouldn't want to split them up.'

'That's very considerate of you. I was going to suggest you have a copy made.'

'Even so, I . . . don't think I will. I never knew him as an adult. Perhaps it's better to . . .'

'Rely on childhood memories?'

'Something like that.'

'Like me and Michaela. She's still a teenager to me, still my gorgeous little—' He stopped and cleared his throat awkwardly, then looked straight into my eyes just as a horrifying thought sprang into my mind. Had it begun with Michaela? Just what had gone on in this house – in the bedrooms above my head – during the lost years when I hadn't wanted to know? 'To you Nicholas will always be a small boy, won't he, Mr Napier? The school-friend you lost touch with in . . . when was it they actually left Truro?'

'September forty-seven. Straight after Michael Lanyon's committal. They moved to Exeter so as to be able to visit him in prison. They never went back to Truro.'

'And that's the last you saw of Nicholas – until a month ago?'

'Yes. The very last.'

It was the day after Uncle Joshua's funeral – a Saturday, when I'd normally have gone to Tredower House straight after breakfast. But that Saturday there was no such thing as normality.

I hadn't attended the funeral. Pam and I had stayed at home with Mum, the shop being closed as a mark of respect. Something was said about the ceremony being

154

no place for children on account of pressmen and photographers hanging around, but I suspected we'd been excluded for another reason. It was one event where an encounter with the Lanyons couldn't be avoided. Gran had foreseen my presence might melt the ice that had formed between the two families, and she was determined to keep it frozen solid.

I'd had my suspicion confirmed by a conversation between Mum and Dad. They'd been sitting together in the conservatory a few hours after the funeral, little realizing that I was crouched within earshot just outside the open windows, concealed behind the water butt.

'Cordelia was there,' Dad had said. 'Rose too. They both looked pretty ashen.'

'Did you speak to them?' Mum had asked.

'Not a word passed between us. I know it seems hard, Una, but Michael's responsible for Uncle Joshua's death. They have to stand by him, of course. Which means we have to stand *against* them.'

'That sounds like your mother talking.'

'We're of one mind on this, if that's what you mean. It's the only way.'

'How will it end?'

'It's best not to think about it. Until the trial, they can stay in Tredower House, but afterwards, they'll have to go.'

'Assuming Michael's found guilty.'

'Yes. Assuming that.' A strange silence had followed. Then Dad had added, 'But we both know he will be.'

His words lodged in my mind and had acquired by the following morning a sinister air of unjustified certainty. I knew I was supposed to hate Michael Lanyon for what he'd done, but I couldn't seem to. I still couldn't connect him with the bloodstained pavement at the top of Lemon Street. I still couldn't connect very much at all.

I left the house after Mum, Dad and Gran had set off for the shop, telling Grandad I'd arranged to play cricket with some friends at Boscawen Park. But the arrangement was a fiction. My real destination lay halfway up St Clement's Hill: the cemetery. If I couldn't attend Uncle Joshua's funeral, I could at least visit his grave.

I scrambled in over the boundary wall at the lower end rather than slog up to the main gate, but didn't save myself much effort by the ploy. The graves at the bottom were clearly the oldest. I followed the perimeter path across and up the slope, silhouetted headstones looming like castle battlements in front of me on the grey horizon. It was the first cloudy day in weeks, though already hotter than many a sunny one, airless and brooding. A fly buzzed obstinately around me as I went and my shirt clung clammily to my back. As I climbed, I made out the hummocked shape of a freshly filled grave ahead and saw the splashed colours of the wreaths laid around it. And, in the same moment, I saw Nicky.

He was standing beside the grave, staring at the piled earth, stooping every now and again to gather scattered soil from the grass and toss it in amongst the clods. His mouth was open, his face slack and expressionless, his hair plastered with sweat. He was so absorbed in what he was doing that he didn't see me coming until the very last moment. Then, just as I was about to speak, he started violently and whirled round to look at me. I smiled, but he didn't.

'Mum and Dad wouldn't let me go to the funeral,' I began. 'I suppose you didn't—'

'Your Mum and Dad think my Daddy murdered Uncle Josh. What do *you* think?'

I should have found some reply, but my thoughts on the issue were so confused that I could only stare back at him and venture a hopeless shrug.

156

'Daddy didn't do it. I *know* he didn't. You know too, don't you?' His eyes pleaded with me to say yes – or simply nod my head in agreement. Then we could unite as friends in defence of his father. But my parents and grandparents were convinced of Michael Lanyon's guilt. I didn't know how strong or weak the evidence was, but I knew they believed it. And I was part of their certainty, bound to it just as firmly as Nicky was to his father's innocence. In that instant, I realized what Uncle Joshua's death meant to Nicky and me. I wouldn't have been able to express it in words, but it was clear before me in the force of his gaze. Our friendship couldn't hold. It was crumbling, like the earth in his hand, like the hope in his eyes. *'Don't you?'*

'Nicky, I can't—'

'Say it! Say you're on my side.' His face darkened, his mouth tightened. 'If you're really my friend, you have to.'

'But it's not . . . I mean . . .'

'Are you on my side?' He must have read the answer in my face, but still he waited, for what seemed like minutes but can only have been seconds, while we each retreated into opposing loyalties and stubbornly tried to stare the other out. Then he gave a cry and rushed at me.

It happened so suddenly that he caught me off balance and bowled me over. The next thing I knew I was lying on the ground with Nicky sitting on top of me, beating at my raised arms with his fists while the breath hissed through his clenched teeth and tears welled from his eyes as well as mine – tears of grief and shock and sundered friendship.

'I hate you,' he cried, his voice cracking. *'I hate you.'*

'You two.' I heard a hoarse bellow from somewhere behind me. *'Leave off that game.'*

Nicky's head jerked up as he glanced past me. 'I'll save Daddy without you,' he said, almost in a whisper. 'You'll see.' Then he jumped up and took off at a sprint between the gravestones. By the time I'd scrambled to my feet, he was twenty yards away, running hard towards the gate. I called his name, but he didn't look back. I'm not even sure he heard me.

I was about to run after him when a large hand seized me by the shoulder. A red-faced man in working trousers and collarless shirt was breathing heavily beside me. 'This is a cemetery, boy,' he growled. ''Tis no place for your rattle-cum-skittery.'

'No, sir. I'm sorry.'

He frowned at me. 'No cause to cry, though. I'm not going to hurt you.' With that, he released me, regretting, it seemed, the distress he thought he'd caused. 'You'd better go after your pal.' He squinted after Nicky. 'He's going like a long dog.'

'There's no point,' I murmured.

'Ar. I suppose you know where he's going well enough.'

I nodded in vague agreement. The truth was too bitter and complicated to explain. Nicky's destination was actually irrelevant. Wherever he was going, I couldn't follow. Not any more.

There was nothing else of Nicky's in the tea chest. Considine had told me there wasn't but he didn't seem surprised when I insisted on checking for myself. If Nicky *had* tracked down Tully, then he'd either kept no record of his whereabouts or, which was an even more frustrating possibility, Considine had destroyed it – flung it, along with a hundred other scraps and traces of my dead friend's life, on to the municipal tip, for the rats to nibble and the seagulls to peck.

'Sorry you're leaving empty-handed, Mr Napier,' said Considine as he saw me to the door, his expression suggesting he was anything but.

'It can't be helped.'

'So little can, I find. Shall I be seeing you at the inquest?'

'You're going down to Truro for it?'

'Why yes. The coroner wants me to give evidence about Nicholas's state of mind in recent months. I had a letter from him yesterday. It's scheduled for the twenty-sixth of this month. Didn't you know?'

'No.'

'You surprise me. I thought you'd be asked to testify as well.'

'Perhaps my letter's in the post.'

'Perhaps so. Of course, as you see, evidence as such about my stepson's . . . condition . . . is in short supply.'

'It is now, certainly.'

Considine gave me one of his sly little half smiles. 'Well, as I say, I'm sorry you had a wasted journey.'

'Me too.' I smiled back grimly, content to let him believe I'd gained nothing from my visit. But that wasn't quite true. There were people who knew where Tully was; there had to be. The policeman who'd put him behind bars back in 1947 could well be one of them. According to his retirement tribute, Superintendent Treffry had planned to spend his declining years in a cottage he'd bought overlooking the harbour at St Mawes. The chances were he was still alive and still in St Mawes. Maybe that was why Nicky had kept the cutting. Maybe that was the one piece of evidence I needed.

CHAPTER EIGHT

I telephoned Emma as soon as I got back to Pangbourne. She was as disappointed as me by the slim pickings my journey to Clacton had yielded, but glad there'd been at least some – and relieved, I suppose, that there was no question of my calling off the search.

'I'll go down to Cornwall tomorrow. I have a hunch Nicky went to see Treffry. And I want to know what Treffry told him.'

'So do I. But, Chris . . .'

'Yes?'

'About Considine. You didn't . . . let anything slip, did you?'

'I was careful not to. Though I don't mind admitting there were times, listening to his simpering voice as he talked about you and Nicky, when I wanted to . . .'

'What?'

'Oh, it doesn't matter. *Considine* doesn't matter. Let's try to remember that.'

'He's not who we're after, right?'

'No. He isn't.' Nor was he. Though one day, I sensed, he might be.

I called Mark straight after Emma had hung up. He didn't seem to mind putting in some extra time to cover for me during the week ahead, which was one reason why I wasn't angrier with him for shooting his mouth off to Pauline Lucas. The other reason was that her unexplained visit seemed a minor mystery I could afford to ignore. Emma Moresco's arrival in my life had pushed it to the margins of my thoughts.

I tried to speak to Pam next, in order to beg a room at Tredower House, but got no answer from the private number. The girl on reception seemed to think they could fit me in, though. She was oddly cagey about where Pam and Trevor were, but at the time it didn't seem important; I put the matter out of my mind.

It didn't stay out, however. Nor did the enigmatic Miss Lucas. Just as I was preparing for an early night, Tabitha rang. And it was immediately clear she hadn't done so for an idle niece-uncle chat.

'What's going on with Mum and Dad, Chris?'

'How do you mean?'

'Mum says Dad's gone away, but she won't say where – or when he's due back. And she spent so long assuring me everything was all right it seemed pretty obvious it wasn't.'

'I'm afraid I know nothing about it.'

'I thought she might have confided in you.'

'What about?'

'That's just the point. I don't know.'

'Well, as it happens, I'm going down there tomorrow. How would it be if I called you when I've had a chance to see how the land lies?'

'That'd be great.'

'I'm sure there's nothing to worry about, though.'

'Yeh? Well, I wish I was.'

I was too taken up with my own concerns to make

anything of this. The greatest puzzle to me was Tabitha's bizarre idea that her mother might have confided in *me*. She obviously had entirely the wrong idea about brothers and sisters – probably because she was an only child. I went so far as to try the private number at Tredower House again, but there was still no answer.

Just as I put down the telephone, it rang again, which surprised me. Two calls on a Sunday night were two more than I usually received, and this particular call wasn't so much a rare species as one verging on extinction.

'Where have you been all day?'

'Staying out of your life, Miv. Isn't that how you like it?'

'Don't be like that. It seems I *might* owe you an apology.'

'You have done for years, but I never expected—'

'About the Lucas woman. Or whatever she calls herself. The fact is I think I could have helped her set you up. Inadvertently, I mean. Unintentionally. You know?'

'No,' I said, ratcheting up my concentration. 'I don't know.'

'I mean, I just didn't connect her with— Not at first. But when I thought about it, well, it clicked.'

'What clicked?'

'This girl rang me a few days ago. Said she was a free-lance journalist called Laura Banks, engaged by one of the music mags to do a piece on me. Interviewed me over the phone about old times on the road. The usual stuff.'

'You get a lot of approaches for that kind of material, I imagine.'

'Not many, you sarcastic bastard. Now listen. I suppose I *was* flattered. Not that I want to go back to those days, but it's fun to talk about them. Even about my ex-husband – once in an ultramarine moon.'

'Are you saying—'

'She could have been pumping me about you. She was

certainly very curious about you. After you called yesterday, I rang the number she gave me. Just to check.'

'Unobtainable?'

'The operator said even the dialling code didn't exist.' There was a pause. Then she said, 'Sorry, Chris.'

'Never mind,' I said, steeling myself not to blame her. 'It wasn't your fault.'

'Who is she?'

'I don't know.' But I was going to find out. That now seemed to be one certainty sown among many imponderables. When I set out for Cornwall in the morning, she'd be waiting somewhere ahead. She hadn't finished with me yet. Perhaps she hadn't really begun. There was more than one beast, it seemed, hiding in the forest.

'Are you in any kind of trouble, Chris?'

'I'm not sure.'

'Does this have something to do with Nicky Lanyon? I read about him in the paper.'

'Nothing at all.'

'You're lying.'

'No. I'm hoping. Without a lot of confidence.'

If there was anyone in Truro who doubted Michael Lanyon's guilt, other than his own family, they kept quiet about it during the weeks following his arrest. It was easy to say – as my father did – that the police could be trusted to have good reasons for charging him along with Edmund Tully. It's what I assumed myself. I wasn't a rebellious child. I'd been raised to trust authority as well as respect it. If my parents and the police said something was so, then to me it was unquestionable.

Why Michael had done what he'd done and what the consequences were – for him and Nicky and me – taxed me much more than the central issue of his guilt or innocence. Denied a friend to confide in, I wandered around

Truro through the dusty days of late summer imagining all manner of crazy preludes and unlikely postludes to Uncle Joshua's murder. I wanted to see Nicky and heal the breach between us without confronting the cause of it. But I knew that wasn't possible. When we next met – which I supposed we were bound to do when the Truro School year began, on the second Wednesday in September – there was going to be some kind of reckoning. But what kind I couldn't imagine.

'My dad says they're going to hang your pal's dad,' Don Prideaux announced with a gleeful leer when I met him fishing one afternoon down by the Moresk viaduct. 'He reckons they'll string him up by the neck.' He added a choking noise and a roll of the eyes to his prediction. 'Want to see how they tie a noose?'

'It's not a joke!' I shouted at him in protest.

'It's a come-uppance,' Don riposted. 'That's what my dad calls it. Pride goes before a fall. That's what *he* says.'

Don's father wasn't the only one who relished the reversal in Michael Lanyon's fortunes. I was too young to sense it at the time but now it seems as obvious as it was cruel. Michael Lanyon had been raised from the gutter on an old man's whim. That's what they'd have said about him. He didn't deserve the advantages he'd been given. So, by the same twisted logic, he deserved to have those advantages taken away. He deserved to be humbled.

But the law had something far worse than that in store for him. He and Tully were due to have the case against them heard by the Truro magistrates early in September. Until then, they were languishing on remand in Exeter Prison, ninety miles away. While at Tredower House, Michael Lanyon's mother and wife and son sat out the siege as best they could, seen nowhere and consoled by no-one. They too were in prison. There were no bars at their windows, no gaolers patrolling beyond them, but for them as for Michael Lanyon, there was no way out.

I had a single dismal sight of them at this time. It came one morning at the railway station. I'd gone down there straight after breakfast to watch whatever was coming or going from a favourite vantage point on the Black Bridge – the footbridge spanning the tracks and goods yard just west of the station. It was an ideal spot from which to see the first up train from Penzance go through and that's where I was when the eight forty to Bristol pulled in. As the smoke cleared the bridge and I looked down on to the platform, three figures hurried forward to board the train: Cordelia, Rose and Nicky.

They were going to Exeter to visit Michael. I realized at once that was what they were about. The early start would allow them a decent stay before they had to return. Not that I knew the first thing about arrangements for visiting prisoners, nor whether Nicky was going to go in with them or be left outside. Either way, I could glimpse the mixture of dread and anticipation in his expression: pale, fixed, determined, but unequal to what lay ahead of him. I glimpsed that too. Slowly, he was being overwhelmed. This was just one early moment in the process, but perhaps the first moment when I appreciated what it meant to him; when I started feeling sorrier for him than for myself.

I cried out to him, loudly and instinctively. But too many doors were slamming, too many voices shouting. They were gone in an instant, bustling into the carriage. Nicky didn't look up as his mother pushed him aboard. He didn't see me. He didn't hear me. He was gone.

I ran back across the bridge, down the steps and along the road towards the station entrance. I knew it was a hopeless effort. Their train was standing at the farthest platform, and it was already moving when I dodged in through the parcels gate. But still I ran after it, in the vague hope that Nicky would see me and know I really was trying to reach him. I stopped at the far end, where the platform chamfered down to the trackside, and stood there panting, with my hands on my knees, as the train gathered speed and moved steadily away from me, out across the city.

I never found out if Nicky saw me. The chance to ask him was a long time coming. When it finally arrived I didn't take it. And it'll never come again.

A letter from the Truro coroner arrived while I was packing a bag early on Monday morning. As Considine had told me, the inquest into Nicky's death was to be held on 26 October and I, like him, was required as a witness. In a sense, I was pleased to have a deadline to meet. Three weeks would be enough, one way or the other.

I gave the Stag its head and reached St Mawes in the middle of a milk-mild afternoon. The Roseland was looking at its autumnal best: green and rolling and refulgent. The estuary had a clear blue beckoning sparkle, with the slack sails of slow-moving yachts scattered lazily across it.

I traced George Treffry via the post office, where he drew his pension, to Tangier Terrace, a row of narrow, white, slate-roofed cottages off Church Hill, perched vertiginously above town and sea like guillemots on a cliff face. There was no answer at his door, but a keen-eared neighbour looked out and told me this was the invariable hour of 'Mr Treffry's p'rambulation'. I was advised to try the road to Castle Point and to look out for an old fellow in a brown suit and battered trilby with a snow-white moustache, accompanied by an elderly bull terrier.

It was a good description, but I'd have missed him nonetheless if I hadn't happened to glance over the beach wall when I reached the road. His perambulation had evidently taken him no further than a bench in the sunny lee of the wall, where he was enjoying a quiet pipe while his dog pottered aimlessly on the foreshore. I hurried down the nearby flight of steps to join them.

'George Treffry?' I ventured as I neared the bench. He turned a slow frown towards me. 'I don't suppose you remember me.'

'You're right there.' His voice had gruffened with age. He eyed me warily from beneath the brim of his trilby. Perhaps he was worried in case I was an old lag he'd once sent down. If so, he must have concluded I was too young or too respectable, because his tone softened as he added, 'Should I?'

'Chris Napier.'

'Napier?' The frown returned.

'Joshua Carnoweth was my great-uncle. You inter-viewed me after his murder. I'd have been eleven then.'

'Good Lord.' He took the pipe from his mouth and stared at me. 'So you would.'

'Can I sit down?'

'It's a public bench.'

Undeterred, I sat beside him. The bull terrier came panting over suspiciously, but his master reassured him with a pat. A wave broke idly on the beach and a gull curled past us, a shadow flicking across the sun.

'This about the Lanyon boy?'

'We were best friends as children.'

'But only as children. I imagine that ended in the summer of forty-seven.'

'I used to think so. But since Nicky's suicide . . .'

'Conscience troubling you, Mr Napier?'

'Yes. What about you?'

He treated me to a lengthy glare, then smiled faintly, as if he were too old to sustain an outraged front.

'Arthritis is troubling me. Old age is boring me to death. But conscience doesn't give me even an occasional jab.'

'Nicky thought his father was innocent.'

'So would I. If I'd been his son. But I wasn't. I was investigating a murder. That's what I told your pal when he came to see me.'

'When was that?'

'About a week before his death.'

'Nicky came here then?'

'He did.'

'What did he want?'

'I think he wanted me to say I regretted putting together the case against his father. Regretted seeing him hang. It was hard to be sure. He wasn't making a lot of sense. I felt sorry for him, but I had to tell him the truth.'

'Which is?'

'That his father was guilty as charged.'

'You've always been sure of that?'

'Oh yes. It was a depressingly straightforward case, if you really want to know. Not much real detection involved. We apprehended Edmund Tully less than twelve hours after the murder. There were bloodstained clothes in his bag when we took him off the train and the samples later turned out to match your uncle's blood type. There were eye-witnesses who picked out Tully in an identity parade as the man they'd seen running away down Lemon Street. Plus his fingerprints on the murder weapon. He threw the knife into a drain at the bottom of the hill, but it hadn't rained for weeks so it was just lying down there, waiting for us. All in all, there wasn't a lot of work for us to do.'

'What about Michael Lanyon?'

'Tully led us to him within hours of his arrest. He had nearly five hundred quid in his bag, and when he saw the evidence piling up against him he admitted Lanyon had

168

paid him the money to do away with Mr Carnoweth. He was to get another five hundred when the job was done. But he botched it so badly he panicked and made a run for it. He denied it all later. Said we'd coerced him into signing a confession. His barrister cobbled together a story that his treatment as a Japanese prisoner of war had made him vulnerable to the slightest pressure under interrogation. But there wasn't any pressure. There didn't need to be. He admitted that in the end when he changed his plea. Besides, I knew it was the truth as soon as he said it.'

'How?'

'Just a feeling you get in that line of work. What do you do for a living?'

'I restore cars.'

'So you can tell when an engine's running sweetly?'

'Yes.'

'Same with the stories people tell and the way they tell them.' Treffry tapped out his pipe against the edge of the bench and inspected the empty bowl. 'It all fitted together, you see. Tully and Lanyon met at Oxford. Got to be good friends. Toured Europe together. Tully had a wealthy father to pick up his bills just as Lanyon had Mr Carnoweth. Then they drifted apart. Lanyon went back to Truro, Tully to the family firm up north. When the war broke out, he joined the Army and had the bad luck to wind up in Malaya. He was captured at the fall of Singapore and spent more than three years in a Japanese prison camp. That does something to a man. I reckon it's what made Tully a murderer.'

'What made Michael Lanyon a murderer?'

'Temptation. Mr Carnoweth was thinking of changing his will. You know that. You were with him when he went to see his solicitor. Michael Lanyon was the sole beneficiary under the will Mr Carnoweth made when he came home from Alaska and found out how things stood with the boy's mother. I suppose he thought his own family didn't need any help at the time. Later, as he grew older and you and your sister turned up to make him think about the next generation, he decided to share his fortune more fairly. God knows, there was plenty to go round. If Michael had known just *how* much, maybe he'd never have . . .' Treffry shrugged. 'But that's just speculation, isn't it?'

'It seems to me this is all speculation. You can't be sure Uncle Joshua meant to change his will. Or that Michael Lanyon knew what his intentions were. Or even knew he stood to inherit under the old will, come to that.'

'But I can, Mr Napier. Tully told me so. Now, how could he have come by that information, other than through his old friend? And what reason did he have to murder Mr Carnoweth, other than to help his old friend out? He couldn't settle to anything after he came home from the war. There'd been some kind of family feud even before he joined the Army. I forget the details now. But the upshot was that he started leading a nomadic life, drifting from one boarding house to another, drinking too much and spending too much, until he found himself in Truro – largely by chance, to hear him tell it – and decided to touch his old chum from Oxford for a loan. You were there when they met for the first time in about fifteen years. Colquite and Dew's yard. Remember?'

'I *do* remember, yes. Michael looked anything but pleased to see him.'

'That was before he realized what Tully might be able to do for him. Tully hung around Truro because he saw Lanyon had done well for himself and thought he might be persuaded to help him get back on his feet.'

'According to Tully.'

'Not just Tully. There was a witness who corroborated

his claim to have seen Lanyon at the Daniell Arms – slap bang opposite the Lander Monument, mark you – two nights before the murder. That's when the money changed hands. The night after Lanyon withdrew five hundred pounds in cash from his bank account. The witness was a reliable man. What was his name, now? Vigus. That was it. Sam Vigus. Worked for Killigrew's, the removers.'

Sam Vigus was clear in my memory as an overalled figure of some girth likely to be seen humping and heaving at the scene of just about every house move in Truro during the forties and fifties. His wife was even clearer, as one of the slaves to fashion who helped Gran make such a success of credit drapery. I'd forgotten Sam had also played a small but vital part in convicting Michael Lanyon of murder.

'Vigus saw Lanyon give Tully a bulky brown envelope. His description of the envelope matched the one in which the money was found in Tully's bag. And that envelope had Lanyon's fingerprints on it. Vigus also heard Lanyon telling Tully to do what he'd been paid to do soon. He saw them look out of the window at the Lander Monument. *As if choosing the spot.* Tully wrote to Mr Carnoweth next morning, saying he had some embarrassingly intimate love letters sent by Cordelia Lanyon to Tully's late father, which he was willing to sell to the highest bidder. Would Mr Carnoweth meet him at the Lander Monument at midnight the following night to fix terms? That was the set-up.'

'The letter was never found, though, was it?'

'Mr Carnoweth presumably destroyed it before setting out to keep the appointment. Anyway, that's not the point. What it shows is that Tully knew things about the Lanyons only a member of the family could have divulged to him.'

'Yes, but Michael might easily have mentioned his mother was Uncle Joshua's former sweetheart when he and Tully were undergraduates together.'

'What are you suggesting?'

'I don't know. Except that it wasn't quite the open-and-shut case it seemed to be at the time.'

Treffry shook his head pityingly. 'No good, Mr Napier. Lanyon paid Tully five hundred pounds. We know that for a fact. He said it was for old times' sake, but you're not about to tell me you believe that. Tully murdered Mr Carnoweth. We know that for another fact. And I'm afraid a third inevitably follows.'

'You're certain Michael Lanyon deserved to hang?'

'I am.'

'And Tully?'

'Him too.'

'The Home Secretary thought otherwise.'

'That's politicians for you. There was sympathy for Tully because of his war record, and because he eventually owned up. Well, that had a contrived look about it to me. I think Tully knew he was going to be convicted and reckoned a confession, however late in the day, might swing a reprieve. The judge seemed to fall for it and the Home Secretary went along with him. Tully handled the trial a sight better than the murder. I have to hand it to him there. A British prison must have seemed like a holiday camp after three and a half years in Changi Gaol.'

'But Michael Lanyon didn't confess. Even when Tully's change of plea left his defence in tatters.'

'There was no point. No mitigation, you see. It was a strange case in that sense. The man who delivered the fatal blow always seemed less guilty than the man who talked him into it. What really hanged Lanyon was the stark ingratitude of commissioning his benefactor's murder, and the exploitation of his war-ruined friend.'

'There could be another explanation for his refusal to confess.'

'Strangely enough, I think you're right. But it's not the explanation you seem to have in mind.' The bull terrier ambled up and nuzzled his master's knee, as if he'd had enough and wanted to go home. But Treffry was in no hurry to leave. He seemed to be relishing the debate. 'Lanyon's family were so sure he was innocent he couldn't bring himself to disillusion them. Maybe he thought it was kinder to leave them with the memory of a wronged man. From what I saw of his son, though, I reckon he was mistaken. The truth's always preferable. In the end, it's easier to live with.'

'And you're sure you know what the truth is?'

'In this case, yes.'

'How can you be? Absolutely sure, I mean.'

'Like I told you. Professional instinct.'

'What about me, then? How can I be sure?'

'If what I've said hasn't convinced you, then . . .' He shrugged. 'I can't help you.'

'Maybe you can. It's occurred to me, you see, that one man knows the exact truth beyond question.'

'Tully.' Treffry nodded. 'Your pal Nicky Lanyon seemed to have the same idea, as far as I could tell from his ramblings. No disrespect to the boy, but he was pretty confused when he came here. What I did gather, though, was that he was looking for Tully and thought I could point him in the right direction. I had to disappoint him there, I'm afraid.'

'Why? Is Tully dead?'

'Could be. He never struck me as the sort to make old bones. But I've no way of knowing – or finding out.'

'Surely the probation service keeps tabs on prisoners released on licence.'

'They do. But there's a strange thing. Probably just as

173

well the press have never got wind of it. Tully went missing a few months after he was released. They let me know in case he headed this way, looking to settle old scores. But I never saw hide nor hair of him, and neither did anyone else. I had a word with some old contacts after the Lanyon boy's visit and I can tell you nothing's changed. Tully hasn't been seen or heard of for twelve years. Abroad seems a good bet. South Africa. Argentina. Somewhere like that. He'd fit in there, I imagine.'

'You mean he's on the run?'

'Technically, yes. But since he'd already been released, it's a manhunt that'll never get beyond the filing cabinet. Overseas is only my theory. He could be literally anywhere. Or nowhere, of course.'

'And that's what you told Nicky?'

'It is. Seemed to knock out what wind there was in his sails. I'm sorry for that, in view of what happened, but . . .' His weary shake of the head and seaward squint seemed to speak of all the human frailty his working life had acquainted him with. The bull terrier sat down slowly and settled its muzzle on Treffry's boot. 'If Tully isn't dead, he might as well be for all the difference it makes.'

'What about his family? He might be in touch with them.'

'Doubt it. His parents were dead by the time of the murder and there was no love lost between him and his brother. He was the only relative I tracked down when I went up to Yorkshire to check on Tully's background. He'd taken charge of the family firm. A linen mill, as far as I can recall. Probably closed down years ago. And I dare say the brother's pushing up the daisies. He was the older of the two by quite a few years.'

'Where was this mill?'

'Hebden Bridge. Halfway between Leeds and Manchester. Can't remember much about the place. A dull day in a Yorkshire mill town doesn't leave many traces in the memory. And Tully's brother was as tight-lipped as they come. The whole business was an embarrassment to him. He didn't want to know, and I can't say I blame him.'

'So where did Tully go when he left prison?'

'Not Yorkshire. The probation officer he was assigned to, the one who contacted me when he went missing, was based in London. He said he'd set up Tully in a small flat somewhere. Described him as a loner. Well, a lot of ex-cons are. Especially lifers. No mystery in that. And not much in his doing a bunk. He was a wanderer by nature. So, he wandered off. It's only what you'd expect.'

'You make it sound so simple. So predictable.'

'Murder often is. I blame these crime writers for making people think it's complicated.'

'There have been such things as miscarriages of justice.'

'Not on my patch.'

'I wish I could share your confidence.'

Treffry treated me to a benevolent smile. 'I'm afraid sentiment is clouding your judgement, Mr Napier. It does you credit, I suppose. But it won't accomplish anything.'

'Nor will closing my eyes to the remote possibility that Michael Lanyon was a wronged man.'

'Remote is right. Remember this. A man is innocent until proven guilty. Once the verdict's in, it works the other way round. Michael Lanyon is guilty until you prove him innocent. And that you never will.' Treffry stirred the bull terrier gently, levered himself up off the bench and flexed his knees. 'Time I was off home. Buster wants his tea. Come on, boy.' He lumbered off, the dog plodding after him, but he paused at the foot of the steps to touch his hat to me in an oddly courteous farewell. Then he started up to the road and Tangier Terrace and the resting place of a professionally untroubled conscience.

* * *

175

The case against Michael Lanyon and Edmund Tully went before the Truro magistrates on Monday 1 September 1947. It occupied most of that week and a sizeable daily chunk of the front page of the *Western Morning News*. Since it was virtually a taboo subject in the Napier household, at any rate in my presence, the newspaper, examined over Pam's shoulder after she'd surreptitiously rescued it from the bin, was really the only insight into the proceedings I had. A distant glimpse of the crowd that gathered at the rear of the court on Back Quay each morning and afternoon to see the coming and going of the defendants was certainly enough to deter me from seeking a closer view. There was something unsettling about the way they moved and looked; something ugly and vengeful in their eyes; something, I suppose, of the mob that people anywhere can so easily become.

The evidence as set out in the newspaper sounded damning enough, although I couldn't understand why it took so long to present. According to Pam, that was because I had no appreciation of how a court of law worked. I was fooled at the time into believing she did have, but in those pre-television days, with no weekly fix of Perry Mason to shape our imaginations, the legal world was as remote to us as Ancient Rome. We could read what the county pathologist had to say. We could study the versions of events given by witnesses. We could pick our way through Inspector Treffry's painstaking account of how and why his inquiries had led him first to Edmund Tully, then to Michael Lanyon. We could analyse every detail. But how those details sounded in court, what impression they created and whether they allowed any margin for doubt, were matters beyond our grasp.

I often thought of Nicky reading the same newspaper

articles in his bedroom at Tredower House, secretly perhaps, by torchlight beneath the sheets while his mother and grandmother talked anxiously downstairs late into the night. It wouldn't be any clearer to him, I knew. It wouldn't be any simpler. And the fact that the case went unanswered at this stage would only make his mental wrestlings with the evidence more futile.

Neither defendant testified. They both reserved their defence. According to the *Western Morning News* crime correspondent, the magistrates retired for less than fifteen minutes before committing them for trial to the assizes. It seemed like torture by deferral. Three days had been devoted to deciding there should be a trial, something every inhabitant of Truro had known there was going to be for several weeks past. A lot of them thought they knew the outcome as well, and I was beginning to feel I did too.

'Looks bad for young Michael, dunnit?' I heard Mrs Boundy say to my mother one morning at the shop, where I was ostensibly helping out, Pam's school term having commenced a week earlier than mine. 'Fearful what people can do for money, don't you think?'

'It's dreadfully upsetting,' Mum said, accurately enough, though I could detect in her voice the desire to make several other less guarded remarks.

'I saw his mother leaving the court yesterday, drab and drawn as a winnard. She's aged something awful these past weeks.'

'It must be a terrible strain for her.'

'And only like to get worse. My Reg reckons he'll hang for sure.'

'We shouldn't jump to conclusions, Mrs Boundy.'

'Should we not, though?' Mrs Boundy's head swivelled like that of a pigeon eyeing a grain of corn as she looked meaningfully at Mum across the counter. 'Well, I can see as how it's awkward for you, Mrs Napier, of course, considering where old Mr Carnoweth's money is going to end up when this is all over. Like my Reg says, one man's albatross is another man's golden goose.'

I reached Tredower House late that afternoon, my mind filled with long-ago events that had left George Treffry, more than thirty years on, undimmed in his certainty that justice had been done to Michael Lanyon. It was a certainty I'd never shared, however often I'd let others as well as myself believe I did. But still I couldn't say why. And the one man who could resolve every doubt and answer every question was missing. Despondency was creeping in. Resignation was preparing to open its retreat for me.

But a dead end isn't always what it seems. A concealed turning only reveals itself just before you hit the wall. What I'd forgotten was what I'd just begun to understand. This wasn't only about the past.

The receptionist said Pam was waiting for me in the flat – the converted stable block she and Trevor had turned into a comfortable home. It sounded curiously like a summons, so I went straight round to see her.

She didn't have to say a word for me to know something was badly wrong. She looked tired and unkempt and hugged me tighter and longer than usual. We'd never been the most demonstrative of siblings and the way she clung to me sounded even more alarm bells than the dark smudges beneath her eyes.

'I didn't know whether to be glad or sorry when I heard you were coming, Chris. I've not been sure whether I could go on keeping this quiet. But right now I'm grateful for a shoulder to cry on.'

'What's happened? Where's Trevor?'

'Gone.'

'*Gone?* What do you mean?'

'I mean I've thrown him out.'

'Good God. I'd no idea. Tabs phoned me last night. She seemed worried about you both. But . . . I thought it was nothing. What the hell's been going on? What's he done?'

'What hasn't he done – over the years? I've been wondering that. Asking myself just how much I haven't known, and for how long.'

'You're going to have to explain.'

'All right. You may as well know the full sordid details. On Saturday morning, I had an anonymous letter. Well, an envelope anyway. There wasn't actually a letter inside. Just a photograph. Showing my husband having sex with a prostitute.'

'You're joking.'

'No. I wish I were. I opened the post over breakfast, with Trevor sitting opposite me, and found myself looking at a photograph of him in some hotel room with this . . . this . . .'

'I can hardly believe it.'

'Nor could I. But there was the proof in front of me. A one-off, Trevor said. An unprecedented and never to be repeated lapse that weekend when he went to London for the hotel catering fair. The photo was almost as nasty a surprise to him as it was to me. He obviously thought I was never going to know anything about it. Which makes it equally obvious it wasn't the first time it had happened.'

'But . . . who took the photograph? Who sent it to you?'

'You'd better ask Trevor. Perhaps he knows who arranged it. I don't care. A well-wisher, I suppose. Isn't that what they're called? Somebody who thought I should have my eyes opened. Well, they've been opened. And how.'

'I still can't quite believe it. I mean, you've been married for . . .'

'Twenty-four years.'

'And you're saying that's . . . over?'

'I'm certainly not sharing a bed – or a home – with Trevor after this.'

'Do Mum and Dad know?'

'Not yet. You're the first, Chris.'

'They'll take it badly.'

'Perhaps you think I should try to patch things up for their sake.'

'I'm not saying that. Of course I'm not.' Secretly, indeed, part of me was pleased Trevor's image as the ideal son-in-law was to be smashed beyond repair. But already something about the circumstances of its destruction was beginning to worry me. And that worry was diminishing what should have been my sole concern: my sister's state of mind. 'This is a real shock, Pam. Shouldn't you . . . take some time to decide how best to deal with it?'

'There's only one way to deal with it.'

'It must seem like that now, but—'

'You don't understand, do you?' She glared at me. 'You have no idea what it was like. That photograph made me feel physically sick. Not because of what Trevor was doing in it, but because he was doing it with a stranger. And he was loving it. He was having the time of his life.'

'Pam, let's just—'

'See for yourself.' She whirled away to the bureau, wrenched open a drawer and pulled out a large envelope. 'I don't want anyone saying later that I imagined this. That I overreacted. That I got it all wrong.' She moved back to where I was standing and held out the envelope for me to take. 'Have a look, Chris. Have a long look at what my husband gets up to on weekends away. *Then* tell me I need to take some time for reflection.'

I took the envelope from her, reached inside and lifted out the photograph. It was a large glossy black and white print. Small wonder Trevor had been as appalled by it as Pam. For there he undeniably was, naked and grinning, clambering flabbily on to a bed. But one part of him was far from flabby. And the reason was obvious. A sleek-skinned woman wearing some kind of short silk slip was sitting on the bed, the slip riding up around her hips as she smiled invitingly at him.

I caught my breath. Not because of the spy-hole explicitness of the scene, but because of the woman's face. The excitement on it wasn't just synthetic lust for Trevor's benefit. It was the thrill of a trick expertly played. I knew that for certain. Because hers was the face of Pauline Lucas.

CHAPTER NINE

Pam was grateful to me for volunteering to explain her breach with Trevor to Mum and Dad. How it would affect the running of the hotel was something they were going to have to consider, quite apart from the mess it made of the family's cosy self-confidence. I phoned them that evening, casually suggested calling by the following day, and was promptly invited to lunch. There was no way to warn them that by the time we sat down to eat they might well have lost their appetites.

I sat up late with Pam, listening as she refined the marital difficulties of a quarter of a century into hard-edged revulsion at what Trevor had done. I'd never thought their marriage a union of souls, but it had unquestionably possessed staying power. That was all gone now, drained in the few seconds it had taken Pam to open an envelope. It was hard to decide at what level the shock had registered. Like Pam, I didn't for a moment suppose this was Trevor's first sample of illicit sex. But now Pam knew for a fact. Worse still, she'd seen what it actually meant.

What Pam's outrage at her husband's behaviour

blinded her to was what preoccupied me most. Who *was* Pauline Lucas? And *why* had she done this? There was something orchestrated yet unfathomable about her appearance in my life as well as Trevor's. She'd shown she had the power to penetrate our defences. But to what purpose? What did she really want?

I couldn't breathe a word of this to Pam. She was in no mood to accept anything that implied Trevor had been set up, and she might even have thought I was in league with him if I related the little I knew. I had to speak to Trevor, and I had to do it without Pam's suspecting I was taking his side – which I most certainly wasn't. I was as disgusted with him as she was. But we'd both been targeted by the same woman for reasons I had no inkling of. For the moment, that took priority over the brotherly self-righteousness I'd otherwise have been happy to indulge.

I told Pam I'd come down to examine a rare old Lancia in Falmouth which a client wanted my expert assessment of, so she didn't query my early start the following morning. As it happened, I did take the Falmouth road, but only because a discreet word with the kitchen staff had revealed that Trevor had taken refuge with his golfing chum, Gordon Skewes, who ran the Trumouth Motel in Perranarworthal.

The place resembled an American roadhouse, plonked beside the A39 halfway between Truro and Falmouth in a moment of mid-Sixties planning madness. Somebody's had the good sense to demolish it since, and nature wasn't doing a bad job even then, stripping the paintwork with its intrusive fingers and staining the chalet roofs with damp disdain.

Trevor was still in his dressing-gown, grouching round the cramped chalet he shared with a half-empty suitcase and a half-eaten motel breakfast. His expression suggested I was the last person he either wanted or expected to see.

'What the bloody hell do you want?'

'I've seen the photograph, Trevor.'

'She showed it to you? The bitch.'

'I should soften your tone if I were you. We're talking about your justifiably outraged wife.'

'And your pure-as-the-driven-snow sister. What have you come here for, Chris? To gloat? To rub salt in the wound? To tell me this only confirms what you always thought about me – that I'm not worthy of her?'

'Actually, no.'

'Then why? As her messenger boy? Is this the opening of negotiations?'

'I don't think there's much left to negotiate, Trevor. Anyway, that's nothing to do with me.'

'I'm glad you realize that.'

'But we *do* need to talk. About Pauline Lucas.'

'Who?'

'The woman in the photograph.'

'What?' He frowned at me, bafflement competing for his attention with what his periodic winces suggested was a bad headache.

'I know her.'

'*You?*'

'Not in the same way as you do, of course, but we *have* met.'

He gaped at me. 'I don't understand.'

'Then just tell me as much as you can. How did you meet her?'

'You really know her?' He grabbed at my arm, a crazed kind of hope moistening his bloodshot eyes. 'You know who she is?'

'Not exactly. Do you?'

'Of course I don't. If I did, I'd track her down and—'

184

He broke off. 'What did you say her name was?'

'Pauline Lucas. She visited me in Pangbourne on Saturday. Claimed to be Miv's solicitor.'

'Solicitor? That's a good one.'

'It's the same woman, Trevor. No doubt about it.'

'It can't be. Unless—' He slumped down on to the unmade bed, clenched his teeth fretfully on the knuckle of his thumb for a moment, then said, 'I thought it was just me she had her claws into. What the bloody hell's going on?'

'I was hoping you might be able to tell me.'

'Well, I can't. Since that picture came through the post I've been through six different kinds of hell.'

'So has Pam.'

'You think I wanted this to happen?'

'No. But you made it possible, didn't you?'

'She set me up. Don't you understand? She arranged the whole thing.'

'Tell me how.'

'All right.' He plucked a coffee cup from the bedside table and drained the contents with a grimace. 'Though where this is going to get us I don't . . .' He shrugged. 'She stayed a night at the hotel a couple of weeks ago. Registered as Marilyn Buckley. Said she was down from London on business. Looked the part, God knows. Smart, sexy and very, very cool.'

'Pam seemed to think she was a prostitute.'

'Maybe she is – at the top end of the market – but I wasn't paying her bill. I told Pam she'd been to Tredower House, but I don't think it sank in. What happened was that she chatted me up in the bar. Oh, very subtly, very expertly. But I got the message. She said I should look her up next time I was in London. She gave me her number and I said I'd bear it in mind. Some such garbage, anyway. But it wasn't likely I'd forget. She was pretty memorable.'

'And the hotel catering fair was coming up at Olympia.'

'Yes. It was. I'd mentioned it to her. So, while I was up there, I . . . gave her a call.' He sighed. 'She met me at the Ritz for a drink on Friday evening. We went on to dinner at a restaurant in Soho, then some cabaret club she knew. Classy joint in Piccadilly. From there we went back to her place.'

'Where was that?'

'Danby Street, Marylebone. A third-floor flat, expensively done out. By then, well, it seemed fairly obvious to me where the evening was heading.'

'I don't suppose you could believe your luck.'

He glared at me. 'Don't get sanctimonious with me. Most red-blooded males would have done the same.'

'Do you know how the picture was taken?'

'From the angle, I'd say through a two-way mirror. There was a big gilt-framed job on the bedroom wall.'

'I assume an even more compromising picture could have been sent. I suppose you should be grateful.' Unable to resist goading him a little, I added, 'Try any adventurous positions, did you?'

'I never got the chance.'

'What do you mean?'

'I mean nothing happened.'

'Come on, Trevor. Nobody's going to believe that.'

'No. Which is why I didn't even bother trying to tell Pam. Besides, she's convicted me just on intent. As Marilyn Buckley, or Pauline Lucas, or whoever the hell she really is, obviously had in mind. She didn't need to get screwed herself to screw me good and proper.'

'Are you saying . . . you didn't have sex with her?'

'She wouldn't let me.' I almost felt sorry for him then, as he rubbed his hand across his face and recollected the details of his humiliation. 'She suddenly went cold on me, a few seconds after that photograph was taken. Like *ice*. Jumped off the bed, put her clothes back on and told me she thought I ought to leave. I couldn't believe it. Begging for it one moment, ordering me out the next. It didn't make any sense.'

'But it does now.'

'Yes. She'd got what she wanted.'

'What did you do?'

'What do you think I did?' Actually, I'd have said Trevor was the sort who mightn't have taken no for an answer. And something in his tone suggested his departure hadn't been the simple matter he went on to claim. 'I left. I got dressed and I walked out like a good little boy. I told her what I thought of her, of course, in pretty choice language, but I already had her down as a bit of a head-case, if you want to know the truth. I mean, pulling the plug on a fellow like that is asking for trouble. With the wrong type, there's no knowing what might happen.'

'You think she makes a habit of this sort of thing?'

'I did – at the time. But when the photograph arrived, well, that changed everything. I went up to London yesterday to see her and demand an explanation, but there was no-one in at her flat. A neighbour told me she'd moved out a week ago.'

'Shortly after entertaining you.'

'Exactly. Mission accomplished. I hung around all day, just in case, but there wasn't a sign of her. I reckon the neighbour had it right. Which means the whole set-up was for *me*. Me personally.'

'Not just you, Trevor. I seem to be in her sights as well.'

'I can't think of anyone who'd want to go to such lengths to harm me. The whole business is . . . crazy.'

'There has to be a connection,' I murmured, as much to myself as to Trevor.

'Connection with what?'

'Nicky.'

'Nicky *Lanyon*?' Trevor rolled his eyes. 'Come off it, Chris. That's . . . that's . . .'

'Crazy?'

'*Too* crazy, by a long way. Who are you suggesting this woman is? Nicky's lost love, out for some twisted kind of revenge?'

'He never had one.'

'I'll bet he didn't.' Trevor suddenly sat up and snapped his fingers. 'But he had a sister, didn't he? It was in the paper. She'd be about the right age, too.'

'I've seen a photograph of the sister.'

'You have?'

'Not a ghost of a resemblance.'

'Are you sure? People change.'

'Not that much.' I didn't like the direction Trevor's thoughts were taking, being in no position to tell him why I could be absolutely certain on the point. 'She isn't Michaela Lanyon.'

'Got a better idea?'

'Not at the moment. But—'

'Then I might settle for it. If Pam can be made to see I was lured into this . . .'

'She won't believe you.'

'No, but she'll believe you.'

'I'm not going to tell her.'

'What?'

'If you go to her with your half-baked idea about Michaela Lanyon, I'll deny we had this conversation.'

He sagged visibly at that. 'Why?'

'Because I intend to find out who this woman is and what she wants, and I reckon my best chance of doing that is quietly and discreetly.'

'Starting how exactly?'

'I have a few clues to follow.' The lie sounded convincing,

even to my own ears. 'For one thing, we have a photograph of her now, don't we?'

'You mean Pam has.'

'I know where she keeps it. If you lent me your keys to the flat, I could help myself while she was busy in the hotel.'

'What's to stop *me* doing that?'

'The probability that you'd be caught in the act. You're *persona non grata* at Tredower House, whereas I'm a welcome guest.'

'All right.' He looked too tired to be riled by my implication that sneaking in and out undetected was beyond him – as it probably was. 'What's in it for me if I do lend you the keys?'

'The comfort of knowing the photograph won't fall into the hands of Pam's solicitor.'

'Just be shown around by you to all and sundry.'

'I'll cut it in half to save your blushes, Trevor. I'll even give you the negative if I can find Miss Lucas-Buckley and persuade her to part with it.'

'Fat chance of that.'

'Your only chance, I rather think.' He looked up at me grumpily. 'What are you going to do if Pam won't have you back?'

'I'm not short of offers.'

I glanced around. 'Looks like it.'

'This is just temporary.'

'Let's hope so.'

'I saw Tabs in London yesterday,' he said, the defiance draining from his voice. 'After I left Danby Street, I wandered down to the cabaret club in Piccadilly that the bitch took me to. Just in case somebody there knew her. But if they did, they weren't telling. Anyway, halfway down Regent Street, I saw Tabs coming out of one of the

189

shops. I had to dive down a side street to avoid her. Christ almighty, I had to *hide*. From my own daughter.'

'She'll have to know eventually.'

'I wouldn't want her to see that photograph.' He closed his eyes, clearly aghast at the prospect, and I refrained from pointing out that Pam probably wouldn't want her to either. The consequences of stealing the picture hadn't yet assembled themselves in my mind. All I was clear about was that it was easier than trying to explain to Pam why I needed to borrow it. 'You'd better have those keys, God damn it.'

'Attaboy.'

'Pam will blame me, won't she?'

'Naturally. But she won't be able to prove it.'

'That'll only make it worse.'

'What can I say, Trevor? I'm not offering to save your marriage. Just to find the person responsible for wrecking it. Other than you, of course.'

'Thanks a bunch.'

'A bunch of keys is what I need.'

He scowled. 'You're enjoying this, aren't you?'

'I seem to recall you derived considerable pleasure from my break-up with Miv.'

'That was different.'

'You're right. You didn't do me any favours at all.'

'This is a favour?'

'Could be.' I smiled. 'We'll just have to see how it turns out, won't we?'

On the Sunday following Michael Lanyon's and Edmund Tully's committal for trial, all six of us – Gran, Grandad, Mum, Dad, Pam and me – piled into the Talbot and drove up to Perranporth. This profligate use of carefully conserved petrol was justified on the grounds that we needed a break: a dose of seaside normality as well as a breath of fresh air. Truro had closed in around us over the past month, as the consequences of Uncle Joshua's murder seeped slowly into the nooks and crannies of our lives. There would be no break for the Lanyons, of course. For them, dread and uncertainty stretched out into the future. But we didn't mention them while we paddled and pottered away the afternoon. I for one tried not to think about them. They were part of what we were escaping.

And they were also part of what we returned to early that evening. A gently hushed sabbath dusk was settling over Truro as we drove up Chapel Hill and turned into Crescent Road. There was hardly anyone about, and we'd fallen silent in the car, wearied by wind and sunshine, depressed by the close of the day and the end of our journey.

Dad pulled up at the foot of our drive and I scrambled smartly out of the bench seat at the front which I'd been sharing with Pam; opening the garage doors was one of my responsibilities. Mum, Gran and Grandad began to make a more sedate exit from the rear as I started up the drive.

Halfway to the garage, I stopped. Cordelia Lanyon, looking haggard and ill and wearing a long grey overcoat despite the warmth of the evening, was standing by the front door of the house, framed in the arched porchway. She neither moved nor spoke, but stared at me impassively, with a strange expression I couldn't decipher at the time but remember now as infinitely regretful.

I heard the car doors slam and the engine cut out, then cautious footsteps on the drive behind me. I was aware of Gran standing at my shoulder, breathing faster than normal. At the sight of her, Cordelia moved out of the porch and advanced a few paces towards us, her expression stiffening.

'What brings you here, Cordelia?' Gran said.

'I thought you'd like to know, Adelaide.' It was strange to hear Gran's name spoken. Nobody else, even Grandad, seemed to use it. 'We'll be leaving Tredower House tomorrow.'

'Where are you going, my dear?'

'Exeter. We've found lodgings there. It'll make visiting Michael easier.'

'But what about Nicky's education?'

'We'll arrange schooling for him in Exeter. I've withdrawn him from Truro School, if that's what you mean.' It was a bigger bombshell to me than anyone. I'd been assuming I'd meet Nicky face to face in a few days' time at the start of the year. Now, suddenly, that wasn't to be, and I didn't know whether to feel glad or sorry. 'As things are, we'd be in no position to pay his fees even if we stayed here.'

'It must be difficult for you.'

'Difficult?' Cordelia walked down to where we were standing and stopped in front of us. Closer to, her gauntness was still more apparent. Her skin, stretched taut over her high cheek-bones, had acquired a bluish translucency. Her eyes seemed larger than I remembered. 'It's been that and no mistake.'

'You mean to shut up the house?'

'No. The Ellacotts will look after it.' Mr and Mrs Ellacott had worked for Uncle Joshua as gardener and cleaner respectively since before the war. They were a reticent and dependable couple. 'No call for you to be concerned, Adelaide.'

'I wouldn't want anything to go wrong. It'd be no bother to—'

'Stay away.' Cordelia's face coloured as she snapped out the words. Her gaze narrowed as she added, 'If you can.'

'It was my brother's home.'

'But not yours. Not yet.'

'How long do you think you'll be gone?'

'Until the trial's over.'

'We must pray . . .' From the corner of my eye, I saw Gran lick her lips nervously. Then she said, 'For a true and just outcome.'

'That we must,' said Cordelia slowly, staring at Gran as she spoke. Then she gave the faintest of farewell nods and walked smartly past us down the drive. Mum, Dad, Pam and Grandad parted to let her through and we all watched in silence as she headed off towards Chapel Hill.

Only when she was out of sight did Dad say, 'I wonder how long she was waiting here just to say that. She could have telephoned. Or written a letter.'

'That wouldn't have been her way,' said Gran. 'She knows she won't be back.'

I stared up at Gran in amazement, realizing the accuracy as well as the sincerity of her words. I'd sensed the awareness of it in Cordelia but hadn't understood what it amounted to. The Lanyons were leaving Truro and they could only return if Michael was acquitted. Then they'd all be vindicated. Otherwise . . .

'They'll never come back?' I murmured plaintively.

'Never's a long time, Christian,' said Gran. 'But that's how long they'll be gone, you may be sure. A precious long time.'

My parents reacted in predictably contrasting ways to the news about Pam and Trevor. Mum wanted to dash up to Truro straight away and envelop Pam in a warm fug of maternal sympathy. Dad veered more towards impatience with both parties. Though willing to admit Trevor might have behaved stupidly, it seemed unreasonable to him that Pam should wish to end a marriage one year short of its silver wedding anniversary on account of a compromising photograph of her husband.

Just how compromising I didn't spell out, but that somebody had it in for Trevor was clear. Dad regarded this as an extenuating factor and declared his intention of underlining the point to Pam once the dust had settled. He apparently believed the breach was eminently reparable, a possibility Mum was also eager to entertain. In the end I gave up trying to point out that what had happened was irrevocable. They'd realize that eventually and probably blame me for encouraging false optimism. Either that or Pam would cave in and have Trevor back, only to regret it shortly afterwards. Between stonewalling Dad's demands to know who Pam's anonymous informant might be and reassuring Mum about the state she was in, I weighed the alternatives in my mind and realized both were equally feasible.

All too soon we became bogged down in a debate about how the hotel would operate in Trevor's absence. My own opinion, that it would run all the better without him, was regarded as unhelpful. But then Dad had never valued my opinion about anything, so I saw no need to put a lot of thought into shaping one. It was obvious where we were heading. Pam had already foreseen the threat and pleaded with me to fend it off. But that was easier said than done.

'I'll have to lend a hand,' Dad declared eventually. 'Pam won't be able to cope without help.' And so saying he bustled off to his study to clear his diary for the rest of the week.

'Don't worry,' said Mum as soon as he was gone. 'It won't come to anything.'

'I hope not – for Pam's sake.'

'But while he's out of the room, there's something else I want to discuss with you.'

'About Pam?'

'No. Nothing to do with that at all.'

'What, then?'

'Well, it's rather odd, actually.' Her voice fell to a confidential whisper. 'It's been going on for a couple of weeks now. Your father says I should ignore him and he'll go away. But I'm not sure he will and, anyway, all he wants is to talk to someone.'

'Who does?'

'I've answered the telephone to him a couple of times myself and he sounds sensible enough, though your father thinks he's probably senile. He won't go into details over the telephone. In fact, he won't say anything. Except that there's something he wants to tell us – something important. Your father reckons it's nothing of the kind and we shouldn't encourage him, and I dare say he's right, but what harm can it do just to humour the poor old fellow if he's—'

'Who? Who are we talking about?'

'Oh, you probably don't remember him. His wife was a good customer of ours over the years though she's dead now, poor soul. He lives at Playing Place. They moved out to a bungalow there when he retired. They used to live in Fairmantle Street, of course, just round the corner from us in Carclew Street. Still, Playing Place isn't far from Truro. Since your father refuses to see him and won't hear of me going, I'd thought of asking Pam. Just as well I didn't, in the circumstances. Anyway, now you're here with some time to spare, I thought—'

'Just tell me who he is, Mum.'

'Didn't I say?' She frowned at me as if the oversight was somehow my fault. 'Sam Vigus. Do you think you could possibly find out what he wants?'

They were gone. I knew they would be, but the fact of it only really sank in as I crept across the empty lawn and

195

stared up at the blank windows. Tredower House was deserted. Uncle Joshua was dead and the Lanyons had departed. There, with the drought-stunted grass rustling beneath my feet and the first tinges of autumn browning the trees around me, I confronted what seemed like the end of childhood.

It wasn't, of course. It was only the end of one phase of it. But also of an era. Though what the new one we were all entering was to comprise I could never have guessed. Everywhere I looked, there was only uncertainty. Michael Lanyon's trial; my friendship with Nicky; my senior-school career: they were formless and unknowable, outside my control even though they were part of my future.

Eleven is too young to glimpse the insecurity of life. It can seem bewildering at any age, but the brink of adolescence is likely to turn bewilderment into oppression. I walked down to the horse chestnut tree in the corner of the garden, sat on the swing and pushed myself aimlessly back and forth, listening to the rope creak on the branch and wondering when or if Mr Ellacott would remove it. I looked up at the knots, knowing Uncle Joshua had tied them, imagining his stubby but nimble fingers manipulating the rope. Then I thought of Don Prideaux, with his cackling talk of the noose, and jumped off the swing so suddenly I nearly fell over as its momentum carried me forward.

My stumbling steps became a run. I burst out from beneath the tree, crossed the lawn at a sprint and turned down the drive. Suddenly all I wanted was to be away from Tredower House, peopled only by a throng of memories, loud only with the absence of voices. I'd had enough of death and doubting. Tomorrow would be my first day at Truro School. I'd expected to dread the event. Now I positively craved it. Slowing as I ran down the road towards Boscawen Bridge, I prayed for the future to speed on and over me, like a wave that breaks but doesn't bruise; and for a sight of clear water beyond.

Playing Place straddles what was once the Falmouth road but is now a quiet lane a couple of miles south of Truro. The fifties and sixties had seen a ribbon of bungalows strung along the route. According to my mother, Sam and Doreen Vigus had moved into one of these after Sam's retirement from Killigrew's. But Doreen was dead now and maybe Sam was losing his grip on reality, living alone away from their old neighbours in Fairmantle Street. That was certainly one way to explain his recent telephone calls.

But I didn't believe it any more than Mum seemed to. And though the stooped and wheezy old fellow who answered the door was a sad and deflated parody of the cheery dough-bun of a removal man I remembered, it didn't sound to me as if his mind had decayed anything like as rapidly as his body.

'Christian Napier. That's who it is, isn't it? Well, I'll be blowed. You'd best come in.' His head sagged and his chin was clumsily shaved, but his eyes were bright and alert. He was wearing trousers large enough for a clown, held up nearly to his armpits by short braces over what looked like a pyjama jacket. There was a cigarette hanging from his lower lip, apparently by some force of its own, and a growly cough lurking behind his every breath. 'Your father sent you, did he?'

'Mother, actually.'

'Ar, well she always had the better manners of the two, so that's no surprise. Come in and take the weight off, why don't you?'

Sam shuffled down a short length of hall and into the sitting-room, where an armchair, an ashtray and a racing paper were waiting for him beside a paraffin stove that seemed to be the only source of warmth in the house. A vast pair of off-white combinations hung drying on a rickety clothes horse in front of the stove. Otherwise the yellowing stacks of old newspapers, stray gatherings of empty cider bottles and random scatterings of cigarette ash suggested he hadn't acquired many of the skills of house-husbandry since Doreen's death. I had to remove a jumble of football-pools coupons and cellophane ciga-rette-pack wrappers from the second armchair before taking up his invitation to sit in it. Tea wasn't suggested and I declined the offer of cider.

'Expect you're wondering what this is all about.'

'My mother is, certainly.'

'But not you, boy?'

'I'm definitely curious.'

'Ar, and we know what curiosity did.' He let out a long rattling cough. 'Hear about Nicky Lanyon?'

'Yes. As a matter of fact, I was the one who found him.'

'Were you? The papers didn't mention that. Kept it quiet, did you?'

'Not exactly.'

'Your family's always been good at keeping things quiet. Or getting them known. Depending which serves them better.'

'Is there something you want to tell me, Mr Vigus?'

'There is. And to ask you. Though I reckon I know the answer in your case. With you and Nicky being pals and you nought but a lad anyway, there'd have been no cause for you to know a thing about it. I just want to know who cooked it up, see. Whether it was all of you or just the one. I'm not going to do anything about it. No sense. Besides, I come out of it worse than anyone. It's eaten at my conscience all these years. I can stand it eating on for the few that are left to me.'

'Does this concern the evidence you gave at Michael Lanyon's trial?'

'That it does, boy. That it does.'

'What about it? It was the truth, wasn't it?'

'Well, there was truth in it. I suppose I can say that.'

'You saw Michael Lanyon hand an envelope to Edmund Tully in the Daniell Arms two nights before the murder.'

'I did.'

'You overheard him telling Tully to get the job he was being paid for done quickly, and you saw them looking across at the Lander Monument as if selecting the spot where it was to be done.'

'Ar, well, that's where the truth finishes, if you really want to know, and something a sight more fanciful takes over.'

'What do you mean by that?'

'I've been turning it over in my mind since Nicky Lanyon strung himself up, wondering if that tale I told back then might have made the difference. I mean, did it tip the balance, do you think? It *was* the truth – about the envelope. I saw that right enough. But the rest . . .'

'What are you saying?'

'I made up the rest.' He discarded the remainder of his cigarette and stared across at me, breathing heavily. 'I never heard a word they said.'

I stared back at him, as amazed as I was confused. 'You heard nothing?'

'I wasn't close enough. They were whispering, like they were plotting something. But what they actually said—' He shook his head dolefully. 'I couldn't swear to that.'

'But that's exactly what you did do. You swore to it.'

'Ar. I know. Perjury it was, right enough. I varnished the facts to make things look blacker for Michael Lanyon. I can come out and say that now, with my old lady dead and gone. Leastways, I can say it to you, can't I? There's no fear of it going any further. It'd be the worse for your family if it did. You've more to lose than I have. And I reckon it's time you knew that, assuming you don't already. Time we shared the poison round a bit. When all's said and done, it's as much your fault as it is mine.'

'How do you work that out?'

'Simple, boy. I lied on oath. That's quite a thing to stand up and do. But I did it. And not out of spite or devilment neither. I did it because I was told to.'

'Told? Who by?'

A shameful little smile played around his lips as he replied. 'Your grandmother. Adelaide Napier. It was her idea. It helped hang Michael Lanyon. And now I'm wondering if it helped hang his son as well.'

CHAPTER TEN

'Eli,' Gran seemed to be saying. The word formed on her lips with a slow gathering of effort. She was dying and must have known it, despite the succession of strokes. They might have broken her physically, but behind the swimming eyes and dribbling mouth that tenacious brain of hers was working as well as ever. I could feel its determination, its refusal to accept defeat. Death would be kept waiting a little longer yet.

'Eli.' That's what I thought she said. That's as much sense as I could make of the slurred murmur. I could only hear by stooping over her where she lay, twitching one forefinger in what might have been an attempt to beckon me closer. A schoolfriend I'd never heard of; a sweetheart from her distant youth. That's what I assumed. An old woman was recalling a stray fragment of the remote past in a vain attempt to hold death at bay. Nothing more. Only a few hours later, as rain beat against the windows of her bedroom at Tredower House and a February dusk blackened into night, she drew her last laborious breath. *Peacefully at home, aged ninety-two*, her obituary notice would say, *after a short illness*, Adelaide Napier died, with her family – and her secrets – gathered about her.

'Eli.' I recalled the sound and the word I'd thought it was meant to be as I drove away from Sam Vigus's bungalow that afternoon, not north to Truro, but south to the National Trust garden at Trelissick, where I could walk alone and unquestioned by the steep wooded shores of the Fal and seek for answers in the dwindling autumnal light. I could never say for sure what Gran had intended to communicate on her deathbed nine years before, but now a name was far less likely than a confession.

'He lied.' Yes. That could have been it. That could so easily have been the meaning. For Sam Vigus *had* lied. He'd admitted as much. And my grandmother had been responsible. That too he'd volunteered, without any way of knowing my own memory could supply a partial corroboration.

'Why did you do it, Mr Vigus?'

'Doreen was in over her head with the fancy clothes your grandmother supplied on the never-never. We owed her precious near a hundred pound, and it was going to take me Lord knows how long to pay it off. I would have done, mark you. It wouldn't have been easy, but I'd have done it. If your grandmother hadn't come to me whispering about . . . alternatives.'

'She wrote off the debt in exchange for your false testimony?'

'That she did.'

'I don't believe it.'

'Yes you do, boy. I can see it in your eyes. You already know it's the truth. Michael Lanyon was guilty. We both believed that. What I'd seen at the Daniell Arms was proof enough, to my way of thinking. Your grandmother just wanted to be sure of the outcome, she said; sure of justice.

And since I didn't doubt where justice led, I didn't mind giving it a helping hand. Not when it got me off the hook so quick and simple. Except there's more than one kind of hook. I've been dangling on another kind ever since.'

'Gran told you what to say?'

'No, no. She left that to me. She knew from Doreen that I'd reported seeing Lanyon and Tully together to the police. Well, a tongue like a barn door on a windy day, my old lady had. So, your grandmother came to me and proposed that I say I'd . . . heard something as well as seen. Just to . . . "stiffen the arm of justice" was how she put it. In return, we'd forget the debt.'

'And you agreed?'

'To my shame, I did. I went to Inspector Treffry and told him I'd held back on what I'd heard because of how bad it looked for Michael Lanyon, but conscience had got the better of me. Treffry was angry at first, but he was too pleased with the new evidence to keep that up for long.'

'I'll bet.'

'I thought at the time your grandmother wanted to make sure her brother's murderers didn't wriggle out of answering for what they'd done. But later, when I heard how much came down to her from old man Carnoweth's will, just how much richer he'd been than any of us had thought, well, I felt sicker than a whipped dog, I don't mind admitting. I'd helped her make sure, all right, of putting more noughts on her bank balance than I ate boiled eggs in a week. For the sake of barely a hundred pound thrown away on Doreen's glad rags.'

'You could have spoken out.'

'With Michael Lanyon dead and no-one likely to believe me? Talk sense, boy. Your grandmother could have denied the Holy Ghost without turning a hair. And there was Doreen to consider. She didn't know, see. Not a thing. Thought I'd cleared the debt with back pay from

203

Killigrew's. She was a simple soul, with no head for figures, so she never questioned it. Besides, I'd been taken for a fool right enough, but there's worse things than that to suffer.'

'Like being hanged for a crime you didn't commit on the basis of false evidence.'

'But Michael Lanyon did commit it. You know that sure as I do.'

'If you're so certain on the point, why are you telling me this?'

"Cos doubts creep in here with the draughts and the unaccountable noises I hear when I lie awake at night recollecting his face as he stared at me across the court-room. And I don't see why I should be the only one to bear them.'

To that extent, I realized as I walked through the woods at Trelissick, Vigus had got what he wanted. I shared the burden with him now. I knew. Worse still, I *suspected*. Had Gran confided in any other member of the family? Dad had told Mum to ignore Vigus, to forget all about him. Why? Why so very adamant? I looked down through the trees at the King Harry Ferry and listened to the steady clanking of its chain as I wound in the thread left trailing down the years. One lie was a single crack that could become a thousand shatter-lines in the smooth mantle of my family's past and present. It didn't prove anything. It didn't vindicate anyone. But it meant I couldn't stop.

Tully still held the key, more firmly than ever. Treffry had told me, and Nicky before me, that he could never be found. But then Treffry had called Sam Vigus a reliable man. The truth was that he didn't want to find Tully, whereas I did. Maybe, if Nicky had heard Vigus's con-fession, he wouldn't have given up so easily. Maybe he'd have done what I was now determined to do: track down Edmund Tully, wherever he might be hiding.

Trust was another victim of Vigus's revelations. I didn't know who I could rely on and who I couldn't. Gran had spoken to me, no-one else. She'd been dumb and inert for the best part of two days prior to my arrival, garnering her strength, perhaps, ordering her thoughts. But why try to tell me at all? Because she judged I'd know what best to do with the information? Or because she felt I was entitled to know what others already knew? Mum wouldn't have sent me to see Vigus if she'd had any inkling of what he meant to say. She at least was ruled out. But nobody else was. Even Pam. Which made it so much easier than it might have been to enter the flat at Tredower House under cover of darkness that night and remove the photograph from the bureau while she did her bravely smiling rounds of the tables in the restaurant. The chances were I'd be on my way before she noticed its loss. And, even if I wasn't, it wouldn't occur to her that I might be the culprit.

I drove down to the Trumouth Motel later and left Trevor's keys with the receptionist in an envelope addressed to him. The man himself was out, presumably drowning his sorrows somewhere. I was grateful to be able to slip away without needing to deflect any demands of his to hand over the incriminating half of the photograph. I'd already decided to have a copy made for my use so that Pam could give the original to her solicitor if and when the time came. If a divorce was what she ultimately wanted, who was I to stand in her way?

I looked in on her when I returned once more to Tredower House and was reassured by her calmness. Nothing was amiss, other than the relatively trivial matter of her difficulties with Trevor. She already knew how Mum and Dad had taken the news, because they'd been on the telephone at some length.

'I'm sorry about Dad,' I said, working on the safe assumption that he'd offered to stand in for Trevor. 'You know what he's like.'

'Don't worry. I think I've managed to persuade him I can cope alone. Tabs is coming down for a few days, anyway, so I've been able to say she'll supply all the help I need. Your flying visit's been a real help, Chris. It's made me face up to telling people. And Tabs has come up trumps. No hysterics, no demands for a rethink. Just level-headed practical sympathy. Where have you been since lunch, by the way? You can't have had your head under a car bonnet in Falmouth all afternoon.'

'I called on Sam Vigus.'

'Who?' Her unawareness sounded genuine. She too was probably in the clear.

'An old customer Mum wanted me to call on. When you see her, can you tell her, preferably while Dad's out of the way, that there was nothing to it?'

'Nothing to what?'

'She'll understand.'

'All right. But you can tell her yourself if you like. She'll be here tomorrow night.'

'But I won't be, I'm afraid. I have to make an early start.'

'Business is obviously booming.'

'Well, I'm being kept busy, Pam. That's for sure.'

Once I was back in my room, I telephoned Emma. It was a relief to hear her voice and to know there was at least one person I could be completely open with.

'Something's happened and we need to discuss it. Not over the telephone. It's too complicated. Could we meet somewhere?'

'Yes. Of course.'

'Where and when?'

'I'm on earlies at the supermarket this week. I finish at three. It's in Battersea. Why don't we say Battersea

Park at three thirty? The benches beside the boating lake.'

'All right. I'll be there.'

'Are you on to something, Chris?'

'Maybe.'

'Well, that sounds better than definitely not.'

'Not necessarily.'

'How do you mean?'

'I'll explain tomorrow.'

'All right, but Chris—'

'Yes?'

'Whatever it turns out to be, something *or* nothing, thanks. For Nicky, I mean. You know?'

'I know.'

The turmoil and anonymity of my first few weeks at Truro School enabled me to forget Nicky and his father's forthcoming trial, often for days at a stretch. Everything was new and confusing – teachers, classmates, rooms, books, uniforms: all the intimidating components of senior school life. *'High on the hill, with the city below,'* we sang in the chapel on the first day of term, *'up in the sunshine we live.'* Well, the sun didn't always shine, but the sense of separation from Truro that our lofty setting imbued in us was never clearer to me than then.

Some of the pupils who'd come up with me from the prep department recalled how chummy I'd been with Nicky Lanyon, but those who hadn't were in the majority and were determined to be unimpressed by what they thought was my bid for a dubious kind of fame. I was happy to let my connection with Nicky wither into something minor and inconsequential. Well, not happy exactly, but willing. I knew it was disloyal. I knew it was unworthy. Yet, pulled between the necessities of day-to-day survival and the slowly fading memory of our friendship, I let it happen. Nobody seemed to think it in the least odd that Nicky hadn't taken up his place at the school. After a while, it would have seemed perverse to suggest he'd ever been likely to. He had nothing to do with any of us. He'd become a stranger.

But the name of Lanyon was known to all. And soon it would be blazoned across the front page of every national newspaper, let alone the *West Briton* and the *Royal Cornwall Gazette*. Soon the slack-water weeks of waiting would be over. The trial of Michael Lanyon and Edmund Tully for the murder of Joshua Carnoweth was due to commence on 20 October. Amongst the dates of long-ago battles and long-dead kings that went into my mind and out again with every passing history lesson, that date – which no-one had asked me to remember – lodged stubbornly and firmly. As the calendar rolled round towards it.

A few weeks beforehand, Dad's *Daily Telegraph* reported the hanging at Pentonville of two armed robbers, Geraghty and Jenkins, convicted back in July, when I'd been taking no interest in such things, of the murder of a motorcyclist who'd tried to stop them escaping from a raid on a jeweller's shop in London. Geraghty had done the shooting. Jenkins hadn't killed anyone. That was clear. But both men hanged. I couldn't help imagining that to Nicky, reading the same report in a lodging house somewhere in Exeter, it would seem what he least wanted it to be: an ill omen.

Battersea Park was bathed in crystalline sunlight, gilding the yellows and reds of the trees around the boating lake and etching the lines of the power-station chimneys beyond Queenstown Road. Children on their way home from school were playing with their mothers, the high notes of their carefree voices rising above the plaintive wail of the peacocks and the distant growl of the traffic.

Emma looked odd, if not downright eccentric, wearing her flying jacket over her pale check supermarket uniform. She sat beside me on a bench close to a form-less Barbara Hepworth sculpture, listening patiently as I recounted what I'd learned in Cornwall.

I expected her to react with disbelief or outrage; she was entitled to both. Instead, when I'd finished, she gave me a sympathetic smile and said, 'I'm sorry, Chris.'

'*You're* sorry?'

'It can't be very nice to learn your grandmother stooped to bribing a witness.'

'I'd say it was closer to blackmail than bribery.'

'Whatever you call it, it weakens the case against my father, though, right?'

'It does. But don't get carried away.'

'Do I look as if I'm likely to?'

'Well, no.' She'd looked tired and dispirited when she arrived; the effect, I assumed, of a mind-numbing shift on the supermarket check-out. Even now she remained subdued, saddened perhaps by the thought that Nicky had thrown away the chance to make the same discovery as me. But that wasn't quite true, even though I felt it myself. It had taken Nicky's suicide to flush Sam Vigus out of the undergrowth. Nicky had had to die to make my discovery possible.

'Remember, Emma. This proves my grandmother falsified some evidence. I'd never have thought her capable of such contemptible behaviour, but there it is. What it doesn't prove, however, is that the *verdict* was false. We're still left with the fact that your father paid Edmund Tully five hundred pounds two days before the murder.'

'He said he gave Tully the money for old times' sake.'

'Five hundred pounds. That must be several thousand at today's prices. It's simply not credible.'

'You think Vigus made up something pretty similar to what they actually said, don't you?'

'I think it's still the likeliest explanation. But one man could tell us for certain.'

'Tully.'

'Yes. And no-one's seen him for twelve years.'

'What next, then?'

'I'll go up to Hebden Bridge and see what I can find out. There might be a friend or relative of Tully's there who can put me on the right track.'

'When will you go?'

'At the weekend. I'll have to get some work done before then. You know, the kind that pays.'

She grinned. 'Yeh. I know. Are you in a hurry to get back to Pangbourne? If not, maybe I could buy you a cup of tea. There's a café on the other side of the lake.'

'Thanks. That'd be nice.' We rose and started walking slowly round the perimeter of the lake. 'Unless there's somebody waiting for you at home, of course.'

I was fishing for information, as her smile seemed to acknowledge. 'Like I told you, solitude's a habit of mine. See those flats over there?' She pointed back at the high-rise blocks that loomed like the mesas and buttes of a desert landscape beyond the red-brick Victorian terraces flanking the park. 'One of those windows is mine. And, unless I'm being burgled again, there's no-one on the other side of it.'

'Ever thought of leaving London?'

'Where would I go? And what would I go there with? Most weeks I can barely pay the rent.'

'If it's as bad as that, maybe I could—'

'Don't say it.' She shook her head vigorously. 'I'm not looking for handouts.'

'It wouldn't exactly be that.'

'It would be to me.'

'But if things had gone just a little differently back in forty-seven, your family would have been . . .'

'Rich? Don't think that hasn't crossed my mind.'

'What's the first thing you'd do – if you suddenly came into money?'

She looked up at the sky, as if in search of inspiration. 'Oh, I don't know. Fly to Paris for the weekend, I suppose.'

'Ever been there?'

'Paris? Never.' Her head drooped. 'You need a birth certificate before you can apply for a passport, and Emma Moresco's never been born.'

Even fantasies, it seemed, were forfeit in the shadowy world Nicky's sister had been compelled to inhabit. As we walked on in the silence of her punctured dreams, I thought of how different our lives might have been, hers *and* mine, if Edmund Tully and Michael Lanyon had never met; if Tully hadn't gone to Truro in the summer of 1947; if Uncle Joshua had died in bed a few years later of manifestly natural causes. Then the past would unravel like a rope twisted against its coil, and Michael Lanyon would never have stood in the dock at Bodmin Assizes to answer a charge of murder.

According to the newspaper reports which were all I had to go on, the first few days of the trial, during which the prosecution presented its case, were simply a grander and lengthier rerun of the hearing. And a compelling case it seemed to be. Only now, as I review what went on in that courtroom in Bodmin while I puzzled over algebra or floundered on the rugger pitch at Truro School, does the invidiousness of Michael Lanyon's plight reveal itself to my mind. Edmund Tully's guilt was undeniable, even though, at least at the outset, he *did* deny it. The problem Michael Lanyon's counsel faced was that the joint prosecution implied a joint defence, even though there was nothing of the kind. Lanyon and Tully, the newspapers called them. And so they were in the public mind, as well, perhaps, as the jurors': a partnership in crime. The evidence against Michael Lanyon himself came down to the money he paid Tully and the conversation they had when the money changed hands. By the time he entered the witness box to explain the first and deny the second, the limelight had been seized by Tully's change of plea. It was dramatic stuff, of course. One of the defendants was throwing in his hand, confessing to a capital crime. And since everybody believed his confession, it seemed to follow, given that his co-defendant had a motive for the murder and he didn't, that the Crown's contention was proved. The two men had conspired together to murder Joshua Carnoweth. Both were guilty, and one of them even had the decency to admit it. It looked all the blacker, therefore, for the one who didn't: the prime mover, as the prosecuting counsel called him – the true villain of the piece.

Justice was a summary business back in 1947. Nowadays the case would wait in the legal queue for a year or more before coming to court and would drag on for a couple of months when it eventually did. But it was a different world then, in more ways than one. Tully's change of plea came on the sixth day of the trial. By the eighth, it was done and dusted.

It was Mr Cloke's clerk, I later learned, Mr Rowe, who called with word of the verdict. We were gathered at the dining-room table for high tea when the telephone rang in the hall. Dad went out to answer it, said little more that I could hear than 'Yes', 'I see' and 'Thank you', then returned to the table, announced impassively that

Michael Lanyon had been found guilty and commenced serving the cold cuts with a louring brow that served notice of a ban on all discussion.

He didn't mention the sentence, and I remained in some slight doubt on the point, wondering – however illogically – if the mandatory death penalty for murder really meant the judge had no discretion. I would have asked Dad if his expression had been less forbidding. As it was, I had to rely on Pam's confirmation of my understanding of the law when we conferred in her bedroom afterwards. And even then I didn't quite believe it. Until the headline in the following day's *Western Morning News* bestowed its printed authority on the outcome. TRURO MURDER PAIR TO HANG. There really was, it seemed, no room for doubt.

The Zenith Club in or more accurately under Piccadilly was close to its nadir in terms of seductive ambience when I paid my extortionate temporary membership fee and descended to the bar early that evening. The stage was empty, the music barely audible, the atmosphere lethargic. All of which was as I'd hoped, since it meant that Frankie, the barman, didn't mind talking to me. Although his enthusiasm faltered slightly when I slipped the photograph out of its envelope and asked him if he recognized the woman on the bed.

'Maybe,' he said warily, after amused and prolonged scrutiny.

'Is she a member?'

'Could be.'

'Come here often, does she?'

'Not sure.'

'I need a name and address.'

'More than my job's worth.'

'But is it more than fifty quid's worth?'

'Maybe . . . not.' He shrugged. 'I could ask around. See what I could find out, you know?'

'Here's my number.' I scribbled it on a paper coaster and handed it to him. 'And a down payment.' I laid a ten-pound note on the bar.

'Make it twenty.' He grinned. 'Well, it's not a local call, is it?' I added a fiver to the tenner and he settled for that. 'Can't guarantee nothing, mind,' he said as he folded the notes into his waistcoat pocket. 'Could have registered under a false name, couldn't she? There's a lot of it about.'

How true that was. The odds, I admitted to myself as I drove back to Pangbourne, were that the Zenith Club was a dead end. Pauline Lucas, aka Laura Banks, Marilyn Buckley and a possible clutch of other pseudonyms, wasn't going to leave any clues behind her unless it suited her purposes to do so. When I next encountered her, as I didn't doubt I would, it would almost certainly be at her instigation, not mine. That was what was so worrying.

As it turned out, however, I didn't have to worry for long. I'd not been at home more than five minutes when the telephone rang.

'Where have you been?' a voice I could hardly believe I recognized chidingly enquired. 'This is the fourth time I've rung.'

'Miss Lucas.'

'Yes, Mr Napier. Surprised to hear from me?'

'Not exactly. What do you want?'

'I thought *you* might want a chat.'

'And if I do?'

'Then I'm available. Now. This very evening.'

'Where are you?'

'At your workshop.'

'*Where?*'

'Don't you believe me?'

214

Without further ado, she put down the telephone. Impatiently, I dialled the workshop number. She answered at the first ring.

'You ought to improve your security, Mr Napier, you know that? I mean, you don't even have a burglar alarm. I'm surprised your insurance company doesn't insist you install one. Assuming you *are* insured, of course. But you must be, I suppose, with all these valuable old cars about the place. It's not as if most of them actually belong to you, is it, so the consequences of a fire could be—'

I dropped the telephone and raced from the house. I should have seen this coming, I really should. She'd found my weakness just as she had Trevor's. But how far did she mean to go?

The absence of a clue, however slim, clogged my thoughts like static as I pitched the Stag through the potholes to the road, sped along Pangbourne High Street at approximately twice the speed limit and roared off up the lanes towards Bowershaw Farm. It was a hoax, I told myself, nothing but an evil-minded trick. She wouldn't do it. She couldn't.

But she had. I saw the glow of the fire beyond the bank as I rounded the last bend before the entrance to the yard. I pulled up in the gateway and jumped out, petrol fumes and the stench of burning rubber wafting through the heat towards me. I stopped, my eyes smarting from the smoke as I stared at the roaring inferno visible through the half-open workshop door. Eight years, six classic cars, two livelihoods and one carefully cultivated business were going up in flames in front of me. And all I could do was watch.

CHAPTER ELEVEN

'I hadn't realized it was this bad,' said Pam, climbing from the car to take a closer look. 'There's nothing left, is there?' I'd met her off the train at Reading and driven her out to Bowershaw Farm to see the damage. To view the ruins might be a more accurate description, given the destructive power of spray-paint, petrol, oil, rubber and assorted solvents when ignited under the right conditions. Three days had passed since the fire and all that was now left of Napier Classic Convertibles was piled in two large skips, ready for disposal. The workshop itself had been reduced to its blackened brick walls and concrete base.

'I still have the Bentley Continental down at the showroom,' I said, joining her in the middle of the yard. 'Dominic's father might yet offer me a good price for it.'

'You're not thinking of winding the business up, are you?' Pam turned and stared at me. The hint of resignation in my voice seemed to have worried her. 'I mean, this is a big blow, obviously, but it's hardly terminal.'

'That remains to be seen.' I grinned ruefully. 'Clients aren't going to be keen to entrust their cars to me after this,

216

are they? We're supposed to restore them, not cremate them. And then there's the question of how much I'm going to have to pay out by way of compensation.'

'Isn't that covered by insurance?'

'Not necessarily. Insurance companies get twitchy where arson's concerned. Who's to say I didn't do it myself?'

'They surely don't suspect that.'

'The assessor who came to see me seemed the type who makes a point of suspecting that. And I can't say I blame him. An anonymous and motiveless arsonist doesn't score highly on the plausibility scale.'

'But you said on the phone you knew who it was.'

'Oh, I do. That's why it was so urgent we meet. I'm sorry to have dragged you up here, but with so many clients to grovel to, not to mention *their* insurance companies . . .'

'You don't need to apologize.' Pam let me know by the tilt of her eyes that she knew I was procrastinating. 'Just explain, Chris.'

'All right. Come over to the car. There's something I ought to show you.'

She followed me back to the Stag and we sat inside. I reached across her to the glove compartment, took out the envelope and saw her frown in puzzled recognition. 'Surely that's—'

'The photograph that should be in your bureau. Yes.'

'But . . .'

'Had you missed it?'

'Yes. I assumed Trevor had taken it. I sent Tabs to demand it back from him, but he denied all knowledge. That didn't surprise me. I thought he'd have destroyed it by then anyway. More fool me, I reckoned, for not having the locks changed. But now it looks as if it wouldn't have made much difference.' She glared at me. 'Well?'

'The woman on the bed and the arsonist are one and

the same. I'd already met her, you see, posing as . . . But that doesn't matter. What does is that I needed the picture because it's the only available likeness of her. I've had it copied since. I'd always intended to return the original to you.'

Her glare was becoming one of anger as well as disbelief. 'I don't understand any of this.'

'She's out to hurt us. In any way she can.'

'*Us?*'

'You. Me. Trevor. Maybe Mum and Dad too. You must warn them to be on their guard. Tabs and Dominic as well. Setting up Trevor was one thing. This—' I gestured towards the charred skeleton of the workshop. 'Means I can't say what she mightn't do next.'

'Who is she?'

'I don't know.'

'You must have some idea.'

'No, Pam. I don't. I literally haven't a clue. Except that it's something to do with Nicky.'

'*Nicky?*'

'I think so, yes.'

'That's mad.'

'Well, isn't this? And what she did to Trevor? Extreme, verging on mad. Wouldn't you say?'

'Why didn't you tell me sooner?'

'Because I had no idea she'd go this far.'

'And how far do you think she *will* go?'

'There's no way to judge.'

'My God, the hotel. You don't think she might try the same trick twice?'

'Strangely enough, no. That doesn't seem to be her style. The unexpected's more her stock-in-trade.'

'Just a minute.' Pam's gaze narrowed. 'This isn't some story you've cooked up with Trevor, is it, to make me feel sorry for him? Because, if it is, it won't work. You can—'

She broke off and glanced around, looking suddenly crestfallen. 'Sorry. I'm being rather silly, aren't I? I'm forgetting this really happened.'

'Yes. It really did.'

'Where do you go from here?'

'Commercially, I haven't even begun to think. Maybe I should start again at my beginnings and never breathe a word about my loss.'

'Kipling.'

'That's right. *If—* was printed on a tea towel I kept in the office to dry the coffee mugs. Fine words, but no doubt one of the first things to go up in smoke.'

'Talk to Dad. I know you don't like asking him for help, but you'll be a rich man one day thanks to him, so why not—'

'Thanks to Uncle Joshua, actually.' I gave her a tight little smile. 'Let's not forget whose money it really is.'

'All right, Uncle Joshua. But the point is—'

'The point is I intend to find out what this is all about before I start trying to build the business back up. I don't want the rug pulled from under me a second time.'

'Shouldn't you leave that to the police?'

'They've nothing to go on.'

'They have a picture of the arsonist.'

I grimaced. 'As a matter of fact, they don't. I haven't shown them the photograph.'

'Why not? This is no time to be squeamish. Trevor will just have to—'

'It's nothing to do with Trevor.'

'Why, then?'

'Because it doesn't prove a thing. And, besides, I have this . . .' I gazed through the windscreen towards the green horizon beyond the burned-out shell of my hard-won business reputation. 'I have this feeling the answer's close to home and no outsider stands a chance of finding it.

What's more, if and when we do find it, that we'll be grateful we kept it to ourselves.'

Life went on. Looking back at the autumn of 1947, it's the normality of the daily routine, the absence of emotional response to the grinding tragedy of Michael Lanyon's fate, that seems the most bemusing feature. I went to school from Monday to Friday and on some Saturdays as well; the shop traded as usual; the family functioned as it always had. Or so it seemed. What went on while I was out of the way – what secretive anticipation there was of the material consequences for us of unfolding events – I simply don't know. But then I didn't appreciate just how significant those consequences would be. And nobody was inclined to tell me, because merely to speak of it would have seemed to wish it so, and hence to wish Michael Lanyon dead.

Not that wishing was likely either to condemn him or to save him. The law had its methods and was in the process of applying them. A few weeks after the trial, an appeal was heard and dismissed. Then a couple of days later came the announcement of Tully's reprieve. Gran took this as a personal insult. 'How dare a *Labour politician* come to the rescue of my brother's killer?' she complained, Mr Chuter Ede's party hue serving somehow to exaggerate the offence. 'What on Earth does he know about it?' The question went unanswered, but the judge had recommended mercy in Tully's case, so it shouldn't really have come as such a big surprise to her.

Belatedly, public opinion got in on the act. People suddenly realized that only one of the 'Truro Murder Pair' was to hang and that struck many of them as fundamentally unfair. Both or neither was the gist of letters that appeared in the press, and of more than one editorial, even in the Cornish papers. Only now did people realize

220

what was actually about to happen. The staff of Colquite & Dew got up a petition. Evelyn King, the local MP, raised the matter in the House of Commons. The *Western Morning News* carried an interview with Rose and Cordelia Lanyon, who were still lodging in Exeter. They'd written to the King and Queen pleading with them to intervene. They expressed the hope that hearts would soften in the run-up to Princess Elizabeth's wedding and mentioned the distraught state of Michael Lanyon's son.

Ah, Nicky. How I guarded my thoughts of him as the days and weeks slipped by; how I hid my wish to help him as if it were some vice to be ashamed of. I wrote him a letter at one point, a stilted expression of sympathy that it was probably just as well I didn't send. The lack of an address for him in Exeter was the reason, I told myself, but it was more in the way of an excuse. I saw Ethel Jago in Boscawen Street one Saturday afternoon, and could have asked her for the address if I'd really wanted to know it. But I didn't even speak to her. Instead, I dodged down Cathedral Lane to avoid being seen, and so came to the point at the other end of the lane where I'd had my last sight of Uncle Joshua three months before. I remembered the half-crown piece he'd tossed me twinkling in the sunlight. I still had the coin in my pocket. I'd carried it about with me all that time. It was for the cinema, of course. And I hadn't been to the cinema since. It was for me *and* Nicky. Now, I realized, it never would be spent. Not for its appointed purpose. So I resolved to keep it as a symbol of the ending of things.

I wonder when and how I lost it. In the confusion of a house move, perhaps, or the long careless stretch of my late twenties and early thirties, when reminders of the past, whether sweet or sour, were anathema to me. I wish I hadn't. Not as dearly as I wish other things, but I wish it even so. *'The future's a two-edged sword,'* Uncle Joshua said that day. And he was right. But he might have gone on to mention that the past is sharper, even though it's a single blade.

The royal wedding came and went without news of a reprieve. Letters to the press went unheeded. Appeals for clemency fell upon deaf ears. What the law had decreed it seemed determined to dispense. The appointed day dawned, mild and wet in Truro, unremarked upon in the Napier household, though filling the thoughts of every one of us as we rose and washed and ate our breakfasts and engaged in a pretence of normality. Except that the subdued tones in which we spoke, the silenced wireless and the unopened newspaper, weren't normal at all. Pam and I usually squabbled over the last slice of toast, but that day we left several slices untouched in the rack.

Just before eight o'clock, Michael Lanyon was marched to the scaffold in Exeter Prison. I was on my way to school at the time, trailing listlessly along Quay Street as the City Hall clock struck the hour behind me. My parents were already serving in the shop, while back at Crescent Road Gran was readying herself to join them. A few minutes later, Michael Lanyon was dead. In Truro, nothing marked his going. The rain continued to fall, my footsteps to carry me forward. Life went on.

I headed north on Monday morning. Sunshine and showers chased me along the scarp line of the Chilterns until I hit the M1, then fell away behind as the long grey motorway miles wound out like a reel, the sky leadening as the wind weakened, the day stretching and thinning around me.

Calderdale that afternoon looked autumnally benign, the moors above tamely picturesque. I drove into Hebden Bridge from the east and saw it at its meekest, the chimneys smokeless, the mills silent. I saw it, indeed, as the

222

stone and slate ghost of a dead industry. Only geographically was it the same place Inspector Treffry had come to thirty-four years before. In every other sense it was a world away. The family firm Tully had fled must surely have been buried by history. But history had left abundant traces, in the double-decker back-to-back houses clinging to the sheer valley walls, in the ranks of barrack-block mills crammed along the riverside. The TO LET and FOR SALE signs were up, but Edmund Tully's past was still here, in this town. I sensed it as much as I knew it, driving out for a mile on to the moors, then back down into the tangle of steps and streets and secret ways he'd once called home. Edmund Tully had gone. But he'd left some part of himself behind.

I booked into the White Lion Hotel, then walked out into the town as a grey evening settled over it like a shroud. A group of standard-issue youths sat on a wall in the central square, but there was nothing they could have told me, apart from how grim it was to be young in Hebden Bridge. It was their parents' memories, and *their* parents', that I needed to tap.

The bar of the Albert, a smoky Victorian street-corner local, seemed like a good place to start. 'Tully, you say?' growled an old man in a grimy suit and flat cap, breaking off from glum scrutiny of the *Halifax Courier*. 'It's a good long while since I heard anyone asking after that firm. And a longer one since it were a going concern. When would you reckon Tully's went bust, Bert?'

'Must be twenty years at least,' replied the man standing next to him, a marginally smarter but similarly lugubrious fellow. 'Well, twenty since Henry Tully died, any rate. And that carpet-bagging son of his closed the place down within a twelvemonth.'

'Henry Tully was the original owner?'

'No, no. That were his father, Abraham Tully.' So,

Henry Tully had to be the brother Treffry had spoken to back in 1947. 'You remember old Abe, Wilf?'

'I do. A hard man. And not noted as a fair one.'

'What line of business were they in?'

'Fustian,' said Bert, who was emerging as the more forthcoming of the two. 'Like the rest of the mills here. Cloth for coats and trousers and such. But it all comes in from abroad now. Tully's made good money, till foreign competition finished them.'

'The son – where does he live?'

'Spain, last I heard.'

'None of the family left round here?'

'Not a one.'

'Hold up, Bert,' said Wilf. 'That can't be right. What about the old lady?'

'Oh aye. Miriam. I was forgetting her.'

'Who's she?'

'Henry Tully's widow.'

'And she still lives here?'

'Not in Hebden, no. Old people's home, up Keighley way. You don't want to see her, surely?'

'Why wouldn't I?'

The two exchanged a look. Then Bert said, 'Gone in the head, son. That's what they reckon.'

'Do you happen to know the address of the home?'

'Can't say I do.' Wilf gave a shrug to indicate he had no idea either. 'We're not likely to be haring up there to visit her, are we? The Tullys were owners and the likes of us were workers, till the South Koreans put us all out of a job. Big bugs and littl'uns don't mix, least not in this town. Why'd you say you were interested in them?'

'We might be distantly related.'

'You'll be distantly related to a murderer, then.'

'Oh?'

'Henry Tully's brother, Edmund, murdered a bloke

down south just after the war. We thought he'd swing for it, but he wriggled out of that, just like he wriggled out of Hebden when it suited him.'

'You knew him?'

'By sight and reputation, aye. But it's more than forty years since he buggered off and he's not been back since. They let him out of prison a few years ago, I heard. The good Lord alone knows why. And it's only God who'll know what's become of him since. He'll not be found here in a hurry, that's certain.'

But I wasn't certain. Home is where you start from, and it's the last place to forget you. I rose early next morning and walked up past the Tullys' old house in Birchcliffe Road. It was in the middle of a row of imposing Victorian villas overlooking the town – Snob Row, Bert and Wilf had called it. They hadn't said which one had belonged to the Tullys nor which of the redundant mills clogging the valley floor below had paid for it. I'd have liked to know, but it didn't really matter. One was the same as another. Hebden Bridge; Oxford; Malaya; Truro: that was the route map of his life. I felt I only had to follow the arrows to find where he was hiding.

Back at the White Lion, after breakfast, I started phoning round all the residential homes with Keighley numbers. The third one I tried, Ravensthorpe Lodge, confirmed that Miriam Tully lived there. And that visitors were always welcome.

Murder defines the murderer as well as his victim. Everything else they did and were becomes subordinate to that terminal event. No other way of dying has quite the same binding power. Joshua Carnoweth wasn't remembered in Truro as a tinner made good, a lovelorn wanderer or a sentimental loner, but as the rich old man stabbed to death at the top of Lemon Street in August

1947. Nor was Michael Lanyon recalled as a glamorous war hero or a hard-working auctioneer, only as the avaricious schemer responsible for the stabbing, who'd gone to the gallows a few months later. The rest – their lives and loves, their failures and successes – was discarded as so much unnecessary detail.

I sensed the process taking hold around me as autumn became winter and all the protests and arguments and niggling inconsistencies were forgotten in the face of one pragmatic truth. Both men were dead and buried. Neither was coming back to life, any more than the Lanyons were coming back to Truro. A line had been drawn, an episode closed. It was over.

But its consequences remained to be assimilated. I don't know when or how I realized my family had become rich beyond their most optimistic estimates of Uncle Joshua's wealth. Mr Cloke no doubt dispensed his secrets with a grudging hand. And the settling of a murdered man's estate is presumably a complicated affair. Certainly Gran and my father spent many an hour closeted in Mr Cloke's offices that December. Gradually, however, the awareness seeped into teatime conversation and my own limited view of the future. 'This will set us up nicely,' Dad cautiously admitted one day. But at Christmas, tongue loosened by port, he was more expansive – and rather more accurate. 'We'll be able to live like kings. To think he had so much. And to think it's all come to us.'

To be strictly accurate, it had come to Gran. And, though she was to develop a liking for extravagance, it would remain as it began: purposeful. Moving to Tredower House and fitting it out as a stylish residence would establish us as a family of substance. Expanding a small grocery shop with a one-room credit drapery business above into a regional chain of department stores would seal our reputation for acumen and industry. These ambitions of hers became the destinies of each of us, though it was a long time before I understood what they amounted to.

Meanwhile, undreamed-of luxuries were there to be enjoyed. To celebrate my twelfth birthday in March 1948, we all went up to London for a long weekend at the start of the Easter school holidays, which fell early that year. We stayed at Claridge's, took a boat trip along the river, visited the Tower and went to see the new smash-hit American musical, *Annie Get Your Gun*. I can still remember the sights and sounds of the evening, its intoxicating metropolitan sense of energetic fun. It put right out of my mind – as perhaps it was intended to – all conscious memory of my joint birthday party with Nicky at Tredower House the year before. It was our home now, not the Lanyons'; our future, not theirs. And I was beginning to enjoy the transformation.

Ravensthorpe Lodge was one of several high-gabled Victorian residences on the north-western outskirts of Keighley, leafily tranquil and blessed with what I assumed would have been a panoramic view of Airedale and the Pennines but for the drizzly pall of cloud that had descended as I drove across the moors from Hebden Bridge.

Miriam Tully wasn't in the lounge, where most of the residents were taking morning coffee to the booming accompaniment of a natural history documentary on the television. 'Not one of our more sociable ladies,' the nurse who greeted me confided. Which was just as well. What I wanted to talk to her about wasn't going to be aided by having to shout over a commentary on the grazing habits of wildebeest.

She was sitting in an armchair by the window of her

room, reading a large-print Dick Francis novel. White-haired, slope-shouldered and clearly in physical decline, as her clumsily buttoned dress and the walking frame standing in readiness by the chair confirmed, she nevertheless looked better and more alert than Bert had led me to expect.

'Visitor for you, Miriam,' said the nurse. 'The gentleman who phoned earlier.'

'Phoned?' said Miriam, in a cracked and querulous voice. 'I've phoned nobody. Can't afford to at the rates you charge.'

'I'll leave you to it,' the nurse whispered to me as she slipped out, a touch of resignation detectable in her tone.

'You from the council?' Miriam asked, looking up as I approached, her pale-blue eyes magnified alarmingly by her glasses. 'High time you checked up on these people.'

'I'm nothing to do with the council,' I said, drawing up a chair and venturing a smile as I sat down. 'My name's Napier. I'm hoping you can help me.'

'Can't think how.'

'I'm looking for your brother-in-law, Edmund Tully.'

'My brother's dead. And his name wasn't Edmund.'

'Your brother-*in-law*. I'm sure you know who I mean.'

'I don't understand anything.' She pouted. 'Matron will tell you that.'

'Come on, Miriam. I don't think there's anything wrong with—'

'How dare you use my Christian name?' She glared at me. 'Did I give you permission? Perhaps I forgot. They tell me I'm so very forgetful. Or perhaps I didn't and you're merely displaying the presumptuousness of your generation, in which case—'

'Sorry, sorry.' I held up my hands in surrender. 'I stand rebuked. Quite right – Mrs Tully.'

'Who did you say you were?'

'Chris Napier.'

'Never heard of you.'

'Joshua Carnoweth's nephew.'

'*Who?*'

'The man your brother-in-law murdered.'

'Murder?' She grew suddenly thoughtful and carefully set her book aside. 'Such an ugly deed.'

'Do you know where Edmund is?'

'He should be dead by rights. Dead. Like my poor dear Henry.'

'But he isn't?'

She shrugged. 'I don't know. I can only hope so. Your uncle wasn't his only victim. He as good as murdered Henry. Bottling up the shame he felt for what his brother had done took him to an early grave. He'd have kept the mill open, you know. He'd have found a way to make it profitable. Then Richard wouldn't have been able to sell off the family silver and lock me up here.'

'Richard's your son?'

'A thankless child. And therefore sharper than a serpent's tooth. There's a streak in him of his uncle's nature. He sits out there in Spain, running that sports clinic he set up with the money he got from cashing in on two generations of sober industry. He sits there by his swimming pool, sipping Pimm's while I have to—' She broke off and frowned, as if aware she might have said too much. 'Well, well, I dare say this is getting us nowhere.'

'When did you last see your brother-in-law, Mrs Tully?'

'Edmund?'

'Yes,' I said, trying to remain patient. 'Edmund.'

'Oh, many years ago. Before the war. He announced one day that he was off to London to take up a job offered him by somebody he knew from Oxford. Insurance, as I recall. About which Edmund would have known less than nothing. He hated Hebden Bridge. Said it was too small, too hostile an environment for his exotic talents to bloom in. What he really couldn't abide was working under Henry. He thought a university education entitled him to a senior position in the firm, but he wasn't prepared to earn it. He never was prepared to apply himself to anything, come to that. A feckless boy, and a worthless man. I always knew he'd come to no good.'

'Do you remember the name of his friend in London? Or the company he worked for?'

'Gone, I'm afraid. Edmund didn't stay there long.'

'But he didn't come back to Hebden Bridge?'

'Not once. Even to see his mother's grave. She died while he was a prisoner of war. You'd have thought he'd want to pay his respects when he came home, but nothing of the sort. He stayed away. We didn't expect to hear from him and I don't suppose we ever would have – but for the murder.'

'You know he was released from prison twelve years ago?'

'I heard something to that effect.'

'But still no contact?'

'Not even a begging letter, I'm pleased to say.'

'Might he have approached your son?'

'Richard? He never knew him.'

'Some other relative, then?'

'I hardly think so.'

'But surely—'

'There's a wife, of course. I suppose he must have got in touch with her. Though if it was a handout he was hoping for—'

'Wife?'

'Yes. Edmund married a girl down in London just before he joined the Army. We never met her, but they may have had some genuine affinity, given what we

230

learned she was capable of, so I suppose it's possible he crawled back to her after his release.'

'What do you mean – "what she was capable of"?'

Miriam looked past me at some spot on the wallpaper that might have been an irksome stain on her memory. 'It can't do any harm to tell you, I suppose. Henry went to great lengths to keep it quiet, but he's been gone so long and the name of Tully stands for nothing in Hebden Bridge now, so what does it really matter? If it embarrasses Richard, so be it.' She almost smiled at the thought. 'They are cousins, after all.'

'Who?'

'Richard and Edmund's child.'

'There was a child?'

'Oh yes. That was half the problem. I don't think Henry would have agreed, but for the fact that it was his niece we were talking about.'

'Edmund had a daughter?'

'According to his wife. Though I've always thought she might have—'

'How old? How old would she be?'

'The daughter? About thirty-five, I suppose.' She shook her head in wonderment. 'Yes, she must be all of that by now. How time flies.' Then she looked across at me. 'Is there something wrong, Mr Napier?'

CHAPTER TWELVE

There was nothing wrong. There was, in fact, a great deal that was right – that fitted and made a dimly perceived kind of sense – about the revelation that Edmund Tully had a daughter. She'd be about thirty-five years old; more or less the age I'd have put Pauline Lucas at. Well, well, well. When all was said and done, she had to be some-body's daughter. And she had to have some link with the murderous past of Edmund Tully. Why not more of a bond than a link, then? Why not the love of a child for her father?

I said nothing to Miriam of what I suspected. There was no point. It was easier to sit there by her drizzle-misted window, with the unappetizing foretaste of a boiled fish lunch drifting up from below, while she talked on, dipping in and out of a lifetime's worth of regrets and resentments. I was lucky to find her so old and bored and bitter. In earlier times, when she'd had a status and a reputation to defend, she'd have been far less forth-coming. But all that was gone. She no longer handed out the Sunday school prizes at Birchcliffe Baptist Chapel. Her husband no longer chaired meetings of the Hebden

Bridge Wholesale Clothiers' Association. And he and she no longer lived in a big house on Snob Row within sight of the smoking chimney of Abraham Tully Ltd. The chapel was closed, her husband dead, the house sold, the family firm extinct. So, with nothing to lose bar a seat in the Ravensthorpe Lodge television lounge, she was free to speak her mind. Indeed, she was glad to.

Abraham Tully set up in business at Hebden Bridge in the late 1880s, just as the town's domination of the fustian industry was becoming apparent. Treffry had described the works to me as a linen mill, but then what would a Cornish policeman know about such things? Fustian was actually the stuff of hard-wearing working-men's clothes. Tully's turned out trousers, jackets, coats, overalls and boiler suits for sale throughout the Empire. It made the founder a rich man and a top dog of local society. He moved into one of the smart new houses being built on Birchcliffe Road, married the daughter of another fustian magnate and had three sons: John, destined to die of dysentery while serving in the First World War; Henry, whom his father groomed as his successor at the head of the firm; and Edmund, the youngest by some years, doted on, spoiled and ruinously indulged after his brother's death.

That was Miriam's version of events, anyway. Her father ran a dye works in the town, which Tully's later took over. She married Henry while Edmund was at Oxford and came to know him as the arrogant and restless younger brother who contributed little at work, especially after old Abraham's death left Henry in full charge, and only trouble and tension at home. His drunken escapades and unexplained absences made him notorious among the workforce – and hence in the town. When he departed for the bright lights of London in the autumn of 1938, she was heartily relieved. He chose to announce his going one Sunday afternoon, when Miriam, Henry, baby Richard and old Mrs Tully had attended the ceremonial unveiling by Sir James O'Dowd of a memorial stone to Hebden Bridge's war dead. The fact that his own brother was among them had not persuaded Edmund to put in an appearance. When the party returned home, it was to find him packed and ready to go. The last Miriam had ever seen of him was driving off down Birchcliffe Road at a mad speed, leaving his mother in tears and herself in a state of well-concealed delight.

Word of Edmund's subsequent activities came sporadically and was received by Miriam with indifference. His career in insurance lasted less than a year. His enlistment in the Army she saw not so much as a patriotic act, more an alternative to unemployment; his virtually simultaneous marriage not a serious commitment, but a passing whim. Of his wife, Alice Graham, nothing was heard or known. Certainly it was the War Office rather than the new Mrs Tully who let them know he'd been captured by the Japanese at the fall of Singapore. The news cast his mother into a decline from which she never recovered.

When, after the war, the treatment meted out to Japanese prisoners was reported in the newspapers, Miriam concluded that Edmund was unlikely to have survived. Eventually, however, through tangled official channels, they learned he had, though there was still only silence from his wife. From Edmund himself nothing was heard. Had he come to them and asked for help, Miriam insisted, he would not have been turned away. As it was, he never came. And they for their part never went looking. Instead, in the summer of 1947, an inspector called – to announce that Edmund had murdered a man in Cornwall. For money, naturally. It seemed only to confirm his irredeemability. Once again their response was to do nothing. A certain amount of gossip in the town had to be ridden out, of course. That was inevitable. But Henry was not his brother's keeper. He declared that Edmund should answer for what he'd done. There could be no question of speaking out in his defence, since his actions were indefensible. Not that Edmund asked him to speak out. There was no grovelling note from Exeter Prison appealing for a character witness, no message passed on by his solicitor. Edmund, it seemed, wanted nothing from them.

But his wife was a different matter. Just before the trial began, she wrote to them asking for money. Not for herself, naturally, but for her daughter. Edmund's daughter, that was, the issue of their brief post-war reunion, now a babe in arms. Alice Tully wanted to leave London and make a fresh start somewhere else, where her association with a murderer – along with baby Simone's – could be forgotten. Their connection with Edmund hadn't yet reached the ears of the press, but, if no other means of support came their way, then selling her story to the Sunday papers was something Alice would have to consider.

'It was blackmail, of course,' Miriam declared. 'As bold as you like. But it would have been awful to find ourselves portrayed in the press as letting Edmund's widow and child live in poverty. We thought he would hang, you see. And the baby was Henry's niece, of course. He felt an obligation of some kind towards her and never doubted Edmund's paternity – as I must admit I did. With women of that kind, you can't be too sure, can you?'

I refrained from pointing out to Miriam that she actually had no way of knowing what kind of woman Alice Tully was. Maybe desperation had forced her hand, and maybe Edmund had portrayed his brother and sister-in-law as people more likely to respond to threats than pleas for help.

Either way, Henry paid up, and went on paying, in the form of a modest allowance, for the rest of his life. Alice settled in Brighton, where she reverted to her maiden name and turned herself into a seaside landlady. Henry wrote to Edmund in prison some months after the trial telling him of the provision he'd made for his daughter, but received no reply. Typical ingratitude, as Miriam saw it.

Edmund was still in prison, and Alice was still living in Brighton, with Simone by then a teenager, when Henry suffered his fatal heart attack just before Christmas, 1961. When she'd recovered from the shock, Miriam wrote to Alice, making it clear that the allowance would no longer be paid. Simone wasn't *her* niece, after all. And times were hard for a widow with a failing business and a rapacious son to contend with. Alice didn't reply, accepting, Miriam supposed, that time had neutralized any threat she and her daughter might once have posed to the Tullys. And there, so far as she was concerned, the matter ended.

'I don't know what Alice Graham told the girl about her father or his family,' said Miriam. 'Whatever it may have been, the truth or rather less than it, it's never led to any contact with me. And, as you've discovered, Mr Napier, I'm not hard to find.'

'Did . . . Mrs Graham . . . keep you informed about her daughter's progress in life?'

Miriam snorted. 'Certainly not.'

'So she could be anywhere, doing anything, for all you know.'

'Or care. Isn't that what you really mean?' She tossed her head. 'Well, I don't deny it. I was determined from the first not to become involved in Edmund's life in any way. Whatever and whoever he touches tend to be . . .' She wrinkled her nose. 'Soiled.'

'But Simone was your husband's niece. Didn't he ever think of visiting her?'

Miriam looked at me as if I were mad. 'It never crossed his mind. The allowance was ample recognition. More than ample, in my opinion.' It was an opinion I had no doubt she'd favoured Henry Tully with on many occasions. 'Richard was horrified when he learned what his father had paid over.' She smiled. 'One of the few things we *have* agreed about.'

'He's never wanted to see his cousin?'

'He doesn't really want to see *me*, Mr Napier, let alone the daughter of an uncle he can't even remember. Besides, he *has* seen her, strictly speaking. Alice Graham sent us a photograph of the baby when she first asked us for help.'

'Do you still have it?' It was a long shot, but if the baby had a look of Pauline Lucas about her—

'I'm afraid not. I had to dispose of most of my possessions when I moved here. As you can see, the accommodation is not exactly spacious. I was only able to keep a few precious mementoes of happier times. A photograph of Edmund's daughter was, as you may imagine, something I didn't miss.'

'Do you think Alice Graham still lives in Brighton?'

'I haven't the remotest idea.'

'It's just that if I'm to have any chance of finding your brother-in-law . . .'

'You must try your luck in Brighton. My, my, you are persistent, aren't you? From one end of the country to the other. Your energy is quite exhausting, I must say.'

'You don't happen to remember her address?'

'I do, yes.' She arched her eyebrows as if to rebuke me for the smile of surprise that came to my face. 'I believe it's a sign of approaching senility that one's memory is at its sharpest where matters of small consequence are concerned. Twenty years ago, you could have found Alice

Graham at the Ebb Tide Guest House, Madeira Place, Brighton. As for now, who can say? But I imagine you'll find out soon enough. In return for the information, I wonder if I could ask you one small favour.'

'Name it.'

'Take me out to lunch before you leave. I suggest the Brown Cow at Bingley. It isn't far, and with any luck they won't have boiled fish on the menu.'

After the taxman had claimed his slice of Uncle Joshua's estate, Gran was left with about a million pounds in interest-bearing accounts and half as much again in bonds, shares and assorted securities, plus Tredower House and its contents. A million then probably represents ten or more now, of course. What I'm describing is the acquisition of a fortune overnight. Nobody told me or Pam, and there was no way to guess it from our lifestyle, but the fact is that early in 1948 we became a very wealthy family.

Even if Gran had been tempted to indulge in a reckless spending spree, rationing and the austerity economy were there to prevent her. There wasn't a lot to blow money on in post-war Britain and fierce foreign exchange controls meant you couldn't take much of it abroad either. It's a world that seems so remote from the present that I'm surprised it's as recent as my own childhood.

That first summer of our relatively untrumpeted prosperity, though, Gran and Grandad did cross to New York on the *Queen Mary* to celebrate their sapphire wedding anniversary. It was about the only example of conspicuous expenditure an observer could have detected: an old married couple taking their first trip abroad. They returned with tales of the Empire State Building, the Statue of Liberty and dinners at the captain's table, as well as a firm conviction on Gran's part that the future of retailing lay in providing customers with the good things in life she'd seen so abundantly on offer in New York. She'd glimpsed that in a small way in the credit drapery business, and now she proposed to use her recently acquired capital to link the Napier name with a new concept of shopping.

Over the next few years, Napier's Department Stores opened branches in Truro, Plymouth, Torquay, Exeter, Taunton and Bournemouth. Dad gave up slicing bacon and weighing cheese to become chairman and managing director of a large and prestigious business. In the public eye, he *was* Napier's, and he took to the role with enthusiasm, acquiring a Daimler, a chauffeur, a seat on the magistrates' bench, a taste for tailored suits, a liking for golf and, as the Fifties advanced, the jowly air of a successful entrepreneur.

Not quite a *self-made* entrepreneur, of course. Behind his rise to commercial eminence stood Gran. And behind her, Uncle Joshua's money. Ironically, taken over the long term, Napier's was a failure. The good years never outweighed the bad. A lot of people were employed, a lot of customers served, a lot of business done. But it never made anybody's fortune, so it was just as well that Gran's more passive investments brought in such a healthy return.

I see all this with hindsight, but, at the time, Napier's seemed like some sort of financial leviathan, the solidity and reliability it acquired perfectly represented by its Boscawen Street frontage. The Harrod's of Cornwall, they called it. Well, it was never quite that, but it was *the* shop in Truro. And the name spelled out above the entrance in as many large gold letters as there were high decorated windows on either side was literally as well as metaphorically what Gran had hoped it would become: the biggest in the city.

It was also my future, a ready-made career that could one day see me succeed my father as chairman. As I progressed through school, National Service and university, it lay ahead, waiting for me, I sometimes thought, whether I wanted it or not. When Pam married Trevor Rutherford and he was ushered into the business while I was still leading a carefree student's life in London, I didn't see him as any kind of threat. I assumed I could take on as significant a role as I chose at Napier's when the time came. The only question was whether I *would* choose.

I didn't rush into the decision. I even managed to persuade Gran to fund me for a year or so of postgraduate globe-trotting to think it over. The months I spent in the States during that footloose spell, cruising down the freeways in an electric blue Chevrolet Corvette with Elvis Presley booming out of the radio, gave me a fondness for stylishly designed convertibles, not to mention rock 'n' roll and platinum-blonde coffee-shop waitresses, but no great enthusiasm for department-store management.

The truth was, however, that I didn't have any clear idea of what I wanted to do with my life, so, with an exasperated sense of inevitability, I ended up taking my place in the family firm as a twenty-four-year-old trainee manager. No longer, however, was I heir apparent; Trevor had his feet firmly under that table. With my father slowing down as Napier's entered its second decade, Trevor had become the company's guiding force. He greeted my arrival with thinly veiled hostility and engineered my swift departure to the Plymouth store, to be 'knocked into shape', as he droolingly phrased it, by the branch manager, Humphrey Metcalfe.

Miriam Tully's description of her brother-in-law's return from Oxford gave me an insight into what Trevor must have thought of me, an idle and pampered interloper who strayed into his kingdom in the autumn of 1960. I suppose that's exactly what I was. But there was no way of remaining either idle *or* pampered under the tutelage of Humphrey Metcalfe, a man as capable of grovelling obsequiousness to good customers as of red-faced ranting fits at back-sliding staff. The boss's son was a phenomenon he both feared and hated, but my disenchanted semi-detached approach to working life, plus whatever hidden agenda Trevor may have set for him, gave him more to hate than fear. The result for me was a purgatory of menial tasks and stifled complaints. The Plymouth store, a stark white megalith dominating the shopfronts of Armada Way, was sometimes compared to a cruise liner by architectural students. To me it was always more of a prison hulk, where I served out a sentence of errand-running and telephone-answering for a petty dictator. 'Musso' Metcalfe, the staff called him behind his back, the reference to Mussolini implying he was beholden to a Hitler somewhere else. I was never really one of the lads and lasses, of course. I could never quite be trusted. Little did they know I was paid no more than them and treated no better, on the grounds that working my way up should mean precisely that. We were in the same boat, but it never felt like it.

Don Prideaux was about the only friend I had in Plymouth, unless you count the other regulars of the Abbey, the pub closest to my flat, where I took to drowning many of my murderous intentions towards Humphrey Metcalfe. Don had turned up at Truro School at the start of the second year, transferred on a hard-won scholarship from Daniell Road. Despite his never letting me forget that education as well as a career had been handed to me on a plate, whereas he'd had to earn his by dint of effort and application, we met regularly for midweek pub crawls, Friday night double-dates and weekend excursions on to Dartmoor in the frog-eyed Sprite I bought with the handful of cash Grandad left me in his will. The sentimental old fellow knew I was being kept on a short leash and may have thought it was *too* short, but there wasn't much he could do about it.

The last piece of advice Grandad gave me, and now I think about it probably the first, was to ignore the unanimous urgings of my sister, father, mother and grandmother to marry and settle down. Freedom from financial pressures had come to him too late in life to be properly enjoyed, so I suppose he was effectively telling me what he'd have done as a young man if he'd had the same opportunities as me.

The only problem was that I wasn't so very young any more. I was twenty-seven in 1963, the year of Profumo and the Beatles and the Great Train Robbery and the slow stirrings of the permissive society. I faced a choice between doing what was ever less patiently expected of me and breaking free of what I saw as a charade of trainee respectability; between a dull, safe, suffocating future and the great and glorious unknown.

I took a week off in October to catch up with some old university friends in London and remind myself what fun life was supposed to be. Most of them were married by now and pursuing careers with more commitment than me. Fun, it turned out, was becoming a stranger to them as well. But not in *every* case. Johnny Newman, whom I'd shared some lodgings with in my final year, had always fancied himself as a rock 'n' roll singer. When I met him at a party in Hampstead thrown by a mutual former girl-friend, it transpired that he was about to go on the road full-time with his band of three guitarists and a drummer: the Meteors. Johnny was reluctant to sign up with a Tin Pan Alley agent. He reckoned they'd be better off managing themselves. But he also reckoned the five of them should concentrate on music-making. What they needed was a non-playing member of the band to make bookings, organize transport, arrange accommodation and keep some rudimentary accounts.

It took me most of that very late night plus a black coffee encounter with the others next day to persuade Johnny to recruit me as the sixth Meteor on the basis of my experience at Napier's as a manager *and* salesman. Just as well he wasn't likely to ask Humphrey Metcalfe for a reference. I was in.

And out of the family firm. Dad was horrified, naturally. 'Have you taken leave of your senses, boy? You can't be serious.' But I was. And so was he – in making one thing absolutely clear. 'You'll be on your own if you walk out on this job. You'll get no handouts from me or your mother. There'll be nothing to fall back on. Do you understand that?' I assured him I did, although the truth was more ambivalent. I didn't think he was giving me a once-for-all ultimatum, nor that I was cutting off every possibility of a retreat. Only later did I discover how stubborn we could both be – how unforgiving *and* unrepentant. Even when forgiveness and repentance were badly needed.

The Meteors turned out to be aptly named. For a few months in 1964, they soared and shone. 'Wasting the Night' reached the Top Twenty. The musical press talked up their prospects. A lucrative and exhausting round of gigs and recording sessions edged them ever closer to fame and fortune. I proved my worth by maintaining a ramshackle kind of order in their lives – managing the money, planning ahead, talking to journalists, negotiating with record companies. I even, single-handedly, kept the van in which we travelled the country on the road and in serviceable condition – an heroic achievement in itself.

But the Meteors' flaw was human rather than mechanical. The lead guitarist, Andy Wicks, had real musical flair and a yen for self-destruction to go with it. He didn't so much succumb to alcoholism and drug addiction as embrace them like friends. In that sense, he died with his friends about him, choking on his own vomit in a basement flat in Lewisham at the end of a lost midweek.

Johnny and the others put a brave face on it, reckoning they could go on as a four-man band. But Andy had supplied the best of their lyrics and given their playing much of its heart. Without him, the Meteors burned out in a long night of slow and ultimately squalid decline. I had no idea that was how it was going to be. None of us had. The world tilted only gently at first beneath our feet, but eventually it was to become a sheer slope down which we careered.

Somewhere near the middle of that slope, with Andy less than a year dead and hope still giving us a run for our money, though not much of one, I talked our way into a series of gigs along the south coast. It was hard going by then to keep the band to any kind of itinerary. The entanglements of their love lives and drug habits, not to mention *my* heavy drinking, combined with the creeping awareness of a downward trend, resulted in more botched performances, no-shows and ugly disputes with night-club managers than the Meteors' plummeting reputation could bear.

Brighton was only one of the places where things went wrong, but Johnny reacted so badly to being booed off stage by a student audience at the university that he smashed up the room I was sharing with him. Not a hotel room, in best pop-star tradition, but an attic in digs near the railway station. I suppose that's when I realized there wasn't going to be a comeback. As disasters went, that night in Brighton was in a class of its own. It took me sixteen years to realize it could have been worse. We might have stayed at the Ebb Tide Guest House, Madeira Place. Then the landlady I had to pay fifty pounds to cover the damage and keep the police out of it . . . would have been Edmund Tully's wife.

'Mrs Graham?'

'That's right.' She was about sixty, trying with some success to look a good deal younger, dark hair swept back from a fine-boned face that age was only just beginning to harshen. She wore an elegantly cut pleated skirt and crisp white blouse; there was nothing of the traditional seaside landlady about her. 'A room just for yourself, is it?'

'Yes. Just for myself.' We were standing in the porch of the Ebb Tide Guest House with a streetful of low October sunlight behind us, traffic noise and the screech of gulls mixing in the Brighton air. I'd got home from Hebden Bridge late the previous night and driven down to the Sussex coast through the middle of the day, plotting my strategy as I went. 'You do have a vacancy?'

'Oh yes. It's a quiet time. I can even do you an *en suite* room at the standard rate. Seven pounds fifty bed and breakfast. Would that suit you?'

'Sounds fine.'

'Come in, then.'

The façade of the Ebb Tide had looked smart enough, area and balcony railings gleaming, cream stucco basking warmly in the sunshine. The interior was clean and homely too, the carpet thick beneath my feet. I followed her along the passage to be shown the airy dining-room, then we doubled back to the stairs.

'Somebody recommend me, did they?'

'Not exactly. The . . . accommodation bureau . . . pointed me in this direction.'

'It's just, since you knew my name, I assumed some-body must have put you on to me.'

'Oh, the woman at the bureau mentioned it.'

'Really?' She looked round at me doubtfully as we reached the landing. 'Well, I must be doing something right. This is it.' She opened a door and stepped back to make way for me. It was a small but neatly furnished room, scented with just too much air freshener. The window promised a sea view, though; the bed a firm mattress.

'Very nice. The whole place is. Been here long, Mrs Graham?'

'A good while, yes.'

'Do you run it single-handed?' Seeing her frown, I added, 'I mean, is it a husband and wife operation?'

'I'm a widow.'

'Oh. Sorry to hear that. Any children to help out?'

Her mouth tightened and a stiffness entered her pose. 'Are you sure it was the bureau who sent you here, Mr . . .'

'Napier.'

'Only most of my guests ask me about hot water and mealtimes, not my family history. And they don't tend to know my name unless they've been before, which you haven't.'

'I suppose I'd better come clean, then.'

'Why don't you?'

'I'm looking for your husband, Edmund Tully.' She didn't so much as blink in surprise. I had to admire her coolness. But the way her gaze flicked across my features told me she was thinking fast and evasively. 'Don't try the widow routine. It won't wash.'

'Who are you?'

'That doesn't matter. I simply want to know where Tully is.'

'I think you'd better leave. The accommodation's no longer available.'

'Then I'll have to go elsewhere. The street's full of B & Bs, all with vacancies. Your neighbours, Mrs Graham. Since you use your maiden name, I have an idea you don't want them to know who your husband is and what he did. If you won't help me, I might have to enlighten them.'

'Bastard.' She spoke in an undertone, with such a distant look on her face that it wasn't clear who she meant – me, or Edmund Tully.

'Just his whereabouts.'

'Like I told you. I'm a widow.'

'Prove it.'

'I don't have to prove anything.'

'Why are you protecting him?'

'I'm not.'

'Then tell me where he is.'

'I can't.'

'I think you can. Look at it this way. You don't owe Tully a thing, so why not help me find him? Isn't that preferable to having your friends and neighbours know how you extorted money out of Tully's brother to set yourself and your daughter up here?'

'My daughter?'

'Henry Tully's widow told me all about it. You can drop the pretence.'

Some decision – some acceptance of expedient necessity – drained the defiance from her. She closed the door softly behind her, crossed to the window and squinted out into the sunlight, then turned to look at me. 'You said your name was Napier. As in Napier's Department Stores?'

'Yes. Since you mention it.'

'Then why are you asking me where Edmund is? Whose behalf are you acting on?'

'My own.'

'Is Melvyn Napier your father?'

'Yes.'

'Does he know you're here?'

'No. But I can't see—'

'Why do you want to find Edmund?'

'To learn the truth about the murder of Joshua Carnoweth.'

'Well, I can't help you. I haven't seen Edmund in years. He could be dead for all I know.'

'What about your daughter? Could she be in touch with him?'

Alice Graham smiled grimly. 'There's no chance of that.'

'Are you sure you know her well enough to say?'

'Oh yes.'

'I believe I may have met her, you see. Quite recently. Going under the name of Pauline Lucas.'

'You can't have.'

'I've got a photograph of her. Not a very nice photograph, I'm afraid. Not very nice at all. But you'll recognize her, I'm sure.'

'No, Mr Napier. I won't.'

'Take a look.' I reached into the inside pocket of my jacket. 'Then you'll—'

'I don't have a daughter.'

'What?'

'I don't have any children, living or dead. I'm childless. Got that?'

'But—'

'I lied to the Tullys. They'd never have paid me a penny on my own. For a niece, on the other hand . . .'

'You sent them a picture of the girl.'

'A picture of *a* girl. The daughter of a cousin of mine, born just after the war. I knew they'd never want to see her. One picture was more than enough for them. And for me.'

'I don't believe you.'

She shrugged. 'That's your privilege.'

'Look at this.' I slid the photograph from its envelope and held it out for her to see, as determined to force the issue as I was reluctant to let Pauline Lucas slip through my fingers again. 'You recognize her, don't you?'

But it was clear from her disinterested pout of disgust that she didn't. 'I've never seen her before in my life.' Then she caught the scowl of frustration on my face. 'Looks like you've made a major misjudgement, Mr Napier. I suppose having this kind of picture taken is an expensive business. It must be galling to learn you've wasted your money.'

'You're lying.'

'No, I'm not. I have no daughter. If I did, she wouldn't be Edmund Tully's. He and I – Well, I'll say this. When he came back from the war, he was incapable of fathering a child. The Japanese . . . hadn't exactly been lenient with him.' She waved a dismissive hand at me or the past or the reflection of one in the other, walked back to the door and opened it. 'I think you ought to leave now. I've told you enough.'

'You've told me nothing. Where is he?'

'What makes you think I either know or care? I married Edmund because he was handsome and flattering and because I was too young to know better. I made the kind of mistake lots of girls of my generation made, and I don't need you to remind me of it.'

'Maybe I wouldn't be in a position to, if you hadn't decided to cash in on your mistake.'

'All right.' She closed the door again – and briefly closed her eyes as well. 'I cheated Henry Tully. But his brother played a far worse trick on me. I have nothing to apologize for. Not to you, anyway.'

'How could you be sure of getting away with it?' I said,

still chasing the hope that there really had been a daughter. 'What if he'd demanded to see the girl?'

'Then I'd have been found out. But he'd never bothered to see *me* and I'd been married to his brother for seven years. Besides, neither he nor Edmund told the police I even existed. That made it pretty obvious I was an embarrassment to both of them. So, I reckoned the odds of getting away with it were pretty good. And it didn't much matter if I failed. I was as poor and desperate as I'd wish my worst enemy to be during those post-war years in London. I had nothing to lose, and a better life to win. So, I tried it on. And it worked.'

'But Edmund must have known what you'd done. Henry wrote to him in prison.'

'Yes. And Edmund said nothing. He always did have a warped sense of humour. He thought it was funny – Henry paying out to support his non-existent daughter. He thought it was a really good joke. That's what he told me, anyway, when he tracked me down after his release. I thought I'd shaken him off for good, but, thanks to Henry, he knew where to find me.'

'So it was a shock – Edmund turning up here twelve years ago?'

'Oh yes. A very unpleasant one.'

'Did he stay long?'

'He didn't *stay* at all. He came for some money, knowing I'd be willing to pay to see the back of him. It was Whit week. I had a houseful of holidaymakers. I didn't need an ex-con husband hanging about the place. So, I filled his wallet and sent him on his way.'

'His way to where?'

'That's what I don't understand about your visit, Mr Napier. I haven't seen or heard of Edmund since then. And I'm not about to complain, believe me. It doesn't matter to me what he was up to. But if you really want to know, well, you didn't have to go to all this bother to find out. Just ask your father.'

'My father? What do you mean?'

'I mean that I didn't ask Edmund where he was going when he walked out of this house twelve years ago, but he told me anyway. He said he was going to Truro. To see Melvyn Napier.'

CHAPTER THIRTEEN

'He said he was going to Truro. To see Melvyn Napier.' I recalled Alice Graham's exact words, and the puzzlement in her eyes, as I drove out of Brighton late that afternoon. She couldn't have missed my flinch of surprise, nor the irony that it sharpened into the kind of joke Edmund Tully might have relished. 'You really didn't know, did you? You had no idea.' None whatsoever. She was right there. I felt as if I'd woken suddenly, to discover I was no longer in the room where I'd fallen asleep. 'I'm afraid your father must have been keeping you in the dark, Mr Napier.'

'Maybe Tully didn't go through with the visit,' I'd managed to say.

'He seemed determined to. There was money in it for him, he said. And he must have got some, because if he'd thought better of the idea or been turned away empty-handed, he'd have come back here for another handout. But he never did.'

'Why should he have thought my father would give him anything?'

'You'll have to ask him, won't you?' Yes. I would have

252

to ask him. But could I trust him to give an honest answer? 'Edmund always seemed to think there was money to be made in Truro. That's why he went there in the first place.'

'I thought he just drifted into town.'

'Hardly. He told me once he had an old chum in Truro he could squeeze for cash if he needed to. Somebody he was certain wouldn't refuse him.'

'How could he be certain?'

'I took it he meant to blackmail the man.'

'Blackmail? What would he have had on Michael Lanyon?'

'Who knows?' She'd flushed a little at that, some remembered grievance still burning inside her.

'I have the distinct impression you do, Mrs Graham.'

'Well, I could take a guess, it's true.'

'And what would you guess?'

'That he was one of several "chums" of Edmund's. I realized pretty soon after I married Edmund that he preferred men to women. He hid a bundle of letters at the back of a wardrobe in the miserable little house in Stepney we moved into after getting married. I came across it while he was away. They were from men he'd had affairs with.'

'And Michael Lanyon was one of them?'

'I don't know. But they were close friends at Oxford. They toured Europe together. It would make sense, wouldn't it? Michael Lanyon was married himself by then, with a son. And he had a well-paid job. Ideal prey for Edmund. Especially if he genuinely loved his wife.'

'I think he did.'

'There you are then. Edmund only stayed with me for a few months when he came back from the war. Long enough for me to see how it had changed him, though. He'd always been selfish and idle. Now he was cruel and vindictive into the bargain, as if he wanted to repay his torturers by torturing others in turn. When he left he took the letters with him.'

'When was that?'

'December forty-six. Just before Christmas.'

'And the next you heard from him?'

She'd smiled grimly at the memory. 'I simply read about his arrest in the newspapers nine months later like everyone else. Edmund kept quiet about me, and I was more than happy to keep quiet about him. I'd moved by then, anyway, hoping he wouldn't be able to find me again, so there was no-one to connect us.'

'Why do you think he let the police think he was single?'

'Because of what I might have told them about him. I suspect he'd been calling in old debts with the contents of those letters for months. Being exposed as a black-mailer wouldn't have helped his defence, would it?'

'It might have helped Michael Lanyon's.'

'Might it?' She'd eyed me defiantly. 'Well, that was nothing to do with me. As far as I was concerned, Edmund and his "chum" could—'

'Go hang?'

She'd paused before replying, as if to deliberate on the point. 'Yes. Exactly.'

But only one of them had hanged. The other had returned, like a dog to its vomit, to the murder he still hoped to profit by. But how? What pressure could he apply? What threat could he make – so long after the event?

My father knew. *Had* known, for twelve years. Or maybe longer. Sam Vigus's perjury and Gran's complicity in it weren't enough. There had to be something Tully could prove beyond doubt that would hurt the family badly. Nothing less would work. And evidently it had worked. Well enough to set up Tully somewhere beyond the reach of the law, able to afford the relative luxury of leaving his wife in peace.

I telephoned my parents as soon as I reached home, intending to tell them I'd be down the following day on urgent business, though without giving them any inkling of just what that business might be. Not for the first time, however, I was unprepared for the course events were taking. Mine wasn't the only hand prising open a long-closed door.

'Chris?' Dad barked. 'What the hell is going on? First Pam tells us some kind of madwoman is pursuing a vendetta against you, then . . . then this, for Christ's sake.'

'What? What's happened?'

'We went to Truro today to have lunch with Pam and Tabs and discuss how to sort out this God-awful mess with Trevor. When we got back here, just a few hours ago, we found the house had been ransacked.'

'You've been burgled?'

'Oh no. Nothing so damned reasonable as that. As far as we can tell, nothing's missing. Not even your mother's jewellery. But the place looks like a bomb's hit it. Ornaments smashed. Paintings slashed. Armchairs ripped. And red paint daubed everywhere. As if it was just thrown around. On curtains, carpets, walls. You have no idea. She was thorough, all right. There isn't much she didn't ruin in some mean-minded way. And what I want to know is—'

'Who she is?'

'You bet I do. The police think it was vandals. Yobbos high on drugs. But it wasn't, was it?'

'Probably not, no.'

'Mrs Hannaford didn't come in today. And we were in Truro. It's the first chance she's had to do this. Now, who is she? And what does she want?'

'I don't know. But maybe you do.'

'Me? What the hell's that supposed to mean?'

'I can't explain over the telephone. There's too much involved.'

'Then you'd better get yourself down here and *explain* to my face.'

'For once, Dad, I agree with you. I'll leave first thing in the morning.'

Whit week, 1969. According to Alice Graham, that's when Edmund Tully had left Brighton, bound for Truro and the execution of a money-making scheme he'd had twenty-two years to devise and refine. Whitsun normally fell in late May or early June, close to my grandmother's birthday. That year, she'd been ninety, the occasion for a full-scale family celebration at Tredower House. I should have been there. It was expected of me, if not required.

But expectations and requirements didn't mean much to me in the late Sixties. The slow sputtering fall to earth of the Meteors in the two years following Andy Wicks's death dragged me down into a drink problem that became, at some indefinable point, outright alcoholism. Then sleek-bodied sweet-voiced Myfanwy Probin, alias Melody Farren, came to my rescue. But it was a short-lived salvation. We met when the Meteors were briefly her backing group, in the autumn of 1966, and were married the following spring, shortly before she realized there were better and more attractive propositions in the pop music business than me. Well, undoubtedly there were, though even she'd admit she didn't choose wisely, which is why her singing career fizzled out so rapidly.

Our marriage fizzled out even sooner. The eighteen months we were notionally together I store now in the deepest basement of my memory, not so much because of the nerve-sapping remorselessness of our rows as because of the pitiful shambles it reduced me to. During the winter of 1968/9, I was living in a bedsit near Archway tube station, deluding myself, thanks to a bottle of vodka a day, that I wasn't so far gone that I couldn't reclaim a normal and respectable existence any time I chose. I'd lost a wife and at least two careers, and it was easy enough to make the choice between caring and drinking.

Occasional telephone calls to my mother and sister kept up a front for the benefit of my family. I was too ashamed to admit to them how low I'd sunk, and too proud to ask for their help. Whether they believed my claim to be spending Christmas at Johnny Newman's villa on the Costa del Sol – he didn't have one and wouldn't have invited me there if he had – I wasn't sure. But even in my addled state I knew that Gran's ninetieth birthday on the last day of May, 1969, was a family gathering I couldn't dodge.

I actually meant to go. I even managed to scale down the booze intake for several days beforehand, my will to do so strengthened by the thought of how ashamed they'd all be of me if I didn't. By then there were too many symptoms of what I still hadn't admitted was a disease for them to miss. But an interlude of relative sobriety enabled me to gain control of the more obvious ones. I set off for Truro by train on the 30th looking far better than I felt and determined to fool everyone at Tredower House with a well-rehearsed imitation of a healthy and contented member of the family.

Around the same time, Edmund Tully headed for Truro as well. My resolution failed me before I was halfway there. But Tully didn't turn back. Already, I felt certain of that.

My mother was directing clean-up operations at Lanmartha when I arrived on Wednesday afternoon. Mrs

Hannaford had drafted in her daughter to assist and they told me the place already looked a lot better than it had, with many of the smashed items disposed of or bundled up for repair, the damaged furniture shrouded in dust sheets and most of the paint, if not exactly erased, at least reduced from blood-red daubings to salmon-pink shadows on walls and carpets. The house smelled of shampoo and polish and disinfectant, but it also had the hollow scoured feel of somewhere that was no longer home.

My father had spent the morning on the golf course, Mum told me, without any noticeably beneficial effect on his temper. He was still in a black mood, holding me partly responsible for what had happened.

I found him in his study, deep in a deskload of paperwork. 'I'm checking to see if any of my financial records have been disturbed,' he explained, seeing me raise an eyebrow at the stacks of bank statements, share certificates and accountants' letters. 'It occurred to me the vandalism could have been a cover for finding out how much we're worth.'

'I don't think so, Dad.'

'Then what do you think?'

'I think it was done to hurt you. Simple as that. Pam's marriage. My business. Your home. All natural targets in their way. Things we valued, and things Pauline Lucas had the ability to harm.'

'So, now you're here, are you going to tell me who she is?'

'I don't know.'

'But on the phone you said—'

'That *you* might. Yes. I think it's more than possible.'

His lip quivered, but he held a sneer at bay. 'This had better be good, boy,' he said, with that shake of the head he'd given me so many times before, in which carefully judged measures of disappointment and disapproval were mixed with a dash of contempt.

'It's something to do with Edmund Tully.'

'Tully?'

'I know from his wife that he came to see you shortly after his release from prison twelve years ago.'

'What?'

'You can't have forgotten his visit.'

'*Forgotten?*' He jumped up from his chair and rounded the desk to confront me. 'What the bloody hell are you talking about? I saw Tully in court thirty-four years ago and that's it. I've never spoken to him in my life.'

'He travelled to Truro in the spring of sixty-nine. He told his wife he had business with you.'

'He had no "business" with me. And so far as I recall he had no wife. Have you taken leave of your senses?'

'No, Dad. I'm just beginning to use them. Think back to Gran's ninetieth birthday in May sixty-nine. That's about when Tully would have called.'

'Tully, Tully, Tully. Will you stop babbling that name at me? I'm surprised you want to dredge up memories of your grandmother's ninetieth in view of how you celebrated it. Drunk in a ditch, wasn't it?'

'Not exactly.'

'It might as well have been. What have you ever contributed to this family, Chris? Tell me that. What precisely have you ever done that entitles you to start cross-questioning me?'

'I wouldn't call this cross-questioning.'

'Then what would you call it?'

'I'd call it a search for the truth.'

'The truth? My God.' He gestured towards the papers behind him. 'There's the truth, boy. There's the reality of what I've done for you. Shrewd hard-headed financial management. One day you'll benefit from that. One day you'll be rich. Not because of your own efforts, which God knows have been feeble enough, but because of mine. *My* bloody efforts. So don't preach to me.'

'What's the matter?' I asked mildly. 'Why are you so angry?'

'I have every right to be angry. Have you seen the state of this house?'

'Yes. And I've seen the state of my workshop as well. It's a good deal worse. But I haven't blamed you for that, have I? Not yet.'

'What's that supposed to mean?'

'It means I'm still waiting for an answer. Why did Tully come to see you?'

'You've had your answer. He didn't.'

'I don't believe you.'

'*What*?' If he'd been twenty years younger, or even ten, I think he'd have hit me then. Calmly and deliberately, I'd laid it on the line. He was lying, and I wasn't prepared to let him rant his way out of it. He was lying, and we both knew it.

'Tully was blackmailing Michael Lanyon with some letters proving they'd once been lovers. That's why Michael paid him five hundred pounds. *And* why he couldn't explain his reasons for doing so.'

'Rubbish. It was proved at the trial—'

'Sam Vigus lied.'

'Oh, he lied, did he? And the evidence was planted and the police were corrupt? Is that your brilliant new theory?'

'No.'

'Then tell me, Chris. Why should Sam Vigus have lied – on oath?'

'Because Gran forced him to.'

'Gran?' He glared at me and in his face I read the hint of artifice I'd been looking for. He was angry all right. But not as angry as he was trying to appear. Something was hiding beneath the excess, and I was close to finding out what.

'Vigus told me all about it.'

'You've spoken to him?'

'Yes. Last week.'

'Your mother put you up to this, didn't she?'

'She told me Vigus had been phoning you, yes. But it was my idea to go and hear what he had to say. He couldn't understand why you hadn't responded to his calls.'

'Why should I want to speak to the old fool?'

'No reason at all, I suppose, if you already knew what he was going to say.'

'All I know is that he's not worth listening to.'

'You mean now – or thirty-four years ago?'

'I mean any time. If he perjured himself at the trial, that's his affair. It's nothing to do with me.'

'But it is. It's to do with all of us. Gran put Vigus up to it so she could be sure of inheriting Uncle Joshua's money. But she miscalculated. She assumed Michael really had paid Tully to commit the murder. But I don't think he had. And who better to know that for a fact than Tully himself? If I'm right . . .'

'Yes? What if you *are* right?'

'Then no wonder he headed for Truro after his release. He knew Vigus was a perjurer. But he didn't come to see Vigus, did he? He came to see you.'

'He did not.'

'He must have done. And you must have paid him to shut up, otherwise he would have gone on to Vigus.'

'You're talking absolute bloody nonsense.'

'How much did you pay him? And what for, exactly? He had no way of knowing it was Gran who'd twisted the evidence. It was simply his word against Vigus's. And who'd have taken the word of a convicted murderer? Or

261

cared anyway? Nobody would have been—' I stopped and stared into my father's wary eyes. Suddenly, I understood. And in that instant I could only wonder at why I'd not done so sooner. 'But the Lanyons would have cared, wouldn't they? That's what he threatened to do. Tell them the truth: that Michael had played no part in the murder; that the only thing he was guilty of was a homosexual past. Proof wasn't the issue. He knew you'd pay up rather than risk having the Lanyons try to reopen the case. They couldn't have succeeded, but they might have caused us a lot of embarrassment.'

'You're the embarrassment, Chris. You and this . . . this . . . half-baked crusade. What's it for? To ease your conscience about Nicky?'

'Yes. And why not? My conscience isn't clear. I'm not pretending it is.'

'Well, mine is. And I'm still waiting to be told who broke into this house yesterday and did their best to wreck it. *Who* and *why*.'

'I'm waiting too. The only way to answer your question is to answer mine. Find Tully and I reckon you find Pauline Lucas. So, did you pay him to leave the country? Was that the deal? It would explain why—'

'*That's enough.*' He slammed the flat of his hand down on to the desktop, then seemed to lean against it for support, his age showing in the flagging of his energy and the hoarsening of his voice. 'I'm not going to stand for any more of this. You're my son. The least I'm entitled to demand of you is that you accept my word. I've never spoken to Edmund Tully and I've never paid him a penny. Do you understand?'

'No. I don't. You're not telling me the truth.'

'If that's what you think . . . then get out.' He walked slowly round the desk to his chair and clasped the back of it. 'I'll not be called a liar in my own house by my own son.'

'Very well.' I moved to the door and looked back at him from there, letting him see how completely he'd failed to rattle me. This was a temporary stand-off; we both knew that. Sooner or later, we'd have to resolve it, but for the moment, there was no way of knowing how. 'I'm not going to give up, Dad.'

'Aren't you?' His chin jutted as he tossed out the words. 'I wouldn't be so sure. You've spent your whole life *giving up*.'

'Well, maybe that's how I *can* be sure,' I said, treating him to a smile that was sarcastic at my own expense as well as his. 'It won't happen this time.'

Addiction saps the will to such a degree that the firmest of intentions fade into the dimmest of hopes. Two and a half hours on the train from Paddington that Friday afternoon in May 1969 were enough to undermine the small amount of determination I hadn't drowned in vodka long before. I started anticipating the kind of atmosphere that would prevail at Tredower House – one heavy with the unspoken implication that I'd let them all down with the way I'd led my life. I began to imagine the exchanged glances I wouldn't be expected to see, the censorious frowns and despairing shakes of the head. I confronted a realization I'd been able to evade while they were in Truro and I was in London: I was nothing to be proud of. Whichever way you defined me – uncle, brother, son *or* grandson – I didn't measure up.

I left the train at Exeter, already half-drunk after an hour in the buffet car. It was opening time on a warm spring evening and I picked my way across the city from pub to pub, with no destination in mind, telling myself

I'd carry on to Truro later, but secretly knowing I wouldn't because I'd slid down this slope too many times before to mistake the descent for something reversible.

It was a shock to find myself near the prison, blearily recalling, as I wandered past the gate, that this was where Michael Lanyon had been hanged – and buried – twenty-two years before. I walked up an alley beside its soaring eastern wall, listening to the indecipherable sounds of voices beyond the lofty barred windows. There was a small pub at the end of the alley, where I sat and drank steadily until all memories of the summer and autumn of 1947 had vanished. I took an overnight room at the next pub I went to and woke late on Saturday morning, memory as patchy as it usually was, but crystal clear on one point: I was supposed to be in Truro. And I could still have made it, though only just. But I couldn't face myself, let alone my family. I scrawled a hasty letter of apology to Gran, claiming I'd been laid up with flu, and posted it before boarding the train back to London.

It's pitiful, looking back. It would be funny, if it weren't so pathetically incompetent. Alcohol was making me stupid as well as unreliable. An Exeter postmark on my letter, after all, was just about the most certain way to discredit its contents, and me with it. Perhaps, sub-consciously, that's what I wanted to do. Perhaps I was aware by then that I couldn't sink much lower.

Pauline Lucas's latest outrage had failed to lessen Pam's determination to end her marriage. When I reached Tredower House late that afternoon, it was to find her just back from a meeting with her solicitor. Tabitha had gone along to boost her mother's morale and to make it clear which side her sympathies lay on. Whoever Pauline Lucas was and whatever her motives might be, Trevor had been too willing a victim to be forgiven. My father had pleaded with Pam to think again, or at least to postpone a decision, but she was adamant: there had to be a divorce.

We discussed the ramifications of this over tea. Or rather Pam and Tabitha discussed them while I listened with half an ear and struggled in my mind with a more sinister problem. Eventually, when they'd talked themselves to a standstill, I raised the question my visit to Lanmartha had failed to answer.

'Do either of you remember anything strange happening around the time of Gran's ninetieth birthday party?'

'What on Earth makes you ask?' Pam was clearly taken aback by the seeming irrelevance of the enquiry. 'That must be twelve years ago.'

'It could have some bearing on what's happening. I think Edmund Tully came back to Truro after his release from prison in May of sixty-nine.'

'Well, I certainly saw nothing of him.'

'And I wouldn't have recognized him if I had,' said Tabitha. 'He's only ever been a name to me.'

'As for Gran's ninetieth,' said Pam, 'well, Chris, what I most remember that for is somebody who *didn't* come back to Truro. A place was kept for you at the birthday lunch, you know. Right up to the last moment, Gran seemed to think you might arrive. We all hoped you would, Dad especially. I'm not sure you've ever lived that down with him.'

'Nor ever will.' I smiled grimly. 'But forget about my blotted copybook. I only mentioned the birthday to help you tie down any . . . unexplained incidents.'

'Like what?'

'I don't know. If not Tully turning up here in broad daylight, then a weird phone call or . . .' I shrugged. 'Just something out of the ordinary.'

'Nothing's stuck in my mind,' said Pam. 'And Tabs

would have been away at school until the day of the party, so she—'

'No I wasn't,' Tabitha intervened. 'Great-Grandma's birthday was at the end of my half-term holiday. I was home all that week.'

'Were you, darling?'

'Yes. Don't you remember? On the Friday, you took me to a gymkhana at Wadebridge. Flossy and I won a prize.' Flossy was one of the ponies Tabitha had ridden in her horse-crazy teens. His stable had been incorporated into the annexe for the private flat when Tredower House had been converted into a hotel. 'You can't have forgotten. It was our one and only first prize.' She laughed. 'I still have the rosette.'

'Yes, of course.' Pam smiled at the memory. 'We were so proud of you.' But she couldn't help adding, 'Well, *I* was.'

'Come on, Mum. Dad was proud of me too.'

'Was he?' Pam seemed inclined to disagree. 'As I recall, you were very upset that night because he took so little interest in your victory.'

'Yes, but that was unusual. Normally, he'd have—' Tabitha broke off and looked across at me. 'You were asking if anything out of the ordinary happened, Chris. Well, I suppose that was. In its way.'

'What happened?'

'As soon as we got back from Wadebridge, I went to find Dad so I could show him the rosette. He was with Grandpa in his study. They were . . . Well, it's funny, now I look back. I couldn't seem to get their attention. They were . . . arguing.'

'What about?'

'I don't know. I wasn't interested. I just wanted to tell them how well Flossy had jumped, but they hardly seemed to notice I was there.'

'The poor girl came to me in tears,' said Pam. 'She wanted to impress her father with what she'd achieved, but he couldn't spare her even a few minutes of his valuable time.'

'Nor could her grandfather,' I pointed out. 'Why, I wonder?'

'It'll have been about business,' Pam replied with a dismissive toss of the head. 'When wasn't it? They probably—' She stopped and snapped her fingers. 'It's all coming back to me now. Yes. What a night. Tabs upset. Final arrangements for the party to be made. And then Trevor announces he and Dad have to go out to dinner with a supplier in Plymouth. He was only in the country for a few days, apparently, and had to be buttered up. So, off they went, leaving me to drive back and forth to the station every time a train from London was due, just in case *you* were on it.'

'Perhaps that's what they were arguing about, then,' I suggested. 'Whether they really had to go.'

'Oh, Trevor wouldn't have minded. Anything to get out of helping me would have suited him. Besides, where business was concerned, he never said no to Dad.'

'That's true,' Tabitha contributed. 'But that's what's so odd about it. Grandpa had asked him to do something – I don't know what – and he didn't want to. I mean, he was objecting. Strongly. They were really at loggerheads. I'd never seen them like that before.'

'And you've no idea what they were at loggerheads about?'

'None at all.' Tabitha frowned. 'But it must have been important.' She looked at Pam, then back at me. 'Mustn't it?'

CHAPTER FOURTEEN

Arguing with my father was something Trevor had always been happy to leave to me. The secret of his success, both as a son-in-law and a deputy managing director, was a degree of compliance he'd have called loyalty and I'd have dismissed as servility. Back in May 1969, the last thing he'd have wanted to do was step, even slightly, out of line.

It was clear from Tabitha's recollections, however, that he'd nevertheless done so. The sudden announcement that he had to accompany Dad to Plymouth suggested his resistance hadn't lasted long. But dinner with a supplier, however inconvenient, was still too trivial a cause. There had to be more to it. According to Pam, they'd got back late; very late. And by the next morning everyone was on their best behaviour for Gran's party, so there was plenty to camouflage the disagreement, not least the scandal of my continuing absence. But still it must have been there, simmering beneath the surface. Whatever Dad had asked of Trevor that night, it had nearly been too much. But not quite. And there was the weakness in

Dad's refusal to admit buying off Tully, for I felt certain Tully was behind their dispute. And with Trevor as absorbed in self-pity as he now was, I had a good chance of finding out how.

I let Pam and Tabitha think I was going to my room for an early night when I left them, but a late one seemed altogether more probable. I went straight to my car and headed for Perranarworthal.

At the Trumouth Motel, I was told Trevor was out. But I'd parked beside his car and without it he wouldn't have gone far. The Norway Inn, on the other side of the road, looked a good bet.

Sure enough, Trevor was there, propped on a stool at one end of the bar. As one who knew the signs well from personal experience, I reckoned he was halfway between drunk and very drunk, head and shoulders wallowing, eyes bleary, the ashtray in front of him well-filled. He winced as he took another gulp of lager – an extra-strong brand, by the look of him.

'Hello, Trevor.'

'Oh, God.' He glared fuzzily at me. 'Can't you leave me alone?'

'Solitude doesn't seem to be doing you many favours.'

'Well, it beats the alternative, believe me.' He did his best to think for a moment. 'You can buy me another drink if you insist on staying. Carlsberg Special.'

'All right.' There was no point arguing with him about it. That too I knew from personal experience. I ordered what he wanted and a fizzy water for myself, then sat on the stool next to his. 'How are things?'

'You should know. I'll bet Pam's told you. In loving detail.'

'She seems determined to press for a divorce.'

'Yes. And I don't have much choice in the matter, do I?

269

Not while she has that damned photograph. Which *you* promised to keep from her.'

'I didn't promise anything. Besides, the fire at my workshop changed all that. You're not the only one to have suffered at Pauline Lucas's hands.'

'No? Well, I suppose that's some comfort. But don't kid yourself I believe it's why you let Pam have the picture back. You were never bothered about me. *I'm* not a Napier, am I? Not a fully paid-up member of the authentic bloodline. So I can be hung out to dry whenever it suits.'

'Trevor—'

'But I don't care. Not any more. I've had it with your family. Pam can have her divorce. She can have anything she wants. Except me on a plate. I'm off. I'm cutting the ties that bind.'

'What do you mean?'

'You think I'm going to sit it out here all winter while Pam bleeds me white? Think again. I have friends in sunnier climes. It's time I looked them up.'

'What friends are these?'

'Better ones than you'd like to believe.' He prodded my chest for emphasis, tilting the glass in his hand as he did so and spilling lager down my shirt. 'I'll be welcomed with open arms.' Then he giggled. 'And legs.'

'When do you leave?'

'Sooner the better. This'll have to be a farewell drink for you and me, Chris, I'm far from sorry to say. Which reminds me. My glass is nearly empty.'

I bought him another lager and steadied his lighter for him while he lit a cigarette to go with it. 'Before you rush off, Trevor,' I ventured, 'there's a minor mystery you might be able to clear up for me.'

'You mean why I married Pam in the first place? Well, I'll tell you. It was for her money. Her grandmother's

270

money, I suppose I should say. Which I'm going to see precious little of now.'

'It concerns Gran, certainly. Remember her ninetieth birthday party?'

'Yeh. I do. But you don't, do you?'

'You had a row with Dad the night before.'

'Did I?'

'What was it about?'

He frowned woozily at me. 'Why should you care?'

'Something to do with Edmund Tully, was it?' Shock registered dully on his face and I knew I was on the right track. 'Dad bought him off, didn't he? Paid him to shut up about Michael Lanyon. But how were you involved, Trevor? What did he want you to do? Deliver the money? Or get Tully out of the country? Was that why you went to Plymouth?'

He looked at me a long time before responding. 'Why don't you ask the old man?'

'I have. He denies everything.'

'I'll bet he does.'

'But I'm right, aren't I? It was to do with Tully.'

'Maybe.'

'What was the deal?'

'There wasn't one.'

'There must have been. Otherwise he wouldn't have dropped out of sight so obligingly.'

'That's all you know.'

'If I've got it wrong . . .'

'You have. As usual.'

'Put me right, then. Tell me what really happened.'

'No can do.' He took a large gulp of lager. 'Strictly no can do.'

'Why not?'

He grinned crookedly. 'I don't think you're ready for the shock.'

271

'Try me.'

The grin chilled. 'I preferred you as an alcoholic, Chris. It stopped you asking questions.'

'A straight answer would do the same.'

'Maybe it would.' He leaned closer. 'Of course, it was because you were an alcoholic you didn't make it to Truro that day. If you had . . .'

'Yes?'

'Well, you might have walked in at just the wrong moment.'

'And seen Tully?'

'If he was there to be seen.'

'Stop playing games, Trevor. Was he or wasn't he?'

'Maybe he was both.'

'It's one or the other.'

'Not necessarily.'

'Just tell me. What did Dad want you to do?'

'Your father? What a man, eh? What a piece of work. After all I've done for him, all I've put up with . . . he lets Pam pull the plug on me. Can you beat that? He doesn't seem to realize how much he owes me. But for me, he'd be—' Trevor broke off and stared at me, sobered a little by the force of his feelings. 'Perhaps it's time you knew what kind of a father you've got – what he's capable of.'

'What did he want you to do, Trevor?'

'Help him.' Trevor leaned closer still and lowered his voice to a whisper. 'To bury Edmund Tully.'

The ugly farce of my non-appearance at Gran's party wasn't, as it turned out, the bottom of the barrel. I had to scrape a little harder to find that, halfway through the following winter, on a pouring wet day in Shaftesbury Avenue. It was mid-morning, but I was already drunk. Standing in the refuge between two bollards in the middle of the road, waiting for the traffic to thin, I caught sight of my reflection in the window of a taxi as it came to a halt in front of me, slowed by congestion ahead. I was looking even worse than usual, sodden by the rain, my face drawn, my eyes hollow, the flesh beneath them dark enough to have been charcoaled. I looked what I was: a man who'd lost his grip.

Then I saw the passenger in the back of the taxi staring out at me in horror and amazement. It was Miv. She was every bit as beautiful as she'd ever been – and expensively groomed to boot. Her mouth fell open. She really was appalled. She sat forward in her seat and reached for the window, intending, I think, to lower it and speak to me. But at that moment the traffic eased, the taxi moved forward and she was gone. And I was left behind, leaning against a bollard for support, as the rain sluiced down and shame lanced through me.

In the months ahead, with the professional help I finally admitted to needing, I weaned myself off alcohol. I recalled the expression on Miv's face that day whenever I wanted to remind myself of the price of weakening. It wasn't easy. There were setbacks, God knows, and relapses into the bad old ways and days. But eventually, by Christmas 1970 – the season of every reformed alcoholic's severest test – I could claim to have wrestled the habit into submission, even if kicking it altogether could only be as certain as how long had elapsed since the last drink.

That had stretched to three years when, with Miv's help, I set up Napier Classic Convertibles. I asked my father to put some money into it as well, but even though Gran's death the year before and his subsequent sale of the department stores had left him with more cash in hand than he knew what to do with, he refused, an act of meanness for which I was eventually grateful.

Since moving to Pangbourne, I'd been making a living

as a roving motor mechanic in the Thames Valley, repairing cars, vans, lorries, tractors, even combine harvesters. There was something wonderfully therapeutic about getting failing old vehicles back on the road. My time with the Meteors hadn't done much for me, but the hours I'd put in on their temperamental van paid off in the end. I began specializing in classic convertibles because they paid better and were more interesting than your average Ford Escort. I rented a workshop from a farmer whose Land Rover I'd nursed back to life on several occasions, in order to tackle more ambitious jobs. Word of mouth and selective advertising brought me more and more customers. In 1973, I decided to make a proper business of it. And I never looked back. Until Pauline Lucas put a match to what I'd spent all those years achieving, leaving me to scrabble through the wreckage in search of the truth about her and Michael Lanyon and . . .

Edmund Tully. I knew where he was now. Trevor had told me. Along with more, perhaps, than I really wanted to know. We'd left the Norway Inn and I'd driven him down to Falmouth, where we stopped in a deserted car park at the far tip of Pendennis Point. We stepped out to the railings and leaned against them, staring into the damp velvety night as the waves broke like a whispering chorus on the rocks below us. Then Trevor, sobered into coherence by the cool October air, but with resentment of his plight still loosening his tongue, spilt out his twelve-year-old secret.

'It seems Michael Lanyon really was innocent. Of murder, anyway. He and Tully had been lovers at Oxford – and after, I suppose. Lanyon had written him some pretty explicit love letters, which Tully had hung on to. Down on his luck after the war, and knowing Lanyon was married and doing well, he decided to blackmail him with the letters. That's all it was supposed to be: extortion. Rather than have his wife learn the truth about him, Lanyon paid up: five hundred quid. Easy money. But Tully had kept his ear to the ground while he was in Truro and had learned that Joshua Carnoweth was worth a bit and Michael Lanyon was the apple of his eye. So he decided to squeeze the old man as well. It wasn't love letters from Cordelia Lanyon to his father Tully put up for sale. It was love letters from Michael to Tully himself. He'd kept some back, just in case he needed to pull the same trick again later. But why wait when there was so much money sloshing around? Tully thought he'd hit the jackpot.'

'But Uncle Joshua didn't play ball?'

'He was too hard for the game. I suppose you don't claw a fortune out of the Alaskan tundra only to hand even a fraction of it over to a blackmailer. Seems Uncle Joshua told him to go to hell, *and* mentioned that Michael Lanyon would inherit his fortune one day whether or not he'd been exposed as a homosexual in the meantime.'

'Why did he make that appointment with Cloke, then?'

'Who knows? Maybe Tully's try-on prompted him to think about his will afresh and he resolved to share his wealth more equally. He's not likely to have told Tully that, is he? And since he didn't live to keep the appointment, it's just so much speculation.'

'But why did Tully kill him?'

'Pure rage, apparently. Pique at being turned down. He just lashed out, then fled the scene.'

'And the letters?'

'He left them at his lodgings. Hidden under the floorboards in his room. Since the police never found them I suppose there's a good chance they're still there.

Wherever *there* is. Tully told Melvyn he could retrieve them if he needed to. But I suppose that might have been a bluff.'

'Why did he leave them behind?'

'Because they linked him with the murder, and because they undermined the story he dreamed up that night. The story he decided to tell if he was caught. Seems he had it in for Lanyon good and proper. It came down to envy. He knew Uncle Joshua's death made Lanyon a wealthy man, and he didn't fancy hanging with that to show for his efforts. So he cooked up an alternative motive; one that Lanyon came out of even worse than he did. He'd have preferred to get away scot-free, of course, but if that didn't prove possible, he could at least try to drag Lanyon down with him. And it worked, didn't it? Tully knew Lanyon could never bring himself to admit the truth. He wouldn't have been believed even if he had, because, naturally, he'd already destroyed the letters Tully had sold him. That left him with no plausible explanation for paying over the money in the first place. And then, to cap it all, there was Sam Vigus.'

'Thanks to Gran.'

'Yes. Well, she was always one for corset *and* girdle, wasn't she? She had the money in her sights and, to do her justice, firmly believed Michael was guilty. Spicing up Vigus's testimony struck her devious mind as a sensible way of making absolutely certain Uncle Joshua's fortune stayed in the family. Only Tully didn't hang, did he? And Tully was well placed to know Vigus had lied.'

'Gran was certainly angry about Tully's reprieve.'

'Because she was afraid her distortion of the evidence would come back to haunt her. Just as it did – a few days before her ninetieth birthday.'

'You're saying Tully contacted Gran?'

'No, no. It was Melvyn he went to – the man with most

to lose. Tully phoned him and set up a meeting in Boscawen Park. That's when he revealed what had really happened back in forty-seven and what he was willing to do if Melvyn didn't pay him the small matter of a hundred thousand quid to make himself scarce.'

'Spill the beans to the Lanyons?'

'Exactly. Tully had it all worked out. He'd been studying the law while he was in prison and reckoned that if he could convince the authorities he'd framed Lanyon they'd have to grant the poor bastard a post-humous pardon. That would invalidate the grounds on which Uncle Joshua's will had been set aside and mean his estate had to revert to the heirs of the original benefi-ciary. Are you with me, Chris? The house, the money, the whole lot, would go back to the Lanyons. Together with compensation, damages and God knows what.'

'Is that true?'

'You'd need to consult a lawyer for a definite answer. It sounded convincing enough to Melvyn, though. Especially since he was harbouring a guilty secret about the evidence that had sent Michael Lanyon to the gallows in the first place. Gran had told him all about it. He knew what she'd done. It hadn't seemed so bad when you could argue it was all in a good cause. But if Tully carried out his threat, they might find themselves charged with conspiring to pervert the course of justice – and bankrupt into the bargain.'

'But Tully would have gone back to prison if he'd admitted lying at the trial.'

'True. But he said that would be water off a duck's back to an old lag like him. And it would have taken a steelier nerve than Melvyn's to call his bluff.'

'So Dad agreed?'

'Yes. Tully gave him forty-eight hours to get the money together. The handover was fixed for Friday afternoon in the car park at St Erth railway station.' St Erth was a junction most of the way down the main line to Penzance, where passengers changed for the St Ives branch. Guessing I'd be puzzled by the choice of rendezvous, Trevor explained: 'Tully didn't want to hang around Truro in case he was recognized. He was planning to stay in Penzance until Friday and pick up the money *en route* to London. St Erth's pretty much deserted between trains and the car park isn't overlooked by houses, making it a nice discreet setting. It suited Melvyn too. He didn't want to be seen consorting with a convicted murderer. He even borrowed my car to drive down there, feeding me a cock-and-bull story about the Daimler's starter motor being on the blink.'

'You had no idea what was going on?'

'Not the foggiest. I still hadn't been dragged into it. He told Gran, of course. She was all for defying Tully to do his worst. Like brother, like sister, I suppose. Melvyn talked her round in the end and she stumped up the cash. He left the office after lunch, supposedly to play golf. Instead, he drove down to St Erth and met Tully off the train. It should have been a straightforward transaction. Over and done within minutes. But . . . something went wrong.'

'What?'

'They were standing at the back of the car, apparently, with the boot open and the bag containing the money inside. Tully was checking it, slowly and methodically. There was nobody around. The London train was long gone and so were the few other passengers who'd got off. They had the place more or less to themselves. Melvyn was watching Tully fingering his way through the wads of notes, wondering if he'd ever finish. Eventually, he did. "It seems to be all here," he announced. "And very nice to be going on with." Who knows what he really meant?

It could have been a hint he'd be back for more later. Certainly Melvyn took it that way. Well, you know how short-tempered he is. Something snapped. Just like that.' He paused. 'Hit you much as a child, did he?'

'Off and on.'

'But not with a wheel-wrench over the back of the head, I imagine.'

'Good God. Are you saying . . .'

'He gave Tully a whack with the first thing that came to hand: my wheel-wrench. Tully fell forward into the boot, out cold. Melvyn panicked – as you would. He bundled Tully's legs in after him, closed the boot and drove off, hoping nobody had seen what he'd done. A few miles down the road, he pulled into a farm gateway and got out to check how Tully was.'

'And he was dead?'

'Had been since the wrench struck him at the base of the skull. Seems Melvyn should have been in the Commandos rather than the Catering Corps.'

'My God. I'd never have thought . . .'

'Him capable of it? No, neither would I. Neither would *he*, I suspect. But he was. And it could only get worse before it got better. You can't exactly ignore a dead body in the boot of your car, can you? Not for long anyway.'

'So what did he do?'

'Drove back to Truro like a bat out of hell and told Gran what had happened, hoping she'd snap her fingers and make the body disappear. Instead she told him to snap his – and get me over there from the store sharpish. She reckoned it would take two of us to bury him. Just think. If you'd made it to Truro on time you could have taken my place – and been welcome to it.'

'If you think—'

'No, Chris. I don't. I expect you'd have called the police and happily seen your father sent to prison, your sister

279

and niece turned out of house and home and Napier's Department Stores renamed Lanyon's overnight. But I don't have your finely chiselled moral sensibility. I wasn't exactly enthusiastic about what Melvyn wanted me to do, but in the final analysis I couldn't see we had much choice. Tully was dead. But nobody was going to miss him. Or come looking for him. And he *was* a murderer. Let's not forget that. Of Michael Lanyon as well as Joshua Carnoweth. We couldn't leave him where he was. We either went to the police or . . .'

'Where did you bury him?'

'Bishop's Wood, late that night. While we were supposed to be wining and dining a supplier in Plymouth. Back-breaking work, I don't mind telling you. We'd had quite a bit of rain in the previous week, so the ground was fairly soft, but even so . . .' Trevor sighed. 'I've had a healthy respect for gravediggers ever since. They're scandalously underpaid.'

'You think this is a joking matter?'

'I certainly didn't at the time. I thought it was a waking nightmare, if you want to know the truth. I thought your father had dragged me into an even deeper hole than the one we had to dig for Tully. I was frightened enough to tell him exactly how I felt. That's what Tabs walked into the middle of. But it didn't change anything. We had to go through with it or face some pretty hideous consequences. Tully's body was in *my* car, remember. Melvyn never said as much, but there was a hint he might try to saddle me with the blame if push came to shove. But we got away with it, didn't we? Nobody saw us. Nobody suspected a thing. And nobody ever unearthed Edmund Tully.'

'Is that supposed to justify what you did?'

'Don't get sanctimonious with me. I was just helping to clear up the mess. *Your family's mess.* Remember that. I didn't help convict an innocent man. I didn't murder anyone. Your grandmother did one and your father the other. They're the ones to blame. Not me. And you'll profit by their crimes eventually. Remember that as well. I've no doubt you'll get a lucrative mention in Melvyn's will. But I won't, you can be sure of that. As things have turned out, it looks like I strained every nerve and sinew planting Tully six feet under that night in Bishop's Wood for precisely no personal gain whatever.'

'What do you want – my sympathy?'

'It wouldn't go amiss. But don't worry, I'm not expecting you to clap me on the back and say, "Nice one, Trev. You did what had to be done. I'm proud of you." I don't even expect you to acknowledge that it was a bloody awful fix to find myself in. But you could satisfy my curiosity on one point. Now you know what really happened, what are you going to do about it? What *exactly* are you going to do?'

'Eli,' Gran had muttered to me on her deathbed at Tredower House in February 1972. 'Eli.' And now the interpretation of her faltering farewell had changed again. 'He lies.' Was that it? 'He lies in Bishop's Wood.' It could have been. It certainly could.

Bishop's Wood fills a stretch of the valley of the River Allen above Idless, a few miles north of Truro. There's an Iron Age fort preserved in the middle of it, which Nicky and I used to defend against Roman soldiers whenever we strayed that far on all-day rambles from Truro. By night it would be a dark and secret place, where the desperate and determined could bury a dead man in the realistic hope that he'd never be discovered.

'He was a short, thin, old man,' Trevor had said. 'But still it was almost too much for us, carrying him to the hole it had taken us hours to dig. Then the filling in and covering over. The camouflaging with leaves by failing torchlight. God, it was one hell of a business.'

That last I would easily believe. The consequences of murder often are. They seemed so to me as I drove back alone to Truro after dropping Trevor at the Trumouth Motel: an innocent man hanged; his son driven to suicide; his daughter to the twilit life of a fugitive from her own identity. And after it all, just one question to answer. 'What *exactly* are you going to do?'

I didn't sleep much that night. I lay in bed wondering what I'd have done if I'd learned the truth while Nicky was still alive. I wanted to believe I'd have told him everything and given him the proof he craved of his father's innocence. But would I? Would I really, when there was so much at stake? I was far angrier with Dad for covering up Gran's responsibility for Michael Lanyon's conviction than I was for his murder of Edmund Tully. I found that quite forgivable. I was almost glad he'd done it; glad the man who should have hanged in 1947 had gone on to meet a violent death and been buried in unhallowed ground. But murder was murder. To reveal one part of the truth was to reveal all. Maybe, even if Nicky could have heard me, I'd have stayed silent.

It was to reject that notion, to distance myself from what my own flesh and blood had done to his flesh and blood, that I left the hotel before dawn next morning and drove out to Idless. I watched a cloud-streaked sunrise over the enfolding green hills that rolled away beyond Bishop's Wood towards St Austell and ran it all over in my mind until I was sure what I had to do.

Then I rang Emma from the telephone box in the village. She sounded as if she wasn't properly awake. But what I said soon roused her into alertness.

'Can you take the day off work and come down to Cornwall?'

'What? Just like that?'

'It's important. Just about as important as it could be.'

'Well, I suppose I could go sick, but—'

'Do it. Believe me, Emma, it's vital you come.'

'All right, then.' Her voice altered. 'I will.'

'There's a train from Paddington at seven forty. Can you be on it?'

'Just about.'

'Buy a single to St Erth. I'll meet you there.'

'St Erth? Why not Truro?'

'You'll understand when you get there. I promise you, Emma, pretty soon you'll understand everything.'

CHAPTER FIFTEEN

'I'm glad you told me,' said Emma, squinting out towards the Atlantic rollers crashing against Chapel Rock. 'I'm glad you felt you could.' We were at Perranporth, late that cool October afternoon, a chill wind whipping in off the sea as we sat on the low perimeter wall between the car park and the promenade and watched the tide sliding in across the sand. The sky was grey and turbulent, but the past was a slate washed clean of secrets. She knew now. And through her knowing I'd made my peace with Nicky. 'Thanks, Chris.' She laid her hand on mine. 'It means a lot to me.'

'It isn't a pretty story,' I reflected, as much to myself as to her. The station car park at St Erth; the muddy rides of Bishop's Wood; the manicured gardens at Penmount Crematorium: we'd visited them all in the last few hours as I'd set out for her the dismal facts of her family's tragedy. 'But you had a right to hear it.' And she'd heard it all. I'd made sure of that. Her father's innocence and my father's guilt were clear between us. There was nothing left to hide. 'Now you know the truth, Emma. What you do with it . . . is up to you.'

'What do you expect me to do?'

'I don't know. You'd probably have grown up the pampered daughter of rich and doting parents but for us Napiers. We cheated you and Nicky, and we helped Tully murder your father. We've got a lot to answer for.'

'None of it was your fault.'

'But I gained by it. Gran was trying to look after the interests of the next generation, however misguidedly. I was part of her excuse.'

'What she did she did for her own reasons. If she was still alive, I'd want to make her suffer. I admit that. Tully too. *Especially* Tully. But they're both dead. It's too late to go looking for revenge. Your father and brother-in-law are guilty of doing away with a man I'd have happily killed myself in the same circumstances. Am I supposed to hate them for that?'

'You could hate them for stealing your inheritance. We're talking about millions of pounds, Emma.'

'Are we? Well, if the life I've led has taught me anything, it's that there are some things more important than money.'

'Even so, it's rightfully yours.'

'But to get it I'd have to persuade the courts to pardon my father. And they're not going to, are they? There's too much for them to untangle. And too much embarrassment waiting for them if they try. Thanks all the same, Chris, but I think I'll pass on that.'

'Maybe there's an easier way.'

'How do you work that out?'

'It came to me while I was waiting for you at St Erth. I mean, it lets everyone off lightly I realize, but . . .'

'What?' She turned to look at me.

'My father's seventy-six years old. He can't live for ever. I imagine I'll inherit rather a lot of money when he dies.'

'So?'

'You'd be welcome to it. Every penny.'

'What?'

'I don't want it. I'm not sure I ever did, really. And now I know I'm not entitled to it, well, why shouldn't you have it?'

'You're crazy.'

'We could have a legal document drawn up, transferring title to any bequest I receive from him to you, if that would set your mind at rest.'

'My mind doesn't need setting at rest.' She stared at me incredulously, almost angrily. 'You say you don't want the money. Well, frankly, I'm pretty hurt that you think I want it either.'

'But it belongs to you.'

'I'll say this just once more, Chris. *I don't want it.*' Her anger softened. She looked back out to sea. 'Do you know something? I've never been to Cornwall before in my life. I've never dared to. I'm glad you forced me into it.'

'It's where you should have been born.'

'That's what Nicky used to say. He promised to bring me down here for a holiday when I left school. To show me all the places he remembered from his childhood. I think he hoped we could move down here together when I was too old for Considine to stop me. But by then . . .' She shrugged. 'We could have stayed with Auntie Ethel at Nanceworthal to start with, I suppose. It might have worked out.'

'You still could,' I ventured. 'She'd be overjoyed to discover—' I was cut off by the gentle pressure of Emma's fingers against my lips.

'Don't say it,' she murmured. 'It's too soon for that.' Her hand fell away.

'You could still come down here. For a holiday. Stay somewhere like this. I'll pay.'

286

'We're back to money again.'

'Only because I have some and you don't. I'd like to show you Cornwall. Like Nicky wanted to, I suppose. It's something I could do – for both of you.'

She looked at me long and thoughtfully before she said, 'It's certainly tempting.'

'It's quiet down here in the autumn. And beautiful too.'

'I *am* owed a week off.'

'Take it, then.'

'When?'

'After the inquest?'

She frowned. 'You're giving evidence at that, aren't you?'

'Yes.'

'Don't say anything about . . . all of this, will you? I mean, even if the idea crossed your mind . . . of bringing it into the open . . . I wouldn't want you to. It's simply not worth it. Besides, no-one would believe you.'

'No,' I concluded ruefully. 'I don't suppose they would.'

'What will you say to your father?'

'Nothing. I don't want to hear his explanations and evasions. He had a chance to tell me the truth himself, but he chose to lie instead. As far as I'm concerned that pretty well finishes it between us.'

Our eyes met and she shrugged apologetically. 'Sorry.'

'Don't be. I'm not.'

'Really?'

'Well, not as sorry as I'd be if you didn't let me treat you to a holiday as soon as the inquest's behind us. What do you say?'

'Maybe,' was what Emma eventually said, halfway back up the A303 to London that evening. I had to settle for a

287

definite 'Yes' to Sunday lunch in Pangbourne the following weekend and the promise that she'd make up her mind about Cornwall by then.

I'd happily have driven her all the way to Battersea, but she insisted on finishing the journey by train. Her reluctance to accept help was easily explicable in psychological terms. She'd been taught from an early age that gifts came with strings attached, strings that could cut as well as bind. But it also lent her an air of mystery I was beginning to find attractive. I'd done what she asked of me out of a sense of obligation to Nicky, and now she asked no more of me. The end of our strangely vicarious relationship was in sight, but I didn't want it to arrive.

As for the truth about her father, entangled as it was with the truth about mine, like her I could see no alternative but to let it lie. Dad would be wondering if I'd honour my pledge to him: *I'm not going to give up.* For the moment, I was content to let him go on wondering. Eventually he'd conclude he'd read me right after all. But one day, I promised myself, he'd have a rude awakening.

All this, of course, assumed I was free to decide what was or wasn't revealed. But that was a dangerous assumption, as Emma pointed out to me after lunch on Sunday, when I took her for a drive and showed her what was left of the workshop.

'You still have no idea who Pauline Lucas is?'

'None.'

'Or what she wants?'

'Not a clue. I thought she was involved with Tully, you see. It didn't make a lot of sense, but nothing else seemed to fit. Now . . . I just don't know.' I grinned perversely. 'I think that's why I need a holiday.'

Emma grinned back at me, but gave no other hint of her intentions until we returned to Harrowcroft. She asked if I'd salvaged anything from the wreckage of the workshop and I pointed to a boxload of tools, some of them still fire-blackened, standing in the garage.

'This is all there was left?' she asked, stooping to take a look.

'All that was serviceable.'

'She did a thorough job, didn't she?'

'I'm afraid so.'

'Then I think you're right.' She straightened up and smiled. 'You *do* need a holiday. How about Cornwall – at the end of the month?'

And so it was settled. She'd take the week of the inquest off and find a small hotel or guest house to stay in somewhere a safe distance from Truro. I'd stay at Tredower House and spend the days with her exploring the Land's End and Lizard areas. It would be her first real break from London in years and it was clear the prospect excited her, try as she might to disguise the fact. It excited me too, for a jumble of reasons I wasn't ready to analyse. Her life in the shadows had left her so unsure of herself that she seemed younger than she really was, innocent and vulnerable, in need – as I saw it – of brotherly protection. Only I wasn't her brother. And I didn't aspire to be. But I didn't want her to walk out of my life either.

It was possible, I was soon to be reminded, that I needed protection more than Emma did. I'd hardly stepped indoors that evening after driving her into Reading to catch her train when the telephone rang and I found myself talking to the woman who seemed to have decided to become my tormentor.

'Pauline Lucas here, Mr Napier. I got your message.'

'What message?'

'The one you left with Frankie at the Zenith Club. I gather you've been looking for me.'

'Does that surprise you?'

'Nothing you do surprises me.'

'What do you want?'

'To meet.'

'That's what you said last time.'

'I mean it. Interested?'

'Do I have a choice?'

'Of course. But if you want to speak to me face-to-face, go to Baker Street tube station at five o'clock tomorrow afternoon. Wait on the westbound platform of the Circle Line. Stand by the fire extinguisher cupboard halfway along.'

'Hold on. Why—'

'If you're not in that exact position at that exact time, you won't see me.' She paused for a second before adding, 'But if you are, you will.' Then she put down the telephone.

Baker Street at the start of a Monday evening rush hour was a crowded warren of stairs and platforms, the convergences of four different Underground lines producing a bewildering tangle of interconnecting passageways. I stood where I'd been told to, watching the trains as they rattled in and out, scanning the jumbled faces of the commuters as they surged on or off and glancing up at the footbridge linking the westbound and eastbound platforms. I waited patiently, knowing Pauline Lucas would keep her word in her own way and wondering what that way would be, aware of the people coming and going around me and the minutes till five o'clock steadily ticking away. I'd arrived early, naturally. But she, just as naturally, hadn't.

A train pulled in just before five and pulled out again, leaving me momentarily alone, though almost immediately more passengers started flooding down the stairs to join me. I looked up at the clock and saw it register the hour. 'Where are you?' I murmured under my breath. I looked further along towards the footbridge and the tunnel mouth beyond and let my gaze track back along the eastbound platform.

And there she was, exactly opposite me, smiling faintly and cocking her head as our eyes met. She was wearing a pale raincoat and looked like any other working woman returning home from the office, except there was no trace of the end-of-day dishevelment most of the commuters around her displayed.

'Hello, Mr Napier,' she said, her voice carrying across the gap between us. 'Nice to see you again.'

'Is this what you meant by face to face?' I complained. On most Underground stations I'd have been looking at a concave wall full of advertisements. Here the platforms faced each other and she could speak to me secure in the knowledge that she was out of my reach. Behind her was a cut-through to the rest of the station. If I tried to cross the bridge to her side, she'd have time to slip away through the crowds to one of the other lines. She could dictate our parting as well as our meeting.

'I'm here, aren't I? You can see me. And I'm listening.' So were several people around us, roused from their *Evening Standard*s by the strangeness of the spectacle. 'Don't you have anything to say to me?'

'I'd like an explanation.'

'Of your family's recent misfortunes? Why should you think you're entitled to one? After all, they were scarcely undeserved, were they?'

'What do you mean by that?'

'You know what I mean. You just can't bring yourself to admit it.'

'Does this have something to do with Nicky?'

'Who's Nicky? A friend of yours?'

291

'He was, yes.'

'Why the past tense?'

'Because he's dead.'

'Really? How did he die?'

'I think you know.'

'Tell me anyway.'

'He killed himself.'

'Did he?' She glanced down the line, hearing, as I could, the approach of an eastbound train. Then she looked across at me again. 'Perhaps you should take better care of your friends, Mr Napier.'

'Who are you?'

But the train arrived before she could answer, even supposing she meant to. The doors hissed open and my view of her became a chaos of milling figures. I dodged back and forth, trying and failing to catch a glimpse of her. Then the train moved out and I saw her again, still standing in the same place.

'How does it feel?' she asked as soon as it was quiet enough to be heard. 'To suffer and yet not to know why?'

'How do you think? I worked hard to make something of my business.'

'Just like your sister worked hard to make something of her marriage. And your parents to make something of their home.' She nodded. 'Oh, I believe you. I wanted each of you to miss what I took away.'

'Why do you hate my family?'

'I don't. Not any more. It's over. You haven't suffered enough, but then you couldn't, could you? That wouldn't be possible without—' To my astonishment, her voice faltered and she looked suddenly distressed. She raised a hand to her forehead. A man standing a few yards away stared at her in evident puzzlement. The calm reasserted itself. 'Don't worry, Mr Napier. I don't propose to turn the villains into victims.' Her voice was back under control.

'This is goodbye. You won't hear from me again.'

'Who are you?' I repeated.

'A friend of a friend, you might say. And in the final analysis not a much better one than you.' With that she turned and headed down the cut-through towards the Metropolitan Line, moving slowly, as if tempting me to follow.

I knew the layout of the station was against me and so did she, but I couldn't just watch her walk away. I started running along the platform, up over the footbridge and down the steps towards the other end of the cut-through. There was no immediate sign of her, though one dark-haired raincoated figure among so many was easy enough to miss. I reached the Metropolitan Line platforms and moved as fast as I could through the crowds to the top of the stairs leading down to the Bakerloo and Jubilee Lines.

And there I stopped, recognizing the futility of what I was doing. I could blunder on in random pursuit, but I stood no realistic chance of catching her. She could have taken any one of half a dozen different routes. It was as if she wanted me to understand her mastery of the situation. And so I did. But still there *was* a chance, however slim. I could guess right, or I could see through the deception. The least likely course was probably the one she'd followed.

Trusting the hunch, I doubled back towards the Circle Line, sighting an eastbound train standing at the platform as I neared the footbridge. I ran towards it, but already the doors had closed and it was pulling out. And there, strap-hanging calmly in the second carriage to pass me, was Pauline Lucas. She smiled as she caught sight of me and raised one hand in ironic farewell.

Then she was past me and gone. The train accelerated away into the tunnel, until only the fading rumble of the engine and the dwindling sparks of static on the track could be heard. Silence descended in the stale air, as vast as it was brief. I stared on into the black mouth of the tunnel. But I saw nothing.

Frankie's story, painfully extracted over three exorbitantly priced mineral waters at the bar of the Zenith Club, was that he had, as promised, asked around about the woman I knew as Pauline Lucas – without success.

'Nobody knew nothing, mate. Or, if they did, they weren't telling.'

'Then how do you account for her knowing about our arrangement?'

'Word must have got back to her. Can't say I'm surprised. She looks like one of the sisterhood.'

'What sisterhood?'

'The high-class hookers who bring their clients here for an appetizer. They don't all patrol King's Cross in fishnet stockings and miniskirts, do they? There's a smarter set for your more discerning customer. We get quite a few of them in. They tend to stick together. Know what I mean?'

'So, you think she's a prostitute?'

'Well, from what I remember of the picture you showed me, she's no nursery schoolteacher.' He grinned. 'Unless that's the day job.'

'Thanks for nothing.'

'No problem. But, here, before you go . . .' He leaned confidentially across the bar in a gust of spearmint. 'Why are you so desperate to find her? When it comes to special services, there's always someone else.' He winked. 'I could give you a personal recommendation.'

Who was she? A friend of a friend, by her own description, which surely had to mean a friend of Nicky. But nobody who'd known him had mentioned anyone who fitted her description. The consensus was that Nicky had

294

had precious few friends of either sex, and Pauline Lucas seemed a singularly unlikely acquaintance for an emotionally insecure librarian in Clacton. But perhaps his CND days held the key. Perhaps they'd met on an Aldermaston march. Hadn't Considine said something about a girl involving him in the campaign in the first place? Yet that would imply she was about the same age as Nicky and me, whereas I'd have put her at a good ten years younger. Whichever way I turned, there was no obvious answer.

Next morning, I was breakfasting late, the dismal prerogative of the unemployed, wondering how or if I could find out about more recent friendships Nicky might have struck up, when a possible method presented itself literally at my door.

I thought it was the postman when I went to answer the bell. Instead I found Neville Considine standing outside in a shabby raincoat, smiling foxily as if relishing the unpleasant surprise his visit represented.

'Good morning, Mr Napier. I've just walked round from Grayson Motors. They told me I might find you here. I gather there's been a fire at your workshop. Most distressing for you, I'm sure.'

'What can I do for you?'

'Could you spare me a few moments of your time?'

'I suppose so. You'd better come in.' I walked back to the kitchen and reluctantly offered him tea, about which I had little choice since a fresh pot was standing conspicuously on the table. He accepted and I was aware of him eyeing me as I poured a cup and handed it to him. I had the impression he knew what I really thought of him, and I could almost believe he knew why I couldn't afford to disclose my opinion. 'What brings you here, Mr Considine?'

'I'm thinking of trading in my car. You remember the Fiat?'

'I remember it.'

'I need something more reliable. It occurred to me, since you're in the trade, so to speak . . .'

'The only car I have for sale is a Bentley Continental. You probably saw it at the showroom.'

'I did, yes. Very classy.'

'But probably out of your price bracket. I doubt I can help you. But maybe you can help me.'

'How so?'

'You once mentioned a girl who you blamed for introducing Nicky to the ban the bomb campaign.'

'Yes. Gillian Hendry. She was a bad influence on him.'

'How old would she be now?'

'Goodness me, Mr Napier, what a question. Let me see.' He drank from his cup with an audible slurp. 'She was a few years younger than Nicholas. Forty, I suppose.'

'No younger than that?'

'Not much. Why?'

'Could this be her?' I took the photograph from the pocket of my jacket, which was hanging behind the door, and handed it to him. He glanced down at it and the glance became a stare. For a fraction of a second, no more, it seemed clear he recognized the woman. But he said nothing. 'Well, could it?'

'No.' He cleared his throat. 'Definitely not.'

'Some other friend of Nicky's, then?'

'I don't think so.' He handed the photograph back and looked straight at me. 'I'm not acquainted with this woman.'

'Are you sure about that?'

'Certainly.' He gulped down some more tea. 'When was the picture taken, might I ask?'

'Why should you want to know, if it's the picture of a total stranger?'

'Oh, mere curiosity.' He dredged up one of his leering grins. 'After all, it's scarcely an everyday snapshot, is it?'

'It was taken quite recently.'

'And have you . . . met the woman?'

'Yes. As a matter of fact, I believe her to have been responsible for the destruction of my workshop.'

'Really? But you . . . don't know her name?'

'Not her real one, no.'

'It's a pity I can't help you.'

'The man she's with is my brother-in-law. The photograph's led to the break-up of his marriage. There's been an attack on my parents' house as well. It seems awfully like a vendetta, which is why it occurred to me there might be a connection with Nicky.'

'If there is, I'm unaware of it. I'm sorry to hear of your family's difficulties, Mr Napier, really I am. And I'm even sorrier to have to add to them, but . . .' He drained his cup and set it down on the table. 'Needs must.'

'Whose needs are those?'

'Mine. They amount to rather more than a new car, I'm afraid. That's why I've called on you. I've never had the pleasure of meeting your father, but I gather he's a man of considerable substance, not to say great wealth. I'm wondering if you might feel able to make certain representations to him on my behalf.'

'What kind of representations?'

'The financial kind.' He took a few steps to the window and gazed out into the garden, slapping one hand thoughtfully against the other behind his back in perfect time with the dripping of the tap in the sink beside him. It seemed he was about to ask me to negotiate a loan of some kind, but the idea was so preposterous I knew something else was coming. He turned and gave me a tight-lipped smile. 'I require a million pounds, Mr Napier.'

'You *what*?'

'One million, to be paid into a specified bank account, of which I'll supply the details. I require ten per cent by the end of this week, as a deposit, so to speak, and the balance within another week. Adequate notice, I think, for your father to liquidate sufficient assets.'

'What the hell are you talking about?'

'Failure to comply will oblige me to notify the authorities of the manner by which Edmund Tully met his death twelve years ago – and the reason for his murder. I have the letters Tully left at his lodgings in Truro in August 1947 and I have, from your brother-in-law, an estimate of where in Bishop's Wood his body's to be found. I also have, as next of kin to Michael Lanyon's widow, a legally sustainable right to the entire estate of the late Joshua Carnoweth. Hence I think you will agree – and be able to persuade your father to agree – that the sum I seek in settlement is . . . entirely reasonable.'

CHAPTER SIXTEEN

The viewing enclosure at Culdrose Royal Navy Air Station was loud with the whirr of helicopters, the noise reverberating even through the closed windows of my father's car. Two days had passed since Neville Considine's delivery of his ultimatum and they looked to have added as many years to Dad's age. He sat in the driving seat, shoulders hunched, face set and brooding, his lower lip protruding in a sign of pent-up anger, his eyes following the take-offs and landings with pointless concentration. I'd broken the news to him by telephone, knowing I'd have to confront him in person before the way ahead became clear. Now, here we were, conferring in secret under the improbable camouflage of helicopter-spotting. Each of us blamed the other for what had happened, so deeply that we would infinitely have preferred not to meet, let alone speak. But Considine had forced us to do both.

'A million pounds,' Dad grumbled. 'My God, he doesn't do things by halves, does he?'

'Depends how you look at it,' I countered. 'A million's roughly half what Michael Lanyon would have inherited from Uncle Joshua.'

'And he seriously expects me to pay him that much?'

'He's certainly serious about what he'll do if you don't. Starting at the inquest.'

'Hell and damnation.' Dad rubbed his forehead and I noticed a scab on his jaw where he'd cut himself shaving. He was having a nerve-wracking time of it and I was surprised by how momentarily sorry I felt for him – even though it was in so many ways richly deserved. 'Why did Trevor do this?'

'You know why. Because he resents being cast adrift, as he sees it, and because divorce is likely to cost him dear. I suppose he saw the secret you and he shared as an asset to be cashed in.'

'But he comes out of it just as badly as I do, for God's sake.'

'Not quite. Besides, I imagine he's pretty confident you'll pay up. In which case, he'll come out of it with whatever cut Considine has promised him.'

'He's a fool to trust a man like that.'

'Well, that's his problem, isn't it? I don't know what kind of deal they've made and I don't care. Frankly, neither should you.'

'They can't prove a damn thing.' His brow furrowed in hopeful thought. 'What do the letters amount to – assuming Considine really does have them? How can Trevor be sure where we buried Tully – when I wouldn't know to within a quarter of a mile? Who's to say this isn't just a try-on – a bloody ramp?'

'No-one. Considine claims he tracked down the address of Tully's landlady from old press reports of the evidence she gave at the trial and paid the present owner of the house to let him search for them. But he could be lying. So could Trevor about how accurately he recalls the burial spot. It could be one gigantic bluff. If that's what you think . . .'

'I could tell Considine to go to hell.'

'Exactly.'

'But then he'd shoot his mouth off at the inquest. And even if he didn't have any real proof, the papers would start digging into it and like as not track down that old fool Vigus and drool over his every word and from there . . .' He shook his head. 'I can't risk it. I simply can't risk it.'

'So you'll pay Considine the million?'

'You think I deserve this, don't you, Chris?' He glared round at me. 'Being made to squirm by some oily little schemer. Well, just remember one thing. Whatever I have to pay Considine you effectively pay him as well. Your mother and I can live off our income quite comfortably, thank you. This will have to come out of capital. And what's left Pam will have first call on.'

'That's fine by me. You can give it to Battersea Dogs' Home as far as I'm concerned. Money started all this off, Dad. Don't you understand? Uncle Joshua's money – and the lengths Gran was prepared to go to in order to be sure of getting it. One lie. Then another. And another and another and another. You could have told me the truth last week – just as recently as that – and I might have been able to forgive you. But you left me to hear it from Trevor. The truth now is that part of me wishes you'd refuse to pay. Then maybe the whole story would come into the open.'

'If that's how you feel, why did you agree to act as Considine's messenger boy?'

'Because it's only how *part* of me feels. The other part fears what the truth would do. To Pam and Tabs. To Mum. And to you, of course. When all's said and done, you *are* my father.'

'Pity you didn't remember that sooner. But for you lifting up every blasted stone to see what was hiding under it . . .'

301

'Considine wouldn't have you dangling on a hook? Is that how you see it? All my fault, is it?'

'In large measure, boy, yes.'

I stared at him, knowing I should feel angrier than I did. But his eagerness to blame me was too pathetic even to be contemptible. It was the thrashing of a drowning man. I sighed. 'What do you want me to do, then?'

'Find out where Trevor's hiding. When I think of everything I've done for him . . .'

'Nobody knows. I told you that. He booked out of the Trumouth Motel last Thursday saying he was going abroad for a holiday – somewhere in the sun, with a friend, by implication female. I asked Pam who and where she thought that meant, but she hadn't a clue, and I couldn't press the point without making her suspicious. Tabs is equally in the dark, likewise the hotel staff: the grapevine has its limits and Trevor's old girlfriends are beyond them.'

'The letters, then. We ought to check Considine's story. If he can trace the address where Tully stayed from old newspapers, so can you.'

'All right. I'll try. But it could be a time-consuming job. And you only have until tomorrow to pay Considine the hundred thousand, otherwise he says his piece to the coroner on Monday.'

'Yes, yes, I know,' Dad snapped. 'Do you think I'm stupid?'

'What I think you are is short of options. Do you want me to tell Considine you accept his terms?'

'Yes. God damn it.' He grasped the steering wheel and slowly straightened his arms, leaning back against the headrest. 'I'll have the down payment transferred to his account by close of business tomorrow. As for the rest, well, once the inquest's out of the way, he has no ready-made audience for his claims and we have some breathing space.'

302

'Not much.'

'Any's better than none. Let him believe I'm caving in. It'll give me a chance to put out some feelers about where Trevor's bolted to, while you find out if the letters really exist and whether Considine's got them. If I can get Trevor back onside, they won't matter so much. And they won't matter at all if they're not in Considine's possession.'

'All right. If that's how you want to play it.'

'You have a better suggestion?'

'I don't have any suggestion at all. Besides, you're not likely to break the habit of a lifetime and listen to my advice.'

'I need your help, Chris.' He tried to make the appeal sound genuine, but he couldn't drain his voice of an inflexion that suggested my help was something he shouldn't have to ask for. 'I can't do all that needs to be done without your mother smelling a rat.'

'It's OK. I'll do most of the running around.' I looked at my watch and opened the door. 'I'll let you know if I turn anything up.'

'Chris—'

'Yes?' I looked round, challenging him to admit his actions were indefensible but knowing him too well to expect he would.

'You have to see it from my point of view. By the time I realized what your grandmother had done, Michael Lanyon was dead and buried. There was nothing I could do to set the record straight without destroying the family. Surely you can understand that.'

'But you have destroyed it, Dad. That's exactly what you've achieved. Love. Trust. Loyalty. Whatever happened to them, eh? We've lived Gran's lie – and Tully's – for thirty-four years: a lie you're still trying to sustain. And now, God help me, I'm doing the same.'

'Because you know it's for the best.'

'No. That's the worst of it. I'm doing it because there's nothing else I *can* do.' I climbed out. 'I'll be in touch,' I added. Then I slammed the door and walked away towards the Stag.

Tully's landlady wasn't a witness who'd stuck in my memories of newspaper reports of the trial. She can't have had much to say and could easily have been overlooked altogether. None of the articles, however thorough, amounted to a transcript. And the papers held at the library in Truro were the Cornish weeklies, which I spent a couple of hours plodding through to no avail that afternoon. The *Western Morning News* had carried daily and hence more detailed reports, but that meant a trip to Plymouth and by then it was too late to travel there and find the library open.

Pam was glad of my company now that Tabitha had gone home, but clearly puzzled by my curiosity over Trevor's whereabouts, given my claim to have lost interest in events at the time of Gran's ninetieth birthday. She was even more puzzled when I quizzed her about the identity of Tully's landlady in August 1947 – and quite unable to help.

An early start the following morning had me installed in Plymouth Public Library shortly after it opened with a dusty back-volume of the *Western Morning News*. Reports of the hearing yielded nothing, but the trial itself received such concentrated coverage that my hopes rose, only to be dashed when I opened the edition for Thursday 23 October 1947 and found a corner of one page missing. The last few paragraphs of the report of the previous day's proceedings at Bodmin Assizes had been torn out. Considine had learned what he wanted – and tried to stop anyone else learning as much. But he'd reckoned without my access to inside information. The paper was sure to have its own archive, to which Don Prideaux could give me access. I hurried round to their offices, only to learn Don was in court all day following a case.

He looked understandably surprised to see me waiting outside when he emerged at the lunch adjournment, but after a couple of pints at my old local, the Abbey, he was willing to scribble a note to get me past the archivist. On condition that I share with him any startling discoveries I made.

'Wouldn't happen to be the summer and autumn of 1947 you're interested in, would it, Chris?'

'How did you guess?'

'Easily. But guessing exactly what you're looking for is another kettle of fish.'

'Hard to say until I find it.'

'I've got to get back soon. Why don't we meet here later? You can tell me all about it then.'

'All right. See you at opening time.'

But by opening time I was back in Truro, our appointment forgotten. Tully's landlady, who'd testified on the third day of the trial about his movements on the night of the murder, was Mabel Berryman. She let an attic room at her home in Kenwyn Road to commercial travellers and the like and was pretty damning about Tully, who'd left – surprise, surprise – without paying his last week's rent. No street number was quoted for her house, but that obviously hadn't stopped Considine.

Nor me. The elderly occupant of the third house I called at in Kenwyn Road could recall Mabel Berryman – 'Dead and gone these twenty years or more' – as well as her exact address. 'Strange, though,' she added, 'you're the second feller in a week to be asking after that party.'

And so the trail ended with her avaricious neighbour, 'young Warren Dobell', who was actually a man close to my own age. He was sufficiently obsessed with a model

305

railway that had overtaken most of the ground floor to regard some floorboard-lifting in the unused attic bedroom as a trifling matter, especially when the person who'd carried it out had handsomely compensated him for the inconvenience. 'Said as Mabel Berryman, her what used to live here, was his aunt and he was looking for some letters his father had sent her from the trenches. He found them too and took them away with him. Why should I mind? Didn't know anybody else wanted them, did I? You family too, are you?'

It wouldn't have made much difference if I had been, of course. Dobell had the price of a substantial track extension and Considine had the letters – as I was obliged to inform my father in a somewhat one-sided telephone conversation later that evening.

'The letters exist and are in his possession.'

'Damn.'

'Have you paid the money into his account?'

'Yes.'

'And is there any news of Trevor?'

'No.'

'So, I tell Considine on Monday that he'll have the balance by next Friday?'

'Yes. Do that.'

Dad hadn't given up hope of wriggling free, even now. Behind his terse response a stubborn refusal to knuckle under was beating a persistent rhythm. But I for one was inclined to abandon the unequal struggle. Considine had us exactly where he wanted us, and nothing seemed likely to change that.

It was a relief, therefore, to leave my father to his own devices and spend the greater part of the weekend with Emma, who travelled down from London on Saturday and booked into a small hotel I'd found for her in

Penzance. I'd paid for the accommodation in advance, but she wouldn't find that out until she came to leave. Meanwhile, I hoped for some carefree days of cliff-top walking and sightseeing to help us both relax. I'd not told her about Considine's bombshell because it didn't seem fair to burden her with yet another difficulty she wasn't responsible for – and also because I was worried how she might react. The architect of her childhood miseries was poised to walk off with what should rightfully have been hers.

Sunday was, as if by special dispensation, a brilliantly clear day. Emma gazed out at the limitless blue of the Atlantic from Land's End and confessed to a form of colour-shock after the man-made drabness of London. I knew what she meant. Cornwall never loses its capacity to pummel the senses into heightened alertness. I saw the effect on her as we drove back across Penwith in the child-like wonder with which she stared at the scenery and the bubbling exuberance of her conversation. 'God, Chris, I think I'd forgotten just what a beautiful world it is. Now I'm here, I don't think I'll ever want to leave.'

We lunched on fresh crab sandwiches by the harbour at Mousehole, then carried on round the bay to Marazion and walked the causeway out to St Michael's Mount.

'Did you ever come here with Nicky?' she asked tentatively.

'Yes. On a class outing during our last term at prep school.'

'Before I was even born. Hey, who'd have thought that one day . . .' She smiled. 'Why don't I feel sadder, Chris?'

'I don't know, but I know he wouldn't want you to.'

That last was undoubtedly true. Nicky would have wanted nothing to hurt his sister and I owed it to him to make sure nothing did – least of all me. I knew the path we were treading was treacherous as well as beguiling.

That's why I was so determined to tread it carefully.

Later, as we made our way back across the causeway to Marazion, the deep blue of full afternoon fading towards the hazy gold of early evening, she said to me, 'I'm glad you haven't mentioned the inquest, Chris. Let's pretend it isn't happening. I'll stroll around Penzance tomorrow thinking how lucky I am, that's all. Then, on Tuesday . . . where will you take me?'

'The Lizard. It's a place like no other. You'll love it.'

'I feel I already do.' She stopped and looked back towards the Mount, its castle walls glowing in the sun, the sea beyond sparkling benignly. Then she turned and stared at me solemnly for a moment.

'What is it?'

'Nothing.' She smiled, leaned up and kissed me, then walked on along the causeway as if nothing had happened. I stood where I was for a few seconds, watching her go. Until I noticed the water lapping at the cobbles around my feet. The tide was rising, as it always does, come sorrow *or* gladness.

'Don't worry, Nicky,' I murmured. Then I called to Emma and started after her.

When I got back to Tredower House that night, the receptionist said Pam was anxious to see me, so I went straight up to the flat.

'Dad's been here,' she announced. 'He came up to visit Margaret Faull. She's not been well, apparently.' Margaret Faull had been Dad's longest-serving secretary at Napier's Department Stores. Yet something in Pam's tone suggested she'd not found the explanation convincing. 'He was hoping to speak to you. It seemed pretty urgent. He hung around for hours waiting for you to come back.'

'Well, here I am.'

'You'd better phone him straight away.'

'OK.' I tried to sound casual as I added, 'I'll call him from my room.' But Pam still looked puzzled when I left.

Though no more so than my mother sounded over the telephone. 'He'll speak to you from the study, dear,' she explained, then hastily went on in a quieter voice, 'Is something the matter between the two of you? He's been fearfully distracted these past few days.'

'Depressed over the break-in, I expect. I'll try and jolly him out of it.'

'I'd be grateful if you could.' There was a click on the line. 'Here he is now,' she said more brightly. 'Goodbye, dear.' Then another click as she hung up.

'Hello, Dad. News?'

'Where the hell have you been?' If there *was* news, it clearly wasn't good. 'I waited all afternoon for you.'

'I was out. Enjoying the fine weather.'

'The *weather*? Good God, boy, do you realize how desperate our situation is?'

'I realize how desperate *yours* is, yes. Now, what's happened?'

'I've traced Trevor.'

'Where is he?'

'Tenerife. Margaret Faull led me to him. She always knew what was going on between the staff better than me. Trevor had an affair with Eileen Bishop, our clothes buyer, back in the late Sixties. Fairly common knowledge, apparently. It may have gone on after we sold the business as well. She was always a flighty one, I do remember. Runs a swimwear boutique now.'

'In Tenerife, presumably.'

'Yes. Which is where Trevor's holed up.'

'Are you sure?'

'Yes. I've spoken to him. Margaret put me on to Eileen Bishop's mother, who lives in Redruth. She gave me the number.'

'What did he say?'

'That he didn't know what the hell I was talking about.'

'Really?' Trevor obviously had more gall than I thought. 'Well, I suppose he would say that.'

'Only because he thinks he can get away with it on a long-distance telephone line. It'll be a different matter face to face.'

'You mean you're going to Tenerife?'

'Of course not. You are.'

'Me?'

'I want you to fly out there as soon as possible after the inquest and explain to Trevor very clearly that unless—'

'I can't go.'

'What?'

'I have to be in Cornwall all this week.'

'Rubbish. I'll cover your expenses, Chris. All you have to do is—'

'I'm not going.' I thought of Emma and the wide-eyed wonderment with which she'd confronted the sights and scenes I'd shown her so far. There was no way in the world I could be induced to deny her – or me – the pleasure of more in the week ahead. 'I'm definitely not going.'

'You have to.'

'It's out of the question.'

'But . . .' He was beginning to splutter. 'But for God's sake, boy, don't you understand . . . how important this is?'

'You go, Dad. You talk him round.'

'How the bloody hell do you expect me to explain a jaunt like that to your mother?'

'Tell her you're still trying to engineer a reconciliation with Pam.'

'She'll never swallow that.'

'Why not? It won't be the first lie you've told her, will it?'

'Listen to me. You have to—'

'I don't have to do anything, Dad. I'll put on a good show for the coroner tomorrow, and I'll tell Considine you're going to cooperate. For the rest . . . you're on your own. Good night.' I put down the telephone and made a point of not answering when it rang a minute or so later. I felt sure the caller would get the message, though. It was time for him to do some of his own dirty work.

The inquest into the death of Nicholas James Lanyon was held in the same courtroom where the Truro magistrates had once considered a murder charge against his father. The coroner's proceedings were a brief and less sensational affair altogether. The friends and relatives of the deceased in the second inquest due that day boosted what would otherwise have been an audience of four: Neville Considine, Ethel Jago, Don Prideaux and me. Considine, moreover, was probably only there because he'd been called as a witness.

I arrived as late as I reasonably could, limiting Don to a muttered, 'Nice of you to turn up,' as I took my seat. Considine caught my eye but said nothing, though his tight little smile spoke volumes. Ethel Jago gave me the meekest of nods, as if uncertain whether I'd even admit to knowing her.

Then the jury was brought in, followed shortly by the coroner, and we were under way at a businesslike pace. The pathologist was the first witness called. He gave a matter-of-fact account of the mechanics of hanging and sounded almost complimentary in describing how successfully – and probably swiftly – Nicky had ended his life. Detective Sergeant Collins then summarized his inquiries, such as they'd been, and managed to make the connection with the conviction and execution for murder of Michael Lanyon sound both inevitable

311

and unremarkable. Nobody, it was already clear, saw any merit in making a meal of this sombre coda to a largely forgotten crime.

I was called next and was encouraged by the coroner's bland style of questioning to follow the same line. I mentioned that I'd known Nicky when we were children without revealing that we'd actually been the closest of friends. As far as it went, my description of his state of mind that last afternoon of his life was accurate. All I'd subsequently discovered – along with the injustice of what had taken place in the same dusty chamber thirty-four years before – went unreferred to and unhinted at.

The only person present who knew just how reticent I was being followed me into the witness box. Neville Considine, resplendent in the same cheap suit he'd worn for Nicky's funeral, portrayed himself as the most considerate of stepfathers, as distressed by Nicky's suicide as he was regrettably unsurprised. He saw it as the climax to several years of depression and reclusiveness in which Nicky's obsession with his father's execution and the shock of his mother's death were exacerbating factors. Listening to Considine, I could almost believe he sincerely missed his stepson. He was cleverer than he seemed, a disarmingly self-aware brain scheming away behind his fray-cuffed humility. I was only just beginning to realize how formidable an enemy he could be – and how right Emma was to fear him.

Considine was the last witness called, although the coroner did read out a letter from Nicky's doctor in Clacton, sketching in a history of depression, before he invited the jury to consider their verdict. Suicide was their rapid conclusion, 'while the balance of his mind was disturbed.' And though the evidence they'd heard was at best selective and at worst distorted, it was

312

the right verdict. The balance of his mind *had been* disturbed.

'Give my regards to your father,' Considine whispered to me as we filed out of the court. 'I'm glad he's been able to accommodate my request. May I look forward to hearing from him again by the end of this week?'

'Yes,' I replied out of the corner of my mouth. 'You may.'

'Excellent. Thank you so much, Mr Napier.'

Then we were out in the dazzling daylight on Back Quay, where the crowds had assembled to jeer Michael Lanyon and Edmund Tully each day of the hearing. But there was no crowd waiting for us. Sergeant Collins nodded to me, then buttonholed the pathologist and walked off with him. Considine mumbled something about having to start for Clacton and quickly walked away towards the car park. I looked round for Ethel Jago, only to find she'd vanished. And realized that the event was over, the book unceremoniously closed on the life and death of Nicky Lanyon.

'That was quicker than I reckoned it would be,' said Don from close behind me. 'Plenty of time for lunch, over which you can clear up a couple of minor mysteries, such as friend Considine's hasty exit and your failure to show up at the Abbey on Friday night. What's going on, Chris? You can tell me.'

Don was none the wiser after an hour and a half with me in the City Inn. He'd worked his way through the same back copies of the *Western Morning News* as me after being stood up at the Abbey, but, not knowing what I was looking for, had come away empty-handed. Nor had the inquest enabled him to pin down his suspicions. But Considine's behaviour – '*I'd have expected him to hang around, hoping I'd buy him lunch'* – added to my circumspect performance in the witness box – *'You sounded as if you were walking a verbal tightrope'* – meant they couldn't be dispelled.

'You're up to something, Chris, and I want to know what it is.'

'I've no idea what you're talking about.'

'Yes you have, so spare me the po-faced denials. All I ask is one favour for an old friend. If this – whatever it is – blows up into a big story one day, give me the jump on it, will you? I could really use a nationwide front-page scoop. You know? Just one – before I hang up my note-book for good.'

'That's years away.'

'And I've waited years to get this close to the real thing.'

'How do you know you are close?'

'Reporter's instinct. It's never let me down yet. Is it a deal?'

'Yes – so long as you don't seriously expect me to deliver.'

Don's instinct was sound. I had to give him that. His liver was an altogether dicier proposition, though. I left him to abuse it some more and made my way back to Lemon Quay, where I'd parked the car. I wondered if I mightn't drive straight down to Penzance and tell Emma what had happened at the inquest instead of waiting until the morning, when I'd arranged to collect her at ten o'clock for our day on the Lizard.

I'd more or less decided to head for Penzance without delay when I caught sight of Ethel Jago walking past the *West Briton* offices. She was moving slowly and had a dejected look about her. Two bulging supermarket carrier bags dragged at her arms. She was making for the bus station, which surprised me, since I would have assumed she'd driven up from Nanceworthal. A bus journey seemed likely to be a tortuous affair. My conscience stricken by not having talked to her earlier, I called out and hurried to catch her up.

'Why, Christian, 'tis you.'

'Haven't you got the Land Rover, Ethel?'

'Failed the MOT. Dennis is working on it now. He'd have come with me else.'

'Would you like a lift back?'

'Don't want to put you out.'

'It's no problem, honestly. Let me take those bags.'

She was too weary to protest much. I loaded her and the shopping into the Stag and we started off. She'd heard about Pam throwing Trevor out and said how sorry she was. I asked her how the farm was doing and she admitted Dennis was finding it harder to cope as he grew older, though she didn't mention the most obvious reason: the lack of a son to help him – and one day succeed him. She asked me about the classic car business and I told her about the fire – without mentioning that it was arson. We were both a little wary of each other, reluctant to venture beyond superficial exchanges of news for fear of where we might stray.

Perhaps that's why we didn't talk about the inquest until we were aboard the King Harry Ferry, waiting for other cars to be loaded behind us as the Fal drifted languidly past the ramp and cloud-dappled sunlight played across the autumn-tinted woodland on the Roseland shore.

'That's the end of it, then,' said Ethel. 'The world's finished with Nicky now, at long last. May he rest in peace.'

'Amen to that.'

'I miss him still, even though I never saw him from one year's end to the next. It's a funny thing. I suppose it's

315

knowing as I'll never see him makes the difference. What with our Tommy gone as well, and Michaela . . .' She shook her head dismally and I resisted the temptation to tell her there and then that one tragedy at least hadn't really happened. Her niece was living and breathing even as we sat there. I knew where she was. I'd talked to her the previous day. We'd laughed and walked together. She was all right. And soon . . . But I said nothing. I was sworn not to, and I was determined not to break that trust. Ethel sighed. 'It makes you wonder, it really does. Poor Nicky. Such a sad and lonely boy. I don't think he ever made another real friend after you, Christian.'

'I'd be sorry to believe that,' I said, as the gates clanged shut behind us and the ferry started moving. 'We all need friends.' Then I remembered Pauline Lucas and her description of herself. '*A friend of a friend.*' Considine's ultimatum had distracted me from the search for her identity. He'd denied knowing her with something less than total conviction. If he'd been lying, for whatever reason, then it was just possible Ethel might be able to point me towards the truth. 'Let me show you something, Ethel. I want you to tell me if you recognize this woman. Perhaps as an acquaintance of Nicky's. It's a bit of a long shot, but take a look anyway.'

I took the photograph out of my pocket and slid it half out of its envelope so that Ethel could see the woman on the bed but not the man about to join her. Ethel squinted down at it, then fished her reading glasses out of her handbag and peered closer. She drew a sharp breath and reached out with her left hand to steady the photograph against the vibration of the ferry. But no vibration could explain the trembling of her fingers as she did so. 'My Lord,' she murmured. 'My dear sweet Lord.'

'What is it? Do you know her?'

'Where'd you get this, Christian?'

316

'Never mind. Do you know who she is?'

'Was this took recent, like?'

'A few weeks ago, but—'

'Then she's alive? She's really and truly alive?'

'Who? Who do you mean?'

'Michaela.' Ethel stared at me. 'It's her.'

'Michaela?'

'Yes. I swear it is.' She looked at the photograph again and I saw tears glistening in her eyes. 'It's Michaela come back to us.'

CHAPTER SEVENTEEN

She must have seen me pull into the hotel forecourt from her room, because a few minutes later she came out, smiling and casually dressed in jeans, her flying jacket and a bright yellow sweater I hadn't seen before. It suited her and I'd probably have said so, if this had been the kind of day it had promised to be. But it wasn't. Not by any stretch of the imagination.

'Hi, Chris,' she said as she climbed into the car. 'Are you OK?'

'Fine.'

'You look . . . pensive.'

'The inquest was a sombre business.'

'Yeh. I read the report in the paper. It can't have been as matter-of-fact as they made it sound.'

'It certainly wasn't.'

'But it's over now.'

'Yes. It is.'

'So, are we going to the Lizard? Maybe some fresh air will cheer us both up.'

'Yes. Let's go.' I gritted out a smile and started driving, east out of Penzance and round Mount's Bay towards

Helston. The more I thought about it, the worse it became. She wasn't Michaela. That was a lie she'd concocted with Considine. They'd been in it together from the outset, even to the extent of planting a childhood photograph of Emma, or whatever her real name was, amongst Nicky's possessions. I'd seen a genuine childhood photograph of Michaela since then, fetched from the attic at Nanceworthal by Ethel Jago to banish my lingering doubts about her identification of her niece. There were nearly thirty years between it and the picture of the woman on the bed, but the face was the same. The face was Michaela's.

Then it had all fallen into place. Emma had impersonated Michaela in order to play on my conscience and so persuade me to ferret out the family secret Considine was using to blackmail my father. Considine had supplied the information she needed to pull it off, confident in his belief that Michaela had been murdered by Brian Jakes. But their plans had gone awry. Michaela wasn't dead. Nicky's suicide must have touched her so deeply that she decided to punish my family for benefiting at his expense. I couldn't really blame her. In one way, I was actually grateful to her. Without the photograph she'd used to wreck Pam's marriage, I'd never have seen through Emma's ploy. Until I was meant to, of course. At some point, not very far down the line, I'd have had to discover the extent of my manipulation. But by then it wouldn't have mattered. She and Considine would have pocketed the million pounds and disappeared.

They only needed a few more days. Just a few days, during which I could go on believing Trevor was Considine's informant and I was the best thing ever to have happened to Michaela Lanyon. By rights, they should have got clean away with it, leaving me to carry the can. I had no proof Emma even existed. I'd done as she'd asked and told no-one about her. When Trevor finally convinced my father he'd had no part in the plot and they came to me as the only other person who could have told Considine about Tully's murder, what was I going to say? How was I going to explain what I'd unwittingly done?

I felt bitter and angry, bewildered by how completely I'd been deceived. If only I'd not been so pitifully eager to believe she was Michaela.

But there was one bleak consolation. It wasn't yet beyond recall. The location of Tully's grave was exposed as a bluff now Trevor was in the clear. That left only the letters. If I could frighten Emma with the threat of turning her over to the police as an extortionist, maybe she'd agree to retrieve them and call it quits. What linked her with Considine I had no way of knowing, but it seemed unlikely to be a bond of trust. Maybe he'd forced her into it. Maybe he had some kind of hold over her I could offer to loosen. He'd recognized Michaela when I'd shown him the photograph. That was obvious now. But he hadn't warned Emma of the danger it meant she was in, otherwise she'd surely never have risked coming to Cornwall for the week. And did she know just how much money he was demanding? It would have been uncharacteristic of Considine to deal fairly with anyone, even his partner in crime.

My mind ran through ways of driving a wedge between them as I headed south-east, through Helston and out along the Coverack road past the satellite dishes of Goonhilly. I recounted what had happened at the inquest as I went, as naturally and methodically as I could, praying she wouldn't notice the flatness in my tone or the hardness behind my sidelong glances at her. I was aiming for the long straight minor road that branches off across Goonhilly Downs towards Cadgwith, reckoning she'd have nowhere and no-one to run to if I stopped some-where along it. The morning was cool and cloudy, with a strangely silvery quality to the light out on the wide Lizard heathland. We were alone, unobserved and unconcealed, our destination travelling with us.

'Where are we going?' she asked, when my account of the inquest dribbled away at last into a silence I couldn't hold at bay.

'It's not far.'

'But where? On the coast?'

'No. Not the coast.'

'There's something wrong, Chris. Why don't you tell me what it is?'

'What could be wrong?'

'I don't know. That's the point.'

'You don't know?' We passed a small conifer planta-tion and I began to slow. 'Oh, I think you do.'

'What is it? You're talking in riddles.'

'Riddles? Am I really?' I slowed to a crawl, pulled up on to the tussocky verge and stopped. When I turned off the engine, there was suddenly only the wind whispering in the gorse, the flat heath to either side, the ribbon of tarmac ahead and behind, the grey sky above us and the narrow space between. 'Solve this one for me, Emma. If you can.' I turned and looked straight at her. 'You remember Pauline Lucas? I showed you her photograph.'

'Yeh. What about her?'

'You didn't recognize her, did you?'

'No. Of course not.'

'That's odd.'

'Why?'

'Because you must have known each other as children.'

She stared at me, blinking rapidly. 'Sorry?'

'You must have done. Your aunt has a photograph of Pauline, you see, taken when she was a child.'

'I don't understand.'

'Neither do I. But like all riddles, there *is* an answer. It's just not very obvious until you find out what it is. But when you do, everything else makes sense.'

'What do you mean?'

'Pauline Lucas is Michaela Lanyon, Emma. That's why she's pursuing a vendetta against my family, and why your little scheme has just gone off the rails.'

Her face froze. There was something startled but also resourceful in her eyes. She said nothing, but I could sense her brain racing to find a solution to the problem I'd sprung on her. What was it to be? A straight denial, or some more serpentine manoeuvre? Would she go on playing her part to the end, or abandon it here and now?

'Considine assured you she was dead, didn't he? Then he invented that oh so plausible version of a life for her and persuaded you to pass it off as the real thing. It couldn't go wrong, could it? Not once you'd convinced me you were Michaela and sworn me to secrecy on the grounds you were still frightened of the man who'd abused you as a child. A neat touch, that. Very neat. Based on the truth, perhaps. Considine doesn't like to waste anything – even the details of his own perversions. Still, nothing for you to worry about. All ancient history. Except that Michaela isn't dead. Which makes your impersonation of her look all the sicker and means – just in case you were considering it – that going on with the pretence is pointless.'

Still she said nothing. She licked her lips and glanced out through the windscreen, then looked back at me, weighing her options carefully, seemingly too pre-occupied with her predicament to show even a hint of shame.

'I know what you've done and so do you. You made me trust you and like you and regard you as a friend. You

322

exploited a dead man and a damaged woman to implement a sordid scam. And what I want to know is: why? Don't tell me it was just for the money. Firstly because you'd have to be a fool to trust Considine to share it with you. Secondly because it would make this whole thing so utterly contemptible. And I'd like to believe – I really would – that your motives weren't totally mercenary.'

'They weren't.' Her gaze fell as she spoke. 'I'm sorry, Chris. God, I'm sorry.' For a moment, I thought she was about to cry.

'It's a bit late to be sorry.'

'Yeh. I know. But—' She looked up at me. 'There's so much you don't understand.'

'What?'

'Here, I'll show you.' She leaned forward, gathered up her handbag from where it had been resting on the floor and settled it in her lap. 'It's all so crazy, really.'

'Does Considine have something on you?' I asked, preparing to sound sympathetic.

'Not exactly.' She unzipped the bag and reached inside. 'More the other way round, actually.' Then she smiled and I saw the gun in her hand, pointing straight at me. She clicked back the trigger. 'You'd better believe this is loaded, Chris. I'll use it if I have to.'

I gaped at the rock-steady muzzle of the gun, wondering for a second if I was dreaming. But when I looked up into her cold hard eyes, I knew I wasn't. 'You wouldn't do it,' I said, feeling less than confident of that.

'Yes I would. I think you know that. I wouldn't have got this far without being prepared to take drastic action if need be.' Her voice had changed. The fragile persona of Michaela Lanyon had been sloughed off like a snake's skin. The steely calculating woman who was holding a gun on me was the real Emma Moresco. 'Put your wallet on the dashboard, then get out and start walking, straight ahead. Leave the keys in the ignition. I'll take the car. We part here, I'm afraid.'

'Hold on—'

'Just do it. No debate. No delay.'

I slowly lifted my wallet out of my pocket and tossed it into the angle of the windscreen. 'Short of cash, Emma?'

'You'll get it back. The car too. I'll leave them in Pangbourne. I just need to slow you down. Long enough to make pursuit useless.'

'I'll find you sooner or later.'

'No you won't. The supermarket job; the high-rise flat; the London phone number: they're all about to vanish. Along with me.'

'What about Considine?'

'Just make sure he has the rest of the money by Friday. He'll destroy the letters on receipt.'

'How can I be sure of that?'

'You can't. But once you've made him a millionaire, he can hardly expose your father as a murderer without exposing himself as an extortionist. What you can be sure of is that he'll use the letters to destroy your family if he isn't paid on time. Now, get out of the car.'

I opened the door and climbed out, an awareness of my own folly growing as fear subsided. I'd chosen this spot to place her at a disadvantage, but suddenly the disadvantage was all mine.

She'd slipped out of her side of the car as I left and was training the gun on me now across the roof. 'Start walking.'

'It doesn't end here, you know.'

'For you and me, it does. Get moving.'

I began to walk away, listening to my footfalls on the tarmac, judging the gap as it stretched behind me. A minute or so passed. Then I heard the familiar note of the Stag engine starting. I swung round to see it complete a bumping U-turn between the verges of the road, then roar off into the distance, back the way we'd come.

I stood where I was for a moment, watching it dwindle from sight, then listening as the sound of its accelerating engine faded away. Finally, there was only a blank horizon and a silent sky. I swore, turned on my heel and strode away.

It was about a mile to the first hamlet. I had enough loose change to phone for a taxi from the call box there, but it took half an hour to arrive and Emma had the best part of a two-hour start by the time I reached Tredower House. I persuaded Pam to pay off the taxi driver, loan me the train fare to Pangbourne and drive me to the station. She was clearly sceptical of my claim to have been the victim of a car thief, since if that was the case I would have been reporting the matter to the police rather than racing to catch the next train home. And she also suspected a connection with the bizarre behaviour of another of her relatives.

'Dad left for Tenerife this morning,' she announced as we sped around the bypass. 'To see Trevor, according to Mum. Do you know anything about it?'

''Fraid not.'

'He's been behaving oddly of late, apparently. I suppose you wouldn't know anything about that, either.'

'You're right. I don't.'

'What are you two up to?'

'Nothing.'

'I don't believe you.'

'For God's sake, Pam, what *could* we be up to?'

'I don't know. But I still don't believe you.'

It was early evening when I arrived in Pangbourne, wondering if Emma really had left the car there. My house keys were on the same ring as the ignition key, so I was going to be in dire straits if she hadn't. But about that at least she'd been as good as her word. The keys were actually hanging in the front door lock, with the Stag stowed neatly in the garage and my wallet lying on the passenger seat. I'd had long enough on the train to plan my next move and it still seemed the best – the only – thing I could do. So, despite the weariness that was beginning to drag at my thoughts, I got the car out and headed for Clacton. Emma would be long gone, wherever I chose to look for her. I knew that. But I also knew how far her ruthlessness had surpassed my expectations. It meant she wasn't the junior partner; she was altogether too self-controlled to be Considine's pawn. Perhaps it was, as she herself had said, more the other way round. If so, Considine was the weak link. And he was going to find it rather more difficult to vanish into thin air.

Drizzle was blurring the amber haloes of the street lamps when I climbed out of the car four hours later and walked along the damp deserted pavement towards 17 Wharfedale Road, Clacton. Considine's windows were in darkness, the curtains open but revealing nothing beyond the neon-splashed back of a dressing table in one of the bedrooms. I pressed the bell and heard it ring inside, but no sound of movement followed. It looked and felt like an empty house. It looked and felt, indeed, as if Neville Considine had done a bunk.

I rang a few more times and tried the knocker, all to no avail. Then I prised open the letter box and peered through, but could only see the vague outline of the staircase. There was no sign of life.

But next door was a different matter. As I stepped back out of the porch, a bedroom window in number nineteen squealed open and a voice carried tetchily down to me. 'Give it a rest for goodness' sake, will you? There's no-one at home.'

'I'm sorry if I disturbed you,' I replied, squinting up at a pyjama-clad shape. 'I'm looking for Neville Considine.'

'So I guessed.'

'It's a matter of considerable urgency.'

'Well, he's gone away.'

'Do you know where – or for how long?'

'For a few days, he said. No idea where. Do you want me to tell him you called?'

'No thanks. That won't be necessary.'

So, Considine too had gone to ground, presumably warned by Emma that I might come looking for him. My hopes of finding a crack in their allegiance were dwindling, along with my hopes of setting eyes on either of them before Friday. I drove down to the seafront and trudged out on to the beach, where the waves were breaking slackly beneath a starless sky. Like the Lanyons in their flight from Truro, I'd come to the end here, where the Essex coast shelved gently into the North Sea. Considine must have guessed there was a secret waiting to be uncovered in the tragic history of the Lanyons, but he'd needed the help of an insider to discover what it was. I was his choice, and he'd gone into partnership with Emma Moresco in order to recruit me. How amply I'd repaid his efforts. Oh yes, I'd done his work well. All too well. My reward was to know the truth at last and to watch others profit from it. There was a kind of justice in it: the harsh and arbitrary kind that had claimed Michael Lanyon. There was almost a rightness about it, but the taste it left in my mouth was bitter. And it was growing more bitter all the time.

*　　*　　*

327

I knew what would happen next. I went home and waited, judging I wouldn't have to wait for long. And I was right. By Thursday, my father was back from Tenerife, looking for answers. He arrived in Pangbourne that afternoon, straight from the airport, and as soon as I opened the door to him, it was clear he was even angrier than I'd expected.

'Trevor didn't tell Considine.'

'I know.'

'Then how the bloody hell did he find out?'

'I told him.'

'*You?*'

'There was a girl. They set me up between them. I don't have any excuses, and I don't think you want to hear any explanations. The fact is . . . I'm responsible.'

'Good God, I can't believe it. Even of you.'

'You're going to have to.'

'How could you be so stupid? A girl. Is that all it took?'

'Say what you like. Nothing's going to change. I was tricked into confiding in somebody who was actually working for Considine. The result's the same. Pay up – or suffer the consequences.'

'A million pounds because you couldn't hold your tongue?'

'If that's how you want to look at it, yes. They don't know where Tully's buried, but they have the letters and the ability to do you a lot of harm. The choice is yours.'

'What kind of choice is that?'

'The kind you face.'

'Thanks to you.'

I shrugged.

'And what guarantee do I have that they'll destroy the letters?'

'None at all.'

'Marvellous. Well, you can kiss goodbye to any kind of an inheritance after this, boy, that's for sure.'

'I already have.'

'You'll get nothing out of me from this moment on.'

'I never expected to.'

'I mean it, Chris. I can overlook a lot. But betraying your own family. It's too much. It's too bloody much.'

'As far as betrayal goes, maybe we're about even now. Either way, I don't need a lecture from you about anything. The door's over there.'

'You ungrateful fool.'

'You've said enough, Dad, and so have I. Just go. Leave me alone.'

'That's exactly what I mean to do. I'll leave you well alone in future. In fact, I'll do my best to pretend you don't even exist.'

'Fine.'

'I don't understand you at all, you know that?'

'You never have.'

'As far as I'm concerned, boy, you can go to hell.'

'Goodbye, Dad.'

After my father left, I did something I hadn't done for more than ten years: I went out and got drunk. You're never cured, only reformed, they say, and that night proved the point. I felt demeaned by my failure to understand whose purposes I'd really been serving over the past few weeks; diminished by the loss of what had turned out only to be a sham of growing affection; above all dejected at the emptiness I was left with. Alcoholism is partly a loss of self-respect. Well, I hadn't so much lost it as had it stolen from me, but the result was the same. I took one drink, knowing I'd take another, and another after that. Then nothing mattered any more. The future was unimportant, the past couldn't touch me and the present was a blur.

I encountered Mark Foster in one of the local pubs. He was keen to discuss his employment prospects, but my condition must have made him rate them pretty poor where Napier Classic Convertibles was concerned. He ended up taking me home and all but putting me to bed.

I woke next day to a steam-hammer hangover and a black cloud of self-disgust. I was horrified by how easily I'd slipped back into using alcohol as a prop and by what the lapse suggested. Was I just a fair-weather abstainer? If so, every day since I'd pulled myself up out of the gutter had been a waste of time and effort.

I couldn't let myself believe that. The possibility was not only appalling but sobering. As soon as a gallon of tea had blunted my hangover, I drove up on to the Lambourn Downs and walked for a mile or so along the Ridgeway into the teeth of a cleansing westerly. That seemed to give me the perspective I needed. However gullible I'd been, however culpable, I'd only make a still bigger fool of myself by giving way to self-pity. It was time to put my house in order.

When I got back to Pangbourne that afternoon, I telephoned my bank and made an appointment to see their loans manager on Monday: I'd need an advance on however much the insurance company ultimately coughed up if I was to get the business back off the ground. Then I went to see Mark and told him the score. He was visibly relieved that I was stirring myself and happy to forget all about my exhibition the previous night.

I planned to devote the weekend to spying out possible new premises and preparing a realistic set of figures to show the bank. The irony didn't escape me that, while I was scraping around for funds, my father had just handed a million pounds over to a stranger. At least, I assumed he had. In the circumstances, I didn't expect him to keep me informed. As to the letters, their destruction was, as Emma had implied, a technicality. A million pounds verifiably paid over would look too much like hush money if it ever came to light for them to risk asking for more. Besides, who needed more than a million? They'd surely be satisfied with that, just as I'd have to be satisfied with whatever the future held for a hard-pressed car restorer on the brink of middle age.

But if I thought drawing a line under the recent past was a decision for me alone to take, I soon had a rude awakening. I'd just got home from a tour of potential workshop sites on Saturday afternoon when the telephone rang. The caller's voice was instantly and bewilderingly familiar.

'You made it back from Cornwall OK, then?'

'Emma?'

'Yeh. Don't put the phone down, Chris.'

'Give me one good reason why I shouldn't.'

'You don't know the whole story. I'm just as much a victim as you are.'

'You said something like that on Tuesday. The second before you pulled a gun on me.'

'I had no choice. I had to get away from you. Otherwise Considine would have . . .'

'Would have what?'

'I can explain now he has the money. And I'd like to. Honestly. I don't want you to hate me. Please listen to me.'

'I'm listening.'

'I can't tell you over the phone. Could I . . . Look, can I come to your house this evening? We have to talk. Please, Chris. Give me one more chance.'

'I can't stop you coming here.'

'But will you hear me out if I do?'

'Maybe.'

'I suppose I'll have to settle for that. Will you be alone?'

'Yes.'

'All right. Look, it could be late. I have to make sure – Well, I'll be there. OK?'

'If you say so.'

'See you later, then. And Chris—'

'Yes?'

'I *am* sorry.'

And so she should have been as it turned out, because the phone call was evidently just a farewell hoax. I waited all evening, with ever decreasing patience, and there was no sign of her. The telephone rang just after midnight, when I was about to give up and go to bed, but, as soon as I answered, the person on the other end rang off.

I didn't know what to make of her failure to show up. Everything else she'd done had served a purpose, however devious. But what purpose could there be in stringing me along now the ransom had been paid? The only way I could find to spite her was not to exhaust myself thinking about it. I couldn't put her out of my mind. Not yet. But at least I could behave as if I had.

By Monday morning, I was thinking more about my pending interview at the bank than Emma Moresco's machinations. I was on the point of setting off, dressed in a suit I judged would look businesslike but not affluent, and was giving my tie a final adjustment in the hall mirror, when the doorbell rang.

My visitor was a stockily built, hard-faced man in a raincoat, dark hair streaked with grey ruffling in the wind above heavy-lidded eyes that gave him a look of boredom mixed with scepticism.

'Mr Napier?'

'Yes, I'm Chris Napier. What can I do for you?'

'Detective Inspector Jordan, Essex CID.' He flourished a warrant card. 'Mind if I have a word?'

'Well, I'm in a bit of a hurry, actually.'

'Won't take long.'

'All right. Step inside.'

'Thanks.' He followed me into the lounge, closing the front door behind him.

'Essex, you say, Inspector? Aren't you rather a long way from home?' Getting no response, I added, 'How can I help you?' Already I was apprehensive. Essex meant only one thing to me: Neville Considine.

'This yours, sir?' Jordan held out one of my business cards for inspection. Since I handed them out by the dozen at classic car shows, it was hardly a collector's item. I nodded in confirmation. 'And you're the proprietor?'

'Yes.'

'Though not of very much at present, I gather. I called at the address shown in Station Road. They said you'd had a fire at your workshop recently. Gutted, apparently.'

'That's right. But I don't quite see—'

'We found your card in the wallet of a man murdered in Essex over the weekend. Wondered if he might have been a client of yours.'

'What's his name?'

'Neville Frederick Considine.' Seeing the startled look of recognition that crossed my face, he went on, 'I take it you did know him, sir?'

'Yes. I did. Though not as a client. What . . . what happened?'

'We're still trying to establish that. Do you know Clacton at all?'

'Slightly.'

'Jaywick?'

'I've . . . been there.'

'Really? It's not exactly on the tourist route.'

'I didn't go as a tourist.'

'As what, then, sir?'

'I used to know someone who lived there. Look, are you—'

'Jaywick's where Mr Considine was found. By the old sea wall, where the chalets fizzle out and the marshes begin. A man out walking his dog came across the body yesterday morning.'

'How long had he been . . . I mean . . .'

'We think he was killed late Saturday night. Where were you on Saturday night, incidentally, sir?'

'Here.'

'Alone?'

'Yes.'

'Nobody who could corroborate that, is there?'

'No. But there wouldn't be. I live alone, Inspector.'

'Quite, sir, yes. Take your point.'

'Where was Considine – I mean, was he killed at Jaywick or dumped there afterwards?'

'Why do you ask, sir?'

'I just can't think of any reason for him to go there.'

'Know him well, then, do you, sir?'

'I wouldn't say so. It's just—'

'We're more or less certain he was killed *in situ*. His car was parked back down the road. If you can call it a road. Since you're familiar with Jaywick you'll know what I mean.'

'I'm not exactly fam—'

'When did you last see Mr Considine, sir?'

'A week ago.'

'In Clacton?'

'No, Truro.'

'What took you both there?'

'An inquest. We were witnesses.'

'Really?'

'Considine's stepson was an old friend of mine. He committed suicide in Truro two months ago. You

334

probably read about the case. It got quite a lot of publicity at the time.'

'Nicky Lanyon.' Jordan snapped his fingers. 'Of course. Son of Michael Lanyon. I didn't know Neville Considine was his stepfather.'

'Well, he was.'

'Really?' Jordan frowned. 'Been to Clacton since the inquest, have you, sir?'

'Yes, as a matter of fact. The day after.'

'To see Mr Considine?'

'Yes, but he'd—'

'Gone away?' Jordan flipped out his notebook and consulted it. 'A neighbour told us a man was hammering at Mr Considine's door in Wharfedale Road late on the night of the twenty-seventh. That you, sir?'

'I wasn't hammering. I simply—'

'It *was* you?'

'Yes.'

'"A matter of considerable urgency." That's what you told the neighbour. You declined to elaborate. Care to do so now?'

'I was . . . hoping to be able to . . . obtain a memento of Nicky.'

'Hardly an urgent errand, surely, sir.'

'I suppose not. That was just a . . . turn of phrase.'

'Not called again since?'

'No. I phoned a couple of times, but . . .' I ventured a smile. 'No luck.'

'Really? The neighbour said Mr Considine came home on Friday. But you didn't catch him in?'

'It seems not.'

'Think of any reason why Mr Considine should be in danger?'

'No.'

'Anyone who might wish him harm?'

'No.'

'Or harbour violent feelings against him?'

'No.'

'Sufficient to beat him about the head with a tyre lever and leave him to die in a ditch?'

'I told you. No, I don't.' Alarm bells were ringing inside my brain, more loudly with every question. 'How . . . do you know it was a tyre lever?'

'Abandoned by the body, sir. The murderer must have dropped it in a panic. You know the kind of tool I mean?'

'Naturally.'

'Being in the car restoration business yourself. Yes, sir, I do see that. No doubt you possess several.'

'Just the one.'

'Not lost in the fire?'

'No. I . . . retrieved quite a few tools . . . from the wreckage.'

'A tyre lever among them?'

'Yes.'

'Where is it now?'

'In the garage.'

'Mind if I take a look at it? Just to check it's still there, I mean.'

'Not at all. Follow me.' We walked slowly out of the house and round to the garage, my thoughts racing ahead as we went. I had no alibi for Saturday night. By setting up a meeting with me, Emma had ensured I wouldn't have. The anonymous late-night phone call could have been her checking I'd waited in. And she'd had access to the garage when dropping the car off. A very ugly fit-up was beginning to take shape. 'Here we are,' I announced, unlocking the garage door. 'I think I can remember where I left it.'

'Let's hope so, sir.'

I swung the door open, switched on the light and

walked down beside the car to the box standing against the wall in the corner. The tools didn't look to have been disturbed, but, even as I began to sort through them, I knew the tyre lever wasn't going to be there. It was in a forensic science laboratory in Essex, bagged and tagged, with Considine's blood and my fingerprints all over it. Emma Moresco had proved herself too clever for both of us.

'Found it, sir?' asked Jordan from the doorway.

'No.' I stood up and turned to face him. 'I'm afraid not.'

CHAPTER EIGHTEEN

He was going to arrest me. That was the thought clamouring loudest for my attention as I looked at the approaching figure of Detective Inspector Jordan. He was going to arrest me on suspicion of murder and, before the day was out, I'd find myself formally charged with beating Neville Considine to death. The murder weapon belonged to me, I couldn't prove where I was on the night in question and I'd been seen behaving suspiciously outside Considine's house. It already sounded like an open and shut case and Jordan was about to close it.

'The tyre lever's not there?' he said, his expression hardening in the silty light cast by the dusty fluorescent tube above us.

'No.'

'Then where is it?'

'I'm not sure.'

'Are you saying you don't have it?'

'No.' My mind was a tangle. What should I do? Tell him the whole story and hope he believed me? Admit nothing and deny everything? Neither course seemed likely to serve me well. Emma Moresco sounded like a figment of my imagination even to me. But I knew she was real, and that my only chance was to do whatever she hadn't anticipated. 'It's here somewhere. I'm not . . . the tidiest of people.'

'There aren't that many places to look.' Jordan glanced around at the cobwebbed corners and I realized he too was struggling to catch up with events. He'd come here to tie up a loose end, not to nail the prime suspect. 'I'm going to have to insist on seeing it, Mr Napier.'

'Of course.' I slapped myself on the temple. 'I remember now. It's in the cupboard.'

'What cupboard?'

'There. Under the bench.' I pointed to the workbench running along most of the rear wall of the garage and the double-doored cupboard beneath it. The front bumper of the Stag was resting a few inches from the door handles. 'I cleaned up some of the tools over the weekend and put them in there. The tyre lever must be among them. I'll back the car up and you can have a look for yourself.'

'OK.' He frowned at me. 'If you're sure that's where it is.'

'I'm positive. Hold on.' I squeezed past him, climbed into the car and started the engine, aware of him watching me and forcing myself to move slowly. Then his attention switched to the cupboard as I eased the car back.

'That'll do,' he called, raising his hand to signal that the gap was sufficient.

But it was also the signal for me to put my foot down hard on the accelerator. The Stag roared backwards out into the lane and, as I swung it round, I heard the rear wing crunch into a parked car. Then I slammed it into drive and took off through the potholes. In the mirror, I saw Jordan run out of the garage and fling himself into the car I'd hit. He was bound to see which way I turned on to the main road. I chose right, towards Reading, narrowly missing a Post Office van in the process. But I didn't have a big enough lead. Jordan would contact the local police on his radio and pretty soon every squad car in Reading would be on the lookout for me. It was going to be a short chase to nowhere. Unless—

I took the first left, checking the mirror to be sure he wasn't yet in sight and slowed to an almost unbearable thirty miles per hour as I followed the quiet residential road round towards its end. There was an access track, as I remembered, leading under the railway line to the sewage farm, and a footpath beyond that across the fields to the river, where it linked with the towpath. I could walk back into Pangbourne by that route without being visible from the road and catch a train at the station, either into London or up to Oxford and from there . . . But it didn't matter where for the moment. I simply had to hold my nerve and get well clear of the area before Jordan and his reinforcements realized I'd abandoned the car.

I parked outside the last house in the road, locked up and casually walked away towards the railway bridge, wondering if at any moment I'd hear Jordan shouting for me to stop. But I heard nothing. He'd fallen for it. As soon as I was out of sight of the houses, I stepped up my pace, bludgeoning my brain to think as I went. Making a run for it as I had would spell certain guilt in the minds of the police. In the space of half an hour, I'd turned myself from a reputable local businessman about to negotiate a bank loan into a fugitive who'd soon be the target of a nationwide manhunt. It was difficult to hold panic at bay. What could I hope to achieve? What in the name of sweet reason could I possibly accomplish by such a mad course of action?

I had no answer, except that I knew who'd really murdered Neville Considine: Emma Moresco. No-one but me would even believe she existed, let alone try to find her. Once I was in police custody, she was free and I was finished. But if I could just stay one step ahead of the law for long enough, I might be able to get the better of her. I was angry as well as frightened. Using me to trick money out of my father was one thing, framing me for the murder of her accomplice quite another. I wanted revenge now as well as justice. I wanted to wipe the smile I could all too easily imagine off her face for good, to finish it between us on my terms rather than hers.

It was a grey and gloomy morning, with a chill edge to the breeze and a threat of rain in the air. I wasn't dressed for riverside strolling and I felt acutely conspicuous. But I knew I wasn't really. The few ramblers and dog-walkers I encountered on the towpath passed me without a second glance. No-one was interested in me, although later, when my name and likeness were flashed up on the local television news, they might think back and realize who I was. But for the moment I had a good chance of putting a lot of miles between me and the places where I was known.

So long as my nerve held, at any rate. When I reached the bridge, where the Whitchurch road crossed the river, I took a long hard look up and down before dashing across and cutting round to the railway station. The mid-morning lull seemed almost too profound to be believed. The first train due was London-bound. But going through Reading, where the search would be at its keenest, seemed even riskier than sitting it out on the platform for an extra ten minutes until I could catch an Oxford train. Those ten minutes millimetred their way by uneventfully, then a train pulled lethargically in, I climbed aboard and put Pangbourne behind me at last.

It was a half-hour run to Oxford, and on the way I began to assemble a plan of action. I reckoned the police probably didn't yet know about Considine's recently acquired wealth. The account he'd wanted the money paid into was at a City of London branch of an international bank; discretion was doubtless their byword. Emma had to have access to the money, since cutting out her partner was the obvious motive for murdering him. So it was presumably a joint account. But she couldn't simply withdraw the whole lot now because the timing, if it ever came to light, would look highly suspicious. If I'd been her, I'd have bided my time and waited for me to be arrested and charged, and the hue and cry to die down generally, before pocketing the loot and disappearing. While I was on the run, she was vulnerable – but only if I could find her, along with some hard evidence of her involvement with Considine. Then maybe the police would listen to me. But where was I to start looking for her? How could I hunt her while others were hunting me?

At Oxford, I walked into the city centre, drew as much as I could against my credit card from a bank, bought a raincoat, a bag, some toiletries and underwear, then went back to the station and caught the next train to Birmingham. The anonymity of a big city was the best refuge I could think of and, with any luck, the transactions in Oxford would have them barking up the wrong tree for a while.

From New Street station I headed out more or less at random and booked into the Holiday Inn under a false name. I lay low in my room for the rest of the day, watching the grey afternoon darken over the city and resisting the powerful temptation to get wrecked on the contents of the minibar. The early evening news on the television didn't mention me *or* Considine, but I knew a full-scale search would nevertheless be in motion.

When it was dark, I went out and watched the rush-hour traffic surging round Paradise Circus, ate a fast-food dinner and walked the streets aimlessly. Every pub I passed sang a siren song, and only the thought that I'd be handing victory to Emma on a plate by drinking myself into oblivion gave me the strength of purpose to walk on by. Eventually, when I was weary enough to sleep, despite all my anxieties, I crept back to the hotel.

Although I hadn't made the national news on television, the national newspapers were a different matter. The bunch I bought from a shop near the hotel well before dawn next morning all carried inside-page reports that the police were seeking 'a Berkshire businessman who they believe might be able to assist them with their inquiries into the brutal murder of a Clacton old-age pensioner over the weekend'. Detective Inspector Jordan of Essex CID was widely quoted in urging 'forty-five-year-old Christian Terence Napier' to 'contact them without further delay'. A couple of the papers also printed a muddy photographic likeness which I recognized as the forty-two-year-old Christian Napier in attendance at his niece's twenty-first birthday party. The family photograph album was the only possible source and it was all too easy to imagine how distressed my mother must have been at having to relinquish it. My father, however, was evidently maintaining a stiff upper lip. At the tail-end of one of the reports, he was quoted in support of Jordan. 'We want our son to contact the police and sort all this out as soon as possible.' I could have done with an expression of confidence in my innocence, but if he'd made one it had been edited out.

My father, of course, was likely to be almost as hard-pressed as I was myself, guarding his tongue and his secrets zealously while coping with my mother's no doubt distraught reaction to events. It wouldn't be long, I reckoned, before he bolted to his customary haven at times of stress: the golf club. Sooner or later, I'd be able to catch him at the nineteenth hole. I made my first foray to a call box around noon. My third, a couple of hours later, was successful; I gave the barman the name of Dad's accountant and was handed over without demur.

'Anton?'

'No, Dad. It's me. Listen, I realize you can't speak freely, but do your best. I'm in one hell of a fix. I didn't kill Considine.'

'I . . . never thought you did.'

'Pity you didn't tell the papers that.'

'I'm in a difficult position myself.'

'Do the police know about the money?'

'Apparently not.'

'And you haven't told them?'

'No.'

'Well, I may have to. You do appreciate that, don't you?'

'I'm not sure I do.'

'The girl killed him, Dad. The one who set me up. For the money, presumably. So, it's hard to see how I can get out of this without revealing that Considine was black-mailing you.'

'You'll have to.'

'I'm trying to tell you that just may not be possible.'

'I'll do everything I can . . . to ensure it is.'

'What do you mean?'

'I took the precaution of employing an intermediary in the transaction. I'm assured that will render it deniable. If you take my meaning.'

'*Deniable?*'

'I'm incurring a heavy financial loss and I feel, in all fair-ness, that should be the full extent of my involvement.'

'You . . . what?'

'In the circumstances, there's nothing more I can say.'

And with that, quietly and conclusively, he put down the telephone.

Desperate situations call for desperate remedies. Standing in the call box with my father's parting words echoing in my mind, I knew I had to act decisively. Skulking around Birmingham, waiting to see whether my luck ran out before my money, wasn't going to achieve anything. I had only one slim hope of nailing Emma Moresco and it was time to take it. I picked up the telephone and started dialling.

'Hi there,' Miv answered.

'It's me. Chris.'

'*Chris?*'

'Sounds like you've seen a newspaper.'

'Yes. And I couldn't believe what I read in it.'

'Then don't. I didn't do it, Miv, believe me.'

'Then why have you gone on the run?'

'Because I'm the only person who knows who really did it, and I have to stay free until I find them.'

'Can't you just tell the police?'

'They wouldn't believe me. But I'm hoping you would – if you heard it. I need your help, Miv. You're the only one I can turn to.'

'What about your family?'

'The police will be watching them. But they may not have found out about you yet. Have you heard from them?'

'No.'

'There you are, then. Besides, why would I turn to my ex-wife in my hour of need – after the things she said about me in the divorce court?'

'Exactly. Why would you?'

'Remember the day you caught sight of me drunk in Shaftesbury Avenue as you rode past in a taxi?'

'I remember.'

'That's the reason. I'm not drunk, but I am in dire straits. I need you to stop the taxi and get out, Miv. Will you do that? Will you give me a chance? It's all I'm asking.'

'You look terrible,' said Miv by way of greeting three hours later. The reflection I could see over her shoulder in the night-blackened window of the buffet at Crewe railway station suggested she was understating the case, but I comforted myself that the worse I looked the less I resembled my photograph in the newspapers. Miv, by radiant contrast, demonstrated the beneficial effects of the outdoor life and a vegan diet, her clear-skinned beauty defying all attempts at camouflage. She was clad in a weird mix of hippy and army surplus, but somehow managed to wear it like a cocktail dress.

'Thanks for coming,' I mumbled, sipping at my coffee. 'I wondered if you'd have second thoughts after I'd rung off.'

'I did.'

'But you still came.'

'You gave me plenty of experience of being stood up when we were married, Chris. I wouldn't want to make anybody feel that way.'

I winced. 'If that's how you feel . . .'

'It is, but I'm here, so you may as well say your piece. Things must be even worse than the newspapers made them sound for you to ask me for help.'

'They're as bad as they can be,' I said, leaning across the table towards her and lowering my voice. 'I've been fitted up by a professional.'

'And would this professional be the woman who posed as my solicitor?'

346

'No. But you could say they're related.'

'So, I'm partly to blame for the trouble you're in. Is that it?'

'Not really. But if believing you are will make you help me . . .'

She sighed. 'What do you want me to do?'

'I want you to phone Essex CID when you get home and tell them I've been in touch. Say I'm short of money because I'm afraid to make any traceable withdrawals from my bank account and have asked you to tide me over. Say you've agreed to meet me tomorrow afternoon at Holyhead ferry terminal to hand over some cash.'

'Holyhead?'

'Invent whatever details you like. Say I'm thinking of slipping over to Ireland or something. It doesn't matter. Just so long as you focus their attention a long way from where I'm going to be.'

'And where's that?'

'Clacton.'

She raised her eyebrows. 'The scene of the crime.'

'Perhaps that'll convince you I'm innocent.'

'Oh, I'm convinced. But are *you*? Convinced I won't tell them the truth, I mean.'

I looked her straight in the eye. 'Yes. I am.'

'How can you be so sure?'

'Because you've always been painfully honest. That's why you left me, if you remember.'

She let slip a reluctant smile. 'What happens if I crack under questioning after you fail to show up in Holyhead?'

'You won't. They'll just think I got cold feet or spotted their surveillance team. They won't blame you. Especially if you lay on the embittered ex-wife routine with a heavy hand.'

'And later – if they find out you were in Clacton?'

'They'll assume it was a deliberate blind. Besides, by then it'll all be over.'

'How do you mean?'

'I only get one chance, Miv. If I blow it, I may as well turn myself in. This is it. Make or break.'

After seeing Miv off on the train back to Llandudno, I caught a cross-country stopper to Nottingham and holed up overnight at a cheap hotel near the station. Next morning, I headed on east to Norwich, then struck south to Colchester and picked up the branch line to Clacton. It was a strange journey, of leaden November skies and empty trains, of edging closer to my destination without seeming to approach it. I was consciously avoiding London and anywhere I was even vaguely known, yet unconsciously I was also delaying the moment when my carefully considered plan took effect. I'd weighed the options and reduced them to this solitary throw of the dice. But the odds were stacked against me. I didn't expect to succeed, yet I knew I couldn't afford to fail.

I was pinning my hopes on Considine's suspicious and secretive nature. I felt sure he'd have foreseen the possibility of Emma moving against him and reckoned *he* might well have planned to move against *her*. Emma's anonymity was her crucial advantage, so logically that was what he should have sought to undermine. If so, somewhere in his house, there ought to be a clue to her identity and whereabouts: an incriminating piece of paper; a tell-tale scrap of clinching evidence. The police might have removed it, of course, in the search for evidence against *me*. But I was willing to bet they were content to await my capture before pursuing the question of a motive. Four days had elapsed since the murder. If they *had* rooted around 17 Wharfedale Road, their rootings should certainly be at an end by now. With any luck, the investigating team would be in Holyhead, staking out the ferry terminal. Leaving the way clear for me to put my fragile theory to the test.

I reached Clacton at the listless outset of a dull Wednesday afternoon, my anxiety heightened by the knowledge that my photograph was bound to have been splashed around more widely here than in Birmingham or Nottingham. I'd bought a soft-brimmed tweed hat that I wouldn't have been seen dead in before leaving Birmingham the previous day and wore it now to make myself less recognizable. But I actually put more faith in the improbability of what I was doing. Nobody would reasonably expect to see me walking the streets of Clacton.

Doing so seemed little short of lunatic to me when I confronted the terraced length of Wharfedale Road in cold blood twenty minutes later and started along it on the even numbers side. A woman with a child in a pushchair bustled out of a gate ahead of me and passed by as if I didn't exist. Then I came abreast of number seventeen. There was no policeman guarding the door, nor any other sign of murder recently done. If Considine had been beaten to death on the premises, it would have been a different story, of course. As it was . . .

I moved on before anyone behind a net-curtained window could start thinking I might be loitering with sinister intent, counting the houses beyond number seventeen as I went. Wharfedale Road ended in a T-junction, where I turned left, crossing over to follow the flanks of the back gardens on Considine's side of the road. Between them and the back gardens of the houses in the next parallel street was a narrow service alley, running straight as an arrow between the rear walls of each. Wooden gates were set in the walls, giving access to the gardens beyond, but no view into them. Still, it was a simple matter to count back to the gate serving number seventeen. Relieved to find the alley empty, save of dented dustbins, cat-gnawed refuse sacks and sicked-up Chinese takeaways, I headed down it.

Reaching Considine's gate, I tried the handle. Predictably, it was locked. After a reassuring glance in both directions, I grasped the top of the gate and pulled myself up far enough to see over. There was no-one visible in neighbouring gardens; I looked to have a clear run. I got some sort of a foothold on the handle and scrambled over.

I'd somehow expected Considine's garden to be a wilderness, but it was actually neat and keenly worked, with a greenhouse, vegetable patch, clipped lawn and recently creosoted shed. This meant I had no choice but to walk straight up the concrete path to the back door and pray nobody saw me from the houses on either side.

So far as I could tell, I made it unobserved. Then the real complications started. The door itself was solidly constructed, which left me a straight choice between the conservatory and the scullery window. I chose the conservatory. I grabbed a broom that was propped against a drainpipe and was about to spear a hole in one of the panes when I noticed that the stay on the other side hadn't been secured. The window was sitting slightly proud of its frame, as if the wood had expanded and it didn't quite fit. Relieved to be able to operate in relative silence, I abandoned the broom, took from my pocket a screwdriver I'd brought along for just such contingencies and prised the window ajar. Then I pulled it fully open with nothing worse than a creak and gingerly clambered in.

The conservatory seemed to be halfway territory between Considine's horticultural punctiliousness and his domestic squalor, a prickly forest of healthily plump cacti flourishing amidst rusting birdcages and rotting deckchairs. I hurried through to the back living-room, where the mildewed roof of the conservatory added a sallow subfusc to the gloom. It was furnished after a fashion, but the chairs and tables were overwhelmed by an obstacle course of cardboard boxes. According to the labels, they contained bulk purchases of baked beans, tomato soup, tinned fruit, ham, tea, soap, salt, sugar and God knows what besides, hoarded as a hedge against inflation or worldwide famine or some arcane calamity of Considine's imagining. I picked my way between them, sighting nothing in the way of cabinets or cupboards where the sort of thing I was looking for could be hidden, emerged into the hall and headed for the front room where he'd entertained me a month before.

The room was as I remembered. There was no immediate sign the police had searched it. A bureau stood in one corner and was an obvious place to start. But first I made for the tea chest in the alcove next to the chimney breast. It was still there and still full of the odds and ends Considine had removed from Nicky's flat. But at least one item was missing: the scrapbook. Had the police taken it? If so, why? If not, what *had* happened to it?

Then I spotted the tortoiseshell frame of the trio of pictures Considine had shown me: of Nicky as a young man; of Freda as a baby; and of Michaela. I lifted it out of the box and held it up to the light.

The photograph of Michaela was different. Gone was the swimsuited teenager who'd matured into Emma Moresco. In her place was the little girl who'd become Pauline Lucas. There she was, in the selfsame shot Ethel Jago had a copy of; where she'd been when the picture stood at her mother's bedside; and where she'd have gone on being – but for the need to deceive me.

I dropped the picture back into the box, crossed to the

bureau and lowered the flap. The contents looked innocent enough: household bills, a stack of seed catalogues, a litter of old envelopes on which Considine seemed to have carried out long division and multiplication exercises and a scatter of paper clips, pencil stubs and rubber bands. The drawer beneath the flap seemed more promising at first glance. There were half a dozen dog-eared notebooks inside, interleaved with scraps of paper. But inspection revealed them to be account books relating to freelance electrical work he'd carried out over the past forty or fifty years, the loose sheets to be notes of the names and addresses of clients. The cupboard below the drawer was no better, crammed as it was with what looked like several decades' worth of *Reader's Digest*.

I tried the glass-fronted cabinets next, checking the china vases and EPNS teapots and varnished ornamental boxes for hidden documents. But there was nothing in any of them.

I went out into the hall, opened the cupboard under the stairs and glanced in at a museum-piece vacuum cleaner lurking amidst a cobwebbed jungle of pipes, cables, meters and junction boxes. There was no prospect of joy there. I closed the door, moved to the foot of the stairs and ran up them two at a time.

The doors of the upper rooms stood open. A bath was visible beyond one, a loo beyond another. The next room I could see into as I reached the landing contained a bed and wardrobe. I turned towards it. As I did so, there was a faint noise to my right that made me freeze in mid-stride.

It was the sharp drawing of human breath, as unmistakable as it was unnerving. For a fraction of a second, I thought I'd misheard. Then my eyes swivelled towards the room at the far end of the landing and I glimpsed a figure sitting on the bed within. The hairs on the back of my neck bristled. There was somebody there, rising now and staring straight at me: a woman, her face cast in shadow by the window behind her.

'You,' she said, almost in a whisper. And I recognized her voice at once.

CHAPTER NINETEEN

She was dressed plainly, in black sweater and jeans. Her dark hair seemed even shorter than I remembered. She was wearing neither jewellery nor make-up and her face looked unnaturally pale. She was frightened. I could tell that by the shallowness of her breathing and the staring wideness of her eyes. She didn't know why I was there or what I might do to her. There was no electrified railway line to keep us apart. She was the one who'd been taken by surprise this time. A man wanted for murder, whom she'd gone some way to ruining, stood between her and the stairs, blocking the doorway of the room she'd chosen to hide in. Potentially, I posed a grave threat. But she wasn't intimidated. She wasn't about to give way. I had the impression that was the last thing she'd ever do.

Not that she need have worried. To her, if to nobody else, I posed no kind of threat at all. Not now I knew who she truly was.

'Hello, Michaela,' I said, as calmly as I could, stepping slowly into the room. 'What are you doing here?'

'Michaela?' she murmured disbelievingly.

'Yes. Michaela Lanyon. Your name, until sixteen years

ago.' I glanced around. The room was small, more of a boxroom than a bedroom. A single window looked out into the street. The furniture comprised a narrow dust-sheeted bed, a cabinet beside it, a rickety-looking desk stationed beneath the window and some empty shelves along one wall. The faded wallpaper sported the replicated ghost of a Mabel Lucie Attwell cherub in pyjamas and slippers, with a halo above her head. I gazed at the image and suddenly understood. 'And your room,' I said, looking at Michaela. 'Until sixteen years ago.'

She stared at me for several long silent seconds, then said, 'How did you find out?'

'Ethel Jago recognized you from the photograph.'

'I didn't think your sister would have the nerve to show it to anyone.'

'And I didn't think your aunt would recognize the woman pictured in it.'

'You ought to have guessed.'

'Maybe I would have done, but for the fact that you're not the only one who's been putting me through the wringer these past few weeks.'

'Why did you kill Considine?'

'I didn't.'

'The police seem to think you did.'

'They're meant to.'

'*Meant to?*' A frown of apparently genuine bafflement crossed her face. 'What are you talking about?'

'I was set up. Framed by somebody who operates even more smoothly than you do.'

'Who?'

'That's a good question. She took me in by claiming to be . . . you.' I saw her start with surprise. 'That's why I'm here. To find out who she really is. If I can.'

'You're mad.'

'I'd have some excuse to be, after everything the two of

355

you have done to me. But, no, I'm as sane as you are. And I'm speaking the absolute truth.'

She shook her head. 'I don't think so.'

'Tell me why you're here, Michaela.'

'I don't have to tell you anything.' She made to move past me, but I put out an arm to block her path. 'Get out of my way,' she said, staring at me coldly.

'Not until you've heard me out. You see, I think I know why you're here. It's because Considine's dead, isn't it? So it's safe to come home at last. To open the door with the key you've kept all these years and walk into the house where you spent your childhood. However much of a childhood that was with Considine for a stepfather.' There was a flicker of shock in her eyes as the remark registered. 'It was him you were running from, wasn't it? Him – and the things he did to you. But running away meant you had to leave Nicky to cope alone – *and* to believe you were dead. You didn't set out to hurt me and my family just because we had what you and Nicky should have had. You did it to ease your conscience for deserting him. Isn't that right?'

'You know nothing about it,' she said grimly.

'What did you think when you heard me moving about downstairs? That I was Considine come back from the dead to torment you? Is that why you were too frightened to make a run for it?' I saw her shudder and glance away. It took a lot to rock her self-control, but even in death Neville Considine could do it. The thought made me feel suddenly and vastly sorry for both his stepchildren. 'Did Nicky know Considine abused you, Michaela? Did your mother? Did she have any idea what kind of man she'd entrusted you to?'

She eyed me narrowly. 'Who told you?' she asked, her voice low and suspicious.

'Emma Moresco. Your impersonator. And who told her? Why, Considine, of course. Who else?'

'That can't be.'

'But it is. And there's more. Ask yourself this. Why would I kill Considine? What possible motive could I have? And if I *had* killed him, why would I come here in broad daylight only a few days later? What kind of sense does it make? Unless Emma Moresco killed him and saddled me with the blame. Unless I'm here because I'm hoping Considine hid some clue to her identity in this house. Unless, in other words, I really am speaking the truth.' I slowly dropped my arm, but she made no move. 'Go downstairs and phone the police if you like. I won't stop you. Or stay and listen to what I have to say.'

'Why should I?'

'Because you're her victim too. If you let her get away with it.'

'How do I know you're not making all this up?'

'You don't. But you know Considine's dead, and somehow I don't think you still believe I killed him. I need your help, Michaela. I need to find Considine's most secret hiding place. I need you to lead me to it.'

'What makes you think I can?'

I risked a rueful smile. 'Desperation.'

A moment passed. Then she took a cautious step back. Her expression softened fractionally.

I looked at her. 'Does that mean you'll help me?'

'It means I'll listen,' she said levelly. 'That's all.'

But that, of course, was all I'd asked.

She heard me out in silence, sitting on the bed, her arms clasped around her, rocking slightly back and forth, while I stood by the window, nervously scanning the street as I described the sinister dance Emma Moresco had led me.

I told her everything, just as I'd told Emma everything, and for the same reason. Only this time I knew the risk I was running. She could refuse to believe me and telephone the police. She could even accept the truth of what I said and still telephone them. Emma, after all, had avenged Nicky more completely than his real sister had dreamed of doing. Why should Michaela side with me against Considine's executioner? Why should she want to help someone she'd earlier tried to ruin? Why should she lift a finger to save a member of my family from injustice after what we'd done to her father?

In the end, when I'd said all I had to say and she knew every one of the discoveries I'd made, it was she who told me why.

Still sitting on the bed, her face averted, she spoke in a strange low voice that was scarcely her own, clogged with a kind of exasperated ferocity. 'I'd have thought I could happily turn my back on you in a situation like this. I ought to hate you now you've admitted Nicky was right all along and your own grandmother faked some of the evidence that hanged our father. I ought to throw you to the wolves and hope your whole family gets torn apart in the process. But I can't do it. I find, of all the supreme ironies' – and here she paused to look over her shoulder at me – 'that I actually feel sorry for you. It seems Nicky didn't choose his friends as badly as I thought.'

'I should have searched out the truth a long time ago, Michaela.'

'Yes, you should. But then I should have done, openly and honestly, what Emma Moresco did so cunningly in my place, shouldn't I? I was just too angry to see it. And frightened as well, I suppose, after all these years of leading another life. The result is that a woman I've never met has made a fool of both of us. But she's also made one crucial mistake.'

358

'Which is?'

'She's been greedy. She embarked on this assuming I was dead and she hasn't allowed herself to be deflected by learning that I'm not. She thinks she can still get away with it. And so she might have done, if she'd been content to split the proceeds with Considine. But she wanted it all. Or maybe Considine left her no option. Either way, she's gone for broke. And it isn't going to work.'

'Why not?'

'Because you're right. Considine was a great one for secrets. He loved to hoard them like trophies. That's why I came here today. To collect . . . his trophies of me.' She bent forward and pulled a leather attaché case out from beneath the bed, where it had been obscured by the dust sheet. It was worn and scuffed with age. The initials N.F.C. were stencilled on the lid. 'He planked out the loft and set it up as a darkroom for his photographic hobby. But photography was just an excuse to keep himself locked away.' She stopped and took a long calming breath, then went on. 'And sometimes me with him.' She swallowed hard. 'I remember the very first time he opened this case and showed me the pictures and magazines he kept in it. I didn't understand. I had no idea. Later . . . there were pictures of me in it as well. They were his guarantee I'd never tell Mum what he did to me. He said she'd think I'd led him on and the pictures would prove it and I was stupid enough to believe him.'

'You don't have to tell me this, Michaela.'

'No, I suppose I don't. But it's why I could never come back before, you see. I was always afraid Considine would die and Mum or Nicky would find this and open it and see me and . . .' She gave a long shuddering sigh. 'So much fear, for so long – and for nothing, now they're all dead. Mum and Nicky . . . and Considine too.'

'You came here for the contents of the case,' I prompted

mildly, anxious for her to reveal what I sensed lay behind her words, but reluctant to disregard the years of suffering they skated over. 'I understand.'

'Yes.' She nodded. 'And it was where it had always been, stowed away in a panelled recess in the loft. Not locked, though.' She frowned at the thought and snapped open the catches. 'Considine must have stopped locking it once he found himself living alone.' Slowly she raised the lid. 'I was worried the police might have taken it away, but it didn't look as though they'd even been up there. I brought it down here to check that it still contained . . . what it used to contain. And it did. But there was something else as well.' She reached into the case, lifted out a buff envelope and handed it up to me, letting the lid fall shut beneath her.

It was a letter, addressed to Considine by hand and recently postmarked. The contents felt thin to the touch – no more than a single folded sheet. 'What is it?' I asked.

'See for yourself. But for that, I'm not sure I'd have listened to you. It answers your question. And raises a few others.'

I squeezed the envelope open, slid out the piece of paper inside and unfolded it. I found myself staring at a birth certificate, or rather a copy of a birth certificate, issued only a few weeks previously by a London registrar, detailing a birth back in February 1947 at an address in Stepney. The father's name was recorded as Edmund Abraham Tully, the mother's as Alice Jane Tully, formerly Graham. The child was female. Her first name was Simone, her second . . . Emma.

Michaela's MG ate up the miles south-west along the A12 through Essex as the grey afternoon faded rapidly to dusk. We said little or nothing to each other, an undeclared truce putting reminiscence and recrimination to one side until the issue of the moment was resolved. There would be a time to face the wrongs we'd done each other and those dear to us, but that time was not now.

It was dark by the time we reached the Dartford Tunnel and early evening, cold, damp and Channel-raw, before we were walking back from a parking place near the Palace Pier in Brighton towards Madeira Place. Alice Graham had lied to me once, but nothing less than the truth would be good enough now.

Yet lies, of course, are only one way to avoid a reckoning. As soon as I saw the closed door and blackened frontage of the Ebb Tide Guest House, I knew she'd resorted to another.

'The birds have flown,' said Michaela, when I rejoined her at the foot of the area steps after several pointless stabs at the doorbell. 'It was to be expected.'

'But flown where?' I snapped.

'Her neighbouring landladies might know,' she replied, countering my exasperation with calm logic. 'She may have had to farm out some guests if it was a sudden departure.'

'Which it probably was,' I said, feeling a touch more optimistic.

'Exactly. Wait down by the pier and I'll see what I can find out.'

I did as I was told, skulking around in the anonymous and sparsely populated shadows of the promenade near the pier entrance for twenty very long minutes until Michaela appeared at the bottom of Madeira Place and waved me over.

'Mrs Beavis at the Rock Pool says Alice Graham went away on a spur-of-the-moment holiday last Sunday. No idea where – or for how long.'

'That figures.'

'I said I was looking for Alice's daughter.'

'And?'

'Mrs Beavis said she hadn't seen her in years. But there's no doubt she exists.'

'I know that.' I sighed. 'Sorry. It's not your fault. The fact is, though, we're not getting anywhere, are we? They've done a bunk. And Emma's probably taken good care to cover their tracks.'

'She's not infallible. And remember she goes by her first name: Simone.'

'You're sure of that, are you?'

'Yes, because I tried it on Mrs Beavis and she bit. She's a hopeless gossip. That's what took me so long. I claimed I'd been to school with Simone, but had lost touch since and was trying to organize a reunion. She kindly supplied the name of the school without realizing it and filled me in on Simone's subsequent history. Not that she knew much, as you'd expect. Simone's a bit of a mystery. But when I asked if she'd ever got married, the answer was yes. And divorced. With a son to show for it. The grandmother dotes on him. Guess what he's called.'

'Haven't a clue. Does it—' I broke off and seemed to see her eyes twinkle in the gloom. 'Edmund,' I murmured.

'That's right. He's eleven or twelve, apparently. Lives with his father.'

'Where?'

'Surrey stockbroker belt.'

'We need to be more precise than that.'

'I know. But Mrs Beavis is a gossip, not an address book.'

'Then an address book's what we've got to lay hands on. I wonder if Alice Graham has taken hers away with her.'

'Hard to say.'

'True. But we're going to have to find out, aren't we?'
'Yes.' Michaela nodded. 'My thoughts exactly.'

Six hours later, we made our move. Michaela kept watch while I went down the narrow steps to the front door of Alice Graham's basement flat armed with a length of scaffolding pipe I'd taken out of a builder's skip further along the seafront. Punching a hole in the glazed panel in the top half of the door seemed to make enough noise to wake the occupants of the local mortuary, never mind the sleeping residents of Madeira Place, but nothing stirred, so I went ahead and reached in to slip the latch, then let myself in. Housebreaking was beginning to agree with me.

Luck was with me, because virtually the first thing I saw by the light of Michaela's torch was a telephone standing on a small table just inside the door. And on a shelf beneath was a padded leather address book. I picked it up and beat a retreat, reckoning I could always come back if the book led us nowhere, but fervently hoping I wouldn't have to.

Nor did I. It took a while to find what we were looking for, because Alice Graham had recorded the information – not surprisingly – under the initial letter of her grandson's surname, Morrison. There was little Edmund, listed with his father, Ian, and stepmother, Sally, at an address in Larchdale Avenue, Weybridge.

There were no fewer than seven successive addresses and telephone numbers listed for Alice's daughter, the first elsewhere in Brighton, then one in Horsham, two in London, one in Paris, one in Amsterdam, and another in London. But all of them had been crossed out and I knew better than to think any of them had the slightest value. She would be long gone from anywhere she'd ever been before. But a blood tie was one link she couldn't break, and there was a good chance it would prove her undoing.

The Paris address, however, stuck in my mind as we drove out of Brighton in the dark and empty second half of the night. I remembered asking, that day we'd met at Battersea Park, if she'd ever been there. And I remembered her answer. '*Paris? Never.*' The lie had come, so slickly and swiftly, just as they always had, I suppose. But now she'd begun to stumble. One lie too many, one risk too great, one step too far. We were going after her, and we were going to find her.

We laid up at a large and anonymous hotel serving Gatwick Airport for the rest of that night and most of the following morning. I tried to sleep without much success, resisted the temptation to call Miv for fear her phone might be tapped by now, watched the television and scanned the newspapers for further word of me – there was none – and tried to formulate a detailed plan of campaign.

In the end, though, we both admitted we'd have to play it by ear. Emma's – or rather Simone's – ex-husband wasn't likely to be in on her schemes, nor disposed to protect her. Somehow, I couldn't imagine him refusing to help us if we could convince him of the urgency of the case. On the other hand, he was an unknown quantity, and I couldn't afford to make even one mistake. If he recognized me or took against us, we were finished before we'd even started.

Reluctantly, therefore, I agreed to leave face-to-face contact to Michaela. We booked out of the hotel, drove up to Weybridge and traced the Morrisons' address to a broad avenue of well-to-do detached houses on the affluent fringe of St George's Hill. Theirs was a large double-fronted, red-brick family residence set far enough back from the road to be well screened by the mature garden in front of it. We parked a little way short of the entrance, watched the golden leaves falling from the kerbside trees and waited for Ian Morrison to return from work. There was a car parked in front of the garage beside the house that looked like it could be his wife's, but there was no sign of her and, even if there had been, we'd ruled out approaching her on her own. Simone wasn't likely to be a happy memory for either her or Ian. The best way to trade on that probability seemed to be to catch them together and exploit any embarrassment the memory engendered. We had no way of knowing how long they'd been married, nor whether Sally had been on the scene before the divorce. To us, they were total strangers; nothing more than names in an address book. But they were a vital part of Simone Graham's past – and Emma Moresco's present.

We didn't have to wait as long as we'd expected, because, well before any schoolchildren started trailing home, a stocky fair-haired man of about forty, wearing a dark suit and overcoat and carrying a briefcase, came striding along the road from the direction of the railway station and turned down the Morrisons' drive. By rights, he shouldn't have been back from the office so early, but nevertheless there he was. Michaela gave him a ten-minute start, then went in.

She came out again a quarter of an hour later, walked casually to the car, climbed in and started away.

'Well?' I asked.

'Nice couple,' she said. 'Pleasant, ordinary people. He came home early to build a bonfire for their fireworks party this evening. It's Guy Fawkes' Night, remember?'

'So it is.'

'Life goes on.'

'For nice, pleasant, ordinary people, you mean?'

'I suppose I do. I hope they have a great time. That'll probably be Edmund now.' As we reached the corner at the end of the road, a boy in ill-fitting school uniform came round it, heading towards the Morrisons' house. He had his father's blond hair, but the slender build of his mother. He reminded me of Nicky and of myself when we were about his age, back in the summer of 1947, when his grandfather murdered an old man in Truro and with him a childhood friendship. 'They don't know, by the way,' Michaela went on. 'About Tully. I tried the name on them but they just looked blank. Simone's always styled herself Graham. Even when she was married.'

'Do they know where she is?'

'No. She's become more and more elusive of late, apparently. No address, no telephone number. *She* contacts *them*. Or they can get in touch through her mother. But I had the impression they'd be in no hurry to. The divorce was a long time ago, reading between the lines, the marriage pretty brief and bruising. Neither of them would say much about Simone, but they exchanged a lot of meaningful glances. She's someone they'd prefer to forget.'

'So would I. If I could.'

'Then you and the Morrisons are in the same boat. Simone exercises her right to visit her son, much as they'd like her not to, every other Sunday. Except she's missed several in a row lately.'

'Too busy stitching me up.'

'Probably. But that won't apply this Sunday, will it? Besides, she's promised Edmund she'll take him to the Tower of London.' Michaela glanced round at me as she waited for a break in the traffic on the main road. 'With Granny.'

'Has she indeed?'

'The Morrisons said they'd ask her to contact me when she called round to pick up the boy. I left my phone number, even though they didn't seem confident she'd ring me. Which is just as well, since I wouldn't be at home to take the call if she did.'

'No.' I nodded my agreement to what she was implying. 'I don't suppose you would.'

'She won't let her son down.' Michaela pulled out and we headed north, some destination evidently fixed in her mind, although the only one in mine lay a short distance behind us. 'And *we* won't let *her* down.'

Michaela drove into London through another fast-falling dusk, explaining as we went that she thought I ought to lie low at her flat until Sunday. How strange it was, I couldn't help thinking, that after all the weeks of searching and hiding, we now found ourselves thrown together as allies. We had our reasons, as we'd had them before, but they weren't enough to hold bemusement at bay. By the end of this, we were going to know each other better than she'd ever intended and I'd ever have dreamed possible. But what form the end would take I had no way of foreseeing. Neither of us would have the final say.

The flat turned out to be an elegantly furnished penthouse in a mansion block near Sloane Square. She must have seen the look of surprise on my face as she showed me in. It was a long way from Emma Moresco's fabricated life in high-rise Battersea.

'It didn't start out so very differently from how you were led to believe,' she said, reading my thoughts, 'but the rest was wishful thinking on Considine's part. He'd have liked me to be a loser in life.'

'Instead of which . . .'

She shrugged. 'I get by.'

'How?' I smiled awkwardly. 'If you don't mind me asking.'

'What if I do?'

'It'll seem a long time till Sunday.'

'I'm sorry, but I don't feel ready to bare my soul to anyone.'

'If you say so.'

'I do.'

'It's strange, though.'

'What?' The look she shot me then was pure Nicky.

'I have the distinct impression you will be. By Sunday.'

I was shooting a line, but I turned out to be right. Soul-baring overstates the case, but certainly by Saturday night Michaela was prepared to tell me more about herself than she'd ever told anyone else. We'd been cooped up in the flat for forty-eight hours by then and the pressure of waiting had taken its toll on both of us. She'd gone out a few times to buy food and had conducted several telephone conversations behind her closed bedroom door, but whatever normality comprised for her had made no other intrusion. I'd paced around and drunk coffee and flicked aimlessly through magazines and stared out broodingly across the London skyline, wondering if we'd get the better of Emma Moresco, enduring as best I could the nerve-stretching excess of physical inactivity and mental turmoil.

I deliberately refrained from asking Michaela anything about her life and ignored the few clues that presented themselves: the arrival in the post of letters addressed to Miss C. A. Forbes; a book collection biased towards furniture, architecture and interior design; an accumulation on her mantelpiece of gilt-edged invitations for Caroline Forbes to attend a swish party here and a select reception there. My guess was that she had some lucrative foothold in the world of design, but I was determined to let her keep as much of her hard-won privacy as she wanted. She'd stopped hating me and I'd ceased to be angry for the harm she'd done me. But what took the place of such feelings – except a shared desire to strike back at the woman who'd outwitted us – was far from clear.

On Saturday night, however, there came a sliver of an answer. We had to decide what we were going to do when we travelled to Weybridge the following morning. Yet the decision depended on the personality of Emma Moresco, somebody neither of us knew anything about beyond her capacity for deception.

'I think she's a little like me,' Michaela admitted.

'How exactly?'

'She's used to pretending. So much so that she pretends even to herself.'

'What does she pretend?'

'That she doesn't need other people.'

'And that's what Caroline Forbes does as well, is it?'

'She has to.'

'Why?'

'Because she always has. Since childhood.'

'When did you decide to run away?'

'Why do you want to know so badly?'

'I don't. But I badly want you to feel you can tell me. We're going to have to trust each other tomorrow, and you know all there is to know about me.'

'So you see it as quid pro quo?'

'I see it as inevitable. Emma Moresco told me the story of your life. But it was a lie. Don't you think you should set the record straight?'

She stood up and stared out of the window, crossing her arms defensively. 'Sometimes it's better not to fill in the blanks.'

'But not always.'

'Always . . . in my experience.'

'That's the thing about experience, though, isn't it?'

She turned around and looked at me. 'What do you mean?'

'It doesn't prepare you for the unexpected.'

There was a silence of several seconds, during which a firework held back from Thursday performed a noiseless starburst behind her, somewhere over Belgravia. Then she said, 'Let's take a walk, Chris.' It was the first time she'd called me by name and the clearest indication I could wish for that her defences were slowly coming down. 'I need some fresh air.'

So it was that I learned the truth about Michaela Lanyon at last, walking along Chelsea Embankment at midnight, with Battersea Park facing us darkly across the Thames. And with the truth came certainty about what I had to do. The reckoning was drawing close as we left the riverside. But I was ready for it.

CHAPTER TWENTY

Sunday morning in Weybridge was still and grey, with those layers of silence only autumn and the sabbath combined can wrap around an English suburb. We parked in a cul-de-sac off Larchdale Avenue, from where the Morrisons' drive was visible across the road, and watched the comings and goings of newspaper delivery boys and smart old men with shabby dogs on leads and polished cars on low-gear errands. The pace was slow and aimless, the locale subdued and eventless. Nothing happened, nor seemed likely to happen. Until, with the stealthy suddenness of a shark's fin, she appeared.

A white Ford Granada drew unshowily to a halt just short of the Morrisons' house. Then, the second after I recognized the passenger as Alice Graham, her daughter – the woman I knew as Emma Moresco – emerged from the driver's side of the car and walked briskly along the pavement. She was dressed in grey suede boots and a black fur-trimmed coat. Her hair was less curly than I remembered and more professionally styled. This was Simone Graham, undisguised.

'Let's go,' I said as soon as she'd turned down the

Morrisons' drive and vanished from sight. Michaela nodded and we climbed from the car.

We moved fast, knowing Simone wouldn't linger, but banking on the mystery of the message Michaela had left with the Morrisons to delay her for several minutes at least. Michaela headed for the driver's side of the Ford, whilst I marched up to the passenger door and made Alice Graham start with surprise by rapping my knuckles on the window. The colour drained from her face as she looked out at me, then she jerked round to see Michaela sliding into the driver's seat. Before she had a chance to react, I opened the rear door and climbed in behind her.

'Good morning, Mrs Graham,' I said quietly. 'Surprised to see me?' She glanced round at me, her eyes darting and anxious. 'You may be even more surprised to learn that my companion is the woman your daughter impersonated: Michaela Lanyon.'

'I don't know what you're talking about,' she said hoarsely.

'You should be denying you have a daughter, far less one who impersonates people, but I'm glad we don't have to waste time on that.'

'Get out of this car.'

'Tell me, are you an accessory *before* or *after* the fact? I mean, did you know she meant to murder Considine?' There was a shocked intake of breath and a sudden frown as she turned to look at me. 'Or didn't you know she'd murdered him at all?' She was frightened now, and of something worse than the trap we'd sprung on her. She was frightened of the truth about her daughter. 'Killing Considine could be regarded as a public service, but, believe me, I don't intend to carry the can for it.'

'Leave me alone.'

'I'd be happy to, if only your daughter had left *me*

alone. But she didn't. She made a fool of me. OK, I can live with that, but being framed for murder is in a different league, isn't it? That amounts to what you might call serious interference in my life.'

'If you're in the slightest doubt on the point, Mrs Graham,' said Michaela, 'let me tell you that what he's saying is the absolute truth. Maybe you thought helping her to cheat the Napiers was all it amounted to, but I'm afraid it went well beyond that.'

'That's why it has to end, here and now,' I resumed. 'She has to be stopped. For her own good, and her son's.'

Alice Graham's voice dropped to a defeated murmur. 'What do you want me to do?'

'We want you to stay here and help me entertain your grandson,' said Michaela. 'While Mr Napier has a chat with your daughter.'

'And to answer one question,' I added.

'It'll have to wait,' Michaela put in urgently. 'Here they come.'

I looked up and saw Simone Graham and beside her little Edmund, clad in jeans, trainers and duffel coat. They were at the top of the Morrisons' drive. As I watched, they turned towards us. Simone's hand stiffened in the act of ruffling her son's hair. She'd seen us. I opened the door, climbed out and slowly walked towards her.

'Who are you?' piped Edmund as I approached.

'A friend of your mother's.'

He looked up anxiously at Simone and she patted his shoulder reassuringly. 'It's all right, Edmund. There's nothing to be afraid of.'

'There's another friend in the car,' I said, smiling at him. 'Why don't you wait with her and Granny, while your mother and I . . . have a word?'

He looked up at Simone again. 'Yes,' she said brightly. 'You do that, Edmund. We won't be long.' But he hesitated, frowning at me suspiciously. 'Go on. I expect Granny has a present for you.'

Reluctantly, but obediently, he trailed past me, Simone watching him go while I watched her. Then I heard the car door open and close behind me.

'What do you want?' Simone demanded, her voice and expression chilling as she returned her attention to me.

'What do you think?'

'Rather more than a word, I imagine.'

'Let's walk a little way.'

'All right.'

We headed along the pavement side by side, past the Morrisons' house and on at a slow matching pace.

'How did you find me?'

'It's a long story.'

'Who's the woman in the car?'

'Michaela.'

'I should have guessed.'

'The real Michaela. Just like you're the real Simone.'

'I underestimated you. I admit that.'

'It's not all you're going to have to admit.'

'I wouldn't be too sure.'

'This isn't Goonhilly Downs. There are plenty of witnesses, your own son among them. Shooting me wouldn't do a lot for your visiting rights.'

'I don't have a gun with me. Respectable members of society don't carry such things on days out with their children.'

'And that's what you are, is it – a respectable member of society?'

'Yes. And I'm willing to prove it, by turning a wanted murderer in to the police.'

'It won't be that easy, I'm afraid.'

'Why not?'

374

'Because it's two against one. Michaela will back me up in every detail – *and* supply me with an alibi for the night of Considine's murder. We can prove who you are. We even have your birth certificate. And frankly I don't think you can rely on your mother to withstand much in the way of interrogation.'

'You can't tie me to the murder.'

'Don't be too sure. So long as the police think I made up your very existence, fine. But they won't now. And the chances are there'll be something of you on Considine's body or in his car or his house – some tiny scrap of forensic evidence you won't be able to explain away.'

'It'll never be enough.'

'I think it will. And I think you do too.'

'No.'

'You're going down, Simone. Can't you feel the ground crumbling beneath your feet?'

'If I do, I'll take your whole family with me – the dead as well as the living.'

'I wouldn't count on it. My father's an expert at damage limitation. He'll wriggle out of anything you allege.'

'The papers will crucify him. And you.'

'Empty words, based on the false assumption that I care about him. I'm not sure I do any more, thanks to you.'

'You're bluffing.'

'No, I'm negotiating. I admit you can give my family a very hard time – a nasty taste of scandal and embarrassment, maybe worse. And I admit there's a lot for me to talk my way out of. But the odds are heavily against you finishing in the clear. Which is why I'm prepared to make you an offer.'

'What kind of offer?'

'A generous one, in the circumstances.'

We took a few paces in silence, our feet squelching faintly on the fallen leaves scattered damply along the pavement. Then she said, 'Go on.'

'You go to the police and admit killing Considine. Plead manslaughter on the grounds that he was black-mailing you with some obscene photographs he took of you as a teenager. He picked you up while you were on an off-season holiday in Clacton with your mother back in the late fifties or early sixties. She'll have to corroborate that, of course. But the stuff they'll find at his house will corroborate quite a lot on its own.'

'And where are these photographs?'

'You burned them immediately after the murder.'

'What about the tyre lever – *your* tyre lever?'

'You stole it from my garage. I'm a friend of yours.'

'Which you'll confirm, of course.'

'Yes.'

'Why did you make a run for it?'

'I panicked when I realized what must have happened. Eventually, I tracked you down and persuaded you to confess.'

'And the money? Pretty odd, surely, for a blackmailer and his victim to have a joint bank account with a million pounds sitting in it.'

'The police have no reason to go looking for hidden bank accounts. Besides, it won't be sitting in it. You're going to instruct the bank to pay the whole lot back to my father.'

'Am I really?' She glanced round at me.

'I'm afraid so.'

'Surely the police will smell a rat. Especially when they realize my "friend" and I were independently acquainted with Considine. It's too much of a coincidence.'

'It's no coincidence at all. We met at his house. I was there to talk about Nicky. You were there to plead for the return of the photographs. We got together afterwards and you told me he was blackmailing you.'

'What about the letters? I've still got them, you know.'

'Do what you like with them. They don't matter now.'

'I see you've worked this all out very carefully.'

'It's your least worst option. I suggest you take it.'

'Why should I? What's in it for me?'

'A much shorter sentence than you'll get if the police learn the truth – as I'll make sure they do if I have to. Take your pick.'

We'd reached a T-junction at the end of Larchdale Avenue. Crossing to the other side of the road, we slowly started back the way we'd come.

'So, what's your answer?'

'First tell me how you found me.'

'Considine had obtained a copy of your birth certificate. It was hidden at his house. Michaela knew where to look.'

'She would, of course.'

'Yes. You should have quit while you were ahead, Simone, you really should. Going through with the murder and the frame-up after you knew Michaela was alive was plain foolhardy.'

'I had no choice. Considine would have tried to cheat me out of my share if I'd let him live. He didn't squirrel away a copy of my birth certificate out of genealogical curiosity. He was preparing some devious move against me, you can be certain.'

'But probably nothing quite so drastic as murder.'

'He deserved to die. You know that. So does Michaela, I imagine. I had no qualms about doing it.'

'I never thought you had.'

'Besides, sparing him would have let you off the hook. I didn't go into this just for the money.'

'Why, then?'

'To find out what happened to my father. I never met him. Not once. My mother said he'd deserted her while she was carrying me and vanished without trace. She never told me about the murder, or his relatives in Yorkshire. She kept the whole thing a closely guarded secret. I was out of the country when he called on her after getting out of prison, so she was able to keep that from me as well.'

'When did you find out?'

'Not until his name was splashed all over the papers after Nicky Lanyon's suicide. She had no choice then but to tell me. And as soon as I heard where he'd been going the last time she saw him, I knew you Napiers had done for him somehow.'

'And you chose me as your means of getting at the truth.'

'No. That's down to Considine. I went to him because I realized that, if I was right about my father's reasons for going back to Truro, then he had a financial incentive to help me. Impersonating his supposedly dead step-daughter in order to play on your conscience was his idea. We weren't likely to get far without access to your family's secrets.'

'And who better than a family member to give you that access?'

'Exactly. You were the weak link, Chris – Nicky's childhood friend. It made you the obvious choice.'

'And the ideal candidate for a murder charge.'

'That meant you all suffered. Your parents, sister and brother-in-law would be tainted by association. You'd all be given a taste of your own medicine.'

'But your father *was* a murderer, Simone. He wasn't framed. Why was he worth avenging?'

'Because he deserved better than to be driven to blackmail when he came home from the war. He needed help and compassion, not rejection. You made him a murderer, and then you let him rot in prison for twenty-two years before you finished him off.'

'I won't argue with you. I don't accept your portrayal of Edmund Tully. It sounds like an idealized vision of a father you never had the misfortune to meet. But if you want to hang on to a fantasy, fine. I don't think it has much to do with your motives, anyway. I think they're all about money. That's why you took the risk of killing Considine. So you could have it all.'

'And why shouldn't I? The risk would have paid off, but for you giving the police the slip and throwing in your lot with somebody Considine had assured me was dead. I admit, the very first time you told me about Pauline Lucas, I had a nasty feeling she'd turn out to be Michaela. But I was already in too deep by then to pull out. Besides, it didn't really seem possible. I mean, where's she been all these years?'

'None of your business. It's instructive, though – how much more effectively she covered her tracks than you did.'

'What do you mean?'

'She's shunned every form of personal entanglement. That's the key to it, Simone: isolation. But you have a mother, an ex-husband and a son. And you're in touch with all of them. Too many connections to conceal. Altogether too many.'

'So, my downfall is having a son I care about?'

'In a sense. Without him, you could have stayed one jump ahead. But coming here today to pick him up as usual . . .'

'Was asking for trouble.' She sighed and glanced ahead at the car. 'That's the thing with children, Chris. They're hard to let go of. He was looking forward to our day out. And you know what? So was I.' She stopped, as if reluctant to reach the point, not far off, where the occupants of the car would become clearly visible: the expressions on their faces; the looks in their eyes. 'I thought, with the sort of things a million pounds could buy, I might be able to establish my credentials as a mother once and for all.'

'Why have they been in doubt?'

'Because of a criminal record, if you must know. There are some previous convictions that might come back to haunt me in court.'

'Convictions for what?'

'Drug trafficking. And one or two other things. This isn't the first time I've tried to make a million. Or failed.'

'There's nothing I can do about that.'

'There's nothing *anyone* can do.'

'What's your answer, Simone? Time's nearly up.'

'My answer?' She looked round at me, a cynical self-mocking smile playing at the corners of her mouth. 'Oh, I think you've known what that would be all along, haven't you, Chris? Before you even posed the question.'

CHAPTER TWENTY-ONE

And so the deal was done – a deal I've had cause to regret since. Not that I can think, even now, of a better way to have played the cards I held at the time. The lies I was obliged to tell at Simone Graham's trial for murder eleven months later seemed worth telling to avoid the public exposure of some older and much darker lies. Simone herself played her part so well I sometimes believed her imaginary teenage encounter with Neville Considine had actually taken place. She had the advantage, of course, of being able to describe the Considine-Lanyon household as it must have been twenty years previously with uncanny accuracy. A stockpile of hard-core pornography found in the garden shed at 17 Wharfedale Road and the evidence of assorted neighbours left nobody mourning for her victim. For all that, she was convicted of murder and given a mandatory life sentence. But there were so many mitigating factors that according to her solicitor – who seemed to think I'd want to know – she wasn't likely to spend much more than five or six years in prison.

Alice Graham told me quite a lot about her daughter before and during the trial – including the answer to the question I'd tried to put to her at Weybridge. Alice's biggest regret was that she'd not told Simone the truth about Edmund Tully from the outset. Then she'd never have been able to develop such a romanticized view of him. No doubt the lack of a father explained, at least in part, her wild and ruthless nature. Marriage to Ian Morrison and the responsibilities of motherhood had only sharpened her appetite for glamour and excess. When her marriage had foundered and her unstable lifestyle had cost her custody of her son, she'd renewed the criminal contacts she'd originally made in the Brighton drugs scene and gone in pursuit of quick riches the illegal way. But in her case crime hadn't paid.

Not, at any rate, until her imprisonment for murder. The trial had received more and more publicity as it went on and the verdict released a deluge of sympathy for a woman portrayed in the media as a kind of heroine of our times, who'd survived sexual abuse as an adolescent and refused to give in to blackmail as an adult, only to be victimized all over again by the law. What sort of a crime was it, editorials pondered, for her to turn at last on the man who'd persecuted her? What sort of a country was it, feminist pressure groups demanded to know, where such an act was even regarded as a crime? Questions were asked in Parliament. Bishops were quizzed about it on television. Everyone had an opinion. Except those who knew the truth. We stayed silent, for our own very good reasons, while the world turned Simone Graham of the winsomely photogenic smile into a poignant symbol of social ills and legal wrongs. Don Prideaux was just about the only journalist in the country who didn't swallow it whole. Not that even he was able to work out what had really happened. He went on hoping for his nationwide front-page scoop. But he hoped in vain.

By the time Simone's appeal came round, a full-scale campaign for her acquittal was under way. When it failed to sway the judges, those dedicated to the cause resorted to demands for her early release. At first they seemed to fall on deaf ears, but I had little doubt the authorities would give way in the end. It was in fact a year short of her solicitor's most optimistic estimate that Simone was set free. Within weeks, she'd sold her story to a Sunday newspaper for an undisclosed sum, but strangely she didn't offer me a share of the fee, despite my creative role in the fiction of her past. She managed to write me out of the picture almost completely – for which I was duly grateful.

I never forgot about her, of course, but she gradually slipped to the back of my mind as her name faded from the headlines. Once she was free and everything her supporters had worked for had been achieved, she was forgotten with surprising speed. The years passed and I heard no more of her.

During those years, the real Michaela, not the false one, dominated my thoughts, for reasons I found at first disarmingly unexpected and later fulfillingly obvious. It took time and a lot of effort to lure her out of her secure anonymity, to reunite her with the Jagos and her own true identity. I told myself my devotion to the task was attributable to guilt for abandoning Nicky, but eventually I faced the fact that I was falling in love with her. And around about the same time I discovered, to my astonished delight, that *she* was falling in love with *me*.

I remained the only person she'd ever trusted with the truth about her flight from Clacton as a seventeen-year-old schoolgirl and her subsequent triumph over a succession of miseries and misfortunes to become Caroline Forbes, an interior designer in her mid-thirties, with a considerable reputation and an expanding clientele among the chic and affluent of London. The shared secret of her past became a bond between us that time seemed to strengthen. By a series of unpremeditated transitions, we became first friends, then lovers, then husband and wife. And only later did we wonder why it had taken so long.

Marrying Michaela raised a barrier between me and my family that I'd have regretted more if I'd loved her less. Pam had divorced Trevor by then and sailed happily into a second marriage, to the owner of a flourishing boat-building business in Falmouth. But she still held Michaela partly to blame – as she undoubtedly was – for her breach with Trevor and simply couldn't come to terms with her as a sister-in-law. My mother shared Pam's uncomprehending disapproval, though I think we'd have won her over if she'd lived to see the birth of her grandson. What view Trevor took of the matter I never found out. He didn't stay long in Tenerife, or anywhere else over the next few years. According to Tabitha, the only member of the family who didn't turn her back on me, he manages some kind of country club in Kenya these days. She and Dominic took Trevor's grandchildren out to see him recently and returned with the unsurprising news that the climate doesn't agree with his drinking habits. Tabitha seemed worried about him, though not perhaps as worried as she should be.

Some part of me would have relished my father's reaction to acquiring a Lanyon for a daughter-in-law, but he died while we were still nurturing our relationship in secret, succumbing to a massive stroke halfway through a round of golf. He'd never brought himself to thank me for retrieving the money he'd paid Considine, but turned out to have expressed his gratitude by refraining from disinheriting me. I became a wealthy man under the terms of his will and an even wealthier one when, shortly afterwards, Pam sold Tredower House, enabling me to capitalize the stake in the hotel Gran had bequeathed to me. I tried to insist on handing the whole lot over to Michaela, only to encounter her steadfast refusal to accept a penny of it. But her refusal counted for nothing in the end. What was mine and should have been hers became ours instead. And our son's of course. He was born in the second year of our marriage, a few months after my mother's death. We christened him Nicholas Joshua, and soon found ourselves calling him Nicky.

We bought an old farmhouse shortly after we got married, up on the dip slope of the Chilterns near Nettlebed, and live there still, leading a happy and contented family life – something neither of us ever expected to have and relish all the more as a result. Michaela gave up her interior design work when Nicky was born, but I've kept the car restoration business going, pursuing it now more as a hobby than from any kind of financial necessity. The farm came with enough well-spaced barns and outhouses for me to start dreaming of establishing a classic car museum to run alongside the workshop, though God knows why I'd want to share the peace and quiet I enjoy there with coachloads of visitors. Maybe it'll remain a dream. That's what Miv seemed to recommend when she descended from her Snowdonian fastness recently to check up on her ex-husband's welfare.

'I suppose, after all those years of falling flat on your face, you had to land on your feet eventually, sweetie. You've got it made here. Lovely wife and son, beautiful surroundings. I wouldn't change a thing, if I were you.'

But change isn't always voluntary, or even avoidable. Our life – Michaela's and mine – is everything we could want it to be. Yet part of its perfection is the awareness we share of its fragility. I made a deal with Simone Graham, but I could never have said for certain that would be the end of it. I hoped and I prayed, but I knew hope and prayer wouldn't necessarily be enough. Not in the long run. And I was right. Which is why what happened yesterday morning wasn't entirely unexpected. This, after all, *is* the long run.

We rent a small chalet in the Swiss Alps, near Montreux, where we ski in winter and walk the mountain meadows in summer. Nicky's school had just broken up for Easter and we'd decided to slip away to Switzerland for the duration of his holidays. The weather was fine and I was planning to drive the Stag down through France, taking in the annual *Avant-Hier Mobile* show at Reims on the way, while Michaela and Nicky flew out to Geneva and went on by train to Montreux. I was in the workshop, putting the car in order for its long run, when the telephone rang – and went on ringing. Michaela had gone into Reading with Nicky to buy him some new shoes. I had the place to myself and little inclination to answer, but the caller was persistent, so eventually I relented.

'Hello,' I said, on picking up the phone. And in the strange suspended second before the caller spoke, I knew whose voice I was going to hear.

'Chris, I'm sure you know who this is. We have to meet.'

'Why?' I asked after a lengthy pause for unavailing thought.

'I'll explain when we do.'

'Explain now.'

'No. Truro, tomorrow afternoon, at the cemetery where your great-uncle's buried. Meet me by his grave at four o'clock. And come alone.'

'Look, Simone, whatever you have to say can—'

'Just be there. Or suffer the consequences.' Then the line went dead.

I stared into the dust-moted sunlight shafting through the workshop door. I could guess what she wanted. I'd had long enough to anticipate her demand. But still I couldn't guess what my answer would be.

I said nothing to Michaela about the call. I felt sure she'd refuse to let me go alone if I did, but this was a problem of my making and I wanted her and Nicky a long way away when I tried to solve it, fully *and* finally. Simone's timing had given me the chance to ensure that was the case and it was a chance I wasn't about to pass up.

I drove Michaela and Nicky to Heathrow early this morning, letting them believe I'd be heading for Dover as soon as I'd seen them off. But my destination lay west, not south. A long fast run down the well-remembered road through Wessex got me to Cornwall by midday. I reached Truro in the early afternoon, booked into the Tredower House Hotel for the night and set off for the cemetery on foot, in ample time for my appointment. I still didn't know what to do. But soon the past and the present would meet – to become the future. And then I would know.

TOMORROW

I woke early this morning, while dawn was still only a faint grizzling of the night. For a fraction of a second, I thought Michaela was lying asleep beside me. Then I remembered where I was – and why. The needs of the present rushed into my mind before the past could throw off the last trappings of a dream. I was alert and fully awake – and as ready for the day ahead as I would ever be.

I left Tredower House in strengthening grey light as rabbits preened and nibbled on the lawn and a squirrel leapt from branch to branch of the horse chestnut tree. The air was cool and vernally new, the city as serene and empty as a closed museum. Unconscious almost of what I was doing, I retraced the route I walked with Uncle Joshua that last afternoon of his life nearly fifty years ago, down the hill and round by Old Bridge Street to the cathedral, where we parted.

But this morning there was to be no parting. I followed his unseen fast-striding figure along Cathedral Lane, across Boscawen Street and up the broadly curving slope of Lemon Street towards the beckoning dawn-blurred finger of the Lander Monument.

And now, as I near the top of the hill, I see I'm not the only one to have woken early and found their footsteps leading in this direction. A figure appears from the far side of the monument as I approach. Our eyes meet, and in the instant of mutual recognition I feel suddenly and immensely relieved. There's no need to wait until this afternoon. She can have her answer here and now.

I thought it all through last night. I didn't hurry. I didn't ignore any of the ramifications of what it meant. I let the certainty grow on me in the encroaching darkness until I was sure beyond question. To drag it all into the open now, to exhume so much more than a long-buried body in Bishop's Wood, carries more risks for Simone than me. We're both guilty of perjury, but she stands to forfeit her parole on a life sentence for murder, whereas Edmund Tully's murderer is out of her reach as well as the law's. Her advantage – her incentive – is her determination to get the better of me. Yet anything less than total victory will taste like defeat to her. She wants the money. Of course she does. But she wants the pleasure of extracting it from me even more. She wants to win where Edmund Tully lost.

And I'd let her, I really think I would, but for the fact that it isn't me who'd be giving it up. The money is only technically mine. Morally it's Michaela's. And Uncle Joshua's, of course. He hewed it out of the Alaskan wilderness ninety years ago and died for the considerable satisfaction of denying a blackmailer so much as a penny of it. As I grow older, I feel closer to him – and ever more reluctant to let him down.

In the final analysis, however, the choice wasn't mine to make. The decision, like the money, was Michaela's. I telephoned her at the chalet as soon as I judged it late enough for Nicky to be asleep in bed – and broke the news. At first she was angry with me for holding out on her. But her anger didn't last long. She knew who I'd been trying to protect, and she knew, as I did, that there was only one way to do it.

'What are you doing here?' Simone demands as we confront each other from adjacent corners of the plinth at the foot of the monument. She seems almost to resent my presence – to regard me as an intruder on her property. 'Trouble sleeping?'

'Trouble *waiting*.'

'Then don't wait any longer. Accept my offer now and we needn't meet this afternoon – or ever again.'

'If only I could believe that.'

'You can.'

'No. If I pay up this time, there'll be another time, and another after that. You'll always come back for more. You can't help yourself.'

She smiles, as if I've paid her a compliment. 'You'll just have to take that risk.'

'I'm afraid I'm not prepared to. You're right. We needn't meet this afternoon – or ever again. But only because I'm not going to let you blackmail me. Now – or in the future.'

'What are you saying?'

'I'm saying it's no deal. You're not going to get half a million pounds from me. You're not going to get the loose change from my pocket.'

'You refuse?'

'Absolutely and irrevocably.'

She stares at me disbelievingly. 'You don't mean that.'

'I do.'

'I can bring your cosy world crashing down around your head. Have you forgotten that?'

'No.'

'Then you *must* accept.'

'But I choose not to. You see, I think you're bluffing. You can hurt me, it's true, but only by crippling yourself in the process. And you're too sensible to throw away what you've got.'

'What have I got?'

'Freedom. At a price.'

She moves closer. Her gaze narrows. 'You're wrong. I'll go through with it. And I'll drag you down with me. It'll be worth it. For the money. For the thrill of seeing whether I can get away with it. And for the satisfaction of seeing my father properly buried.'

'You'll never achieve that.'

'Won't I? Trevor Rutherford could show the police where to dig. And I reckon he'll be forced to when I've said my piece.'

'It won't make any difference.' I pause, debating even now whether to tell her what her mother never has. Then the cold hard glint in her eye closes the debate. 'Edmund Tully wasn't your father.'

'What?'

'He was just a name for your mother to put on your birth certificate. He was her husband, but your father in law only. It's why he left her after coming home from the war. Because she was carrying another man's child.'

'You're lying.'

'She told me so herself. Ask her if you don't believe me.'

'You know I can't do that.' A spasm of something between grief and hatred crosses her face. 'My mother died three months ago.'

'Did she?' I ask, genuinely surprised. 'I'm sorry. I hadn't heard.'

'You must have.'

'No. But it explains why you waited till now, of course.

She perjured herself on your account, just as I did. But I'm fair game, whereas she—'

'It *explains* why you think you're free to lie to me.' Her face is flushed with anger, her voice quivering. '*That's all.*'

'I'm not lying, Simone. Your mother told me the truth, in strictest confidence. And I'd have respected that confidence – if you'd respected our bargain. But you chose not to, so you must accept the consequences, however unwelcome.'

'Who do you *claim* my real father was?'

'I don't. Your mother declined to say. A holidaymaker? A travelling salesman? A neighbour? You'll never know. She's taken the secret to her grave.' I take a step towards her and lower my voice. 'As for *our* secret, I suggest you do the same. For your father's sake.'

'Bastard,' she murmurs. 'This changes nothing.'

'I think it does. In you. I think it severs a link that never truly existed.'

She stares at me, hating me more for this single revelation than she ever could for outwitting her in the past or defying her in the present. 'I'll still go through with it. That's a promise. I'll do it – if only to spite you.'

'Spite won't take you far.'

'Far enough to ruin you.'

'I don't think so. I'll deny everything.'

'You won't be able to. I still have the letters.'

'Fine. Publish them. Raise some doubt about Michael Lanyon's guilt. I don't mind. Throw as much mud as you like. It can't stick to the dead. *My* father, *your* mother, Sam Vigus, Miriam Tully: they're not here to confess to anything. As for me, I'll take my chances. It'll be your word against mine. I wonder who'll be believed. A self-confessed liar who's taken the money and run? Or – what was it you called me? – a committed family man. Your mother's death shortens the odds in my favour. You can sell your story and make everyone who campaigned for your release look ridiculous. You can make life difficult for Michaela and me. But not impossible. That's the point. Whatever you do, we'll survive. And do you know why?'

'Tell me.'

'Because she's the real thing.'

'And I'm not, I suppose.'

'You said it.'

'What about this, then?' Her hand moves deftly inside her coat, and suddenly I see she's holding a gun and it's pointed straight at me. I find myself wondering, with fleeting irrelevance, whether it's the same gun she pulled on me at Goonhilly all those years ago. It certainly looks the same. 'Is this real enough for you, Chris?'

'You're not going to shoot me, Simone.'

'Aren't I – when it would make such a big story?'

'No-one would pay you for it.'

'No. But they'd listen to me, wouldn't they? They'd believe me. They'd have to, because you wouldn't be around to contradict me.'

'You still won't do it.'

'Why not?'

'Because being believed doesn't matter that much to you. To Edmund Tully's daughter it might, but not to you.'

'Don't be so sure. I was famous once. I was a heroine. Now . . . what am I? Poor, lonely and middle-aged. My mother's dead. My son neglects me. Nobody pays me any attention. Nobody cares what I do or think. Well, I don't like that, Chris. I don't like being ignored.' In the lines of her face and the dulling of her eyes I glimpse her secret faltering self and realize greed may no longer be the driving force behind her actions. 'This way I'd be famous all over again.'

'But not a heroine.'

'Well, I never really liked that role anyway.' She steadies the gun with her other hand, raises it at arm's length and clicks back the trigger. 'This one fits better. Like father, like daughter. Still think I'm bluffing?'

'It's all over, Simone. Don't you understand? It's finished.'

She nods. 'For one of us.'

'For both of us, I rather think.' At the very edge of my vision I see a milk float trundling gently towards us along Daniell Road. I sense normality slowly stirring in the city behind and below me. Tomorrow has become today. And yesterday. Compressed into one. 'Goodbye.' I swing round slowly and start away down the hill, fixing my gaze on the distant unblinking eye of the City Hall clock I once heard strike the hour of Michael Lanyon's execution.

'Stop,' Simone cries after me, her voice cracking.

But I don't stop. I don't even look back. I walk on at a steady pace, squaring my shoulders and filling my lungs with the clear unhandselled air of as many mornings as I may live to see.

THE END

LONG TIME COMING

Robert Goddard

For thirty-six years, they thought he was dead...They were wrong...

Eldritch Swan is a dead man. Or at least that is what his nephew Stephen has always been told. Until one day Swan walks back into his life after thirty-six years in an Irish prison. He won't say why he was locked up - only that he is innocent of any crime.

His return should interest no one. But the visit of a solicitor with a strange request will take Swan and his sceptical nephew to London, where an exhibition of Picasso paintings is the starting point on a journey that will take them back to when the pictures were last seen - on the eve of the Second World War.

Untangling the web of murky secrets, family ties and old betrayals that surrounds their mysterious reappearance will prove to be a dangerous pursuit for the two men. Because watching their every step is a sinister enemy who will do whatever it takes to stop the truth emerging...

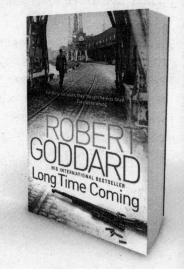

'The master of the clever twist'
SUNDAY TELEGRAPH

FOUND WANTING

Robert Goddard

The past will never let you go...

'The car jolts to a halt at the pavement's edge, the driver waving through the windscreen to attract Richard's attention. He starts with astonishment. The driver is Gemma, his ex-wife.

He has not seen or spoken to her for several years. They have, she memorably assured him, nothing to say to each other. But something has changed her mind – something urgent...'

Immediately Richard is catapulted into a breathless race against time that takes him from London, across northern Europe and into the heart of a mystery that reaches back into history – the fate of Anastasia, the last of the Romanovs. From that moment, Richard's life will be changed for ever in ways he could never have imagined...

'Everybody involved is double, triple and quadruple crossing everybody else...Goddard writes and plots with accurate precision; you feel he knows every setting and was witness to every scene'
LITERARY REVIEW

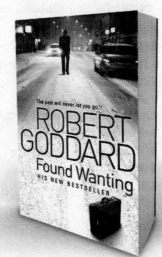

NAME TO A FACE
Robert Goddard

A centuries old mystery is about to unravel...

When Tim Harding agrees to do a favour for a friend by bidding on his behalf for an antique ring at auction, little does he know of the secrets that tie the ring to three tragedies: the sinking of HMS *Association* off Scilly in 1707, a murder in Penzance thirty years later and the drowning of a journalist diving at the *Association* wreck site in 1999.

But the ring is stolen before it can be sold, and a shocking murder follows. Harding is quickly drawn into a web of conspiracies surrounding the ring's origins and finds, close to the heart of the mystery, a young woman he is certain he recognizes, even though they have never met. As he goes in search of her identity, his life begins to fall apart. Somewhere, a perilous truth awaits him, coupled with a dreadful realization: those who uncover that truth are not allowed to live...

'The master of the clever twist'
SUNDAY TELEGRAPH

'Second to none when it comes to duplicity and intrigue...
A master of manipulation'
DAILY MAIL

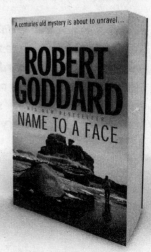